THE PASSAGE

IRINA SHAPIRO

Copyright © Irina Shapiro, 2015, 2023

The moral right of the author has been asserted.

To request permissions, contact the publisher at rights@stormpublishing.co

Ebook ISBN: 978-1-80508-146-3
Paperback ISBN: 978-1-80508-147-0

Previously published in 2015 by Merlin Press LLC.

Cover design: Debbie Clement
Cover images: Shutterstock

Published by Storm Publishing.
For further information, visit:
www.stormpublishing.co

ALSO BY IRINA SHAPIRO

Wonderland Series

The Passage

Wonderland

Sins of Omission

The Queen's Gambit

Comes the Dawn

PROLOGUE

MAY 1685

Surrey, England

Just as a hint of lavender stained the pristine blue of the spring sky the soldiers reconvened on the village green, their faces glistening with sweat and their feet sore from hours of walking. The villagers threw them curious looks but averted their gazes before eye contact could be made, afraid that they would be accused of being complicit. The village was abuzz with talk, but everyone spoke in whispers, their heads bent together as they conveyed the news to one another, shaking their heads and speculating as to what might have happened.

Captain Humphries looked from one tired face to another and felt a twinge of pity for his men. They'd been on their feet for hours, searching the countryside, turning the manor house upside down, going house to house in the village and intimidating the inhabitants in the vain hope of finding some trace of the missing man, but they turned up nothing.

"It was magic, it was," a young soldier named Dawson whispered to the man next to him, but, to his misfortune, the captain overheard.

"There's no such thing as magic, Dawson," Captain Humphries barked, although deep down he wasn't so sure. His father, who was a learned man, always told him that there was a reasonable explanation for most things, but as far as he could see, there was no reasonable explanation for what had happened that day.

"There is, sir," Dawson persisted. "I saw a hare turn into a crow once. It flew straight into the air, wings soaring, and circled over my head thrice. I thought I was done for," the young man confided with a shiver of fear.

"You're an ignorant fool, Dawson, as is the lot of you. This wasn't magic; this was a well-planned escape, an affront to His Majesty, and another nail in that traitor's coffin. Find him!!!!" Humphries roared and watched as his men shuffled off toward their horses. They'd been hoping for a cup of ale and a meal, but instead they'd have to make a pretense of searching for the man when they all knew that he wouldn't be found.

Humphries walked to the public house, tied up his horse, and took a seat in a shadowy corner, gesturing to the barkeep for a tankard of ale. He was a man who needed to understand the way things worked in order to make sense of the world around him, but what he witnessed that morning defied all reason. The man was there one minute—gone the next. He simply vanished. There was nowhere he could have hidden, no other door he could have slipped through. How was that possible, unless there really was such a thing as magic?

Captain Humphries took a long pull of the cool ale and rubbed the bridge of his nose, his eyes watering with fatigue. What was he to tell his superiors? How was he to explain that four soldiers of His Majesty's guard allowed one unarmed man to slip through their fingers? Someone would have to take the blame, and that someone was him. For a brief second, Humphries wished he could disappear as well, for that was much more preferable to what he'd have to face once he arrived back in London.

ONE

MARCH 2013

Surrey, England

Was it possible to change history or prevent something that had already taken place? Those were not questions I would normally ask myself, but had I known that my life was about to change irrevocably, and that, in less than a week, I would be questioning everything I'd believed up until that moment—I might have. But, as I rolled down the motorway on a sunny, but frigid March morning I wasn't pondering philosophical enigmas; all I could think about was the promise of a good night's rest. I'd always had trouble sleeping in strange places, and the past week had been particularly tiring, since I'd barely got any sleep at all, more due to personal worries and less to strange beds at out-of-the-way village inns. My job as a location scout for an independent film production company took me to many different locales, but at least this time I got to stay in England, which was a relief.

The new project was an eight-part series based on the life of Charles II, who'd been invited to return to England following the death of Oliver Cromwell and the demise of the Protectorate after the abdication of Cromwell's son, Richard. After the execution of his father, Charles I, the royal family fled to the Hague, where Charles spent the greater part of his youth. He finally returned to England on his thirtieth birthday and was crowned shortly thereafter; beginning a period in British history known as the Restoration.

Personally, I'd always had a soft spot for Charles II. He was the handsome, tolerant, good-time king who wanted to live, love, and be left to rule in peace. It was a wonder that he had time to rule, since he had several mistresses and sired a legendary number of bastards, twelve of whom he'd acknowledged as his own. Sadly, his wife, Catherine of Braganza, couldn't give him a legitimate heir, a tragedy which resonated for decades, spawning rebellion after rebellion either to depose a Catholic king or put a Catholic king back on the throne.

After years of bloody conflict, political strife, and joyless drudgery perpetuated by the Puritans, Charles reopened the theaters, and introduced music and gaiety back to the people, which earned him the title of the *Merry Monarch*. The Puritan black, white, and gray were replaced by vibrant color, frothy lace, and excessive ornament. The fashions were much like the man who sat the throne—flamboyant and over the top, and for the first time in decades the masses were content.

Shooting the series was going to be great fun, considering the amount of fornication Charles II indulged in, and the undoubted effect this was going to have on the cast and crew. There was usually at least one pregnancy that was the result of a long production, sometimes more, and countless affairs that rarely lasted past the wrap party. Casting had already begun for the various parts, and it was my job to find the right location for our production. It had to be affordable, historically appropriate, weather-cooperative—if such a thing were possible in England —and close enough to a village that would provide lodging. A decent pub large enough to accommodate a thirsty gaggle of actors, directors, cameramen, costumers, set designers, and various assistants who would descend on it after a day of shooting was also an absolute necessity, as was sufficient parking for all the vehicles and equipment, and an amiable landlord who was willing to allow us to overrun his property with minimal amount of meddling and complaints.

I'd already visited three locations in the past week, declaring them all to be unsuitable for various reasons. I'd left Everly Manor for last, hoping that this would be the one. I had to admit that I was secretly predisposed to it since Everly Manor was located in the village of Cranleigh, where one of my all-time favorite *Doctor Who* episodes was filmed. Everly Manor had all the right qualifications in terms of location and setting. The 'old' manor house and gardens were from the right era and were open to tourists five days a week. All that remained was checking out the village, agreeing on a fee, drawing up the legal documents, and taking numerous photographs and measurements, which would be required for set design and other preliminary preparations.

Lord Everly wouldn't hear of my staying at the pub, so I was offered room and board while I worked, assuming that a deal was reached on which both parties agreed. I took the exit off the motorway and headed toward the village of Cranleigh, the peaked roof of Everly House visible in the distance above the stark lacework of bare branches that bisected the sky in their naked splendor. I never enjoyed winter, but I could appreciate the barren beauty of the landscape and the vastness of the sky, which never seemed as encompassing during the summer months as it did on a cold winter's day; the gray-white expanse of the heavens endless and impenetrable to the weak rays of the sun.

I slowed down as a huge tour bus rolled through the gates of the estate and made its way down the lane toward me, several people still taking photos of the receding manor house through the bus windows. The tourists might be a problem, but I was sure Lord Everly took that into account.

I parked my car and gazed up at the "new" manor house, which was a fine example of eighteenth-century Palladian architecture. The house was made up of three blocks, the middle one dominated by a grand portico complete with six Corinthian columns and a sweeping staircase. I made my way up the steps to the front door, which flew open as if by magic, and Lord Everly himself appeared, beaming from ear to ear as if I was the answer to his every prayer. I was taken aback by the man, having expected him to be older. Lord Everly was in his mid-thirties, with a mane of dark hair, warm brown eyes, and an athletic physique that suggested hours at the gym and lots of outdoor activity, judging by his complexion.

"Miss Ashley, I presume?" he asked as he skipped down the steps and scooped the carrier bag from my hand. "Max Everly. A pleasure to finally meet you. Do come in. We have much to discuss, but first I'm sure you'd like to rest and have some refreshment. I'm afraid Mother is a little under the weather, or maybe she's just sulking because she's as much against shooting a film here as she was against opening the old house to the public, but needs must, and so here we are."

I smiled at the man's effusive charm. I could see that he was slightly nervous beneath the nonchalant exterior, and I wondered why that should be. Maybe things with Mother were more difficult than he led me to believe, but as long as the offer was still on the table, I wouldn't worry about it. That was something he'd have to work out for himself.

"I'm afraid we're rather short-staffed," Lord Everly explained as he set my bag down on the black-and-white tiled floor of the foyer. "In its heyday, this house boasted a large staff, including a butler, housekeeper, and every type of servant from scullery maid to boot boy, but now we must make do with only a housekeeper and a maid-of-all-work. Women are not as eager to go into service these days as they were before the First World War. They have much better opportunities."

"It must be very difficult for two people to take care of such a large establishment," I mused as I looked around the spacious foyer.

"Actually, we only use the East Wing these days, it being just the two of us. The staterooms have been closed for some time, and the West Wing is empty as well, to make things easier for Mrs. Harding to manage." He shrugged apologetically as a middle-aged woman appeared from a door at the back of the foyer, her face flushed with embarrassment.

"I do beg your pardon, Lord Everly. I didn't hear the bell. Will this be Miss Ashley then?" she asked, in an attempt to defuse the awkwardness of the lord of the manor having to open the door like a common butler.

"Not to worry, Mrs. Harding, not to worry. Miss Ashley never rang the bell; I saw her from the sitting-room window and went out to greet her. Why don't you show her up to her room?" Lord Everly suggested and turned to me with a smile. "I'm sure you'd like to rest and freshen up," he said as if I'd just traveled for days. In fact, I'd been on the road no more than an hour and a half, hardly enough time to get tired. "We can meet in the sitting room for tea, then turn our attention to the business at hand." He gave me a slight bow before disappearing into a room just off to the right, which I thought might be the library judging by the crammed bookcases I'd glimpsed through the door.

My room faced the back of the house and had lovely views of the park. It was decorated in the softest butter yellow which gave the room a sunny appearance despite the gray sky outside. A four-poster bed dominated the space and suddenly looked very inviting.

"You have your own private bath, Miss Ashley," Mrs. Harding informed me as she set down my bag and glanced around in the manner of a general preparing for battle, casting her eye over the well-dusted surfaces and fluffy bath towels just visible through the door. "Do let me know if you need anything. I'll bring you some lunch shortly."

"Don't trouble yourself, Mrs. Harding. I had a late breakfast, so I'm not very hungry. I'd much rather have a bath and a nap, actually."

"Very well, madam. Shall I run a bath for you? We have some Yardley bath salts," she added, as if sharing a great secret.

"Thank you, but I can manage."

I hadn't meant to sound dismissive, not being used to having servants, but Mrs. Harding seemed to take it that way. She gave me a slight nod and retreated, closing the door softly behind her. It felt odd to be treated so deferentially, but I might as well enjoy it while I could, I told myself as I rummaged in my bag for my dressing gown and turned on the taps.

* * *

Lord Everly was already downstairs by the time I arrived and went about pouring out the tea like the best of hostesses. He smiled as he urged me to try a piece of Victoria sponge.

"My absolute favorite. No one makes it like Stella—Mrs. Harding, I mean." He winked at the scandalized housekeeper and put a thick slice on my plate.

It was indeed heavenly, and I took a sip of tea and let him talk while I took his measure. Max Everly was well-groomed, expensively dressed, and very charming. His brown eyes sparkled with good humor, and he was quick to smile—a trait that I found very appealing in people, especially when the smile actually reached the eyes. Having spent several years around actors whose egos needed to be stroked every hour of the day, and who were usually acting even when not in front of the camera, I was perhaps quick to pick up on certain techniques used for putting people at ease and winning their trust, which Lord Everly was using with or without actually meaning to. Despite his rank and wealth, he spoke to me as if I were his equal, serving me rather than allowing the housekeeper to do it, and talking to me in a manner I could only describe as confidential, as if I were an old friend rather than a woman he had met only a few hours ago. Max Everly seemed to be an old hand at winning people over.

"I hope your other locations didn't suit," he said with a wicked grin. "Or, if they did, Everly Manor is sure to outdo them. As I mentioned on the telephone, we have two houses: the rambling Georgian manor in which we now sit, and the Tudor-era mansion which is now the museum. The 'new house,' as we call it, was built in the late 1700s after my great-great-great-grandfather made a fortune selling gunpowder to the army during the Revolutionary War. He moved the family here and left the old house to crumble. I had it restored and opened it to the public nearly a decade ago."

I set down my cup and leaned back in the chair, feeling pleasantly full. "You mentioned earlier that your mother objects to the museum..." I let the sentence trail off, hoping he would fill in the rest.

"Yes, she does," Lord Everly said as he poured himself another cup of tea and took a second slice of cake, silently offering me one as well.

I knew I shouldn't, but I accepted nonetheless and tucked in, enjoying the mouthwatering goodness. The cake was so moist and light that it didn't make one feel stuffed. It just settled pleasantly, giving a feeling of utter contentment.

"Mother is a proud woman, reared in a different time and with different values. Believe it or not, there are those in her circle who still see any kind of business venture as 'trade' and think it 'common.' I don't know where these people think money comes from, other than inheritances and trust funds.

The truth is—and I'm not ashamed to admit it, although it makes Mummy turn puce with rage—that a house like this takes a fortune to maintain. There are just the two of us, and we have twenty bedrooms. There's always a leaking roof, dry rot, termites, or plant fungi—you name it. I would gladly sell the lot and move to my flat in London, but Mummy won't hear of it—family seat and all that. She won't allow herself to die until I produce an heir, so there's no rest for the wicked."

I couldn't help laughing. He was so easygoing and amusing that I fervently hoped I'd like his offer and get to work with him for the next few months.

"Can you show me the museum now?" I asked, putting down my empty plate and resolutely refusing another helping of cake.

"I'd rather do it tomorrow, if you have no objection. The museum closes to the public at 4 p.m., and then there are still people in the gift shop and the tearoom, and I'd like it to be empty when we visit. Since it gets dark so early, we'd need candles, which would make it kind of authentic. There's no electricity, you see. The house is as it was in its heyday. It's fully furnished, and there are trunks and trunks of clothes, which you would be welcome to should you choose Everly. Some of the dresses are rather elaborate, and I had them cleaned and preserved. Some of the more interesting ones are on display downstairs."

"Lord Everly," I began, but was interrupted.

"Please, call me Max. Lord Everly was my father."

"All right, Max; would you not mind closing the place to tourists for a few months?" I knew what he'd say, but I still had to ask.

"Not at all. The tourists will flock to this place once they hear that a movie was filmed here, especially if someone famous was in the cast. It will give us much-needed marketing clout, if you will. The house and grounds would be completely at your disposal, as well as the car park. The villagers would welcome the additional business as well, and what's good for them is good for me. They still view me as something of a feudal overlord, I'm afraid, since we own some properties in the village, and they feel as if they work for me."

"All right, tomorrow it is then." I glanced at the light beyond the window, which had grown a deep shade of violet while we talked. It would be dark in a few minutes, and I was grateful for the merry fire that crackled in the fireplace and the warmth of the tea. My room at the inn last night had been drafty and uncomfortable, so I was glad to be warm and snug.

"I do hope you'll join me for dinner tonight. I had Stella prepare something special in your honor," Max said, smiling at me warmly.

"There was really no need. A sandwich in my room would have been just fine," I replied, somewhat embarrassed to be the object of so much attention. I didn't expect to be entertained, but Max Everly seemed determined to treat me like an honored guest.

"There was every need, and I won't take no for an answer. We dine promptly at eight," Max announced, "and I think Mummy will come down to meet you. Her bark is worse than her bite. She's actually quite a charmer when she cares to be, and I think you and her will get on like a house on fire."

"I'm sure we will. I'll see you at dinner then." I certainly hoped I wasn't expected to dress for dinner. I had only brought one nice dress just in case. In the meantime, I'd take a little walk in the wintry garden. There was plenty of light from the windows to light the path, and I was feeling restless after my nap.

I dashed upstairs, took my coat and gloves and made my way out into the garden. The flower beds were nothing more than dark circles, and the rose bushes had been pruned and covered for the winter, making them look like shapeless globs in the near darkness. A biting chill quickly turned my nose and cheeks red, but I huddled deeper into my coat and continued to walk. The inky sky was strewn with countless stars, which paled in comparison to the nearly full moon which shone like an electric torch in the darkened heavens.

I tilted my head upwards, filled my lungs with the wintry air and closed my eyes, suddenly realizing that it'd been several hours since I'd thought of anything other than the forthcoming project. This was definite progress, and I smiled to myself and turned toward the door, ready to dress for dinner and meet Lady Everly.

TWO

Lady Everly wasn't quite as formidable as I expected, I mused as I got dressed the following morning. She was well into her eighties, and likely had his lordship later in life, which accounted for the doting looks she had cast his way during dinner. I could tell that she wasn't thrilled with the idea of the film being shot on the Everly estate, but, deep down, I thought she understood her son's reasons very well. She might think that speaking of money was vulgar, but she'd lived too long not to realize the necessity of having it, or the importance of having to pretend that one was financially sound. Naomi Everly did nothing to discourage me, and was very gracious, asking me numerous questions about my work and my life in London. I could see where her son got his beautiful manners, as well as his ability to charm.

Max Everly met me in the foyer just before 9 a.m., dressed in tweeds and ready to tour the house and grounds. The museum wouldn't open until 10 a.m., so we had ample time to visit every nook and cranny of the old manor house before the first visitors of the day arrived. I had to admit that I was excited; I had seen the old house from my window this morning, and it was everything I hoped it would be. If pictures did it any justice, it was the perfect location for the shoot.

Our boots crunched on the gravel path as we walked toward the house. It was built entirely of gray stone, with a steeply pitched slate roof and numerous chimney pots rising into the nearly colorless March sky. The Everlys must have been wealthy at the time of construction since the casement windows, which were usually narrow due to the cost of glass, were wider and arranged in groups of three panes. The leaded glass reflected the morning light and brightened the façade of the otherwise severe-looking structure. The house was built in the traditional Tudor E shape, which I found pleasing to the eye due to its symmetry. The recessed front door was covered with a stone arch and decorated with heavy black hinges shaped in fanciful curlicues, but it opened smoothly, the hinges having been oiled recently.

"There were several outbuildings, but I had them torn down," Max explained as we stepped inside. "We've turned the old stables into a tearoom; the visitors seem to like the rustic feel of the place, but the rest were destroyed to create a car park large enough for tour buses. There are days when we get several tour groups at the same time, you see, so it gets rather crowded."

I felt a chill as I stepped into the square foyer guarded by a shiny suit of armor, which looked as if it would spring to life at any moment. Lovely tapestries decorated the walls to my right and left, their colors still surprisingly vivid after several centuries. I supposed that not being exposed to electric light and hanging in the dim foyer helped preserve them from becoming faded. The manor had no central heating, so the house was as cold as a tomb, and just as silent. A massive, carved desk stood just to the right of the entrance, its surface neatly stacked with brochures detailing the history of the manor house and family, showing glossy pictures of the gardens in full bloom, and providing general information about the museum and the website.

"Is this the ticket counter?" I asked as I looked through the brochure.

"No, the tickets can be purchased at the tearoom. The manor house has no electricity, so we can't process credit card purchases or print receipts," Max replied as he led me into the front room.

I stopped in the middle, feeling as if I'd just stepped back in time. It seemed as if nothing had been touched and the owners of the house would come back at any moment and go about their usual business. The wooden furniture looked anything but comfortable, but it was beautifully carved, with embroidered cushions added for comfort. I paused to admire the marble mantelpiece just as a young man walked into the room.

"Good morning, Barry," Max called out. "Barry is here to make a fire. We light fires in all the rooms during the winter months to avoid the visitors complaining of cold. Besides, it makes things appear more authentic, don't you think?"

"I'm sure it does, and the warmth doesn't come amiss, I daresay," I replied, shivering in my coat. It was actually warmer outside than it was in the house. I stood closer to the hearth as the fire began to crackle and fill the room with the pleasant smell of burning wood. The rest of the room was still frigid, but my spot was growing warmer by the minute, and I dared not move until I got warm.

Max took a seat on one of the hard-backed chairs, ignoring the sign that asked visitors not to touch anything or sit on the furniture, and held out his hands to the fire.

"Barry will have all the fires lit soon, and the house will feel considerably warmer. Sorry, I should have taken that into account, but I wanted to show it to you before the crowds descended," he said apologetically.

"Do you get visitors here all year round?" I asked, looking around the well-appointed room.

"Oh, yes. I have an arrangement with several large tour companies. I give them a price break, and they include us in their tour. They won't be too pleased if I close the museum down for several months, but they will just have to wait until we reopen."

"You seem sure that you will get the contract," I teased Max good-naturedly.

"I know we will. I could see it in your face the moment you walked into this room. This is just what you were looking for, isn't it?"

"I'd have to see the rest of the house to answer that, but, yes, I think this would be suitable. This place has a certain aura. It's like stepping into a bygone era," I said.

"It is. That's why I thought the museum would be such a good idea. The money doesn't hurt either; this place is a cash cow." I could see that Max was very proud of his 'baby' and couldn't blame him. The house really was a gem.

"Come, show me the rest."

"It will be my pleasure," Max replied as he sprang to his feet and led me back out into the hall.

The rest of the house didn't disappoint. The rooms were large and well proportioned, decorated with period paintings and exquisite tapestries. The furniture glowed from frequent polishing, and the heavy drapes and bed hangings were still vibrant and not terribly faded from age and sunlight. The clothes on display were spectacular as well, ranging from the early 1500s to the end of the eighteenth century. I didn't want to gush too loudly and cause Max to increase the asking price, but most of the furnishings and some of the clothes could be used on set in lieu of bringing in our own. It would cut production costs considerably, which was always a bonus.

In my mind's eye, I could already see how several rooms

could be transformed into the chambers of Whitehall Palace and Charles's private apartments. Of course, the façade of the palace would be computer-generated since the original palace was destroyed in the fire of 1698. All we had were some drawings and paintings to remind us of what the palace looked like, but with today's technology, recreating the palace was a matter of a few keystrokes.

Max and I left the house and stepped into the formal gardens situated behind the house. Of course, at this time of year it was nothing more than brown stumps and evergreen hedges, but come spring, the gardens would be glorious and perfect for shooting several key scenes.

"So, what do you think?" Max asked as he rubbed his hands in anticipation. I could see the suppressed excitement in his eyes and was glad not to disappoint him.

"I think it's perfect. I'd just like to look at the church. There's a scene that takes place in the crypt. Is there one?"

"There is, as it happens," Max replied happily, "and it's perfectly sinister, as one would expect. I don't think anyone's been down there in ages. I'd love to escort you, but I have a meeting in the village. Will you be all right on your own?"

"Of course."

"Excellent. I'll walk as far as the church with you," Max offered as he waved a greeting to an employee who was just opening up the tearoom. I wondered how much the cost of admission was and made a mental note to come back later and check, and maybe have a cup of tea and browse the gift shop. I couldn't help admiring Max's business acumen. Life had presented him with an opportunity, and he'd exploited it to its full potential.

The walk to the church took a good half-hour, but it was downhill, so it was easy going, especially since I had company and good conversation. I was chilled to the bone by the time Max finally left me at the gate of St. Nicolas's Church. Weak sunshine shone through gaps in the wispy clouds but offered no warmth, and the brisk wind had a bite to it that left my cheeks rosy and my fingers stiff with cold. I was glad to duck into the church and feel the breath of warmth that instantly enveloped me, physically and emotionally. I wasn't much of a believer, but I always liked churches, with their air of serenity and the promise of something bigger than oneself.

I sat down in one of the pews and just closed my eyes, inhaling the familiar scent and allowing my limbs to thaw before going about the business at hand. I wished I could pray, as there was much I needed to discuss with God, but this wasn't the time. I had a job to do, so my personal turmoil would have to wait a little longer, although it was hovering at the back of my mind every moment of the day, the pain of my loss still fresh, slicing through my heart every time I thought of the past few months.

I opened my eyes and gazed around the church. I'd done some research before I came, so I knew something about the history of the building. It'd been built in 1170 and by the mid-fourteenth century was much as it appeared today, at least from the outside. The church had been restored in 1847, and several key elements had been added since, such as the Jubilee Window which had been installed to commemorate the Golden Jubilee of Queen Elizabeth II. The window was magnificent; a seamless combination of old and new, with the traditional effect of stained glass combined with a somewhat modern, almost abstract depiction of the subject. Something about it reminded me of the works of Marc Chagall, despite the fact that his work centered mostly on Judaic themes.

There was one feature I especially wanted to see—the twelfth-century carving in the North Transept known as the "Cheshire Cat." According to local lore, the carving had been the inspiration for Lewis Carroll's Cheshire Cat in *Alice in*

Wonderland, so I made my way to the North Transept and stood in front of the strange little gargoyle.

I ran my fingers gingerly over the smiling face, remembering all the times I'd lost myself in the story. *Alice in Wonderland* had been one of my favorites as a child, a magical world I escaped to every time I was sad or afraid. No shrinking potion or evil Queen of Hearts could scare me as much as my own mother, who drank her sorrows away and eventually passed out, only to repeat it all again the next day. She was always remorseful and ashamed in the morning as I got ready for school, but she didn't have the strength of character, or maybe the desire, to get help. Drink was her only form of escape from a life she termed "pointless," and "wasted." I had tried to remind her that I was still there, and I needed her, but I was too young to understand that I simply wasn't enough. I was a reminder of all she had lost; a carbon copy of the man who had walked out on her without so much as goodbye and left her to raise a child alone on a meager salary. The money went to pay for the booze, and by the time I was eleven, I had been taken into care; just another child forsaken by her parents and swallowed up by the system.

I'd been one of the lucky ones; I'd ended up in a good foster home with a nice couple who treated me as if I were their own, but no amount of love they gave me could make up for the betrayal of my own parents. When I was seventeen, I'd heard that my mother had died, but I hadn't even bothered to attend the funeral, despite the urging of my foster mother. I had too much anger and too much resentment to be able to say goodbye, so I had stayed away. I never knew what happened to my father. He might have died as well, or he might be living somewhere, possibly with a new family, completely indifferent to the child he had left behind nearly twenty years ago.

I kissed my fingers and pressed them to the smiling mouth of the carving. "Thank you," I whispered, not really sure if I was

thanking the Cheshire Cat for being one of my favorites or
Lewis Carroll for writing the story.

"Good morning," a cheery voice called out as the vicar came
in with a gust of cold air and removed his hat as a sign of respect
for the house of God. "I'm Vicar Joseph Lambert. Very brisk out
there this morning, isn't it? Winter seems to be lingering this
year."

"Yes, I'm just taking a moment to warm up," I said as I
turned to take his outstretched hand. "Neve Ashley, I'm the
location scout for Legendary Productions."

"Ah, yes, of course. Max mentioned you'd be coming. I say,
it would be thrilling to have our little church in your film. Any
parts for an inspirational clergyman who can convey just the
right amount of gravitas tempered with wry humor and understanding? A secret wedding perhaps?" he asked with an impish
smile.

"As a matter of fact, there is a secret wedding between
James Stuart and Anne Hyde, but it was a Catholic ceremony,
I'm afraid," I replied, amused by his eagerness. The vicar was an
older man, who appeared to be made entirely of spheres. His
balding round head sat atop his rotund body; his moon-shaped
face adorned by round spectacles that perched on a rather
bulbous nose. He did have a wonderful smile, though, which
made him appear as jolly as St. Nick.

"Catholic, you say? Well, I don't suppose the Good Lord
would mind if I were just acting, would he now? It would be
great fun, mind," he added, beaming at me.

"I'll have a word with the director," I whispered confidentially, even though we were quite alone in the church.

"Really?"

"I promise. Now, would it be possible to see the crypt?" I
asked as I stuffed my gloves into my pockets and pulled the
camera out of my bag. Lawrence Spellman would want pictures
from every angle so that he could plan out his scene.

"Oh yes, of course. No one ever really goes down there anymore, but it's quite impressive. A few ancient Everlys are interred there, and there's even a knight who returned from the Crusades only to die a week later of the fever. He has a lovely effigy. It's just down those stairs. Do be careful. They're rather worn and can be a bit slippery. Do you need me to accompany you?" he asked, clearly hoping that I'd say no.

"Thank you, but I'm fine on my own. I just need to take a few photos and measurements."

"Excellent. Please join me for a cup of tea once you're finished. I'll be in the vestry."

"I'd like that," I replied as I made my way toward the hole in the church floor from which well-worn stone steps descended into the underbelly of the church.

Thankfully, there was a light switch which activated a lonely bulb in the center of the ceiling. A golden light filled the cavernous space, making it appear slightly less sinister, but spaces behind the thick columns supporting the ceiling remained lost in shadow, making me feel as if something would suddenly spring on me from the dark recesses of the crypt.

I stood in the center of the crypt and looked around. The vaulted ceiling was low, and the stone walls were decorated with fanciful carvings which at one point probably told a story but were now nothing more than chipped and worn pieces of masonry. There were several tombs lining the walls, the lids covered with a thick layer of dust that hadn't been disturbed in decades, possibly centuries.

This will do very nicely, I thought, *a good place to set the scene.*

The tomb of the knight was just by the back wall, and it was impressive, as promised. The effigy seemed to have lost part of the nose at some point during the last few centuries, but the eyes stared blankly at the ceiling, an expression of boredom on what once might have been a handsome face. I snapped a few pictures from various angles, but I wanted to get a better full-length shot of the knight's tomb. In order to accomplish this, I had to back all the way into the wall, pressing my spine against the stone in order to get the shot.

I felt a slight poke in my lower back and then my ears were assaulted by the sound of scraping rock as a small door opened just behind me, nearly making me lose my balance and fall into the fetid space. I jumped aside and rubbed my back, searching for the source of the poke. There was a flower carved into the stone, the center protruding just a little, like a button. I must have pressed it as I backed into the wall, releasing an ancient mechanism.

I should have just walked away, but curiosity got the better of me, so I glanced into the passage. Stone steps led upward toward a wooden door at the top. I noted that they didn't look as worn as the ones I'd descended earlier, the stone still even and uncracked. This was probably another way into the church or to the outside. In centuries past, people often sought sanctuary at churches, and a secret door might have been used to smuggle them to safety or bring them messages and food from the outside. I examined the stone door to make sure it wasn't going to just close behind me and carefully made my way to the top.

The wooden door opened easily enough; the hinges oiled recently from the looks of them. I stepped into the church at the opposite side from which I had descended earlier and found myself in a shadowed alcove. I hadn't noticed it before when I took pictures in the church, but it had been fairly unremarkable.

I stepped out of the alcove and froze. This wasn't the same church I'd left twenty minutes ago. The stained-glass windows which cast beams of colored light onto the floor and the pews were gone, replaced by solid stone walls, broken only by narrow arrow-slit-like windows high above. The interior was dim despite the early hour, dispelled only by sullen light streaming through the narrow windows and several thick candles which smelled strongly of beeswax. The air inside the church was frigid, making my breath come out in white puffs, which instantly dissipated like wisps of smoke. A three-panel altar-piece depicting the birth, crucifixion, and resurrection of Christ graced the wall behind the altar, which was decorated with an embroidered altar cloth.

I looked around wildly. Had I stepped into a different part of the church? But that wasn't possible. I'd seen the church from the outside, and the interior matched the size of the building, or so I thought. I was just about to take a photo when I realized that my camera was dead, as was my mobile, which I'd charged only that morning.

I was just about to go to the vestry and see if the vicar was there when the heavy wooden door which led to the church porch opened and a man strode in, walking purposefully toward the altar. I quickly stepped back into the alcove, stunned by the man's appearance. The man wore knee breeches with stockings, a narrow, elaborately embroidered coat with lace spilling at the wrist and throat, square-toed shoes decorated with large bows, and a periwig of black curls. A plumed hat was held loosely in his right hand and a sword in an ornate sheath swayed on his left hip as he walked down the nave; the heels of his shoes clicking on the stone floor and echoing through the empty church. My mind was in utter shock, but I was still able to place the man's attire as late seventeenth century. The narrower breeches, almost knee-length coat, and curly wig became popular during the reign of Charles II and lasted into the beginning of the eighteenth century.

The man knelt in front of the altar, head bent, his lips moving as he prayed for a few minutes. I heard a muffled "Amen" before he genuflected and got to his feet. I wasn't sure if I was more shocked by his appearance or the fact that he had just crossed himself in a Protestant church, which was a singularly Catholic gesture. I held my breath in the hope that the man would leave, but he took a seat in the second pew and stared at the altarpiece with a look of fierce concentration that could only mean he was deep in thought. I hoped he would just leave so that I could open the door and sneak back down to the crypt, but he seemed to be waiting for something or someone.

A few moments later, there was another gust of wind as his companion arrived. This man was similarly dressed, but his face was craggier and noticeably older beneath the honey-blond curls of his elaborate wig. He wore a large cabochon ring on his finger, and jewels glinted in the hilt of his sword as he sat down. The man exuded an arrogance which could only mean that he was a high-placed nobleman of some sort, the son of a great house.

The two men whispered urgently for a few minutes, clearly disagreeing on something of importance. I could see that the first man was deferential in his manner, but evidently displeased with what was being asked of him. Finally, the older man rose abruptly after issuing some form of order and stalked from the church as his companion said, "Good day, Your Grace."

He waited for a few moments, then departed, leaving the church in silence.

I pressed my back against the wall, breathing hard. What had I just witnessed and how was it possible? Who was the man addressed as "Your Grace"? He was clearly someone of great importance. And why was I even still here?

I ran through the door and down the steps to the crypt and catapulted back into the church the way I'd come earlier. Gentle sunshine streamed through the stained-glass windows, the smell of polish and evergreen boughs filling my lungs. My mobile pinged, alerting me to a new message, and my camera suddenly came back to life, the lens retracting back into the camera as the shutter closed.

I took a few deep breaths and forced myself to walk calmly

to the vestry. Reverend Lambert was sitting behind a small desk, writing something with a ballpoint pen. At this point, I wouldn't have been too surprised to see him scratching away with a quill as the curls of his wig brushed the parchment. He set down his pen, invited me to sit and took the tea kettle off the hob.

"All finished?" he asked as he poured the tea into the pot and offered me a chocolate biscuit. "What did you think of our crypt?"

"Very impressive. I'm still spooked," I answered honestly. The tea was hot and sweet, warming its way through my body, which was chilled by my recent experience more than the nearly arctic interior of the office.

"As it happens, the church was erected on the site of an ancient Celtic place of worship. Some of the old stones were utilized in building the crypt," the vicar informed me as he reached for a third biscuit.

"What was the church like before the Restoration?" I asked, knowing already that he would describe exactly what I'd just seen.

"There was a magnificent three-panel altarpiece depicting the birth, crucifixion, and resurrection of Christ commissioned by the first Lord Everly in the early sixteenth century and presented to the bishop as a gift. The background was made entirely of gold leaf, and the frame was solid gold as well. It was removed in the nineteenth century and placed in a museum since the elements were slowly destroying the artwork. A terrible shame too; it was beautiful. But we got the Jubilee Window which more than makes up for it," the vicar finished triumphantly. "Stunning, isn't it?"

"Indeed, it is."

I think it was the description of the altarpiece which finally pushed me over the edge. I hadn't imagined it—it had been real —as was the man who'd left such an impression on me. I had no idea what had happened to me, but I felt an overwhelming need to flee and get as far away as I could from this strange place. I hastily excused myself and ran from the church before the well-meaning vicar could ask me any questions. My phone began to vibrate as soon as I stepped outside, but I ignored it, feeling unable to speak with anyone. The cold air felt invigorating, and I took a deep breath as I gazed up Greensand Ridge at the imposing façade of Everly Manor. Everything appeared to be back to normal—except me.

An overwhelming fatigue stole over me as I began the climb back to the ridge. It left me weak in the knees and sweating profusely despite the cold air that seemed to find its way inside my coat and dry the sweat instantaneously, leaving me shaking with cold. I felt physically and emotionally drained by the time I finally reached the manor, so I let myself in through the side door, which was kept open during the day and snuck up to my room where I shucked my coat, climbed into bed still fully dressed, and pulled the blanket over my head.

THREE

On the walk back to Everly Manor, I'd nearly managed to convince myself that what I'd experienced was a result of some rogue pregnancy hormones that were still coursing through my body but knew that couldn't be true. I'd miscarried over a month ago, so whatever hormones had been present were long gone by now. My body was back to normal, even if my heart hadn't quite recovered from the loss.

The phone buzzed again on the bedside table next to me, and I nearly threw it against the wall when I saw Evan's number in the display. We'd hardly spoken since I lost the baby, and I still wasn't ready to forgive. I was well aware that miscarriages frequently happened in the first trimester, but a part of me—well, most of me—blamed Evan. He'd caused me round-the-clock aggravation since I'd told him I was pregnant, and I was certain that it had contributed to the loss of the baby, which was precisely what he wanted.

Tears welled up in my eyes as I put aside my weird experience at the church and thought back to those two months which had turned my otherwise stable relationship with Evan into a battlefield. I knew he wouldn't be thrilled with my news, but

the attack he'd mounted against my pregnancy was wholly
unexpected. His words still rang in my ears day after day,
making me by turns angry and sad.

"Neve, I want you to terminate this pregnancy as soon as
possible, so that we can put all this nonsense behind us and get
back to normal," Evan had demanded, his normally calm face
contorted with rage.

"And what if I want it?" I'd asked, my voice shaking with
emotion as tears rolled down my cheeks. And I did want it,
more than I ever thought possible. I'd never actively tried to get
pregnant. The thought of being a mother terrified me after what
I'd endured at the hands of my own mother, but once the
surprise of the news wore off, I'd felt a fierce love for the little
being inside me—a love that left me breathless with its intensity.

Suddenly, the world didn't seem so empty and cold, but full
of promise and wonder. I lay awake at night, dreaming of the
tiny flame of life inside me, wondering if it would be a boy or a
girl, and whom it would resemble. All kinds of images sprang
into my mind unbidden, images that previously would have left
me feeling threatened and forced me to emotionally shut down,
but now seemed like the very idea of Heaven.

I wouldn't be like my mother, who had always put her
needs and feelings first and ultimately drank herself into the
grave. I would be the kind of mother I'd always wanted: warm,
caring, and nurturing. I would put my baby first and give it the
kind of life I'd always dreamed of.

I knew that having a child wasn't a priority for Evan, but I'd
never expected the kind of vehement revulsion he seemed to
feel at the idea of having a baby with me. It had been a shock to
him, but I honestly thought he'd come around after a few days
and possibly even embrace the idea of being a father again, but
as the days had passed, Evan's resentment seemed to grow
stronger, as did his resolve to be rid of this child.

"Then you will be having it on your own," he'd spat out at

me, growing angrier by the minute. "I already have a child—a child who tells me every other day that I'm rubbish as a father; a child who barely looks me in the face as she plays with her mobile or plugs her ears with buds in order not to talk to me," he'd snarled as he slammed his hand against the glass table, making it rattle dangerously.

"She's supposed to do that—she's sixteen. She'll grow out of it in time." I had tried to reason with him, but he wouldn't hear me.

"Neve, I've just been put forward for silk. If my application is approved and I'm made Queen's Council, I'll be on the fast track to becoming a judge. I don't need, or want, the responsibility of another child. I don't even want the one I already have. Get rid of it!" he'd bellowed, which broke my heart.

Despite the awful relationship Evan had with his daughter, he had a child—but not with me. Natasha was the product of his first marriage, a marriage that fell apart after three years. Evan and Deborah, his first wife, had a more civil relationship now than while they were married, so Natasha spent a lot of time at our flat, lounging on the sofa in her pajamas and generally driving Evan to distraction with her insolence. She was a good kid when she wasn't sulking, arguing, or simply ignoring us, and I was sure she loved Evan beneath the sullen teenage exterior. I think she loved me a little too, although she'd never admit it. I was, however, very close with Deborah, who invited me to lunch at least once a month and listened to me talk about her ex-husband, shaking her head and smiling at my naiveté.

"Neve, Evan is never going to change," Deborah had said as she'd served me quiche made with spinach and feta cheese. "His first priority will *always* be Evan. He's smart, charming, clever, and great in bed, but he will always be selfish to the bone. He wants to be a judge, and nothing will stop him. He has no paternal instinct, if there even is such a thing. He just wants to do what he wants to do. A baby is a nuisance and a liability in his eyes."

"So, what do I do?" I'd whined, pushing away the quiche as a wave of morning sickness had assaulted me out of nowhere, leaving me breathless and clammy.

"You have a termination. If you want a baby, have one with someone who wants a family, not someone who will only leave you high and dry and want no part of his child. Sure, he'll pay the bills, but that will be the extent of his involvement. You're still young, only twenty-five; either accept Evan as he is or find another bloke," Deborah had advised me sagely.

Deborah was right, of course; she always was when it came to Evan. I hadn't really listened to her before, but now I knew that I was at a crossroads, and Deborah had painted a very clear picture of what would happen if I chose to keep the baby. I did anyway.

I moved back to my own flat, which I'd been subleasing on a month-to-month basis. Thankfully, the young advertising executive who had leased the flat from me was looking to move in with her boyfriend, so losing the flat gave her the perfect opportunity to force the issue. It felt strange to be living on my own again, but there was also a certain serenity in coming home to a place that was entirely my own and enjoying the restful silence of the place rather than dealing with Evan's attacks and loaded silences.

Evan had continued to call and harass me about the pregnancy, but I'd held firm. Once I'd calmed down, I could see his side of the dilemma, but I wouldn't be swayed by his arguments. It certainly wouldn't advance his chances of getting silk if his colleagues knew that he was having a child out of wedlock, old-fashioned as that might seem. He either had to marry me—and fast—or get me to abort the baby if he wanted his application to be approved.

I'd stopped taking Evan's calls and concentrated on keeping

calm and taking good care of myself, physically and emotion-ally. I'd given up alcohol, excluded all processed foods from my diet and replaced them with organic produce, and religiously went to yoga at least twice a week to focus my mind and find some peace in the current turmoil of my situation, but fate seemed to conspire with Evan. I lost the baby in my third month, just two weeks short of reaching the second trimester.

I'd woken up in the middle of the night, unsure of what had disturbed me. The house was quiet around me, the January night still and silent, as the wee hours of the morning usually are, just before the morning commute turns the empty streets into a sea of humanity, and the rush-hour gridlock transforms the slumbering city into a heaving mass of revving, honking, fume-exhausting machinery.

I felt a tightening in my lower abdomen, but that wasn't anything I hadn't experienced before. There'd been some sudden sharp pains and a feeling of stretching, which the preg-nancy manual assured me was all part of the embryo implanting itself and my uterus beginning to stretch and distend my bowels. I'd pulled my legs up to my chest and wrapped my arms around my knees as I waited for the feeling to pass, but cramps began to roll through my stomach, making me feel as if I were about to get my period. I felt as if I had, when a wetness between my legs forced me to run to the bathroom.

Within mere moments, the cramps had turned into an unbearable pressure, the pain so intense that it left me trem-bling as I saw the blood running down my legs. I hadn't even had time to call for an ambulance as the bloody lump that had been my baby plopped down on the tiled floor of the bathroom, the sight of it making me sick with regret.

I'd lain on the bathroom floor next to what had been my baby for what felt like hours, but eventually I'd forced myself to get up, clean up the mess, and get dressed for an emergency appointment at the women's clinic.

The sympathetic doctor had confirmed that my pregnancy was over. She put her hand over mine, forcing me to meet her eyes.

"Neve, it wasn't your fault," Doctor Eastman had said quietly. "These things happen; it wasn't anything that you did. Nearly twenty percent of women miscarry in the first trimester. It's nature's way of correcting mistakes. That doesn't mean that it will happen again."

Again—a strange word under the circumstances. I wouldn't go back to Evan, not after the way he'd treated me, so who knew if there ever would be an again. Perhaps this had been my one chance, and nature had decided to correct its mistake, thinking I wouldn't make a fit parent to my baby. And again, I was alone in my body. Alone in the world.

For the first two weeks, I had to keep reminding myself that I was no longer pregnant. There was no baby, not anymore. At that point, I went back to work, accepting the assignment for this film and throwing myself into research, jotting down various details about the time period and searching for suitable locations within a two-hour radius from London. I needed to be away from London, away from Evan, and away from my nagging friends, who kept assuring me that everything would go back to normal. I just wanted to be alone.

I pulled the blanket over my head and allowed the tears to fall. It didn't matter where I was, I was still hurting.

FOUR

By 7 p.m., I finally dragged myself out of bed, took a hot shower and began to dress for dinner. I would have happily just gone to sleep, but it was rude to my hosts not to come down, so I applied a little makeup and pulled out a pair of slacks and a cashmere sweater. I'd worn my dress the night before, so unless they wanted me to wear the same thing every night, slacks and a sweater would have to do.

I stared at myself in the mirror. My brown eyes looked haunted, and my normally abundant blonde hair looked lackluster even after shampooing. I twisted it into an artful bun and slipped on my shoes. They'd have to take me as they found me—tired and depressed.

As I came down the stairs to the second floor, I ran into Max. He was wearing a pinstripe navy suit with a lavender silk tie and looked dashing, in a quietly expensive sort of way. I was sure that Lady Everly would also be dressed as if she were dining with Her Majesty the Queen. The Everlys seemed to take dinner very seriously. Had I been dining at home with just my foster mother, I'd have worn a pair of jeans and a T-shirt.

Max's face lit up as he saw me. "Neve, are you all right? I

was hoping to see you after I came back from the village, but Mrs. Harding told me you were having a lie-down."

I had no idea how Mrs. Harding knew that but had no desire to talk about my strange experience of that morning. Truth be told, I was beginning to think I'd imagined the whole thing and was feeling somewhat embarrassed by my reaction.

"I had a headache," I replied, hoping Max would leave it at that.

"I'm sorry to hear that. I hope you're feeling better." I gave a nod of confirmation, and he went on, "How did you like our crypt?"

"It was everything I hoped it would be. I sent several pictures to Lawrence Spellman, and he texted back his approval," I supplied as Max led me through the gallery. Paintings of various sizes lined the walls; generations of Everlys watching us with that mixture of arrogance and boredom often found in portraits from another time period when people rarely smiled for fear of appearing frivolous. Most of the portraits were of men, the women not nearly as important to posterity as their male counterparts, despite being wives and mothers of the men depicted. Most Everlys seemed to have dark eyes, which followed me as I made my way down the endless corridor. "I met the vicar. He told me something of the people buried in the crypt," I said, suddenly aware of the lull in conversation.

Max tore his eyes away from the portraits and turned to me with an apologetic smile. "He's a lovely old chap, isn't he? I bet he offered you tea and biscuits. He keeps boxes and boxes of them in the vestry. Someone should remind him that gluttony is a sin."

I giggled in response, but my laugh sounded false to my ears. I felt strangely nervous, as if the faces in the portraits were live people who judged me and found me wanting.

Suddenly, I stopped in my tracks, staring up at the wall directly in front of me as my knees buckled. I grabbed onto Max to keep myself from falling, causing him to gaze at me in alarm as he deftly caught me and held me upright. A man of about thirty-five glared at me from the portrait, his eyes boring into mine and his lips stretched in a sardonic scowl. The artist had done such a fine job that the painting appeared more like a photograph, the man disturbingly real. "Who's that?" I cried out in alarm.

"Don't worry, he's long dead, I assure you," Max replied, clearly surprised by my reaction.

"Sorry, I don't know why it startled me," I mumbled as I let go of Max and backed away from the portrait.

But I did know. It was the man I'd seen at the church that morning. He was wearing the same dark, curly wig and his ebony eyes seemed to be mocking me as I defiantly glared back at him. He was real. He'd lived, and died, according to Max.

"That would be Hugo Everly. He seemed to have all the appeal of a scorching case of venereal disease, if you ask me," Max supplied with a chuckle. "Just look at that scowl. He was quite an interesting chap, though."

"In what way?" I asked, my stomach performing complicated acrobatics as I tried to get the words out.

"The most interesting thing about dear old Hugo is that no one really knows what happened to him. He was there one day, gone the next. He simply vanished, without leaving an heir, mind you. His nephew, Clarence, inherited the title, and I'm descended from him."

"What might have happened to him?" I asked, suddenly sorry for the man I'd seen. He'd seemed so alive, so virile. What horrible fate had befallen him?

"I suppose it could have been anything. He might have contracted the plague in London and been tossed into a mass grave, or he might have been set upon by highwaymen, robbed and killed en route to somewhere. No one knows exactly when he disappeared, you see, but it was sometime in May of 1685.

He was rumored to be a great supporter of the Duke of Monmouth, but he vanished before Monmouth even landed in England, so I doubt his disappearance had anything to do with the rebellion. All his correspondence was gone as well. He must have burned it, or someone else had, for fear of what would be discovered. It took some time for Hugo to be declared legally dead, by which point his nephew had reached majority. Worked out rather well for my branch of the family," Max informed me smugly.

"It certainly has. When was this portrait painted then?"

"A few years before Hugo vanished."

"Was he married?" I kept staring at the portrait, trying to reconcile it with the man I'd seen earlier.

"Not as far as we know," Max replied, clearly bored with the subject.

"What does that mean?"

"It means that there was no record of a marriage, which is not to say that one never took place. He might have even had a child out there somewhere, or more than one, but none came forward, legitimate or otherwise."

"Poor man," I sighed, turning from the portrait.

"I have no doubt that whatever happened to him, he brought it on himself. He wasn't a very lovable guy, by all accounts. Shall we go in to dinner? I'm starved actually, and we're having roast beef, potatoes and Yorkshire puds." Max smiled like a little boy who'd been promised an extra helping of cake. He had a way of making me feel lighter, which I appreciated, especially on a day like today.

It wasn't until halfway through the meal that I suddenly realized something that had been nagging at me since we left the gallery. It finally fell into place when Max scowled at something his mother said and threw her a dark look of warning, which went completely ignored by Lady Everly as she continued to regale me with stories of Max's exploits at boarding school when he was a boy. Max greatly resembled the man in the portrait. Of course, he wasn't wearing a wig, and his clothes were fashionable and modern, but the features were very similar, especially when he looked displeased, as he did at that very moment.

"Oh, he was such a little scoundrel," Lady Everly recounted with a smile, her eyes clouded by her memories. "He was actually expelled for trying to plant a kiss on his French teacher. It was rather adorable. He was only eight at the time, but the headmaster took it all way too seriously, didn't he, darling?" she asked Max, who was staring down at his plate in obvious embarrassment. "Of course, it wasn't until he was seventeen that he finally succeeded, with the same teacher, I might add. He had quite the schoolboy crush on her. She was only about thirty at the time. A pretty little thing. What was her name, Max?"

I suddenly got the impression that Lady Everly was purposely trying to humiliate Max. Was it a punishment for inviting hordes of people into her home? Maybe she wasn't as harmless as I thought, or maybe she was just a typical mother who got a kick from talking about her son's childhood pranks.

Max looked up at his mother with an expression so like that of Hugo Everly that I was nearly knocked off my chair by the resemblance between the two men. I was so astounded that I couldn't help remarking on my discovery.

"Max, you look much like your ancestor, Hugo, when you frown like that," I said in a teasing tone. "A curly wig and a sword at your hip and you could be brothers."

"Ah, so you noticed," Lady Everly chimed in. "I always did say that Max looks like Hugo. One of the theories that was put forth in my day was that Hugo's nephew was really his son, but my husband, who was descended from said nephew, rejected the idea, since the boy was the son of Hugo's sister. Of course, it was quite possible that Hugo's sister, Jane Hiddleston, adopted the boy and reared him as her own since Hugo wasn't married.

Jane never had any other children; perhaps she was barren, and Hugo's bastard was a godsend. Or, the child could have been the product of incest between brother and sister. They were said to have been very close. Jane was devastated when Hugo went missing. There were several letters in which she confided to a friend that she was heartbroken and lonesome without her beloved brother. What do you think, Max?" Her eyes sparkled with mischief, and I got a brief glimpse of what she must have been like in her youth—carefree and a little wild, a spoiled rich girl who always got her way.

"Who cares, Mother?" Max hissed. "They've all been dead for centuries, so whether we're descended from one Everly or another, makes absolutely no difference to me."

"No, you don't care about that kind of thing, do you, darling? If you did, you'd have sired an heir by now, but you're too busy chasing skirts in London. Don't think I don't hear what you get up to." The atmosphere in the room noticeably changed as the subject of an heir came up. This was a sore subject between mother and son, and I thought it best to leave them to it.

"If you'll excuse me, I'm rather tired," I mumbled as I rose from the table.

"Oh, don't leave on my account, dear," Lady Everly said, smiling pleasantly. "Max will do his duty sooner or later, whether he likes it or not. And he will do it while I'm still living." I could hear a note of steel in Lady Everly's voice and suddenly felt a twinge of pity for Max. Centuries had passed, but nothing much changed for people like him.

I heard Max's voice rise in agitation as I left the dining room, giving them the privacy they needed to duke it out.

FIVE

My mobile rang seconds after I walked through the door of my bedroom, the sound shrill and alarming in the peaceful silence of the upper floor. I picked it up and glanced at the screen. Evan. Again. I hadn't spoken to him since I had informed him of the miscarriage, but I couldn't avoid him forever, and now was as good a time as any, since I was already in a foul mood, given my episode at the church that morning and the uncomfortable position Lady and Lord Everly had placed me in by involving me in their familial spats.

I accepted the call and pressed the phone to my ear with some trepidation. I would be lying if I said that I didn't miss Evan. We'd been together for a long time, and much of that time had been good. I suppose, looking back, that I loved him more than he ever loved me, but he had been affectionate and kind, if not always very giving, especially of his time. It wasn't until I announced my pregnancy that I saw the manipulative, ruthless side that so shocked me, and belatedly realized that Evan would always put his interests above mine.

"Hello, Evan," I said, hoping I wasn't making a terrible mistake by speaking to him. Being a lawyer, he could usually talk circles around me, and I didn't want to give him the chance to talk me around to coming back to him, if that was indeed what he wanted. Perhaps he wanted to ask me to return the diamond earrings he'd given me for my twenty-fifth birthday, or the first edition of *A Tale of Two Cities*, which was one of my favorites and with which he'd surprised me on our anniversary last year.

"Neve, thank God you finally picked up," Evan exclaimed, sounding nervous and surprised. "Please, hear me out, darling."

I didn't say anything, so he went on, encouraged by my silence. I suppose he took it for consent.

"Look, I've been a villain of biblical proportions," he began.

"Why, have you finally killed your brother?" I couldn't help asking, my voice dripping with sarcasm. Evan despised his half-brother Noah as only one sibling could despise another. Whereas Evan was ambitious, educated, and driven, Noah was the happy-go-lucky brother who never had any money, lived on people's couches, smoked tremendous amounts of marijuana, but somehow still managed to produce canvases of such originality and rare beauty as to make more money than Evan could ever dream of. We never did figure out what he did with the money, since he'd seemed to be wearing the same pair of jeans for the past year, but Noah was one of the icons of twenty-first-century pop culture, always hounded by paparazzi and pursued by gorgeous women who seemed oblivious to his matted hair and paint-splattered shirts.

"Neve, be serious," Evan said in his best "lawyer addressing the jury" voice. "Noah is alive and well as far as I know. Now, please, hear me out."

"All right, go on then," I conceded as I sank down on the bed. I needed to be seated for this conversation.

I expected Evan to start talking, but he suddenly grew quiet, thinking something over.

"Where are you?" he suddenly asked.

"In Surrey, why?"

"I just think we need to talk in person, that's all. This is not the right conversation to have over the phone. May I come and see you?"

"I'm working."

"I know, but it won't take long; I promise. I just want to talk to you face to face. I love you so much, Neve. Please, give me the address."

I took a deep breath and held the phone away from my ear for a moment. Evan was trying to push my buttons, but I suddenly realized that his tactics weren't working. My feelings for him had changed. The love I felt was gone, replaced by hurt and resentment. Those negative feelings would go away in time, but the love wouldn't come back in their place. I had endowed Evan with all kinds of chivalrous qualities in my romantic imagination, but I saw him clearly now. He was a flawed, selfish man who wanted a safe and comfortable life which revolved around his needs. I was sure that he'd find a woman to give him that life, but it wouldn't be me.

I held the phone back to my ear and spoke before Evan had a chance to interrupt me. "Evan, I'm at Everly Manor in Cranleigh. If you want, you can come tomorrow, but I must warn you that it will be a wasted trip."

"Thank you, Neve. I'll see you tomorrow." I could hear a note of triumph in his voice, but I wouldn't let him win. I would, however, give both of us a chance to get closure.

I disconnected the call and tossed the phone on top of a dresser. I felt drained, emotionally and physically, so I changed into my pajamas and crawled into bed, hoping that tomorrow would be a better day.

* * *

I spent a restless night, dreaming of Evan happily playing with a little boy, seventeenth-century cavaliers, modern-day lords, and meddling mothers. Sometime in the small hours, I dreamed of a young woman, no older than sixteen, crying quietly as Hugo Everly stood over her, glowering like a thunderstorm about to break. The girl sat on a low stool, her arms wrapped around her middle protectively as her huge, dark eyes silently appealed to Hugo for mercy.

"You can't keep it, Jane," Hugo said, not unkindly. "You will be confined to this house until the child is born, and then the midwife will take it away. She will place it with a family in the village, and they will receive an annual stipend for the upkeep of the child. It will be well looked after, but you can have no contact whatsoever either with the family or with the child. Is that understood?"

The young woman cried harder, tears streaming down her cheeks and sliding into her open mouth as she rocked back and forth. "Hugo, I beseech you, don't take the baby away from me. Please," she begged as he looked on her warily, his eyes softening just a fraction.

"Janey, you are not married, or even betrothed. How can you keep your child without causing scandal and shaming the family? It's bad enough that you allowed that scoundrel to seduce you, but now you're with child and it's up to me, as the head of the family, to do everything in my power to preserve your honor. Perhaps you'll miscarry. That would be best for everyone." Hugo sounded sad, but firm in his resolve.

"I love him," Jane muttered as she looked up at her brother. "I love him, Hugo. Maybe if he knows there's a child, he'll marry me." She looked so hopeful that her brother cringed as he delivered the final blow.

"Janey, he knows," he said softly. "I went to see him last night. He is promised to someone else, and he let me know, in no uncertain terms, that this situation will do nothing to alter his plans. He is not the saint you believe him to be."

"Hugo, please," Jane wailed. "I will do anything, anything at all, but please don't take it away."

"Anything?" Hugo asked, his eyes narrowing in a way that suggested that he might have an idea.

"Anything." Jane smiled at him, and the innocence and trust in her young face was heartbreaking.

"So be it, sister, but there's no turning back once you've agreed."

"Agreed to what?" Jane asked, suddenly fearful.

"To whatever I propose. Give me a week." With that, Hugo strode from the room, leaving Jane's tear-stricken face aglow with hope.

I sat bolt upright in bed. Had I just dreamed of Jane Everly or was my mind playing tricks on me? This place was having a very strange effect on me.

I stretched and got out of bed, ready for another day of ironing out details, sending information to my boss, Lawrence Spellman, and conferring with him regarding various minutiae before drawing up the paperwork.

I was just putting on my coat to walk over to the museum when I saw Evan's car pull into the car park visible from the foyer window. My first impulse was to run out the back door and make for the woods, but that would be immature, not to mention pointless. He'd track me down sooner or later, and the conversation that I didn't want to have would take place. There was no time like the present, although, in my mind, there was nothing left to say. I said I'd needed time to think, to sort things out, but my heart had sorted things out months ago. Now all I had to do was make Evan understand. Something he had difficulty doing when it wasn't in line with his own wishes.

Zipping up my coat, I walked out the door, desperate to

prevent the confrontation from happening within hearing distance of the Everlys or their staff. I didn't like to wash my linen in public, as Lady Everly seemed to enjoy doing, so I walked briskly toward the car, nodding in response to Evan's greeting.

I hadn't seen Evan in nearly three months and was surprised to see that he'd lost weight off his already lanky frame, and there were a few more grays in his sandy hair. His eyes, behind the fashionable rimless glasses, looked anxious as he studied me for a moment, but his lips stretched into a cautious smile as I drew closer.

"Neve, you look great," Evan said as he leaned in for a kiss, which I avoided by turning my head. He kissed my cheek instead and gave me his arm, turning us toward the bleak garden.

We walked in silence for a few minutes; both of us overcome with deep emotion but unwilling to speak. Finally, Evan broke the silence.

"Neve, come home. Please. I know I've been an absolute shit, but I can't do without you. The flat feels so empty, and nothing is right. Even Natasha misses you." He gave me a look of pure misery, which I would have believed, had I not seen him use it in court to win over a jury and make them feel sympathy for his client.

"I can't," I replied, wishing he'd understand.

"Why? You've lost the child, so the problem is gone. We can start again."

"It wasn't a 'problem,' Evan; it was a human being, one I wanted very badly. It's clear to me that we want different things, so can we just drop the pretense that we are still a couple? My feelings have changed." I didn't want to come straight out and tell him that I no longer loved him, but my meaning was clear.

"I'll make it up to you. How about Paris in the spring or Tuscany in the summer? You know how you love a holiday. It'll be like a honeymoon. We'll have wine-soaked dinners, strolls in moonlit gardens, and nights of making love in some quaint little inn. Think about it."

"Evan, my feelings will not be soothed by meals or walks. You showed me very clearly what matters to you, and it's not me or my needs. You never even wanted to discuss the pregnancy; you just wanted me to get rid of it, as if it were a bag of trash. Would you still want to go on holiday if I were pregnant, expecting a baby you don't want? Would you be there with me when I went into labor or brought home our baby?" I stopped and stared him down, willing him to answer.

"No, I wouldn't be. I made that clear," he said, finally dropping the pretense and staring right back.

"Well, let me make this clear—we are finished. I will collect my things from the flat once I come back to London. Until then, please don't call me or message me. There's nothing to say, and I don't want to nurture this animosity between us."

I turned on my heel and strode from the garden, leaving Evan standing among the shriveled flower beds, the frost sparkling like diamonds in the hazy sunshine. He stood there until I'd walked to the museum and disappeared through the door after one last look at the man whom I'd loved for the past four years. I wasn't happy, but I felt a satisfying sense of closure, which, under the circumstances, was all I could hope for.

I was just entering the foyer of the museum when Max emerged from the library looking extremely shamefaced. "Neve, I was looking for you," he said and beckoned me to join him in the library. "I wanted to apologize for last night. My mother thinks that humiliating me in front of guests will somehow induce me to procreate on demand," he stated with a mulish expression that nearly made me laugh.

"Would it be so awful to marry and have a family?" It was none of my business, but I was curious why Max still wasn't married at his age. He was handsome, charming, titled, and presumably wealthy.

"No, it wouldn't, if I could do it on my own terms. I was engaged to a wonderful girl a few years ago, but Mummy"—he said that with bitter sarcasm that showed plainly how he felt—"didn't approve. She did everything in her power to break us up and eventually my fiancée left me, saying that marriage was hard enough, and she wasn't prepared to deal with the interference of my mother in every detail of our life. Can't say I blame her. I tried to win her back, but she stood firm. She was right, too. My mother would have made her life a misery."

"I'm sorry. That must have been difficult for you," I said, secretly siding with the fiancée. I wouldn't care to deal with Naomi Everly either.

"Well, I'm pushing forty now," Max stated dramatically, "so, my mother is a little more flexible on my choice of bride, but I just haven't met anyone I wanted to share my life with since Lauren. By the by, who was that chap I saw you talking to in the garden?"

"That was Evan, my one-time partner. It's over between us."

"Poor man. Wouldn't want to be in his shoes," Max quipped as he drew a little closer to me. "What had he done to get the boot?"

"It's a long story. I actually have some work to do, so if you don't mind..." I didn't want to be rude, but unbidden tears sprang to my eyes at the thought of Evan and the baby.

"I'm so sorry. I didn't mean to pry. Tactless of me," Max stammered at seeing my distress. "I do apologize. I seem to be doing that a lot. Would you join me for a drink later? I promise, no personal questions or inappropriate comments of any kind." He laid his hand on his heart, and I couldn't help but smile. He really was sweet.

"Sure, a drink would be lovely," I replied, hoping it was at a pub rather than at Everly Manor.

"Say, around six at the Richard Onslow?" Max asked as he turned toward the door.

"Yes. See you there."

SIX

I spent the next few days in a flurry of activity, punctuated by meals and walks with Max. His easygoing manner made me feel comfortable, and for the first time in months, I felt lighter of spirit. The conversation with Evan had helped as well, making me feel as if I'd finally reached the end of that chapter in my life and could turn the page without constantly looking back. I still grieved for the baby, but I was coming to terms with my loss and starting to consider the future. Eventually, I'd have to start dating again, which was a daunting prospect, but for now, I didn't have to make any decisions or commitments. I could just take life day by day and see where it took me. My new resolve was even commented on by Max, who remarked that I seemed happier somehow. I'd noticed a change in my physical appearance as well. The haunted look in my eyes had been replaced by a calmer, more purposeful gaze, and my skin and hair seemed to take on a new glow, whether from my improved mental state or the fact that I was spending time away from the smog of London in the fresh country air of Surrey.

I hadn't had any more strange dreams, but the one I did have had stayed with me. I could still feel the anguish of the young woman at the thought of being parted from her child, and wondered if in the psychedelic realm of dreams, she represented me, struggling to accept the fact that her baby couldn't stay with her. Perhaps my mind was looking for ways to work through the hurt and move on. I hoped so, because I was a happy person by nature and could no longer bear the crippling sadness I'd felt for the past few months.

Thoughts of Hugo Everly often caught me unawares, making me wonder about what happened to the man every time I passed his portrait in the gallery. His dark eyes seemed to follow me, a mixture of amusement and arrogance, so deftly captured by the artist, immortalized on the handsome face that would never age. What had I really seen that day? I believed that what I saw had been real, but my mind couldn't accept the fact that I might have gone back in time. The notion was absurd, not to mention completely implausible. I did some half-hearted research on time travel and found some theories about ley lines, but nothing concrete, of course, since time travel was scientifically not possible. Or was it?

I'd also tried to research the site of the church. There wasn't much to be found online, so I decided to ask Vicar Lambert, who was only too happy to oblige. A brand-new packet of chocolate biscuits had been produced for the occasion, the kettle whistling on the hob as the vicar set out the cups and saucers with great ceremony, practically beaming with the desire to help. He was under the false impression that the information would be used in the film somehow, and I decided not to disillusion him, since the notion gave him such pleasure. At last, the tea was poured, and the vicar settled himself with a cup, leaning back in his chair as he took a dainty bite of the biscuit and surveyed me over the rim of the cup.

"I don't mind telling you, Neve dear, that this church was built on an ancient Pagan site of worship. I think I might have mentioned that before. That was often the case in medieval times, partially intended to take advantage of the structure and materials that were already there, and to bring in the Pagan members of the community to the church. I personally think that it was also done with the purpose of obliterating the original holy place in order to discourage people from continuing to frequent it. Some of these ancient beliefs were so deeply rooted that the only way to keep people from continuing to practice them, was to try to wipe them out altogether."

"Did it work?" I asked, wondering how people reacted to having their place of worship desecrated.

"Not right away, no. There were still those who adhered to the old ways, but eventually Christianity won out, as it always does," the vicar added pompously, "and the heathens saw the light of Christ, shining so brightly and burning away their past sins. The Good Lord would never punish someone for their ignorance. After all, these poor creatures didn't know any better, did they, but they knew enough to accept Christ into their hearts, which is all that matters."

I felt a long sermon coming on and balked at the idea. Clearly, Vicar Lambert was not packing the church on Sundays, so his eloquent preaching was wasted on the precious few who still came. I wouldn't be one of them and needed a way to politely change the subject without offending the good vicar.

"Vicar, please tell me more about the crypt," I asked, hoping that he would warm up to that theme instead. He did.

"Well, the crypt just happens to be part of the old Pagan structure that was here long before the church was built. The builders cleverly utilized the stone floor and the walls but added the columns and the vaulted ceiling before building the church itself."

"Were any alterations made to the crypt since the church was built?" I asked, trying to find some explanation for my experience. Why did I go to the seventeenth century if the crypt dated back to Pictish times? If I tried again, would I end up in the same year? I didn't know what year I went to, but Hugo vanished in 1685, around the age of thirty-five, which meant that I saw him within a few years of that date, judging by his appearance. He couldn't have been younger than thirty-three or older than thirty-five.

"As a matter of fact," Vicar Lambert told me confidentially, leaning in and lowering his voice, as if we might be overheard by some Druids who just happened to be hanging around since the Dark Ages and were just waiting for this little tidbit of information, "the crypt had to be reinforced in the mid-seventeenth century. The walls were cracking, from the weight of the church above it, I suppose, so another layer of stone was added on the inside of the crypt, as well as some handsome carvings. I'm sure you've seen them. Before that, the walls were just plain unhewn stone."

"Were any additional exits put in place then, or any tunnels leading outside?" No one could accuse me of giving up easily.

"I don't believe so. Why do you ask?" The Vicar's face suddenly lit up, understanding dawning, although it wasn't at all what I had meant. "Is there a scene in the film where someone escapes the church by means of a secret tunnel?"

"Not as far as I know, but if there was a tunnel, it might be written in. Viewers just love the romance such scenes create," I improvised, feeling a trifle guilty for misleading the poor vicar.

"I'll tell you what; you have another cup of tea, and I will look for the original blueprints of the church. I'm fairly certain there are no secret tunnel exits, but we must make sure mustn't we, for the sake of art."

I raised my teacup in a toast. "For the sake of art," I repeated as I reached for another biscuit.

To the vicar's great disappointment, the blueprints didn't show any secret passages or forgotten exits leading out of the crypt, but he quickly recovered, asking if I might have had an opportunity to speak to the director about his part. I had asked

Lawrence if he might have use for the vicar, but he had emphatically declined, saying that's what actors were for. I hated to disappoint the jolly old man, but casting really wasn't up to me.

Vicar Lambert looked crestfallen as I thanked him for the tea and left the church, stepping into the deceptively mild March afternoon. I was glad that winter was finally over. I'd always hated winter, and the promise of spring lifted my spirits as I climbed the ridge back to Everly Manor.

SEVEN

I heard it said that once an idea takes root in the mind it's very difficult to dislodge it, and this particular idea kept growing in mine for over a week before I finally had to act on it. I needed to know what had happened to me that day in the crypt and prove to myself that I hadn't imagined the whole thing. I reasoned that as long as I could get back to the present, as I had before, I was in no danger. I had spent the past few weeks researching the seventeenth century for work, so I thought I could easily blend in for an hour or so and see how things stood for myself before I returned to my own time.

I wanted to meet Hugo and talk to him, to know that he was real and not just a figment of my imagination. The notion that two people from centuries apart could come together for even a fleeting moment in time, and make a connection where none was possible, was more enticing than I would admit even to myself. I wasn't looking for validation or glory, and I would tell no one of what I had experienced, but having the ability to do something which no one else had ever done before was too tantalizing to pass up. I had no idea what I would say, and every dialogue that I invented in my mind sounded false and contrived, but I felt a physical need to meet the man, to be in the same room and hear the sound of his voice, to try to find out what had happened to him, and to Jane.

On Saturday morning, I told Max that I was going to London for the day. It was the weekend, so he'd have no reason to expect me to stay at the house, and as far as I knew he had plans of his own, which suited my needs perfectly. I drove my car to a car park in the village and left it there, since I could hardly leave the car at the manor and walk to the church without arousing Max's suspicions. The rest was easy enough. I'd stopped by the museum the day before and selected a seven-teenth-century gown, a chemise and stockings, shoes, and a fur-lined cloak of midnight blue velvet from one of the trunks. I didn't take one of the elaborate gowns on display, but a simple one of brown damask with an underskirt of the same shade of cream as the slashing in the sleeves. It was the gown of a lady, but it wasn't pretentious or expensive, so if it got ruined, I wouldn't feel too guilty. The cloak was a bit extravagant, but it was the only thing warm enough for the chilly weather outside, and I made a promise to myself to take good care of it and bring it back in pristine condition.

I took the holdall out of the boot, locked the car, and walked the short distance to the church. The morning was sunny but cold, and my breath came out in small white puffs as I hurried along. I grew more nervous now that the moment was at hand, but my feet carried me along, moving even faster now that I was hesitating.

Was I mad? I asked myself as I passed through the lichen-covered gate and made for the church porch. Would a sane person do what I was about to do? But my mind demanded answers, and I couldn't live without learning the truth of what had happened to me that day.

I stopped in front of the door and counted to ten to calm my racing heart. I could still turn back, but if I were honest with myself, I didn't want to.

I pushed open the door and entered the church. Sounds of conversation could be heard from the vestry, Vicar Lambert's voice clearly audible as he made a comment and then chuckled good-naturedly, but I didn't hear an answering voice, so perhaps the vicar was on a call. The church itself was blessedly empty, the morning light filtering through the stained-glass windows and filling the church with a rainbow of color.

My footsteps echoed on the stone floor as I made my way down the nave, disrupting the solemn hush of the place. Why was the quiet of a church so different from any other sound? You felt as if you were disturbing God himself if you so much as made a sound. I rushed over to the stairway to the crypt and skipped down before anyone became aware of my presence.

The crypt looked much as it had before, but eerier since I didn't turn on the light. The knight kept his silent vigil over the rest of the residents, his hands gripping the hilt of the sword resting against his breastplate.

"What do you think, Bruce?" I asked him as I quickly changed into my finery. "Have I completely gone round the bend? I feel like Alice about to go down the rabbit hole. I just bet Hugo Mad Hatter Everly is waiting for me at his place, ready to serve tea and banter with His Grace the White Rabbit."

Somehow, I felt even more foolish for talking to an effigy, so I stopped blathering and got on with the task at hand. I stowed away my modern-day clothes in a bag behind the tomb of the knight, and carefully pushed the button in the flower. My hand shook with nerves, and I held my breath, almost expecting nothing whatsoever to happen. Wouldn't I feel the fool standing there in my seventeenth-century garb in front of a solid stone wall, but the stone began to move, a little quieter this time.

I glanced at the stone steps shrouded in darkness. "Here

goes nothing," I told the knight and made my way to the
wooden door at the top.

Thankfully, the church was empty on this end as well. I
looked around to make sure everything looked as it did the last
time. It did. But before leaving, I walked up to the altar and
glanced at the register lying open on the pulpit. There were
lines and lines of marriages, births and deaths, all neatly
recorded in the same hand—the year 1685. This seemed to jibe
with what I'd seen before, so I wrapped the cloak around me
and left the church, steeling myself for the walk to the house.

I was shaking like a leaf, more from anxiety than cold, but it
was a rather bitter morning with a thin crust of frozen snow
covering the ground and making me feel numb within minutes.
Modern clothing was so much warmer and more practical. A
frigid wind blew through the cloak since there were no buttons
to keep it closed. All I had was a tie at the throat, which allowed
the cloak to billow around me like a full sail. The hood kept
blowing off my head and wind whistled in my ears as I walked
toward Everly Manor, which rose out of the mist, stark and
proud, not dwarfed by the Victorian mansion which had put it
out to pasture in the nineteenth century.

I had a speech all prepared in advance, but every last word
fled my memory as I got closer, my mind screaming for me to
turn back and go back to my own time, my own place. I barely
registered the pounding of hoofbeats behind me until it was too
late, and I felt the hot breath of a galloping horse inches from
my face as the horse knocked me off my feet and sent me flying
to the side of the narrow lane, the rider screaming something at
me as I fell ass over teakettle and hit my head on the frozen
earth, my ankle twisting painfully as I landed. For a moment,
everything went quiet and still as I stared up at the colorless sky
and saw a lone raven circling above. Was it a sign of doom? I
wondered dazedly.

The huge horse restlessly stomped its hooves, its nostrils flaring and its round eyes rolling from side to side in panic as the man dismounted and ran to my side. Hugo Everly's face appeared above mine, his eyes full of concern as he ran his hands over my limbs to see if anything was broken. His lips were moving, but I couldn't hear anything he said over the ringing in my ears and the roar of blood pounding through my veins. I tried to form words, but nothing came out. I didn't think I was seriously hurt, but my thoughts were muddled, and I felt suddenly very dizzy and disoriented. Oh, God, did I have a concussion?

I closed my eyes, partially to keep my head from spinning, and partially to hide from that dark gaze that was skewering me mercilessly, then opened them again. Hugo's curls fluttered in the wind, his hat shadowing the top half of his face, making him appear even more menacing.

Hugo effortlessly lifted me off the ground and carried me toward the house, his features arranged in just the same scowl that was immortalized in his portrait. His lips moved from time to time, but I still couldn't hear anything besides the beating of my own heart, which seemed magnified a thousandfold, obliterating all other sounds. I closed my eyes in exasperation. I'd finally met the man and couldn't even talk to him. What a fool I'd been to go off like that. The past was full of danger, not the least of it being a galloping horse that came out of nowhere.

The door flew open, and Hugo strode past a shocked servant, whose pale round face was dominated by a pouty mouth currently frozen in an O of surprise. Hugo settled me on a chaise and turned to pour a drink from a silver decanter. He sank to his knees and held the cup to my lips until I took a sip. It was brandy, and very good brandy, if I was any judge. He continued to help me drink until the glass was empty. My heart rate began to slow down and the ringing in my ears finally subsided somewhat. The room was quiet except for my breathing, which still sounded awfully loud to my ears. Hugo seemed to be holding his breath as he leaned over me.

"Can you hear me, madam? Are you badly injured?" His voice was like the brandy, smooth and calming, and not at all what I expected.

"I... I think I'm all right," I mumbled as I tried to sit up.

Hugo unceremoniously pushed me right back down as he rose to his feet. "Don't try to get up; you'll be overcome by vertigo. Just rest awhile. Would more brandy help?"

Under the circumstances, I had no idea what would help, but I nodded, and he poured another inch into the cup. I accepted the cup from his hand and took small sips between gulps of air, while Hugo removed his hat and tossed it onto a nearby chair, followed by his wig. The simple gesture instantly changed his appearance, making him appear younger and less intimidating. I'd always wondered how men wore their own hair under those ridiculous wigs and was surprised to see that Hugo's hair was shorn short, the dark waves only about two inches long.

He pulled up a straight-backed chair and took a seat next to me, taking my hand gently as he did so. "Hugo Everly at your service, madam. Please accept my heartfelt apology for the mishap. I didn't see you walking there. In truth, I wasn't expecting anyone to be in the lane and wasn't paying attention to my surroundings as I was preoccupied with my own thoughts. Very careless of me. I trust you are not badly hurt?" he asked again, searching my face for confirmation that he wasn't responsible for causing me irreparable harm.

"I just got the wind knocked out of me, that's all. I'll be quite all right, thank you, Lord Everly," I mumbled, suddenly very conscious of my absurd position.

"May I know your name?"

"Neve Ashley." I was surprised to see Hugo look at me with renewed interest; his eyes narrowed as he studied my features.

"The niece of Anthony Ashley Cooper, the Earl of Shaftesbury?" he asked, clearly stunned. "I thought the Christian name was Nell, but I must have been mistaken."

I was about to deny any relation to the Earl of Shaftesbury, who'd been a fervent supporter of the Duke of Monmouth, but then reconsidered. If it bought me a little time, then what was the harm? Not like I was planning to stay and impersonate the lady.

"Ah... yes," I mumbled as I averted my eyes. What if he decided to take me home?

I was so busy considering the what ifs that I hardly noticed what Hugo Everly was saying.

"I'm sorry, did you say something?" I asked, feeling even more flustered.

Hugo cocked his head to the side, appraising my mental state, which he must have found to be somewhat sound as he sat back and continued his train of thought. "I was just saying how sorry I was to hear of your recent bereavement," he said, still watching me like a hawk.

I, of course, had no idea whom he was referring to, so nodded sadly in the hope that he would just change the subject. He didn't.

"I had great respect for your uncle and didn't believe a word of the accusations of treason against him. A blatant fabrication. It's tragic that he had to die in exile, so far away from the home that he so loved."

"Yes, it was," I agreed, hoping I wouldn't give myself away by making some glaring mistake.

I was saved from further discussion of my "uncle" by the appearance of a boy. He was twelve or thirteen, still sweet-faced and childish, but with a hint of impending manhood hovering somewhere behind the eyes and in the silky fuzz that darkened his upper lip. He stopped dead when he saw me on the chaise, but a stern look from Hugo put paid to any speculation he might have had regarding the situation.

"Mistress Ashley, may I present my nephew, Clarence Hiddleston."

Clarence gave me a stiff bow and averted his eyes in embarrassment. Clearly, he thought he had walked into some kind of romantic tryst. Judging by the boy's shock, they weren't a regular occurrence.

"Where's your mother, Clarence?" Hugo asked irritably. "Is she still abed?"

"You know she is," Clarence answered sullenly and gave Hugo a look of such disdain that it nearly made me laugh. Seems teenagers were much the same in any age. "She rarely stirs before noon. Shall I get her?"

"Yes, tell her we have a guest, and be quick about it."

Clarence threw Hugo a defiant look and left the room, walking slowly in hopes of provoking his uncle. I turned away from Hugo to hide my smile.

"Are you hungry? Should I call for some refreshment?" Hugo asked solicitously, suddenly realizing how compromising we looked with me lying down and him leaning over me. He didn't wait for me to answer as he pulled a cord to summon a servant.

A young girl of about fourteen appeared a few moments later. She seemed intimidated by her master, but he was perfectly courteous to her.

"Please ask Cook to send up some refreshments. We have a guest."

"Right away, Your Lordship," the girl stammered.

"And more brandy, Harriet," he called after her as she scampered from the room.

I looked at the departing girl and decided that it was probably time to make my escape. I'd gotten what I came for, and although I had no idea what would eventually happen to Hugo, I wasn't about to find out. I needed to get back to the church and to my own time since I was feeling worse by the minute. I was lying to this man, pretending to be someone I wasn't, and taking advantage of his hospitality. It felt all wrong, and I was ashamed of myself. I could tell that he was brimming with questions about how I came to be on his property and why I was alone and on foot. He was too polite to interrogate me, especially since he thought I was the relative of an earl, but sooner or later, he would ask, and no answer I could give him would make sense. I needed to leave.

I made to sit up, but a wave of dizziness brought me right back down, reminding me that I'd recently hit my head. My ankle was also throbbing in a most alarming way, and I let out a little yelp as I tried to move it.

"Where are you going?" Hugo was instantly by my side. "You just turned white as a sheet. Please, Mistress Ashley, lie back down and rest. Shall I summon a physician? It might take a few hours though, since the nearest medical man is at Blackney."

"No, please don't trouble yourself. I'll be all right. I just need to rest a bit longer."

"You need to rest for several days. I will make sure you're comfortable and my sister will act as chaperone, so you mustn't worry about any damage to your reputation."

I might be concussed, but at least my virtue would be safe, I thought with an inward giggle. Chivalry was alive and well.

"Ah, here's Jane," Hugo announced with some relief as a woman appeared in the doorway.

She was some years younger than Hugo, which placed her at around thirty, and was dressed in a sober gown of charcoal gray. Her hair was pulled back from her face with only a few curls on either side to cover the ears, but she was without question the woman I'd seen in my dream. She was older now, the bloom long gone from her cheeks and her hair sprinkled with silver, but there was no mistaking the doe-like dark eyes and the full mouth that was once quite sensuous, and so like her brother's.

"My sister was recently widowed," Hugo said as he introduced us. "Her husband is greatly missed."

"I'm sorry for your loss," and I was. She looked bereaved, and I briefly wondered if she ever got to marry her lover.

"Thank you. You are very kind," Jane replied. She took the seat that Hugo had vacated a few minutes ago and folded her hands in her lap, clearly waiting for an explanation as to what a strange woman was doing lying on a chaise in the parlor with her brother anxiously hovering about.

"Jane, this is Mistress Ashley. She was walking in the lane when Ronan and I came along and nearly ran her down. I'm afraid she's had a bad fall. I've invited her to stay with us for a few days until she recovers," Hugo explained, sounding awfully guilty.

"I told you that horse was a demon," Jane replied, the color rising in her cheeks. "'Tis only a matter of time before you kill someone."

"He's just young and spirited, that's all." Hugo sounded defensive, but Jane just glared at him as if he were an errant schoolboy.

"It really was all my fault," I interjected, not wanting to see them argue. "I wasn't paying attention and it was rather foggy outside, so Lord Everly wouldn't have spotted me until it was too late."

"Don't blame yourself, my dear," Jane replied, still gazing at her brother. "That horse of his is a menace. Nothing wrong with a good English mare, but my brother must have an Arabian stallion." I could see that she was teasing him now, her annoyance forgotten.

"I won him in a card game off Henry Howard, the Duke of

Norfolk," Hugo explained with a guilty smile. "The Duke was loath to part with him. Ronan is rather volatile, but that's what makes him such a challenge."

"Ronan doesn't seem like a name fitting for an Arabian stallion," I mused, watching Hugo. I could see that he was fond of the horse, possibly because he'd won it off a duke. I couldn't help wondering if it had been the Duke of Norfolk I'd seen him with at the church.

"No. His name was originally Aamir, but Norfolk had it changed to Ronan since the groom refused to go near the 'Saracen Devil,' as he called him. There's much superstition in this country against anything foreign."

"As well there should be," Jane countered. "We have everything we need right here." Jane finally seemed ready to move on from the topic of Hugo's horse, turning to me in a most solicitous manner. "Is there anything I can do to make you more comfortable?" she asked. "I do hope Hugo had the presence of mind to send for some refreshments."

"He did. He was most kind," I answered, hoping that Jane would stop fretting.

A few minutes later, Harriet came bustling into the room with another decanter of brandy and some sort of rolls which smelled heavenly. "Just out of the oven, Your Lordship," she said, setting the tray down and giving Hugo a slight curtsy.

"Ah, thank you," he replied absentmindedly. Hugo looked from me to Jane and back again, as if he suddenly felt caged and needed an excuse to get out. "Jane, I need to go out for a short while. Will you look after Mistress Ashley while I'm gone? I will return before nightfall, but if you should require me urgently, just send Jem with a message to Nash House."

"Don't worry, Hugo. We will be just fine, won't we? I'm a very good nurse. I nursed my husband for two years before he finally left us, may he rest in peace," Jane explained, turning to me. "Can I get you a sausage in a roll? Our cook rather excels at these, partially because she knows Hugo likes them. All the women in this house simply fall over themselves to make him happy."

Hugo just smiled, knowing he was being teased. I could almost bet that Jane was one of the women who fawned over him. She seemed awfully fond of her brother, and his gaze noticeably softened when he looked at her.

"Off with you then," Jane said, shooing Hugo from the room. "We will be just fine, won't we, Mistress Ashley?"

"I'm sure we will," I replied, wishing that I could just flee, but realizing that I would have to spend at least a few hours at Everly Manor before I was well enough to make my way back to the church.

Hugo snatched his wig and hat off the chair, gave me a stiff bow and hastened from the room.

"Just like a man," Jane remarked with an indulgent smile as she watched Hugo through the window.

"Why do you say that?" I asked, warming up to Jane instantly. She'd voiced my own thoughts.

Jane tore her eyes away from the window and gave me a knowing smile. "Why, it's obvious, isn't it? Hugo feels guilty for the injury he's caused you, so he would much rather put it out of his mind and drink and dice with his friend instead. By the time he returns, I will assure him that you are quite well, and he will forgive himself and put the incident behind him."

I couldn't help but chuckle at Jane's summing up of the situation. She was probably right, but that was just as well. There was no reason for Hugo to feel guilty. He hadn't expected anyone to be in the lane and didn't see me in the mist until he was almost upon me. I should have heard the pounding of the hooves, but I was lost in my own thoughts and didn't get out of the way in time. It was an accident, one that brought me in contact with Hugo Everly and his sister. I had to admit that they weren't at all what I imagined them to be, and I would have liked to get to know them better. As it was, I had to get back to my own time, and I would leave as soon as I could manage the walk back to the church. Until then, I'd spend a little time with Jane. She had a serenity about her which I found comforting, and we easily fell into conversation, as women tend to do.

EIGHT

Hugo Everly galloped out of the yard, bound for Nash House. He'd seen Jane's brief look of reproach when he said he was leaving, but Jane didn't know him quite as well as she thought. He wasn't fleeing out of a sense of guilt or responsibility; he needed to see Brad for an entirely different reason.

Bradford Nash was his oldest and most trusted friend, the only person he could confide in. He'd meant to visit him today anyway, but now the visit took on a whole new urgency. Hugo's mind tried to untangle the dilemma, but despite the application of all his powers of reasoning, he couldn't come up with any explanation.

"Hugo, a pleasure to see you," Bradford exclaimed as Hugo was admitted. He was impeccably dressed as always, but his thick blond hair looked as if he'd been raking his fingers through it and there were worry lines around his eyes. "Have you lunched? I was just about to sit down. Join me. I have a good wine you might like; a fine vintage." Bradford ushered Hugo into the dining room and invited him to sit down.

"Is Beth unwell?" Hugo asked, referring to Bradford's wife, who was conspicuously absent from the table.

"She's started her confinement," Bradford answered with a frown. "I'm not allowed anywhere near her bedchamber until well after the babe is born. Praise God, may all go well," he muttered as he poured the wine. "She won't admit it, but she's very frightened. Both her mother and sister died in childbirth, so Beth secretly thinks she might be next. I keep telling her that all will be well, but it's in God's hands. Spending a month in complete isolation can only make her more fearful. The midwife came yesterday and gave me my orders. Beth is to be on bed rest until the birth, with the curtains drawn to keep out evil spirits, candles lit from morning till night, and no emotional upheaval of any kind. Only Beth's servant and the midwife are allowed to enter. I can't even imagine how Beth will cope," Bradford said, rolling his eyes.

Both Hugo and Brad had known Beth since she was a child, and she was never one to sit still for longer than a few minutes. She was a spritely presence, always on the go, whether it was to help the aged and infirm in the village, visit the new mothers, or cut up fruit to make preserves in the kitchen. The thought of her being locked in a dark room for a month at the very least was hard to imagine.

"Beth is strong; she will get through it, Brad," Hugo said, knowing that his words were hollow. Women died in childbirth every day, and no amount of faith or hope could keep them alive. Brad would be devastated if he lost his Beth. He'd loved her since they were children; she was his reason for living and breathing—his better half—but he needed an heir and there was no other way to provide one.

"To an easy birth and a healthy baby," Hugo said, raising his glass in a toast.

"Please God," Bradford breathed and drained his glass.

After that, they changed the subject by unspoken consent. What more was there to say? What happened to women behind closed doors was a mystery which neither of them cared to explore. That's what midwives were for. All they could hope for was a favorable outcome and a male child to carry on the family name.

"Brad, I'm in something of a quandary," Hugo said as he helped himself to some roast beef. He was hungry, but he couldn't eat until he'd discussed the situation with Brad.

Brad tore off a chunk of bread and mopped up some gravy before popping it in his mouth and chewing slowly. "Is it a woman?" he asked with a grin, leaning in to hear the tantalizing details.

Hugo chuckled at Brad's eagerness. A romantic dalliance would be the least of his problems, but for all intents and purposes, his problem was a woman.

"As a matter of fact, it is. I nearly killed a woman today."

"You did what? Why?" Brad exclaimed, his food forgotten.

"It was an accident. She was walking down the lane, and I didn't notice her until I was almost upon her. I didn't expect her to be there any more than she expected me to come charging at breakneck speed. She's had a nasty fall, but she will recover."

"So, what's the quandary?" Brad asked as he resumed eating. "Is she comely? Married? Has dedicated her life and virtue to God?"

"What do you know of Nell Ashley, the niece of Anthony Ashley Cooper?" Hugo asked, finally taking a bite of his own meal. Now that he was talking to Brad, he felt better. They would sort it all out; they always did. Beneath Brad's cavalier attitude toward life and love was a keen mind that always got to the crux of the problem in record time.

"Not a great deal. I believe she died in the Great Plague of London, around 1665. She was seventeen or eighteen at the time. Her mother and younger sister died as well, but I might be mistaken. Why do you ask?" Brad looked intrigued as he took a sip of wine and continued to watch Hugo. This promised to be interesting.

"The woman I nearly ran down introduced herself as Mistress Ashley. She led me to believe that she's the earl's niece," Hugo supplied.

"Did you ask her if she was his niece, or did she tell you?"

"I asked her, but she didn't deny it. She said he was her uncle. What do you make of that? Why would she lie?" Hugo took a deep swallow of wine to calm his nerves. He knew in his bones that something wasn't right, but was it what he thought?

"Hugo, are you suggesting that Monmouth sent this woman to spy on you? To test your loyalty? We both know how mistrustful he can be, especially since his last attempt failed miserably, but why would he send some strange girl? Is she his mistress, do you think? A whore? What?"

"She's not a whore. She's cultured, well-spoken, and modestly attired," Hugo replied, sounding ridiculous even to himself. There were plenty of expensive whores who were all those things.

"Is she beautiful?" Brad asked as he reached for another helping of beef.

"Yes, but not as young as you might expect. Mid-twenties at the very least."

"Hmm, why don't you just bed her and make her reveal all her secrets?"

"Bradford, be serious. You know what's at stake. If Monmouth learns the truth, I'm as good as dead. He'll run a sword through my heart first and ask questions later. I must walk a very delicate line to maintain his trust and still be loyal to our cause. We have much to gain if we succeed, and everything to lose if we fail."

"Hugo, I wish you hadn't involved yourself in this. You know what can happen. I hope you've made a last will and testament, should anything befall you. At least make sure Clarence is provided for, or that sniveling cousin of yours will get the lot."

"Clarence will inherit the lands and the title, assuming they won't be stripped if I get discovered. In the meantime, what should I do with Mistress Ashley?" Hugo refilled his wine glass and gazed at his friend. Brad always thought strategically, even when it wasn't necessary.

"You can either send her on her way or keep her close and learn what she's about. I suggest the latter. If she was sent by Monmouth, you'll discover her purpose sooner or later. If she wants to leave, let her go and follow at a discreet distance. See where she goes and whom she meets. You know what they say, 'Keep your friends close, but your enemies closer.' Sooner or later, she'll betray herself; they always do." Brad nodded sagely, which almost made Hugo laugh.

"Why, have you had many women worming their way into your good graces—aside from Beth, I mean?"

"No, but I'll be ready when they come."

Hugo burst out laughing. Brad always knew how to put matters in perspective.

* * *

By the time Hugo returned home, he was pleasantly drunk and glad to see that the women had retired. According to the housekeeper, Jane had installed Mistress Ashley in a bedchamber adjoining her own and made sure that the lady was comfortable and well looked after. At least Hugo didn't have to face her again tonight. He'd see what tomorrow brought. He was tired, but not ready to retire, so he took a bottle of wine from the cellar and poked life back into the dying embers of the drawing-room fire. The night was cool and dark, the stars bright as shards of broken glass spread across the heavens. A crescent moon hung high in the sky, casting a sliver of light onto the inky landscape outside the window.

Hugo poured himself a generous measure of wine and took

a sip as he stretched his legs before the fire. The talk with Bradford had been helpful; Hugo was just being overly suspicious. James Scott, the Duke of Monmouth, was many things, but stupid wasn't one of them. If he chose to send someone to spy on Hugo, it certainly wouldn't be some insipid woman who was foolish enough to allow herself to be run down by a charging horse. And it was not as if Hugo would conduct any discussion in front of her which would help her learn anything of his plans.

Currently, Monmouth was still in self-imposed exile in the Dutch Republic, but he would sail for England soon and likely land in the southwest. The West Country would be the best place for raising an army of farmers, artisans, and various nonconformists. Most likely, they wouldn't stand a chance against the king's army, but it was wise never to underestimate the common man. Monmouth had tasked Hugo with gauging the loyalties of the nobles in his area and recruiting sympathizers to Monmouth's cause, particularly ones who could provide ample financial support, but Hugo's real purpose had nothing to do with Monmouth's ambition to sit on the throne and dispose of his uncle, King James II. It was imperative that Monmouth never learn the truth.

Hugo knew that James wasn't an overly popular king, or a very good one, but he had been next in the line of succession, which no one could deny, regardless of their religious and political views. However, support for Monmouth had been growing, and as things stood now, Monmouth stood a fair chance of pulling off a rebellion. After the failed attempt at assassinating his father and uncle at Rye House, he was treading more carefully, and amassing his followers before challenging the king. In truth, there were many who supported him, despite his bastard status, believing him to be the true heir to the throne and desiring to see a Protestant monarchy restored.

Hugo took a gulp of wine and stared into the leaping flames, his thoughts turning dour. Monmouth was arrogant, self-indulgent, overconfident, and ridiculously mistrustful. If even a whiff of speculation regarding Hugo's loyalty reached his ears, Hugo would find himself in mortal danger. A man who was willing to kill his own father and uncle didn't get overly sentimental about his friends, not even those he'd known since adolescence. The years they'd spent together at Court would count for nothing if Monmouth found reason to mistrust Hugo, their shared history wiped clean in a moment of suspected treachery. This time, Monmouth would tolerate no mistakes, brook no arguments. He was a man willing to gamble all on the ultimate prize. It was kill or be killed.

Hugo refilled his glass and savagely poked the dying embers of the fire, willing them to last until he was ready to retire. He suddenly wondered if Mistress Ashley was asleep. She was lovely, he'd give her that. Perhaps she had no ties to Monmouth at all, but it would be best for all involved if she took her leave come morning. He would follow her, of course, to see where she went, but, in truth, Hugo would be glad to see the back of her, no matter how enticing the view of that backside might be. Tomorrow, he would offer to take her wherever she needed to go, which would in all probability make her take flight.

Having reached this satisfying conclusion, Hugo finished his wine, heaved himself to his feet, smoored the fire, and made his way upstairs, his gait shaky at best.

NINE

I stared up at the high tester of my four-poster bed, unable to sleep. Jane had offered to close the curtains, but I had asked her to leave them open, as well as the shutters, which she found to be strange, but complied with my request without a word. I couldn't bear the thought of being entombed in complete darkness, surrounded by heavy embroidered drapes that kept out most of the air, as well as the moonlight, feeble though it might be and distorted by the mullions of the casement window.

I had been in this very room not two days ago, but then it had been just a part of the exhibit, the doorway bisected by a thick rope which allowed the visitors to look into the room, but not enter. The furniture had shone with polish, the hearth had been cold and gleaming clean, unlit for decades. The whole house had smelled of old wood paneling and carved ceilings, woolen rugs, and just a hint of dust trapped in the tapestries and the still-tight weave of the curtains and cushions.

It was quiet now, but earlier the house had been alive with the sounds of footsteps, aromas of cooking drifting from the kitchen, and the pleasant smell of burning wood, the crackling of flames soothing and mesmerizing as I'd stared into the fire.

This wasn't just a house; this was a home where real people lived and worked, a home where they loved, suffered, and in Hugo's case, plotted. No amount of period detail or meticulous preservation could capture the spirit of the individuals who'd lived here so long ago and died almost without a trace; their lives deemed irrelevant and quickly forgotten.

It must have been close to midnight when I heard Hugo come up the stairs and close the door of his room, but still I couldn't sleep. I was achy and tired, my head pounding from the blow I'd received earlier, but I couldn't rest. I was terrified of what I'd gotten myself into. What if I got trapped here and had no way of getting back to my own time? What would I do? How long could I pull off this charade? Hugo didn't strike me as being particularly gullible. He'd make inquiries and find out that I had no ties of kinship to the earl. What would he do with me?

I had to get away from here as soon as I could. At this moment, all I wanted was to go back to my messy twenty-first-century life. I would stop looking back and devote myself to the future—a future where I would find a new love and have the family I'd always dreamed of. No more going back and forth with Evan, no more agonizing over the miscarriage. It was no one's fault. My child was gone, and no amount of self-flagellation or blaming Evan would ever bring it back. It was time to move forward, and I would do that as soon as I went home and forgot this insane scheme.

I had to admit, though, that I had enjoyed meeting Hugo and Jane. I'd assumed that Hugo was a hard, callous man, but I saw the kindness in his eyes and the way he looked at his sister. He was capable of great love; of that I was sure. Was there a woman he cared for? He was in his mid-thirties, surely there was someone? I was fairly certain that Clarence wasn't Hugo's son, despite what Max had implied. Clarence bore no physical resemblance to Hugo, or even to Jane, and the relationship between brother and sister appeared to be one of affection and nothing more. One always picked up on sexual undercurrents, especially when looking for them, but I saw nothing untoward in the way the two interacted. My dream must have had some basis of truth, fantastical though it might be.

Jane had fetched her sewing basket and sat by my side all afternoon, keeping me company in her quiet way. She was no more than thirty, but her demeanor was that of a much older woman, a woman who'd known great sorrow. The pretty, passionate girl I had glimpsed in my dream was no more, the fire extinguished and replaced by gentle warmth that radiated from her kind eyes.

"You must miss your husband very much," I had ventured, hoping she'd tell me something of the man she'd married. There was a momentary wariness in her eyes before she had readjusted her expression to one of bereavement.

"Yes, Ernest was a good man and a loving father to my son." The use of "my" instead of "ours" had made me prick my ears, so I'd remained quiet, letting her talk. It always amazed me how much people would reveal about themselves just to fill an uncomfortable silence, and Jane didn't disappoint. Being in mourning, she had probably felt isolated and lonely, so a few hours in the company of a similarly aged female were possibly a gift rather than a burden.

"He was much older than I and not in good health," she had said, stabbing the needle into her work as if it had just given great offense. "In the last two years of his life, he suffered partial paralysis; his eyesight deteriorated, and he often ranted and raved, making no sense at all. The physick initially said that Ernest had an excess of black bile, which would cause melancholy, but he later changed his opinion. There were too many other physical symptoms by that stage. He bled Ernest repeatedly, but his condition only worsened. I would be telling an untruth if I said it wasn't a relief when he finally passed. I

couldn't bear to see him suffer, and his illness was hard on
Clarence as well."

"Was it a love match?" I'd asked innocently, wanting to hear
more.

"Oh, no. I'd known Ernest most of my life, but never
regarded him as anything more than a kindly uncle rather than
a romantic prospect. He spent much less time with us after he
married his first wife. She was a calculating woman, interested
only in bettering her position in life, and Ernest gave her that, to
be sure. She died not long before Ernest and I married and left
an eight-year-old daughter. Hugo arranged the marriage," Jane
had added by way of explanation as to how she came to marry a
man she didn't love. Another stab at the fabric and Jane pricked
her finger and sucked off the blood, suddenly smiling like a
child. "Hugo always tells me not to do that."

"Did you not mind that your brother arranged a match with
someone so much older?" *And someone you didn't love*, I'd
mentally added. No one could accuse me of tact, but I was
burning with curiosity. Would Jane tell me the truth?

"No. Hugo's always had my best interests at heart. Ernest
was a good, kind man who would take care of me. I'd suffered
a terrible blow, you see. The man I loved had deceived me.
He'd promised me a future when he was already betrothed to
someone else. My heart was broken, and I never wanted to
feel that kind of pain again. I knew that Ernest would cherish
me all his days," she had replied absentmindedly as she went
back to her sewing. "He spent much of his time out on the
estate, so it was just Clarence and I, and Magdalene, of
course," she'd added, suddenly remembering her stepdaugh-
ter. "Clarence was such a beautiful baby, always hungry."
Jane had smiled in that quiet way, remembering Clarence as
he had been as a child. "We used to spend hours together
playing games and walking in the gardens when he got older.
By the time he turned six, Ernest arranged for him to have a

tutor, so I didn't seem him nearly as much. I was lonely without him."

"Did you not get on with Magdalene?" I'd asked, wondering what life must have been like for this child whom Jane clearly hadn't loved.

"I tried, I really did, but Magdalene was a willful child, one prone to fits of temper and hysterics. She felt a terrible jealousy toward Clarence, so I tried to keep them apart. I did spend at least an hour a day with her, just the two of us, reading to her from the Bible or teaching her to sew. She enjoyed the stories, but sewing frustrated her. She lacked the patience, you see."

"Where is she now?"

"In London. She married a few years ago, a fine match. Ernest was very pleased. I must say that marriage has changed her. She truly loves her husband, and he seems to return her affection," Jane had remarked, sounding amazed that anyone could love the wayward child she'd had so much trouble with.

"Do you have any other children, Jane?"

"No, Clarence is my one and only," Jane had replied sadly. "I would have liked to have more children."

I couldn't help wondering if Jane ever shared her husband's bed. It was clear that she didn't love or desire him, and since there were never any other children, it was possible that they never shared any intimacy. Why would Ernest agree to such a union? I wished I could ask, but that would have been crossing the line by a mile. Besides, Jane might have never known the details of the arrangement. It seemed, at least based on my dream, that Hugo had kept his promise and made it possible for Jane to keep her baby, but at what cost? Had this poor girl ever known love? Would she have the opportunity to remarry now that her husband was gone, or was this what her life was going to be—a lonely widow whose son would grow and leave her to live his own life and follow his own dreams?

There was so much I wanted to know about Hugo and Jane,

but I'd overstayed my welcome and would never find out what had happened to these two. The thought of something awful befalling Hugo in the near future nearly made me sick, but I reminded myself that I couldn't change history, nor did I have any right to get involved. Whatever Hugo was mixed up in, he'd made his own bed, and he would have to lie in it sooner rather than later. My heart twisted as I recalled that his "bed" was actually a grave, an unmarked one.

My thoughts were interrupted by Jane's soft voice. I could just see her through the partially open door. She'd settled me in the room next to hers and left the adjoining door slightly ajar in case I needed anything during the night. She was wearing a long white nightdress, just like the one she'd lent me, her hair loose around her shoulders as she sank to her knees and folded her hands in supplication, her face turned up to the invisible heavens. The candlelight played softly over her features, and the gray in her hair wasn't visible at all, making her appear much like the girl I'd seen in my dream. In my own time, Jane would still be a young woman, at the height of her power and sexuality, but in this day and age, she was well past her prime, a woman who had few prospects before her.

Jane was quietly praying, and although I felt like a voyeur, I couldn't help listening to what she said. She commended her husband's soul to God and asked him to take care of Clarence, before turning her attention to Hugo.

"Dear Lord, please help my brother see sense and stop this madness before it's too late. You know what he's involved in with His Grace, the Duke of Monmouth, and it can't possibly end well. He thinks he knows what he's about, but I fear he's in mortal danger. Please, spare him; he's the only family I have, besides Clarence, and I couldn't bear to lose him. *In nomine Patris et Filii et Spiritus Sancti.* Amen." Jane crossed herself, kissed her rosary, and rose to her feet with the air of someone who'd just handed off her troubles to someone else.

So, they were secret Catholics, I thought, glad to have at least a piece of the puzzle handed to me. But my satisfaction was short-lived. I couldn't remember the intricacies of the political situation in England at this time, but I did know that Monmouth was Protestant, being the eldest illegitimate son of Charles II, and King James was Catholic. Why would Hugo throw in his lot with Protestant Monmouth? Of course, there was much I didn't know about what they were involved in, but Jane made it sound serious. Mortal danger, she'd said, and she was right. According to family records, something would befall Hugo within two months, possibly much sooner, and Clarence would inherit.

I hadn't realized I was crying until a tear slid down my temple and into my hair. Hugo was so young and full of life, and Jane was so clearly dependent on him. There was real affection between brother and sister. She'd be heartbroken.

I closed my eyes and tried to will myself to get some sleep, but my mind wouldn't comply, so I spent the rest of the night staring at the darkened canopy above the bed, mourning the loss of people who were still very much alive.

* * *

As soon as the pearlescent light of impending dawn penetrated the darkness of the room, I got up, dressed, and, with my shoes in hand, tiptoed to the stairs. My ankle still pained me, but I couldn't afford to dawdle.

I heard movement and the unmistakable sounds of servants about their business in the kitchen, but there was no one on the ground floor. I eased the heavy bolt out of the lock and slipped out the door, closing it softly behind me. I put on my shoes and ran hell for leather toward the church. My ankle throbbed, but I tried to ignore the pain, knowing I had limited time to escape. It was Sunday morning, and I had no idea at what time the church would start to fill up for the service.

My head still ached, I was exhausted from my sleepless night and bruised from my fall, but I put discomfort out of my mind, as well as terrible guilt at just running out without saying goodbye or thanking Hugo and Jane for looking after me. I hoped they wouldn't think too badly of me, but I had no choice. Had I told Hugo I wanted to go to church, he might have insisted on accompanying me and would see me disappear from the crypt. I couldn't let that happen.

TEN

Hugo woke up with a dull headache. He needed a piss, but his cock was stiff as a board, the remnants of his rather pleasant dream still swirling in his head. He'd dreamed of Neve Ashley. It wasn't an illicit dream, but rather one of longing and desire, Neve always just out of reach as he tried to take her in his arms. Her eyes were pleading with him to come to her, but she continued to run away, laughing softly and making him burn with a passion he hadn't felt in some time. He'd nearly forgotten what it was like to be in love, or even in lust. It'd been too long since he'd been with a woman, especially one he desired.

Liza shared his bed from time to time, but not since Jane had arrived. She wouldn't approve of him bedding a maid, even a willing one. He wasn't in the habit of taking servants to his bed, unlike some men he knew whose female servants lived in terror of being molested, but Liza was different. She made no secret of her intentions, and where some masters would have dismissed a servant for such ill-concealed attempts at seduction, Hugo felt that it absolved him of any responsibility toward the girl. If Liza desired him, he'd oblige most willingly, but since the initiative had been hers, he felt no obligation beyond satisfying her and himself. He liked Liza, made sure she was well provided for, and gave her the occasional ribbon and trinket to make her feel appreciated, but no words of affection ever passed his lips. He'd been blind not to realize that the girl was in love with him, but by that point it was too late to turn back. All he could do was be kind to her and make sure she never got with child. He didn't want to cause her any more suffering than he already had.

Hugo glanced out the window as he got out of bed and promptly swore. "Damn it all to hell," he muttered as he pulled on his breeches and boots, grabbed his coat and bolted from the room. Neve Ashley had a healthy head start, but she was obviously headed for the church, and he knew a shortcut through the woods. He wouldn't stop her leaving, but he had to see whom she was meeting, for he was sure she had an assignation. Why else would she go to church at dawn?

Hugo never let Neve out of his sight as he trotted down the overgrown track, cursing himself the whole time for being a trusting fool. He'd managed to arrange his clothing so that he didn't look as if he'd just come from some woman's bed, but had forgotten his hat in his haste. No matter, he'd have had to remove it in church in any case, out of respect.

Neve looked back just before she disappeared through the thick stone wall surrounding the churchyard, but Hugo wasn't far behind. He gave her a few minutes before slipping through the door and looking around the empty church, his head swiveling from side to side. The church was empty. Not even Reverend Snow was about; the man was likely still abed at this hour.

Hugo walked around the church, peering into every corner and behind the altar to make sure Neve wasn't hiding, but there was no one there. He even went down to the crypt, but it was dark and silent. Hugo exited by the side door and spent the next quarter of an hour wandering between the headstones, his mind refusing to accept that the woman had just simply vanished, before heading back home to break his fast.

ELEVEN
MARCH 2013

I burst through the door to the crypt and ran down the steps, making for the passage and closing it behind me just as the wooden door above creaked open, and I heard footsteps on the stairs. I had the feeling I was being followed as I ran to the church, but when I looked back, I saw nothing but greening fields, whispering woods, and Everly Manor, standing solid and forbidding; its stone walls bathed in the rosy glow of a spring sunrise. I dove behind the knight's tomb and breathed a sigh of relief to find my bag, clear evidence that I was back in my own time. I took off the gown, pulled on my jeans, sweater and coat, and switched on my phone. Nothing reassured me as much as the electronic ping that informed me of several missed calls, nine text messages, and seventeen notifications from my Facebook page.

"Thank God, thank God, thank God," I muttered as I made my way up the steps and into the modern church. That's about the most pious I'd even gotten in a church, but my heart was overflowing with joy, my blood singing with hope for the future. I'd returned, and I would never, ever, go back again. I'd been foolish in the extreme, but I'd learned my lesson.

I stepped into the gentle spring sunshine and inhaled deeply, glad to be alive and exhilarated by my escape. I wasn't ready to return to the manor, so I went back to retrieve my car, bought a breakfast sandwich and the largest cup of coffee they had to offer and went for a drive through the countryside, blasting the radio and feeling gloriously alive. I wished I could tell Max of my adventure, but he'd simply think I'd lost the plot and call the nearest psychiatric facility.

As I licked the last crumbs from my fingers and finished my coffee, my euphoria began to wear off, my logical mind returning to the passage. Was someone from the seventeenth century able to go through or was I the only one? Since the church hadn't been modernized yet in their lifetime, was the other exit from the passage even there when someone went down to the crypt? Was it possible that because both exits existed in my own time, I was able to go between the two, but if so, would this apply to any modern person, and had anyone else gone before me? Could it be that both doors lay on a ley line, if there really was one, that passed beneath the church and therefore opened some wormhole into the past? And why 1685?

Of course, there were no answers to any of these questions, so I had to eventually put them aside and turn back toward the manor. It was time to return to real life, answer my calls and emails, and take a much-needed bath. The thought of modern plumbing made me practically giddy.

Tilly the Labrador came bounding up the drive as I got out of my car, her tail wagging in greeting. Her owner was only a few steps behind, not wagging his tail, but smiling from ear to ear as he called out to me.

"How was London?"

"Oh, you know..." I replied with a grin, happy to see a friendly face. It struck me anew how much Max resembled Hugo, but the resemblance ended with facial features. Max looked relaxed and casual in his tweeds, his wellies crunching on the gravel of the driveway as he walked toward me. I tried to picture Hugo Everly dressed in modern togs and failed, allowing him to remain in his courtly dress in the realm of recent memory.

"It was awfully quiet without you, even Mummy remarked on it. We've gotten used to your endless phone calls, arguments with the director, and tirades from your boss. Don't ever leave again." Max said this jokingly, but I saw something in his eyes which made me realize that behind the flirtatious manner was a man who was desperate to be told that he'd been missed as well.

"It's good to see you, Max—very good. Were you going for a walk?"

"Care to join us?" he asked as he scratched Tilly behind the ears. I could see that she was getting impatient, her body practically vibrating with the need for exercise.

"I'd love to, but I have some work to do, and I'm desperate for a bath. I'll meet you for lunch at the pub if you like, though, say noon?"

"The pub gets crowded on Sunday afternoons. Everyone has to wet their whistle after church. How about somewhere a little more private? I know a lovely bistro that does an onion soup and foie gras to die for. Interested?"

"Very." And I was.

"Be ready by noon," Max called out as he set off at a trot after Tilly.

* * *

Max never mentioned that the bistro was nearly an hour away, nor that the drive through the countryside would be so scenic. I pushed away my plate, pleasantly sated with good food and fine wine, and smiled at Max.

"Thank you, Max. This was lovely; best Sunday I've had in some time." And it was true. I'd spent the past few months in a fugue of misery, and this outing reminded me of how much I'd missed.

"So, have I won your heart yet?" Max asked conversationally, making me laugh. He was such a flirt.

"You think that all it takes is foie gras and some wine? My heart is worth a little more than that."

"You'd be surprised what some women will do for foie gras," Max replied with a raised eyebrow, making me snort with laughter. "I just wine and dine them until they are putty in my hands."

"And does this technique work?" I asked, thinking that it probably did.

"Oh, every time. They can't keep their hands off me."

"Max, are you ever serious?" I asked, smiling at him. He was so easy to be with.

"Not if I can help it. By the way, do you like opera?"

"I do. Is there much opera performed in the village?" I quipped.

"Yes, we do have an annual performance staged by our very own company and I avoid it at all cost, but *Tosca* is being performed next weekend at the London Coliseum, and I just happen to have two tickets. Would you like to join me?"

"Will more wining and dining be involved?" I asked, patting my stomach meaningfully. "I quite like duck confit as well."

"Naturally."

"Then I'm all yours," I replied, hanging my head in surrender.

"See? Told you it works."

Max and I left the restaurant in companionable silence, happy to be in each other's company and acutely aware of the possibilities open to us. I wasn't ready for a new relationship, but I was ready to start thinking of the future, and I genuinely liked Max. He was so different from Evan, who was always brooding, lamenting, and looking for signs of subterfuge from his colleagues. For all his ambition, Evan was a pessimist, whereas Max seemed to see life through rose-colored glasses, and I liked the view from his end. I certainly didn't want to lead him up the garden path, so I interjected several comments into the conversation, letting him know that if anything were to develop between us, it would take time and patience on his part. We didn't discuss it outright, but I felt Max understood and that was enough for now.

TWELVE

I was still grinning from ear to ear when I finally sat down at my laptop that night. I needed to prepare for tomorrow, and there was a long list of questions and comments from Lawrence Spellman. I made a few notes for myself and was about to log off when thoughts of Hugo overtook my mind. I'd managed to stay distracted for most of the day, but now that I was alone, I couldn't help but wonder how Hugo and Jane had reacted when they found me gone. I still felt awful for deceiving them, and I needed to know more about what the Duke of Monmouth was up to in the spring of 1685. The answer wasn't difficult to find. Numerous entries for the Monmouth Rebellion popped up in response to my search, and after reading through a few of them, I felt sick to my stomach, my earlier happiness forgotten.

"Oh, Hugo," I moaned, "what have you done?" The Duke of Monmouth had virtually signed his own death warrant when he took up arms against the king, but I didn't care about him. He was an ambitious young man who saw his chance and took it. There were many like him throughout history, those whose gambles paid off, and those whose hadn't. But Hugo was a different story. I don't know why I felt such sorrow at the thought of his fate, but I knew he was on the verge of something catastrophic. Maybe I was subconsciously confusing my feelings for Hugo with those for Max, because they were so alike, but I didn't think that was the case.

I closed my laptop and just sat staring at the lid, brooding. There was nothing I could do. Hugo had made his choice, and it had nothing to do with me. Nothing at all.

* * *

All throughout the following week, I told myself that Hugo's collision course with destiny wasn't of any interest to me, but every time I walked through the gallery and saw his dark eyes follow me from the portrait, I wanted to run and hide. Had his gaze become more guarded and full of accusation, or was I simply being more fanciful since I'd met the man? He didn't know his future, but I did. Maybe Hugo truly believed that Monmouth stood a chance of taking the crown from his uncle and supported his cause, but I knew that he was walking—no, running—toward disaster. Monmouth would pay with his life, but so would Hugo, his body never recovered or given a proper burial, his name all but forgotten by history. Only his sister would keep his memory alive and eventually pass everything to her son, who would be the patriarch of Max's ancestral line.

You could warn him, a little voice said inside my head. It came unbidden but wouldn't leave, arguing with me for days on end. *All you have to do is go back one more time and tell him what you know. He might not listen to you, but at least your conscience will be clear. You'd have tried to save his life.*

"Don't be ridiculous," I hissed at the insistent voice. "What am I to do, just waltz in there once again and announce that I can foretell the future? That would go over well. I'd be lucky if they didn't accuse me of witchcraft and burn me on the village green. Forget Hugo."

I tried—I really tried—but thoughts of Hugo were constantly with me, even when Max and I drove to London the following weekend. I had no idea why I felt so responsible, but the weight of knowledge lay heavy on my mind.

"You're very pensive tonight," Max remarked as he looked at me over his menu.

"I'm sorry, Max. I was just thinking about the opera. It was so tragic." The opera had been truly amazing. I'd seen *Tosca* at least twice before, but I'd still enjoyed every moment, felt every note as it struck a chord in my own heart.

"I see we should stick to comedies," Max replied. "I didn't mean to make you so sad. I just thought all that anguish and romance would work in my favor." He reached across the table and took my hand in his, his face suddenly serious. "I mean it, Neve. Forget that prat, Evan, and give me a chance. I promise I will be very careful with your heart and not rush you into anything you're not ready for. May I court you, my lady?"

Of course, he had to end his speech with a joke, which made me want to walk around the table and give him a hug, but I didn't, nor did I give him permission to pursue me. I liked Max immensely, but something inside me warned me off him. I suppose having had no parents to look out for me from a young age, I'd developed a certain radar for people who could be trusted. I wouldn't say that I didn't trust Max, but I had my reservations about his sincerity. Max's charm and easygoing manner were a façade, one that effectively hid the real man underneath.

I couldn't quite put my finger on it, but there was something about him that put me on my guard. Perhaps he was too charming and too eager to please, always ready with a compliment or a joke, but never serious long enough to betray his real feelings. "Slippery as an eel" was an expression that sprang to mind, one that my foster mother used often when I was a child. Perhaps I was doing Max a terrible disservice, prompted by my bitter disappointment in Evan, but I wasn't ready to give him the green light until I felt I knew him better and could trust him with my wounded heart.

"Max, I'm sorry; I didn't mean to lead you on, but I'm just not ready for anything more than friendship. Not yet."

"That's okay. I understand, but I'm not giving up. I'll win you over yet. Come on, the night's still young. What would you like to do? We can go to a dance club or a bar in Soho, take a walk, or go back home and have a nightcap."

The idea of spending several hours gyrating in the pulsating darkness of a club or screaming over the noise in a crowded bar just didn't appeal to me after the emotional wrench of *Tosca*, and although a walk would have been nice, I preferred to ride back in the open convertible, the night air caressing my face, the stars right overhead, a celestial canopy that made one feel small and insignificant, but very much alive. Was our destiny truly written in the stars as the ancients claimed, or was it just our over-romanticized imagination that wanted to harness the power of the universe and bend it to our will; making it responsible for our choices and future; imbuing it with a collective consciousness more suited to a divine being than an infinite vastness in which we were nothing more than particles of dust, twirling through space until our time was done?

"I'd like to go back if you don't mind," I said, watching Max's reaction. What did he want to do? I could see that I had made the right choice. Going to a club was all bravado. Max just wanted a quiet evening.

"I was hoping you'd say that."

As we drove back to Cranleigh in the surprisingly balmy darkness of the spring night, I suddenly realized once again that I knew very little about Max. He always used humor to deflect personal questions or weighty topics, and although I really liked his easy manner, I needed to know more about the man inside before I could even begin to truly open up to him and allow our friendship to develop. Of course, tonight wasn't the night to start quizzing him about his political views, past relationships, and hopes for the future. Tonight was just a casual second date; time enough for all the rest later.

But weighty topics were still on my mind, and I turned to Max, needing someone to talk to about the guilt that had been eating away at me for days.

"Max, if you knew that something terrible would befall someone you know because of a choice that they'd made, would you try to forewarn them, or would you simply stand back and let it all play out regardless of the outcome?" I asked, hoping that Max wouldn't make a joke. Thankfully, he didn't.

"If I knew for a fact, rather than suspected, that this person would get seriously hurt, then I would try to warn them, even at the expense of overstepping the boundaries of friendship. Most people don't want to be told that their choices are foolhardy or will lead to disaster, but if you are referring to actual bodily harm rather than just ruffled feathers, I'd say step in. Are we speaking of a metaphorical girlfriend who's meant to represent you in this scenario?" he asked with a knowing smile.

"Not exactly," I muttered, ready to drop the subject. "But thank you, you've put things in perspective for me."

I was still thinking of our conversation nearly an hour later as Max poured me a glass of wine and settled on the sofa next to me. The fire was burning low in the hearth, soft shadows dancing on the walls of the parlor, the moon peeking through the uncurtained window, its nearly round countenance resembling a curious face.

Max moved closer to me, and the moon was momentarily blocked out as he leaned in to kiss me. The kiss was tender and romantic, but I found myself unable to respond. My body tensed, and I braced my palms against Max's chest to keep him from getting any closer.

Max pulled away, his eyes never leaving my face as he

traced the shape of my lips with his finger. "I know you're not ready, and I won't rush you into anything. I just wanted to give you something to think about."

"You have," I replied as I tried to ignore the turmoil I was feeling. Max made me feel desired and pampered, but was I using Max as a crutch to help me move on from Evan?

Max put his finger under my chin and raised my face to his, smiling into my eyes. "Neve, don't overthink it. We're not teenagers who'll shag first and then decide if we like each other later. There's no pressure, no rush. We can just be friends and see where that takes us. You can take the lead; I'm happy to let you set the pace. How does that sound?"

"That sounds great," I replied, feeling a rush of affection toward Max. "I'll say goodnight then."

"Goodnight, darling."

THIRTEEN

By Sunday morning, it was time for me to return to London. The legal paperwork had been signed, all the specs had been sent to the appropriate departments, and by the end of the week, a team would come down from London to begin turning the museum into the apartments of Whitehall Palace. Actual shooting wouldn't begin for a few weeks yet, well after Easter, but my job was done for the moment. I would return with the cast and crew to help manage various aspects of production. I doubled as production assistant and saw to accommodations, meals, and anything else that required taking care of by someone who wasn't involved in the creative process. I loved being on set, so I was excited about returning to Everly Manor, and Max. We would see each other in London during the intervening weeks. Max had promised to come up in a few days and take me to dinner and a film, and I was looking forward to seeing him again.

I tossed my bag into the boot of the car, came around to open the door, but stopped to admire the view from the ridge. The morning was sunny and bright, a gentle breeze ruffling my hair and caressing my face, the intoxicating smell of spring in the air. The still-bare branches created a lacework quilt against the cloudless sky and whispered among themselves in the timeless language of their own. I could see the village spread out below me, several cars moving down the street and early risers already going about their business. The tower of the church drew my eye, silently calling to me to stop by before I left. Sunday service would begin in about a half-hour. Already people were walking in twos and threes from the village to take their seats in the hard wooden pews and listen to Vicar Lambert's sermon. Many felt more pious during Lent, but I felt no emotional connection to any of it. I hadn't been to a church service in years, and today certainly would not be the day.

I should have just gotten in my car and left, but thoughts of Hugo continued to nag at me, leaving me angry and annoyed with the situation I'd put myself into. Why couldn't I just let it go? Things were finally going well for me, and instead of rejoicing in a new project and my friendship with Max, I was obsessing over a man who'd died centuries ago, and whose decision to involve himself in a suicide mission had nothing whatsoever to do with me. And yet...

I had to admit that for some inexplicable reason, I wanted to see Hugo again. He'd left a strong impression on me, something that didn't happen often. Most people who touched my life in such a transient way were just a blip on the radar, but Hugo had stayed with me, and so had Jane. There was something tragic about the pair of them, and I'd been drawn to tragedy since I was a kid, perhaps because my own childhood had left me more sensitive to other people's sorrows. I could almost see a Greek chorus positioned at the back of an amphitheater stage, wearing tragedy masks and togas and singing in the background, warning me of danger and imminent catastrophe decreed by the gods, but I'd always been one to tempt fate.

Getting into the car, I drove to the village and parked on a side street in front of a barber shop. It was closed for business today and likely tomorrow as well, so no one would pay much attention to my car if I failed to return today for some reason. I still had the holdall with my seventeenth-century costume in the boot, having forgotten to return the items to the museum after my last visit to the past. I would just pop by for a little bit, warn Hugo of imminent danger, and then return to the present and never go back. What he chose to do from that point on was entirely up to him, but my conscience would be clear.

I tried to ignore the Greek chorus in my head as it chanted louder and louder, their wails predicting impending doom building up to a crescendo, as I pushed open the door to the church and found myself confronted with a gaggle of women who seemed to be discussing flower arrangements for a wedding that was to take place the following weekend. The young bride was near tears as her mother overrode her every suggestion and took charge like Napoleon riding into battle. I smiled at the despondent bride as she slipped into a pew next to another young woman whom she strongly resembled, and just allowed her mother and the florist to make the decision.

The two girls exchanged knowing looks that spoke volumes, making me suddenly sad that I'd never had a sister or known that kind of bond with someone. I was used to solitude, having spent hours entertaining myself and moving the figures around on my makeshift stage as I'd presented play after play to my audience of dolls and teddy bears. Perhaps that's why I'd spent years with Evan, exchanging one kind of loneliness for another. He'd never given me the type of attention I craved or made me feel as if I was at the top of his priority list. There was a time when I'd dreamed of marrying Evan, but that time was long gone. Would I ever have a wedding of my own? I sighed and pushed these thoughts from my mind. I had more important things to do, and I had to do them before the church began to fill up. There were already a dozen people taking seats for the upcoming service, so I had to hurry.

Vicar Lambert appeared from the vestry, putting an end to the argument about the flowers. He was already dressed for the Sunday service, wearing a chasuble over his alb and stole, and carrying the notes for the service in his hand. The mother-of-the-bride addressed him, distracting him enough for me to disappear down the stairs to the crypt without being noticed. The crypt was shrouded in darkness and I felt as if I were descending into the underworld as I reached the bottom step. The light switch was there, but I didn't really need it. I knew this place by heart.

I hastily changed into my gown, cursing under my breath as I tried to reach the laces at the back of the bodice. Stockings came next, then shoes. I pinned up my hair, wiped any traces of makeup off my face and threw the cloak over my shoulders before stowing my bag behind the friendly knight.

"Wish me luck," I said to him as I groped in the darkness for the button that would open the passage to the past. The scraping of stone informed me that I'd found it, and I stopped for a moment just inside the doorway; my mind yelling at me to give up this foolishness and go home. But there was no one waiting for me at home, so there was no reason to rush back to London. A few hours would make little difference to me, but they might make all the difference to Hugo and Jane—if he heeded my warning.

I stepped into the passage and walked slowly up the steps, my heart pounding against my ribs and my breath caught in my throat as the door closed behind me. I had an idea of what I wanted to say to Hugo, but saying it in my head and confronting the man were two different things. I hoped that as a seventeenth-century gentleman, he would be superstitious and that my warning would put him off his plan, but I was sure he was pretty committed to his cause, and it would take much to change his mind.

FOURTEEN

MARCH 1685

The church seemed to be emptying out as I stepped into the south transept, several mothers rounding up their offspring as they scattered down the nave, eager to play hide-and-seek among the pews. The Sunday service must have been earlier in the seventeenth century since most people rose at dawn. Parishioners were filing out into the church porch, no doubt keen for a word with the vicar, before making for their homes and preparing Sunday dinner which they took at midday. There was no sign of Hugo Everly or Jane, so I headed for the side door that led to the cemetery.

The spring day I had left behind was sunny and bright, but it was muggy and gray when I exited into the graveyard, a miserable drizzle filling the air with moisture and instantly making my scalp and face feel damp and chilled. I drew the velvet cloak closer to my body to keep out the gusty wind and pulled up the hood.

Everly Manor loomed out of the fog as I walked on the side of the lane, conscious of every little sound just in case anyone was coming and failed to spot me in the gloom as Hugo had before. The house looked sinister, the edges blurred by the fog and the windows darkened as if it were empty and abandoned. I was glad when I saw a servant girl come around the corner with a basket in hand. She was heading to one of the outbuildings, humming to herself and bobbing her head to the tune. She didn't even notice me, which was just fine.

I lifted the heavy knocker and banged it a few times before Jane herself opened the door. She must have just come from church because she was still wearing her cloak and hat, her side curls dampened by the weather and clinging to her cheeks. "It's you," she announced as if I had no idea who I was. I couldn't tell if she was annoyed or pleased to see me again since the expression on her face never changed. She just stood still, waiting for me to explain my sudden reappearance before she decided whether to let me in or not.

I glimpsed Clarence behind her, his face alight with curiosity at the sudden intrusion. The poor boy was probably bored out of his mind in this vast house with no one to keep him company besides his mother and uncle, so the appearance of a mysterious stranger was an event not to be missed.

"Good day, Jane. I'm sorry to disturb you, but I wanted a word with your brother. Is he at home?"

Jane looked as if she would much rather send me away, but good manners finally won out and she moved aside, inviting me to come into the foyer. It was even chillier inside than it was out, and a pervasive gloom seemed to shroud the house, making me feel uneasy.

Run away. Run away, the Greek chorus in my head sang, but I stood my ground as I waited for Jane to reply.

"I'll tell him you're here. He's just recently returned from..." Jane suddenly realized that she was telling me too much and grew quiet. "I'll tell him. Liza, light the fire in the parlor immediately. This house is as cold as a tomb," Jane called out irritably to the girl I'd seen earlier, who rushed into the foyer to greet the mistress.

"Sorry, my lady, I've only just returned from church," the girl replied, a slight air of insolence in her face.

"Well, don't stand there dawdling, and bring some mulled wine," Jane threw over her shoulder as she disappeared into the library.

She returned for me a few moments later, a fleeting expression of surprise at her brother's desire to see me quickly replaced by the wariness of before.

"Lord Everly will receive you in the library. This way."

Jane didn't follow me inside, but closed the door softly, leaving me to face Hugo Everly.

This room was completely different from the foyer; it was warm and snug, the fire dancing in the hearth and casting rosy shadows on the stone walls and gleaming bookcases that hugged three out of the four walls. Hugo sat behind a massive desk, several letters strewn in front of him and a map of what appeared to be England rolled out and pinned down with an inkwell and a thick volume. He looked up, leaned back in his chair, and crossed his legs at the ankles, as if readying himself for a good story. He raised an eyebrow in inquiry, but didn't say a word, as I stood there glued to the spot, suddenly tongue-tied.

"Good day, Lord Everly," I stammered, feeling a total fool. Now that I was facing him the whole plan seemed preposterous, if not downright foolhardy. What had I been thinking?

Run away, the chorus roared, but I blocked out their wailing and met Hugo's gaze head on.

"Is it?" he asked politely, but with an edge of sarcasm that wasn't lost on me.

"Ah, I wanted to apologize for my abrupt departure," I said in a conciliatory way, but Hugo wasn't having it.

"Yes, it was rather rude, if I recall." He cocked his head to the side, his dark eyes scanning my face in a way that made me want to turn and run back to the church, but I'd come here for a reason, and it was not as if he didn't have cause to be angry with me. I knew he wouldn't be very receptive.

"Lord Everly, there's something I must tell you," I began, but Hugo interrupted me.

"What you must tell me is why you lied to me about whom you are and then ran off without so much as a word. You led me to believe that you were the niece of the Earl of Shaftesbury..." Hugo let the sentence hang as he watched me squirm.

"It was you who suggested I was the niece of the earl," I countered, knowing perfectly well that my argument was less than sound.

"I was mistaken, but you didn't deny it. Is Neve Ashley even your real name, or were you just hoping I'd immediately assume you were Nell Ashley and open my house to you?"

"Neve Ashley is my real name, and if you might recall, you nearly killed me that day, so my faculties were a trifle muddled," I spat back angrily. "I was confused."

"Confused enough to think you were related to an earl?" He wasn't letting me off the hook, and I suddenly wondered why I even cared about his man. He wouldn't listen to me anyway.

"I'm sorry I came. I'll take my leave now," I announced with as much pride as I could.

Hugo pushed back his chair, rose to his feet, and walked toward me with a conciliatory smile, which is exactly why I allowed my guard to drop. I thought he would take my hands as he did before, but he suddenly swept me off my feet and threw me over his shoulder like a sack of potatoes as he kicked the door open with his foot and proceeded into the corridor.

The last thing I saw before he mounted the stairs was Jane's startled face and Clarence's eyes, which were as round as saucers.

"What's Uncle Hugo doing?" he whispered urgently to his mother.

"I don't know, son; I really don't know," Jane muttered as she watched Hugo ascend the stairs with me dangling over his shoulder.

Once I had regained my composure somewhat, I began to pummel Hugo's back with my fists, demanding that he put me down, but he simply ignored me and carried me to the room where I'd spent the night on my previous visit. There, he deposited me on the bed with very little regard for my person, dumping me unceremoniously on my back.

I made to get up, but he pushed me back down, his face dangerously close as he pinned my wrists and straddled me, his thighs holding my legs in place. I was angry before, but now I was genuinely scared. What was he going to do to me?

He must have seen the fear in my eyes because he instantly drew back and let go of my wrists. "You will remain in this room until you're ready to tell me *exactly* who you are and what you're about. Until then, we have nothing more to say to each other."

With that, he left the room, and I heard the scrape of a key as he locked me in and walked away. I scrambled off the bed and made for the window, but one look assured me that there was no escape. The wall outside the window was smooth and made of solid stone, and even if it weren't, the casement window wasn't wide enough for me to climb through anyway. I was Hugo Everly's prisoner, and I could either tell him a very elaborate story or a partial truth—neither of which seemed very appealing at the moment.

FIFTEEN

Hugo attempted to go back to his correspondence, but thoughts of Neve Ashley kept pushing their way to the forefront of his mind, forcing him to read the same line over and over until he gave up and just allowed himself a few moments of peaceful contemplation. He would never admit it, but he'd been glad to see her, and the feel of her body beneath his own when he'd pinned her down on the bed left him feeling distracted and suddenly very aware of exactly how long it'd been since he'd spent a few hours with Liza.

Hugo chuckled to himself as he remembered Neve's face when he threw her over his shoulder. She hadn't expected that, nor had she expected to be locked in; that would teach her to lie to him. But she had been genuinely frightened, and for that he was sorry. He had seen real terror in her eyes, and although he had no intention of hurting her, she hadn't known that and likely assumed the worst. Some men were no better than animals, so maybe Mistress Ashley had good reason to be afraid. He knew nothing of her life or her past, and suddenly realized that twice now the woman had come unescorted and on foot, which was perplexing. She spoke like a lady, although her phrasing of things was somewhat unusual, and was dressed like one. Her clothes weren't gaudy or frivolous but of good quality and in the current fashion, and her cloak was fur-lined and clearly expensive. Where had she come from and what was she doing on his land? Why had she run off without a word and where did she go? If she'd been staying in the village, he would have seen her, and would have noticed her at church, but Neve Ashley had not been in the vicinity since she left over a week ago. So why did she come back?

What had she said—that she wanted to tell him something? Maybe he should have heard her out, but he'd been so annoyed by the way she had given him the slip last time that his pride had got the better of him. Well, it was too late to go back on it now. He'd let her stew for a few hours, then go talk to her and see what it was she wanted to share with him. He'd gladly go see her now, but it hadn't been enough time. She needed to believe that he meant to keep her there until she was ready to talk, so he had to be patient and try to concentrate on matters at hand.

Hugo was just about to resume his letter when Jane poked her head into the library, her expression full of accusation. "Is that poor woman still locked in? Have you asked Liza to bring her some luncheon? She must be famished." Jane glared at her brother as if he'd used his fists on the woman or relieved her of her virtue, rather than lock her in a room and leave her without food for a few short hours. "I'm surprised at you, Hugo. How can you be so cruel? I know she gave you the slip, but if you're honest with yourself, she did nothing wrong other than behave rudely."

That little speech made Hugo feel even guiltier, but he had to stand his ground. He was the man of the house, goddammit, and Jane had had him running circles around her pretty much since the day she was born and his father had allowed him to hold the squirming infant, telling him that he must always look after his sister and protect her at all cost. He had done his best for Jane, although God knew she hadn't made it easy for him. The revelations about Ernest had been shocking, particularly since Jane had kept the truth from him and he'd found out quite by accident. He supposed she was just being a good and loyal wife, but had Hugo known the truth, he would have run his sword through Ernest while he was still well enough to stand and would have felt no remorse whatsoever under the circumstances. Thank God Jane had been spared physically, if not emotionally.

"Jane, leave and shut the door; I'm busy. I will let her out when I'm good and ready and not a moment sooner, and the longer you stand there, the longer that might take."

Jane gave him a look dripping with scorn and shut the door, but not before he saw her smile as she turned away. He knew exactly why she was smiling, and that annoyed him even more, not only with her, but with himself. Was he really so transparent?

SIXTEEN

After nearly four hours of pacing, I utterly exhausted myself and finally lay down on the bed and pulled the quilt up to my chin, resting my head on the bolster. The misty morning had turned into a rainy afternoon, the deluge seemingly increasing by the hour and plunging the room into nearly impenetrable gloom. The fire hadn't been lit, and it was chilly and damp, making me grateful for the warmth that began to spread through me as the goose quilt did its work. The bed hangings kept out the worst of the draft, and I was cozy in my little hideaway, if not very happy. I was hungry, thirsty, and furious, but most of all, I was scared.

Hugo had looked murderous when he threw me onto the bed, and I'd honestly believed in that moment that he meant to hurt me. He'd seemed to reconsider, but that didn't mean that he wouldn't. Why was he so angry? Okay, so I had left without saying goodbye, but that was hardly a punishable crime. I had also lied about my identity, and I could see how that would anger him, but enough to lock me in? Thank God there was a porcelain utensil under the bed, or I would have burst by now, not that I felt comfortable squatting over it as I held my skirts out of harm's way. Several bedrooms had a privy in the garder-obe, but not this one, since it was used mostly as a guest room.

I must have been mistaken about Hugo. The gallant man who had carried me and looked after me a week ago was a total brute who didn't deserve my concern. He'd have to let me out sometime, and I would leave this house and forget I'd ever met bloody Hugo Everly. How foolish I had been to risk my own well-being to come and warn him. That had always been my problem with men; I put their needs first, instead of my own. I'd done it for years with Evan and, in the end, he'd treated me shabbily, just as I always knew he would. Max wanted to take care of me, and I should let him, instead of always trying to prove that I was an independent woman who could look after herself.

The more I thought about the situation, the more anxious and frightened I became, so I stretched out on the bed with my arms at my sides, palms up, pointed my toes outward beneath the heavy quilt, closed my eyes and began a relaxation exercise that I'd learned in yoga. I wasn't able to fully relax, but my heart rate did slow down, and my breathing grew even as I tried to block out all thought and focus on each part of my body in turn, mentally shutting them down. It was meant to make me feel weightless and at one with the universe, but once I got to my stomach, I remembered that it was empty, and all my anger and frustration came flooding back. It's not like I'd never skipped a meal before; I was usually too busy to think about food, but locked in this room I had very little to distract me.

The sound of the rain proved to be more soothing than yoga, and I began to drift off, desperate to find some escape from my predicament. By the time I awoke, it must have been evening because the gloom of the afternoon had turned into full-blown darkness. The rain still fell, but now it was a soft pitter-patter rather than the downpour of earlier. My stomach growled, and my mouth was dry. Did he want me to dehydrate? I thought angrily. Of course, a seventeenth-century man would know nothing of dehydration or its effects, nor would he be very concerned with my lack of nutrition. He wanted to punish me, and he was doing a fine job of it. If he kept me here a few more days, I'd gladly tell him everything.

The house seemed awfully quiet. *Had they all gone and left me here to die?* I thought melodramatically. I just wanted to go home.

Told you so. Told you so, the chorus in my head moaned, but I made a resolution to ignore it. This was not going to be a Greek tragedy; not if I could help it.

It was another hour, at least, until I heard heavy footsteps in the corridor. They had to belong to a man, so I scrambled off the bed and backed into a corner, suddenly afraid. My heart was racing again, and my palms began to sweat as my stomach turned to water.

Hugo opened the door and shone a candle into the room, finally spotting me crouching in the safety of the corner. "For the love of God, woman, I'm not going to hurt you." He sounded vaguely annoyed, but I wasn't sure if it was with me or himself. "Come out of there," he ordered me.

I remained where I was, eyeing him suspiciously. The flickering light from the candle reflected in his dark eyes, the lower half of his face lost in gloom, making him look even more intimidating.

Hugo set the candlestick on a low table by the door and advanced slowly into the room, palms up. "Mistress Ashley, Neve, I apologize for my behavior earlier. I didn't mean to frighten you. Now, please come out."

"Well, you did frighten me, and you locked me in," I shot back, now more angry than scared.

"And I would do it again, but I shouldn't have physically assaulted you. I am very sorry." He gave me an apologetic smile as I inched away from the wall, more so because it was cold against my back than because I believed him. He did appear to be contrite.

"Step out of the room," I said, and he did, allowing me to pass unmolested into the corridor. "What now?" I asked testily, not wanting to lose any ground.

"Now, we go to the dining room and have some supper, over which you will tell me what I want to know," he answered smoothly.

"And if I don't?" I challenged him, daring him to do his worst.

"Then I will have to lock you in again and wait until you come to your senses, but I hope that won't be necessary."

I followed Hugo downstairs and was surprised to see the table set for two. "Where are Jane and Clarence?" I asked petulantly. I didn't care to be alone with him and suspected that Jane would take my side if push came to shove. She might have been annoyed with my rudeness, but I didn't think she held with women being treated with disrespect.

"Jane went to bed with a headache, and Clarence dined earlier with his tutor. I wanted to talk to you alone. Please sit." Hugo pulled out a heavy chair and held it for me as I perched on the end, deeply conscious of him there behind me.

I glanced over the table while Hugo came around and took a seat across from me. There was baked fish and something that looked like mashed potatoes or turnips. I wasn't sure if they had potatoes readily available in the seventeenth century, but turnips were probably plentiful. There was also some kind of pie, fresh bread, and a hunk of very strong-smelling cheese, which was thankfully on the other side of the table. Cheese was one of the great loves of my life, but I liked the semi-soft kind that melted so nicely on top of toast and not the hard, pungent cheese that sat on the plate across from me. I expected to see a servant, but we were quite alone.

"I hope fish is all right. I refrain from eating meat during Lent," Hugo explained as he placed a piece of what looked like stuffed trout on a plate and passed it to me. I made no move to start eating, partially because I wasn't sure how to approach my meal. There was a spoon and a knife, but no fork. I knew that forks were already in existence, but it wasn't until the eighteenth century that they gained popularity and took their place among the cutlery used at table.

"Eat," he said, "you must be hungry."

I was, but I didn't want to give him the satisfaction of obeying him. I poured myself a cup of wine and took a few slow sips, watching Hugo over the rim of the cup. He wasn't looking at me, but I knew he was aware of my scrutiny. He took a few bites of pie, then finally met my eyes.

"What did you want to tell me?" he asked.

I hadn't expected that. I thought he would start by demanding to know who I was and where I came from. This question was easier.

"I came to warn you, but now I'm not so sure I should have bothered." I was still angry, and I wanted him to know it.

"Warn me about what?"

"Monmouth's rebellion will fail, and he will be branded a traitor and executed. I didn't want the same to happen to you," I blurted out, extremely gratified to see Hugo Everly nearly choke on his food. Served him right.

"How do you know this?" His voice was very low, but I could feel him vibrating with tension, food forgotten.

"I just do."

"That's not an answer. You can't say something like that and not give a reason for your suspicions." Hugo was staring at me across the table, his face ashen, his eyes filled with apprehension. I'd scared him.

"It's not a suspicion; it's fact. I can even tell you the date on which he will be beheaded. Would that help?" I was taunting him now and I knew it, but I wasn't ready to let him off the hook, belatedly realizing that I was putting myself in danger by revealing so much.

"How do you know?" Hugo repeated. His hands were balled into fists, but he made a conscious effort to unclench them and lay them, palms down, on the table before meeting my gaze once again. "Please, don't be afraid. I won't hold it against you. I just really need to know." His voice was soft and ingratiating, but I strongly suspected that if I refused to tell him, he'd employ other methods of getting the information from me.

"I have the Sight." Having the Sight was the only way I could think of to convey my message without telling Hugo I was from the future. Had I been a man, I might have told him that I was a divinist or an astrologer, able to predict the future by looking at the stars or interpreting auspicious signs sent by the heavens, but as a woman, not many avenues were open to me. Most people of the time believed in the gift of Sight, which they thought to be more prevalent among women. However, it was a fine line between being a seer and a witch—a distinction which could get me killed.

Accusing someone of witchcraft was the easiest way of making sure they were found guilty, and often fed into the hysteria of superstition so readily perpetuated by the Church, especially when the parishioners began to question the ways of the clergy and protest the penalties imposed by the Church for non-attendance. Fear was a useful tool for keeping the ignorant masses in line, easily invoked when a lesson needed to be taught, and the presence of the devil spied just at the right time.

The Church had devised a convenient way of testing for witchcraft, sure to prove the accused's guilt every time. They bound the victim's hands and feet and threw them into a body of water. If the accused floated, she was a witch, and if she drowned, she wasn't. Either way, the woman died, the only difference being that she got to die by drowning rather than burning, which I guess was preferable if one had to choose the method of one's death. The thought of being burned alive was enough to make my scalp prickle and my heart pound uncontrollably in my chest, but I pushed the thought aside with the firm belief that it would never come to that.

Hugo sat silently for a few minutes, still glaring at me, but seeing something in his mind which made his hand shake. He hastily took his hand off the table and refocused his gaze on me. "I appreciate your concern, but I can't just take your word for it. Can you tell me something that would support your claim that you have the Sight?"

I knew he'd ask for something, so I decided to play my trump card, the only thing I knew would convince him.

"I can tell you that Clarence was not sired by Jane's husband, and that he's your heir in case anything happens to you. You made out a document to that effect last year, probably before you threw your lot in with Monmouth. You knew the risk and wanted to put your affairs in order."

Hugo continued to stare at me as if I'd suddenly revealed myself to be some kind of supernatural creature. I suppose to him I was. Had I made a mistake and gone too far? What if he turned me over to the Church or the authorities? I was suddenly very scared again, so I broke eye contact and began to move the food around my plate, no longer hungry. It was pitch dark outside, the rain steadily falling, its soothing rhythm beating a tattoo against the mullioned windows. The church was probably locked up for the night, my route of escape barred to me until tomorrow. I had gambled with my safety, and now I was trapped in this house until morning, at the very least, at the mercy of this man who looked fit to be tied.

Hugo took a deep breath, gulped some wine to calm himself and faced me across the table, his anger now under a semblance of control. "You are right on both counts, although your Sight is somewhat flawed. There are things you don't know," Hugo said.

"Such as?" I knew I was right about the rebellion, so had I misread the situation with Jane? Had my dream been a fabrication of my mind?

"That doesn't matter. What matters is that you're probably right, and I thank you for your concern for my well-being. I will take care not to lose my head," he replied with a sad smile, "although I can't guarantee it."

"Hugo, don't do it," I cried, suddenly scared for him. "Monmouth has no legitimate claim to the throne, nor the manpower to mount a proper rebellion. If this country wants a Protestant monarch, they will get one very soon." That got his attention.

"What? How?" Hugo had gone white, his eyes bugging out of his head.

I suddenly stopped and stared at him, the penny finally dropping. Hugo was a Catholic; he didn't want a Protestant monarch. Whatever he was doing with Monmouth wasn't as straightforward as it seemed, and I had blundered in, knowing very little of the man or his cause.

"Oh, God. I've got it all wrong, haven't I?" I whispered.

"What will happen to King James?" Hugo demanded.

I couldn't stop now, so I told him the rest in the hope that he would believe me. "King James and his wife will have a child in 1688, a boy, which will ensure a Catholic succession, unacceptable to the predominantly Protestant majority. The nobles will conspire to invite James's daughter, Mary, and her husband, William of Orange, to invade England." I felt my eyes sting with tears as I saw the expression on Hugo's face. He was heartbroken, and I had been the cause. Maybe it would have been better if he found all this out on his own, or maybe he never would have if he died this year. He'd have thought that James would continue to rule and that his death was a noble sacrifice.

"And King James?" Hugo finally asked.

"King James will live out his life in France, known as 'The

Pretender.' His son will try to regain the throne, but there will never be a Stuart or a Catholic king again."

Hugo poured himself another cup of wine and gulped it down in one swallow, his face still as pale as the tablecloth that was now stained with several crimson blobs, soaking into the cloth and spreading like spilled blood.

I wished I'd never come, never spoken. I had just destroyed this man I'd been trying to help. I felt awful and scared. My insides clenched; my stomach burned, the bile rising in my esophagus in a wave of searing pain. I couldn't breathe, and my legs began to shake with the enormity of what I had done to Hugo Everly, but especially to myself.

"Hugo, I'm really sorry," I stammered. "I didn't mean to cause you pain. I thought I was helping." *And the road to hell is paved with good intentions*, I thought to myself. Why couldn't I have just minded my own business and allowed history to take its course?

"So did Cassandra of Troy," he said, giving me a weak smile. "You are not to blame. It's just something of a shock. I suppose that's why we are not meant to know our future."

He grew silent, staring with unseeing eyes at something just over my right shoulder. I could see that he was thinking, considering, speculating, and looking for a glimmer of hope to be found in my prophecy. Perhaps he wouldn't punish me for the news I'd brought, so maybe my panic was premature. I began to take calming breaths, willing my body to relax. I was kind of surprised to see Hugo's eyes brighten and his color return to normal as he suddenly resumed eating.

"You seem miraculously recovered," I remarked, amazed by the change in Hugo's demeanor, which was highly reassuring. Perhaps not all was lost.

"I was just thinking," he said, "that if I heed your warning, I can change my future. I can take a ship to France, for instance, and be nowhere near England when Monmouth makes his decisive push, therefore saving my life and allowing history to take its course."

"Is that what you're going to do?" I asked, hoping that he would do just that. Perhaps my warning hadn't been in vain after all.

"Of course not, but if I can change the course of my life, then it's possible that the future can be altered. What you see is one version of events. Perhaps things will happen just as you say, but if one man can do one thing to alter the present, then the vision of the future might change accordingly with time." He seemed very pleased with this deduction and took a sip of wine as he smiled into my eyes.

"The future cannot be changed, Hugo."

"Maybe not, but one still has to try. What do you suggest, that I barricade myself in the house and wait for all this to blow over? There's more to life than being safe; there's also following your conscience and fighting for your beliefs. My life is worth nothing if I choose safety over my convictions."

"Well said," I agreed, "if you want to be a martyr."

"I have no intention of becoming a martyr. I will simply follow the path I've chosen but keep what you said in mind. I have no desire to throw my life away, if that's what you think."

"Well, I'm glad to hear that. And how does supporting Monmouth further your own goals? You are a Catholic, are you not? So why support the rebellion of a Protestant bastard against the rightful heir to the throne who also happens to be a Catholic?"

Hugo stopped chewing for a moment and considered my question. I could see that he was torn between talking about that which was so important to him and keeping his own counsel. His face showed a few conflicting emotions before he finally came to a decision and nodded, almost to himself. I suppose he wouldn't be telling me anything that most people didn't already know, but he would be incriminating himself, which he'd already technically done.

"I met Monmouth at Court when he first came from Holland. He was plain James Crofts then, until his father created him a duke. I must admit that I rather liked him, and we became fast friends. We'd both lost our mothers, although I could still remember mine; she died shortly after Jane was born. Monmouth never really knew his mother and was brought up by foster parents chosen by his father, the king. He was bright, witty, and had a great sense of adventure and fun. We spent many hours together exploring Whitehall and trying to flirt with the various ladies of the Court. My father was much at Court, you see, so I saw James quite frequently." Hugo grew silent, remembering those happy days when politics had not ruled his life. He was just a teenage boy then, having fun and growing into manhood on one of the world's greatest stages.

"So, what changed?" I asked.

"Titus Oates. I'm sure you remember him. In 1679, Titus Oates came to warn the king of a supposed Popish Plot against him. It was all nonsense, but it started a mass hysteria against Catholics, which is exactly what Oates and his followers hoped for. The revelation that the king's brother was Catholic incited even those who'd previously been tolerant of Catholics, and the king was under great pressure to quell this wave of fear. Prominent Catholics were asked to leave their posts, and the Royal Declaration of Indulgence, which protected the rights of non-Protestants, was nullified. Many of my father's contemporaries and friends were ousted. My father was long gone by then, but he would have been horrified by what was happening in the country." Hugo gazed at me across the table to see if I was following his story. Of course, I'd heard all these historical facts before, but now I was faced with someone who'd been affected by them.

"That still doesn't explain why you support Monmouth," I

ventured, knowing that Hugo had told me very little so far that I wouldn't know myself having supposedly come from seventeenth-century London.

Hugo gave a slight shrug, casting caution to the wind as he warmed to his subject. "The king's succession is ordained by God. James was next in line since Charles II had no legitimate children, and no one would question this if it wasn't for his religious beliefs. Likewise, James's future son is next in line for the throne, Catholic or not. However, there are many out there who support Monmouth and believe that he has a right to rule. They would never condone this anarchy had James been a Protestant, but these people are ignorant and desperate, and they want to see a Protestant on the throne at all cost, even if he happens to be a bastard. As long as the Duke of Monmouth is alive, there will always be plots to assassinate James and his offspring."

I continued to stare at Hugo, trying to figure out where he came in. If he were a Catholic, why would he want to help Monmouth rebel against a Catholic king? What was I missing? "I don't understand," I finally admitted, making Hugo smile.

"You said yourself that Monmouth doesn't have the resources or the support to mount a successful rebellion. The longer he waits, the more support he will gain, especially if James has a son. So, there are those of us who want to see Monmouth try for the crown sooner rather than later and fail. King James will have no choice but to send the army to quell the rebellion and Monmouth will be defeated once and for all. His ambitions will be quashed, and his supporters either executed or disgraced. Monmouth's failure and subsequent execution for treason will put an end to the witch hunt against James and leave him to rule in peace as a Catholic monarch, who will hopefully ensure his succession soon."

"And you have no pangs of conscience about leading your friend to the scaffold?" I tried to keep the scorn out of my voice but couldn't help myself. Hugo spoke so dispassionately about the Duke of Monmouth being executed for treason.

I was gratified to see a veil pass over Hugo's eyes as the full force of my accusation hit him. He lowered his head for a moment, either gathering his thoughts or thinking how best to tell me off. He was silent momentarily and when he looked back at me, I could see genuine sorrow in his gaze.

"I don't want to see him dead," he replied quietly. "I want him to live to a ripe old age, preferably in Holland, and die in his bed surrounded by people who love him, but as long as he harbors ambitions of usurping the throne from the rightful king, he's in danger of losing his life. His father told him that he would never be king, and that he should be happy with what he has, but his ambition is boundless. He will not rest until he either gets what he yearns for or dies trying. I will not be the instrument of his destruction; he will."

I inclined my head, accepting his answer. He was right, of course; the Duke of Monmouth meant to be king, and Hugo or no Hugo, his fate was sealed.

"So, assuming that your plan comes to pass, and Monmouth is no longer a threat to the king, what of William and Mary being invited to rule?" I asked, hating to squash his hopes so brutally.

"The people might not want a Catholic monarch, but James is English and a direct descendant of the house of Stuart. William is a foreigner. I don't believe that as many people as you say would welcome him as the next king. If James rules long enough to prove that he is a just and good king, the people will come to accept him in time and stop fearing his association with Rome. There are too many Protestants in this country for James to really force the issue of returning the country to Catholicism, as they fear. He simply needs time to show the people that he will not be a tyrant as Mary Tudor was, and brand them all heretics fit only for the fires of Hell."

"Do *you* believe them to be heretics?" I asked, needing to ascertain exactly how much of a zealot Hugo himself might be. His explanation so far seemed very rational, but many a religious fanatic managed to sound rational at times.

"No, of course not. I believe that a man should worship as he sees fit. We're all subjects of the same God, are we not? I simply fear that if James is deposed, the future of Catholics in this country will become untenable, and that's not something I'm prepared to live with."

"You might not get the chance to live with it. As a supporter of Monmouth, you will be branded a traitor as well," I reminded him.

"That's a risk I'm willing to take," Hugo responded, a closed look coming over his face. He didn't want to talk about this anymore, and I didn't blame him. I'd hoped I might have distracted him from questioning my story, but Hugo wasn't one to just let things go.

"Enough about me," he said with finality. "I think I've earned the right to ask a few questions. Where are you from, Mistress Ashley, and what brought you here?" Hugo asked suddenly, his eyes narrowed just enough to put me on my guard.

"London." *Stick to the truth as much as possible if you want your lie to be believed*, I told myself.

"So, how come you to be here?" Hugo asked.

"I was scared for my life, so I fled. I took sanctuary at the church," I confided in him, hoping he'd believe me and not ask too many more questions. My so-called Sight was certainly enough to get me into trouble in London, so he might just accept that I'd run afoul of someone who didn't like my prophecy.

"So, what were you doing in the lane that day?" Hugo asked, clearly still suspicious.

"I had no money left and was hoping to beg some food from your kitchens. I was hungry," I replied.

"And I nearly killed you that day, and then I assaulted you and locked you in a room with nothing to eat when you risked your safety to come and warn me of what you've seen." He looked genuinely contrite, and I felt a little more charitable toward him. Maybe he wasn't so bad after all. I knew what I was about, but he didn't, and given his situation, he couldn't be too careful.

"It's all right. I should have just told you the truth, but I was afraid. I'd like to go back to the church in the morning," I added, hoping that he wouldn't object to me spending the night. The rain was lashing at the windows, the wind howling with such ferocity that it rattled the shutters and sounded like someone moaning and crying in the night. Another few hours wouldn't make that much of a difference, and I really was emotionally drained from my ordeal. "Thank you for supper."

I rose to my feet and was about to leave when Hugo's grin stopped me in my tracks. He was leaning back in the chair, his hands clasped across his middle and his head cocked to the side, but I could see that it was a contrived pose. He was up to something.

"Why are you smiling that way?" I asked, suddenly nervous.

"Goodnight, Mistress Ashley. Rest well, since you will most certainly leave in the morning."

I could see that there was more, so I waited silently, forcing him to tell me.

"You and I are going on a journey come morning to visit another devoted supporter of Monmouth's cause." Hugo seemed to be enjoying his little announcement, watching me like a cat playing with a bird it's about to devour.

"What? Why?"

"I can hardly just let you leave here after all that's just transpired, can I? You know enough about me to have me arrested for treason by the king's men, or have me killed by Monmouth should he discover my true purpose. You are also aware of my nephew's true parentage, which can threaten his inheritance, since although he's Ernest's son within the law, he's really a bastard and has no right to the estate. Ernest has a daughter from a previous marriage who would very much like to hear what you've just told me. I'm sorry, my sweet, but I'm not letting you out of my sight."

"And how will you explain my presence to your associates, *my sweet?*" I asked, my tone mocking. I was angry, and I wanted him to know it.

"You're my mistress."

"Your mistress?!" I nearly gagged on the word. "Are you mad?"

"Insanity has very little to do with my decision. It's self-preservation that drives me. Plenty of men bring their wives and mistresses along to make these meetings appear more social than political. After all, no one wants to be accused of treason, especially so early in the game."

The twinkle in his eye genuinely annoyed me. He was having fun at my expense and not only insulting me but seizing control of my life and trying to bend me to his will.

"And if I refuse?" I challenged him. He could hardly force me to act as a mistress would, even if he managed to drag me along.

"By your own admission, you're alone, without funds, and fearful for your safety. I'm offering you a life of comfort and relative security until the coming rebellion. Then, you're free to go your own way as long as you keep mum about my nephew's paternity, which won't matter anymore in any case, since the terms of the Will would have been met by then. Clarence must be thirteen to inherit his father's estate, which he will be in June. I promise you'll be well paid for your silence as a thank you from me. Do we have an agreement?"

"No, we don't. I want to be free to leave. NOW!" *The inso-lent bastard*, I thought angrily. He'd thought of everything while I was under the impression that he was shaken by what I'd told him. His mind was certainly quick as lightning, and he'd prob-ably sorted through all the alternatives, coming up with the only one that guaranteed my silence.

"I'm sorry, but I can't let you go. I need to keep you with me, and I think you might need me as well. You wouldn't have come back had you not felt something for me, however slight, so let's build on it and make it work for us both. Jane has a few gowns and jewels she can lend you. She's not wearing them while in mourning. She can instruct you on how to behave and what's expected of you. You can pose as my mistress, which shouldn't be too hard to do. Your gift of Sight can be a useful asset in the coming months."

"Why would you want me to pose as your mistress?" I cried, still stunned by his suggestion.

"You can travel as my servant if you prefer, but I think you would be much more comfortable as my mistress, and your pres-ence would be more acceptable. Please don't worry; I have no intention of forcing you to fulfill any romantic obligations— unless you really want to," he added with an impish grin. "You will have to pretend to be enamored of me, however, or the ploy will fail. Do you think you can manage that for a few hours at a time?"

"I'm not going with you," I spat out. Could he really force me? I just wanted to get away from this house and this bloody man. It seemed that every time I got near him, something unex-pected happened, and I found myself thrown off balance and not in control of my life.

"Yes, you are. You can come willingly, and we can try to make the best of the situation, or you can come against your will. I have the means and the manpower to keep you locked up," he replied pleasantly and took another sip of his wine.

He finally rose to his feet and took me gently by the elbow, nudging me toward the stairs. I meekly walked ahead of him, knowing that if I were to escape, I'd have to wait till morning anyway.

"Good night, Neve," Hugo said courteously as he shut the door and turned the key.

SEVENTEEN

I spent the night tossing and turning, my overwrought mind searching for a way out of my predicament. I would have one chance to get away from Hugo when we set out in the morning, but if that failed, my chances of escape would dwindle with every passing mile. I had no money and no way to return to the church except on foot, and the further we got from Everly Manor, the harder it would be for me to find my way back and do it in a way that would keep me out of Hugo's way. He would be able to catch me in minutes on horseback.

I finally fell asleep from sheer exhaustion in the small hours but was awoken by the opening of the door and the sour face of the serving girl who brought me hot water for washing. She didn't say anything, but her demeanor oozed contempt, and I wondered why she should be so predisposed against me when she had seemed courteous enough before. Perhaps she'd overheard something, but I couldn't imagine why she'd care one way or the other. I was a stranger who was about to depart and possibly never come back, so why the sudden hostility?

"Good morning," I ventured, but the girl just harrumphed and left, slamming the door behind her.

I rinsed my mouth for lack of a toothbrush, washed my face and hands and brushed my hair with the brush the girl had left behind. Hugo had mentioned Jane's gowns, and I hoped I wasn't expected to try them on as I had my own underwear beneath my dress, and that would raise a few eyebrows.

I was just about to leave the room when the same sullen girl returned, her arms full of clothing and underthings. There were lots of bits and pieces due to the amount of layers that covered a well-dressed woman, and the maid dumped them all on the bed and began to sort through the pile. Her demeanor had vastly improved, since Jane was right behind her, her own face creased by frowning. I wasn't sure what Hugo had told her, but if she knew what I'd told him last night, she would not be too eager to help me.

"Good morrow," she said without preamble. "Hugo asked me to lend you a few gowns and other necessities for the journey. He's rather taken with you," Jane said, eyeing me with wonder, as if trying to understand what it was about me that so captivated her brother. "I've never known him to act rashly when it came to women, but it appears he doesn't wish to be parted from you." Jane smiled, and her face was transformed, reminding me how beautiful she was when I'd seen her in my dream.

So, Hugo hadn't told her the truth after all. He'd led her to believe that I was really going to be his mistress. I couldn't even begin to imagine what Jane thought of me at present, but I couldn't be bothered to decipher her feelings. I had enough problems of my own and being perceived as a trollop wasn't one of them.

"I hope you like the gowns. They might be a trifle out of date. I haven't had any new clothes made while Ernest was ill."

"They're lovely, Jane, especially this one." I held up a silk gown in a gorgeous shade of moss green. The fabric shimmered in the early-morning light, the color rippling like water in a still pond as it moved fluidly, the silk making an almost imperceptible flutter as it whispered of opulence and seduction. It was embroidered with a pattern of dainty golden flowers with red centers, and the full sleeves were slashed with gold and accentuated with deep red ribbons to pick up the red in the blossoms. A decorative petticoat would be worn beneath the overskirt, possibly in a shade of cream or ochre. A pair of red velvet court shoes came with the gown and Jane shyly handed me a case containing a ruby necklace and matching earrings.

"Hugo said you'd need to look beautiful," she explained. "Would you like to try them on?"

"Jane, I don't feel right taking these things from you," I said, feeling embarrassed by her generosity. "They are so beautiful."

"I won't be needing them for a while, and I know you'll return them when you come back. Besides, I want you to look your best for Hugo."

The maid looked as if she were about to be sick, but I ignored her and sorted through the other gowns. She wouldn't be the first woman to have feelings for her employer, and Hugo was handsome, I'd give him that. Besides, I had no designs on him, but I could hardly tell her that, especially in front of Jane. Hugo had his reasons for not telling his sister the truth, and it wasn't for me to straighten her out. If he wanted Jane to think that I was his lover, then he'd have to be the one to explain things to her when I disappeared from their lives.

In the meantime, I had to figure out the intricacies of a seventeenth-century trousseau. Some dresses came in several parts; the bodice separate from the sleeves, and the skirt worn over an underskirt of a different color and fabric. There were silk stockings of various colors, several chemises, an embroidered stomacher, and a fontage headdress to be worn in a place that, hopefully, had high doorways, or it would be knocked right off since it rose inches above my head. I hoped I wouldn't need

any of these things since I would try to make a run for the
church as soon as I ventured outside.

* * *

My hopes of escape were dashed the minute I stepped into the
yard. I'd assumed that Hugo and I would be traveling alone, but
the yard was bustling with activity. Several horses were already
saddled, three of them laden with heavy saddlebags, and several
men were completing the preparations as they bantered cheerfully between themselves. I couldn't help noticing that they
were heavily armed and unusually burly, which was probably
why Hugo had selected them to accompany him. Several dogs
yapped at their ankles, making the horses nervous and filling the
yard with a cacophony of sound.

The rain had stopped, but thick fog swirled close to the
ground, making everything appear as if it were wrapped in
cotton wool. Every surface was slick with moisture, and large
puddles glistened in the muddy yard. The maid, whose name
was Liza, came out and called to one of the men to come get my
valise. She threw me a filthy look and disappeared inside,
leaving me to stand alone on the steps.

My eyes filled with tears of frustration as I felt my hopes
dissipate, but I didn't want Hugo to see me crying. He would
either feel sorry for me or think me a weakling, but neither
opinion would change his mind about taking me along. He
came strolling out of the house dressed for traveling, an elaborately decorated baldrick over his right shoulder leading to the
sword at his left hip. So, he felt the need to be armed as well,
which was even more disturbing. Where was he taking me?

Hugo gave me an elaborate bow and smiled at me as he
looked up, the message in his eyes clear—remember our agreement and play your part.

"Mistress Ashley, may I present Archie Hicks, Arnold Sullivan, and Peter Yates. They will accompany us on our journey," he added by way of explanation.

The three men bowed to me and muttered, "Good day, Mistress Ashley." They were deferential to me, so I assumed that, just like Jane, they were told that I was his lordship's mistress. Peter Yates helped me mount the mare that was assigned to me and I patted the smooth brown neck, hoping that we would get along. Thankfully, I knew how to ride, but I hadn't been on a horse in ages, and the prospect of spending days in the saddle left me wishing once again that I had never followed my instinct and returned to the past.

While the men completed their preparations and mounted their own horses, I had a chance to study them at close range. Arnold and Peter were both close to forty, tall by seventeenth-century standards, stocky, and swarthy, with dark hair, dark eyes and bushy beards. I thought I noticed a familial resemblance, but their surnames were different, so cousins perhaps. Their faces showed very little, their eyes fixed on the task at hand, their movements measured and deliberate. Archie, on the other hand, was a totally different kettle of fish. He was in his mid-twenties, with bright, curious eyes the color of a summer sky and a shock of ginger hair that matched the sprinkling of freckles across his nose. I reckoned he was popular with the village girls, if he wasn't already taken.

Peter and Arnold avoided looking at me after the introduction, but Archie openly studied me, giving me an impish grin when I met his stare. He tipped his hat to me in an exaggerated gesture of gentlemanly behavior, making me wonder if he were laughing at me.

As the horses began to walk out of the yard, I was surprised to see a young boy rush out of the stables, step up on the mounting block and swing into the saddle of a mule that had been placidly standing by. The boy looked to be no more than ten years old, but he had a knowing gaze that belied his years, and a confident manner that left me wondering who he was. Unlike the rest of the men, he was dressed not in homespun, but in a suit of brown velvet and good leather boots. His unruly dark hair was covered by a chapeau which matched his cloak, and he appeared to have a sword at his side made to accommodate his small stature.

"Wait for me," he called out as he dug his heels into the sides of his mule.

No one paid much attention to him besides me, but I couldn't take my eyes off this little boy-man who seemed so sure of his place in Hugo's entourage.

Hugo turned back briefly and tipped his hat to the boy, eliciting a smile of such pure delight from the child that I couldn't help smiling myself.

Jane waved through the window as we rode away, her face dissolving in the fog mere moments after we trudged through the gate. I looked longingly in the direction of the church, but Hugo gave me a warning look that put paid to any idea I might have had of galloping across the open field toward my sanctuary. I didn't stand a chance.

We skirted the village, and within a half-hour were alone on the dirt road, the village far behind. I was surprised to see a signpost that read "Cranley" instead of "Cranleigh" pointing back in the direction of the village, but it wasn't uncommon for spelling to change over time.

"How are you this morning, Mistress Ashley?" Hugo asked as he rode next to me, his wig and plumed hat making him look like a stranger. "I hope you found Jane's gowns to your liking?"

"Yes, thank you, they are beautiful," I answered absent-mindedly. I was trying to focus on the landscape in case I managed to get away, but it all looked much the same: green, wet, and mostly uninhabited, except for the occasional farmhouse with a smoking chimney just visible between the swirls of fog. Even the animals looked depressed, the cows just lying like

huge brown boulders on the ground and the sheep bleating pitifully as they wandered around in search of new grass.

"We'll be stopping for the night at Sir Benedict Nolan's
house. He's a devoted subject of the king and an ardent
supporter of his nephew. I mean to find out which way he'll
lean once he has to take sides, and if we can count on his
support."

I didn't bother to ask if by "we" he meant the Duke of
Monmouth and his lot or the king. I already knew whom he was
referring to. My warning had done nothing to dissuade him, and
I silently cursed myself yet again for being a complete and utter
idiot. The chorus in my head had long since quietened down,
having done their part. Just like Hugo, I'd failed to listen when
being warned, and now I was paying the price, as would Hugo
when the time came.

"You can honor our agreement and stay with me in the
house," Hugo continued, "or you can thwart my plans and stay
in the hayloft with my men. The choice is yours," he offered
smoothly, but, of course, he knew exactly which option I'd go
with. Staying in the hayloft with three strange men was much
more daunting than spending the night with Hugo. I always
believed in choosing the evil I knew versus the one I didn't, so
gave him a nod of acquiescence.

I spent the rest of the morning riding in silence, despite
Hugo's attempts at conversation, particularly after he had
Archie follow me into the woods when I needed a moment of
privacy.

Eventually, I fell in with the boy. He seemed to be getting
rather tired, but perked up as soon as I drew alongside, his back
straightening and his hands picking up the loose reins as he
tipped his hat to me deferentially.

"Good day, Mistress Ashley," the boy said. He had dark
curly hair and soft brown eyes, huge in the pale face that was
still round-cheeked and snub-nosed with babyhood. Two of his

front teeth were missing, the permanent teeth beneath having pushed them out of the way. I found his smile to be very endearing.

"Good day. I don't believe we've been introduced," I said, curious about the child.

"I'm Jem, his lordship's page," he informed me proudly.

"Do you live at the manor, Jem?"

"I do; I sleep in the kitchens. It's nice and warm there and Cook always gives me buns fresh out of the oven when I wake."

"And where are your parents? Does your mother work at the house?"

"Oh no, madam. My mam passed near a year ago, and my da abandoned us afore I was even born. I'm a bastard," the boy announced cheerfully.

"And what do you do for his lordship?" I asked, feeling a strong kinship to this boy who'd suffered the same fate as me, only much worse. At least I had a home, a bed, and a future, unlike this orphan who slept on a bench in the kitchens and had very little besides servitude to look forward to once he achieved manhood.

"Oh, this and that," the boy said mysteriously. "I'm an in-n-teg-ral part of the household." The boy tripped over the word, but finally got it right and beamed at me in a way that made my heart squeeze. He was hardly more than a child.

"How old are you, Jem?"

"Just turned eight," Jem answered, his narrow chest swelling with pride. "His lordship gave me this sword for my birthday. It's only polished wood, but it's good for practicing. He promised me a real sword once I'm a competent swordsman. I practice every day, mostly with Archie."

"And do you like being in his lordship's employ?" I asked, my voice full of suspicion. "Does he pay you?"

"Not in coin. He gives me food, a roof over my head, and the clothes on my back. That's more than enough, if you ask me.

He's a right good master, he is." The poor child seemed so grateful that it nearly made me cry. What kind of a life was this for a little boy?

"Well, I'm happy to have made your acquaintance, Jem," I said. "I hope we get to speak again."

"I've nae doubt we will, madam," Jem replied, giving me a cheeky smile. He really was cute, which for some reason made me even angrier.

I dug my heels into the sides of my mare and urged her to go a little faster until I arrived at the head of the procession.

"Do you really need an eight-year-old page?" I demanded of Hugo angrily as he slowed down and waited for me to draw alongside him.

Hugo's eyebrows momentarily disappeared beneath the brim of his hat. He seemed affronted by the question, but quickly rearranged his features into a bland mask, replying to me in a tone of utmost patience and courtesy.

"No, but I have one all the same."

He infuriated me with his arrogance, which I think was the objective.

"That child should be in school," I retorted, instantly realizing my mistake. There were no schools, especially for children like Jem. He was probably lucky to have a place at all.

"School?" Hugo asked, looking scandalized. "What type of school?"

"Never mind," I mumbled, feeling foolish in the extreme. "Why do you have him? He's just a little boy."

"Yes, he is, and he needs my protection. He's an orphan with no kin to look after him. I took him in for his own good." Hugo sounded defensive, but I wasn't ready to give up being angry with him. I wasn't angry just about Jem, but that was the one thing I could reasonably berate him for.

"Why?" I demanded.

"Because I held his mother in rather a high regard," Hugo replied with a small smile, which suggested a multitude of sins.

"Is he...?" I spat out at him, but he just shook his head.

"Is he my spawn, you mean?" he asked. The corners of his eyes crinkled in amusement, and his mouth twitched with the effort not to smile. He was laughing at me and my indignation, and I was overcome with a desire to kick him in the shins; unfortunately, with both of us being mounted, that was rather out of the question.

"Well, is he?" I persisted, unsure of whether I really wanted to know the answer to that. Hugo wouldn't be the first master to impregnate a servant or a girl from the village. I supposed the fact that he was at least taking some responsibility for the child was a credit to him, but it didn't absolve him altogether.

"No, Mistress Ashley, he isn't. He's just a child who needed a home. And to answer your next question, if I just took him in without offering him employment, every bastard in the parish would be left on my doorstep by its desperate mother in the hope that I would look after it. Besides, Jem needs to feel useful and important, and being a page gives him a sense of purpose and accomplishment, so everybody wins."

"Is that why he's coming with us, to give him a sense of accomplishment?" I asked, amazed that Hugo would just let him tag along. Judging by the amount of weaponry, he clearly thought there might be some danger and didn't think twice about endangering the child.

"Jem has his uses," Hugo explained. "People tend to speak freely in front of a child; as a matter of fact, they often forget he's even there. He picks up all sorts of useful information which he happily passes on to me."

"So, it's not all generosity and charity on your part?" I asked sarcastically, still determined to be angry with him.

"No, not all. I have plans for little Jem, if you must know."

"What kind of plans?" I asked aghast, suddenly worried about the welfare of the boy.

"Why must you assume the worst?" Hugo retorted irritably. "Do you think that I will put him in danger or work him to the bone? I plan to educate him in due time and make him my secretary once he gets older. Does that meet with your approval, madam?" he asked sarcastically. "That's considerably more than he could have aspired to had he grown up as the bastard son of a washerwoman."

"Yes, that's very kind of you," I conceded. "Was his mother a friend of yours?" There I went sticking my nose where it didn't belong again, but I was very curious about this man and what motivated him.

Hugo gave me a sideways glance, no doubt angry himself since I had practically attacked him and questioned his motives. I suppose he had every right to be. He hadn't asked for any of this. I was the one who had waltzed into his life, called everything he was doing into question, prophesied doom, and then got angry when he did the only truly logical thing and decided to keep me on a short leash, should I decide to shout my suspicions from the rooftops. The only person who deserved my ire was myself, and I felt overcome with helpless fury at my own stupidity and naiveté.

Hugo sighed and turned toward me, his face a mask of patient tolerance. He wanted things to be cordial between us, so he decided to be forthcoming, probably against his better judgment. "If you must know, his mother was a scullion when she was a girl. I fancied myself in love with her when I was about thirteen and found excuse after excuse to visit the kitchens, nearly getting her dismissed for encouraging my attentions. I declared my love and promised to marry her as soon as I reached maturity. She had the good grace not to laugh at me or tell my father. My father was a stern man and would have punished me for forgetting my station in life. Social standing was very important to him, so offering marriage to a lowly servant would be considered disgraceful. I would have gotten the beating of my life."

"Did she share your feelings?" I asked, intrigued. What scullery maid wouldn't be impressed with the future Lord Everly, especially when he was as attractive as Hugo?

"She was a few years older than I and already a woman. She allowed me to kiss her a few times though, which is something I'll never forget. Those were some of the happiest moments of my young life." Judging from Hugo's smile, I assumed that was not all she allowed him, but I didn't dare ask.

"So, what happened to her?"

"Margaret was a willful girl, not content to spend her life in servitude. She waited for an opportunity, and one came along some years later. One of my friends who came for a visit took a fancy to her and she followed him to London, convinced that he would make good on his promise and take care of her. He dallied with her for a while, but eventually tired of her and cut off his financial support, leaving Margaret to fend for herself. She tried to survive on her own in London but was ill and destitute when I spotted her on the street one day, begging, or more accurately, looking for custom. I brought her back here and helped her get back on her feet."

"I take it her newfound respectability didn't last long?" I asked, guessing at what was coming.

"No, she took up with one of the grooms and got with child. As it turned out, Ned was already married. He didn't get on with his wife, so he left her at home and headed for London, where I'd hired him a few years before. He took off as soon as he found out Margaret was carrying his child."

"So, she had Jem?"

"Yes, she had Jem. She wasn't a very good mother to him. He was a burden she wasn't ready to deal with and ruined her prospects of finding another man. She died of a fever not a year ago. If you ask me, it was a happy release for her, if not for her son, who was heartbroken."

"You still cared for her, didn't you?" I asked, seeing a closed look come over Hugo's face.

He didn't answer, but he'd revealed enough already, and I was grateful for his confidence. He had showed me a glimpse of himself, and I found it harder to be angry with him when he took it upon himself to care for a boy who had no one and nothing, out of regard for a woman who was kind to him when he was a boy himself.

"That's a sad story. I'm sorry I was rude to you about Jem," I offered. "He's lucky to have you, and he seems very fond of you," I admitted grudgingly.

"As I am of him."

EIGHTEEN

MARCH 2013

Max Everly stood still for a moment and gazed over the expanse of verdant countryside that belonged to the Everly estate. It never ceased to gladden his heart that he was the master of all he surveyed. The estate was always in need of funds, especially when it came to the house, but the land was what gave one power and true wealth. Hundreds of acres of farmland and woodland had remained in the family for centuries, making the Everlys one of the most prominent families in England.

Thankfully, after the mysterious disappearance of Hugo Everly, his nephew had inherited the estate, and, with the help of his mother and the estate manager, guided it into the eighteenth century. Clarence had been a shrewd businessman who kept his nose out of politics and concentrated on amassing the family's wealth. It wasn't until after the First World War that Ernest Hiddleston's holdings had been sold off and the Everly wealth consolidated in Surrey, but Max was eternally grateful to his ancestor for handing him this legacy, one that would never have been his had Hugo not involved himself in the rebellion and got himself snuffed out somewhere.

Max absentmindedly patted his dog, his eyes still drinking

in the beauty around him. He'd given himself time to play, but now it was high time he got down to business. He had to marry, produce an heir, and then turn his sights to politics, as several men in his family had done since the last century. The next time a seat came up in the House of Commons, he would put himself forward as a Conservative candidate. Being an MP would give him the political clout he craved and put the Everly family on the map once again.

At first, he'd thought that Neve couldn't be suitable, but seeing her juggle phone calls from various people while seeing to all the minute details of the deal had made him change his mind. He didn't want some brainless debutante who only cared about clothes and holidays on the French Riviera. He wanted a wife who would be an asset to his political career, and Neve had certain qualities which would make her indispensable. She could be a true partner, not just an accessory to be displayed on his arm. The fact that she was extremely pretty and personable didn't hurt. She could manage his campaign and still inspire women voters, and maybe even sway some voters, to his cause with her working-woman background. Voters liked candidates who understood their plight and marrying a woman who came from a working-class background could only be an asset.

Max smiled to himself, eager to discuss the plan with his mother. For once, she was bound to be proud of him. Naomi Everly was rarely affectionate or supportive, but she was fiercely proud of the family she'd married into and eager to see her son make something of his life, rather than just indulge his various recreational interests and chase pretty girls. She'd been applying pressure for years, desperate to see Max finally accept responsibility and devote his life to something that would leave a mark—and Max needed her support. Lady Everly would be an invaluable asset when it came to campaigning, using her social connections and influence to woo potential supporters and contributors to his campaign. Political ambition ran on a steady flow of financial fuel, preferably supplied by someone else's generosity.

The phone trilled in his pocket, shaking him out of his pleasant reverie. It was an unfamiliar number, but he decided to take the call just in case it was important.

"Lord Everly? Lawrence Spellman here. Sorry to bother you, but I was wondering if Neve Ashley might still be with you this morning. I've tried her mobile numerous times, but no joy. She was supposed to join us for a meeting, you see, but she never turned up." The man sounded nervous, prattling on like a girl, but Max took the time to reassure him. After all, he needed the lovely fee the film company would bring, so best to be as cordial as possible.

"I'm sorry, Mr. Spellman, but Neve left for London yesterday morning. I saw her off myself. Perhaps her battery has died. I've no doubt she'll turn up soon. I'll be sure to let you know if she gets in touch." Max rang off and turned toward the village, eager for a pint. It'd be noon by the time he got there, so he might even have lunch at the pub. They did a nice shepherd's pie on Mondays.

The thought of food made Max's mouth water. He was hungry after his walk, having eaten only a piece of toast for breakfast. He wasn't big on eating first thing in the morning like his mother, who'd had the same breakfast every day for the past forty years. Naomi Everly was a woman of habit and tradition, whereas her son enjoyed a bit of spontaneity and a desire for personal freedom; something she'd never understood.

"Come, Tilly," Max called out to the dog, turning his steps toward the village.

The dog bounded up behind him, sensing a good meal coming up. Tilly was always offered a nice selection of scraps while her owner spent an enjoyable hour or two at the pub, drumming up local support.

Perhaps he should ask if anyone had seen Neve. Where

could she be? Max tried her mobile himself as he walked, but the call went straight to voicemail. He left a brief message and rang off. Perhaps she had just overslept and would come rushing into the office, apologetic and disheveled. He liked it when her hair was in disarray, as it was when ruffled by the wind. It made Neve look more natural. He liked women who looked real, not the plasticky specimens he often met at parties and fundraisers. They looked as if their faces might crack if they smiled too enthusiastically. He wanted a woman to laugh, to ride, to get her hands dirty, and most of all to be an equal partner in bed. The thought of getting Neve into bed was a very appealing one, but he pushed it away, suddenly overcome by worry.

Max doubled back, turned the corner and stopped in front of the shuttered barbershop; his eyes glued to the little blue hatchback parked out front. Yes, it was definitely Neve's car.

He approached it and looked inside. Nothing seemed to be amiss. Was it possible that Neve had spent the night in the village? But to what end? Had she met someone while she was in Cranleigh? Didn't seem likely. She'd spent most of her time at the manor, and she specifically said that she was heading home to London, so why was her car here?

Max walked up and down the street, peering into shop windows and asking a few passersby if they'd seen a woman of her description. Nearly an hour later, he was back in front of the car with no more information than he had before.

Neve had expressed an interest in the church, but that hardly explained where she'd been for over twenty-four hours. Max decided to put off lunch for a while and walked to the church at a brisk pace, Tilly trailing behind him, her gentle brown eyes full of accusation at being denied lunch.

"Vicar, have you by any chance seen Neve Ashley?" Max asked as Vicar Lambert greeted him in the nave.

"You mean the lovely young woman from the film

company? Why, no, I haven't. I was busy finalizing my sermon in the vestry and then held the service. I must say that, to my great surprise, the church was nearly full. You know how lax attendance has been lately, so I was most pleasantly surprised. Must be the fact that it's Lent, wouldn't you say? People always get slightly more pious around Easter, in my experience," the vicar explained, but was silenced by Max's look of patient annoyance. "Has she gone missing then?"

"I'm sure there's a reasonable explanation, but it seems she didn't turn up for work this morning. Said she was going home to London, so she's probably just overslept." Max didn't want to tell the vicar about Neve's car. He had reasons to keep it quiet, but he still needed information.

"Lord Everly," a young woman called out to him. She'd overheard his conversation with the vicar and was now walking toward him down the nave. He didn't know her, but she appeared to be a local. "I was here with my mother and sister yesterday. My sister is getting married at the weekend, so we came to finalize the flower arrangements, and I saw a woman fitting your friend's description go down into the crypt," the young woman said, eager to be helpful.

"Did you see her come back out?" Max asked, now even more confused.

"No, I didn't. We were here for a quarter of an hour after that, but then the service began, and I didn't notice anyone coming or going. It was surprisingly crowded, as the vicar said."

"Thank you, I appreciate your help," Max told the woman as he turned toward the crypt. He didn't expect to find Neve there a day later, but he still had to look.

The crypt was empty, of course, the light illuminating the stone walls and casting shadows into the dusty corners swathed in cobwebs where the walls converged with the ceiling. Max looked around and scratched his head. No, it wasn't possible. It was just a family anecdote, nothing more, he thought as he began to check behind every sarcophagus. It was ridiculous even to think along those lines, but he continued to search until he found the holdall behind the knight's tomb. Max opened the zipper with shaking hands and pushed aside Neve's clothes to find her mobile and car keys at the bottom. He leaned heavily against the tomb, unsure of what to do.

The rational thing would be to call the police, but a missing person's inquiry was about the last thing he needed just then. The shoot might be canceled, costing him the fee he'd already allocated to cover various expenses, and a scandal splashed across the papers, especially London ones, wouldn't help his future political aspirations. People would forget what the story was all about, but they would remember his name and associate it with something lurid and criminal, even though he had nothing to do with whatever happened to Neve.

Max took the bag and stealthily left the church, practically jogging home.

NINETEEN

Lady Everly poured herself a cup of tea and gingerly set down the china teapot before stirring in a lump of sugar and adding a splash of milk. She always took her tea this way, although in the past it had been served to her by a parlormaid. Lady Everly often spoke of the good old days when Everly Manor was fully staffed, the top floor buzzing with gossip and muffled footsteps as the servants retired for the evening. Those days were long gone, faded into history shortly after Naomi Harrison came to Everly as a young bride over sixty years ago, but his mother loved to harp on about them, driving Max to distraction. He waited patiently until Lady Everly took the first sip before finally recalling her attention to what he'd been saying.

"Mother, are you even listening to me?" he asked, annoyed that she didn't have more of a reaction to the news of Neve's possible disappearance. She appeared as calm and collected as always; her perfectly coiffed head bent just so as she considered him from across the room, the teacup delicately suspended in her right hand. "Mother, please tell me this can't be true," Max pleaded. "Can it really be possible that Neve found the passage and traveled through time? Should I go after her?" he asked, knowing perfectly well that this particular question would finally elicit a response from his mother, who'd remained silent until now.

"You will do no such thing," his mother answered, her tone far more businesslike than emotional. "You are my son and the heir to this estate. You will *not* take any risks, you hear me?" she admonished as she set down her cup with more force than she intended.

"You didn't answer my question. Is it true?" Max demanded, growing more exasperated by the minute.

"How should I know?" Lady Everly barked. "It would appear so. Where else could she have gone? Have you searched the countryside? Maybe she's been attacked," she suggested without much hope.

"So, she parked her car in the village, took off her clothes and left her phone and keys and ran naked from the crypt until she came across someone who attacked her? Or, should I say, killed her? Because if she were alive, she'd have shown up somewhere by now. The woman at the church saw Neve going down to the crypt with her bag—unmolested," Max reminded his mother.

Lady Everly gave an almost imperceptible shrug. "The passage must exist then, although I find that bit of nonsense hard to swallow."

"What do you know about it?" Max demanded. He'd heard some story, years ago when he was a child, about an ancestor who had disappeared and came back after suffering a breakdown, but he never paid much attention. It wasn't exciting enough to hold the interest of a small boy. He'd been far more interested in space exploration and new technology than tales of the Civil War and long-dead monarchs.

"I only know what I heard from your father, and I must admit that I wasn't any more interested then than I am now. It all sounded like the ravings of someone's overactive imagination, but your father had been fascinated with the story, having heard it over and over as a boy and having actually known the miscreant at the center of the tale," Lady Everly replied, her haughty face a mask of contempt.

"So, what exactly did you hear?" Max asked, his patience at an end. His mother was doing this on purpose; she'd always done that to him. She'd talk in circles while staring him down in order to avoid telling him a truth she found to be distasteful. Max had learned over the years not to ask his mother anything and find answers for himself, but in this case, there was no one else to ask.

He suddenly remembered asking his mother about the woman he'd seen his father with at the hunting lodge. The woman had been young and pretty, and Max had been mesmerized by her laugh, which had sounded like the tinkling of bells, melodious and magical, as it had floated through the open window of the lodge. His father had laughed too, something Max didn't hear very often at home. Lady Everly, however, had berated Max for traipsing through the woods when he should have been studying and scolded him for looking through windows, a habit most unbecoming to a future lord. She hadn't even acknowledged that there had been a woman at the lodge with his father, nor had she mentioned it ever again.

Finally, driven mad by curiosity, Max had asked his father, who had patted him on the head, told him the lady was a special friend of his who had a particular interest in hunting lodges built during a certain period, and asked him not to mention it to his mother, while stealthily pushing a five-pound note into his hand. That had been the end of that episode, but Max had never seen the pretty lady again, nor had he noticed any strain between his parents. Funny how adults avoided talking about things, he'd thought then, promising himself that he would always be straightforward and courageous when he grew up. He acknowledged with a sudden pang that he was neither and turned back to his mother, who was watching him with narrowed eyes.

"Well?" Max demanded.

"Your grandfather's younger brother went missing one day. This was right around the turn of the century, and he was fifteen at the time. A search party was mounted, but after days of searching, no one found any trace of the boy. The family was mad with grief, desperate for answers. The local police had concluded that he must have drowned; his body carried away by the current. It was summertime, you see, and Henry went swimming nearly every day. One day, he simply never came back." His mother set the cup down, warming up to her story.

"So, what happened?" Max asked, suddenly breathless. Was his mother really about to tell him that the boy had time-traveled?

"Henry turned up several months later. He was dirty and dressed in rags, his arms and legs covered in dry blood. His mind had been affected by whatever happened to him. He kept prattling on about the Civil War and the horrors that he had witnessed, but no one took him very seriously. He'd always been interested in history, particularly that wretched war, so the family doctor just assumed that whatever Henry had experienced had driven him mad. Henry was given laudanum and put to bed. The doctor felt that he needed complete rest to recover from his ordeal, but Henry didn't recover. He stuck with his story, finally forcing his parents to accept that their son was quite far gone. After several weeks, it was determined that Henry should be put in an asylum where he could have round-the-clock care and medical supervision."

"And?" Max asked, resenting his mother for drawing out the story just to torment him.

"And, he eventually regained something of his former personality and was released into the care of his parents. He went on to marry and lead a successful and productive life, but after his death, a notebook was found among his things. It described his passage through a tunnel in the crypt of the church and his arrival in the seventeenth century. He spoke at length of the Civil War and mentioned several key battles. The details included in the narrative were not something a fifteen-year-old boy could have made up. He described the political and social situation of the time like someone who was there and lived it, rather than someone who simply read about it in a book. Since there was never any reasonable explanation for where Henry had been, it was a family joke that Henry had indeed traveled through time," his mother concluded.

"So, you believe it's possible that he was telling the truth?" Max asked, suddenly struck by the fact that they were even discussing this with any degree of seriousness.

"Max, have you known many people who traveled through time?" his mother asked sarcastically. "I haven't. If such a thing were possible, I'm sure it wouldn't be a family secret discussed behind closed doors for fear of having the taint of insanity associated with the Everlys. Perhaps Neve simply ran off with someone. There have been plenty of people who've faked their own disappearance, and even death, for the chance at a fresh start."

Max gave his mother a look of utter incredulity. "Why would she need to fake her own disappearance? She wasn't married, in debt, or accused of a serious crime. She was just a lovely girl doing her job."

"Max, forget about her. Take the keys and pick up the car from the village after dark. Leave it in the old stable by the hunting lodge in the woods and cover it up. No one ever goes there, so no one would think to look. Leave her holdall in the car. Make sure to wear gloves. If Neve Ashley turns up, we don't have a problem. If she doesn't, it has nothing to do with us. Our main priority is to avoid any trace of scandal. The Everly name doesn't need to be dragged through the mud, especially if you have your sights set on a career in politics."

"Should I not alert the police that I found Neve's things?" Max asked, perplexed by his mother's attitude.

"You always were thick, even as a boy," his mother admonished. "Telling the police anything will immediately get your name into the papers. People won't remember your role in the affair, but they will remember that you had something to do with the disappearance of a young woman who was your guest. You know how sordid the press can be. You'll be accused of all manner of things, when you were nothing but kind to the girl. You'll have to stand the trial of public opinion, which will accuse you and condemn you, with or without evidence of your guilt. Let the police do their own dirty work and stay out of it," Lady Everly concluded, ringing for a fresh pot of tea. As far as she was concerned, the conversation was over, as well as their involvement with Neve.

Max took a sip of his own lukewarm tea and turned over what his mother said in his mind.

"Does the notebook still exist?" he asked casually as he leafed through an architectural magazine. He didn't want to appear too eager, for fear of alerting his mother to his interest, but she'd already moved on from the topic.

"Yes, it's in your father's study. In the bottom drawer of the desk, I believe," she replied, not even looking up at Max.

Max took a few more sips and slipped out of the room, taking the stairs two at a time to the second floor and his father's study.

TWENTY

Max lowered the battered notebook and gazed at the purpling sky beyond the window. The first stars of the evening were beginning to appear in the sky, winking at him as if they knew some delicious secret. The table lamp shone brightly onto the faded ink of the narrative, the yellowed pages brittle and curled at the edges. Perhaps now he knew a secret as well. Having read Henry's account, he couldn't imagine that a fifteen-year-old boy could have made this up. Sure, he might have enjoyed writing a story to pass the time, but the details didn't seem like the product of a teenager's imagination. Henry described his confusion, fear, and an encounter with a group of soldiers who took him to Scotland to join Cromwell's army. Henry's account of the battle of Dunbar sent shivers down Max's spine, the chilling details making his hands shake as he held the notebook. No turn-of-the-century boy could have described the carnage in such gory detail, nor invented such a story of survival and subsequent escape back to the twentieth century.

Henry wrote this many years before the start of the Great War, so his knowledge of warfare would be limited to the schoolroom, where no tutor would ever divulge such inappropriate details to a young boy, particularly the bits about the camp followers and the interludes with whores, which Henry described as well. He spoke of losing his virginity to a fourteen-year-old prostitute named Mabel, describing what it felt like and paying great attention to his surroundings, which were sordid to say the least; people coupling out in the open without any shame or need for privacy; men grunting like pigs as they did their business without any consideration for the women they used, paying them in coin, food, or even gin—whatever came to hand. Henry described soldiers waiting patiently as their comrades took turns with a whore, cheering each other on and offering encouragement and advice. Despite rampant prostitution in Victorian England, a boy like Henry would have been sheltered and woefully ignorant of the lurid details, even if he was aware of the basic facts.

Unfortunately, what Henry did not describe was the location of the passage. He said that he found a secret door, but never mentioned where. The crypt was rather large and ran the entire length and breadth of the church building, and although Max had been down there several times, he'd never noticed anything out of the ordinary. He'd have to go explore, but not before the business with Neve resolved itself. It would look too suspicious if he started hanging around the crypt days after people had seen Neve Ashley go down there for the last time.

Thinking of Neve put Max onto a different tack. Henry seemed to emerge in 1649, but did that automatically mean that Neve would go to the same year? Supposing the passage did lead to the seventeenth century, could it be that Neve found herself there earlier or later than Henry? And what if she met Hugo? Max had always had a bit of a fascination with Hugo, partially because of the lack of information about his fate, but what if Neve did something to alter Hugo's destiny? Max's line descended from Hugo's nephew, but what if Hugo didn't die and fathered a child instead? Clarence would never inherit, and

Max would not be Lord Everly or master of the estate. That was a very alarming thought, one that Max tried to push aside. He had absolutely no proof that Neve had gone back in time, nor that she had gone to a time when Hugo Everly would be in residence. And even if she had, would she be able to alter the past or was it set in stone; already a foregone conclusion since the twenty-first century was well under way?

Max watched as the last bit of light leached from the sky, the darkness settling over the parkland visible from the window. The stars were brighter now, the half-moon hanging low, almost skimming the tree line and leaning a bit to the side as if drunk. Getting drunk seemed like an awfully good idea, but Max had to stay alert. He'd wait until midnight to go and retrieve Neve's car. The village would be deserted by then, most inhabitants already asleep in preparation for another day. He would be able to drive away unobserved, taking the car up the narrow track that led to the lodge and leaving it in the old stable under a tarp. There was sure to be a padlock somewhere in the mudroom which he could use to lock the stable.

Max looked at his watch and went to pour himself a drink despite his resolve not to have one. If Neve had gone through the passage on Sunday morning, where was she? What had happened to her? Surely, she would turn around and come right back when she found herself in the wrong time. She was a clever and resourceful girl, not a naïve teenage boy who grew up during the Victorian Era. What if she were hurt or accosted by someone? Max wondered as he took a gulp of his gin and tonic. A part of him wanted to rush to the rescue and play out a childhood fantasy of the knight in shining armor coming to save the day, but another part of him suddenly wished that Neve never came back. Her return would raise all kinds of questions, and what if she decided to tell the truth? This was not the time of confining people to asylums. Her story would cause an uproar and bring all sorts of people to the Everly doorstep: scientists, archeologists, journalists, and all kinds of rabble who wanted to be a part of something sensational or live out their fantasy of living in another era.

Max poured another drink and stared at the clock. Was he running out of time?

TWENTY-ONE
MARCH 1685

We finally reached Sir Benedict's house by nightfall. It stood proudly amid a large park; the thick stone walls rising toward a purpling sky; the windows alight with the last rays of the setting sun just skimming the tree line and glinting off the diamond-paned mullions, and the chimneys merely black stacks against the last of the light quickly fading into darkness. Like most houses built more for protection than beauty, Sir Benedict's house was forbidding and impregnable, but I'd never been so happy to arrive at a destination. By this point, I didn't care if I had to pretend to be the mistress of a baboon as long as I got to get off the horse. My back was on fire after nearly twelve hours in the saddle without any kind of back support, and my legs vibrated with tension and fatigue.

I smelled of horse; my inner thighs were raw from chafing against the saddle, and I was so thirsty, my tongue stuck to the roof of my mouth. I'd had nothing but ale all day, and some water would taste like ambrosia right about now, especially if it came in a clean glass. All I wanted to do was bathe, have something to eat that wasn't bread and cheese, and lie down, but that was not to be. I had to join Hugo and sup with Sir Benedict, a meal which would probably last several hours, during which I had to play the part of the adoring mistress, not a resentful, tired woman who would have gladly strangled the arrogant bastard who'd abducted her and put her through this agony.

I was shown to my room, where I fell onto the bed, desperate for a few moments' rest. A pretty young maid arrived shortly after, followed by a strapping youth who carried two sloshing buckets and grunted with effort. The maid pulled out a hip bath and the boy poured the water into the tub, tugged his forelock at me, and departed happily, no longer burdened.

"Shall I come back to help you dress, mistress?" the girl asked as she openly studied me. Had word already spread that Lord Everly had arrived with a mistress in tow?

"Yes, that would be most helpful," I replied, eyeing the hip bath with suspicion. I'd seen one before but had no idea what one was meant to do with it. Did I just sit in it and soak my nether regions, or did I use the hot water to give myself a sponge bath? People of this time usually bathed in some sort of garment, so I was afraid that if I stripped down and sat in the tub, someone might walk in on me and suffer a seizure from the shock. I opted for the sponge bath and washed hastily, grateful for the warmth of the water after the gathering chill of the night.

I had just slipped my chemise back on when the maid appeared, ready to assist me. I would have chosen one of the less extravagant gowns, but Hugo had asked me to wear my best, so I selected the moss silk. He'd given me a brief set of instructions just before we arrived, but I was still worried, unsure of what was expected of me, especially when it came to our host.

"What if Sir Benedict asks me questions?" I had grilled Hugo, conscious of the fact that I would have a very difficult time conversing intelligently with anyone of this time period. I knew very little of the politics or the social tidbits that any woman would be privy to. I also had no idea what to say if Sir

Benedict asked me anything about my opinions or about my stance on Monmouth's attempted rebellion.

"Don't worry, he won't ask a thing." Hugo had looked at me in a way that suggested that he was holding something back.

"How can you be so sure?" I couldn't imagine that the man would just ignore me for most of the meal and ask me nothing, especially since my presence was unexpected and was bound to cause some speculation on the part of our host.

Hugo had sighed, clearly unhappy to have to explain the facts of life to me, but he had no choice since I was badgering him relentlessly. "Since Sir Benedict has never heard of you or your family, he will assume that I plucked you out of some theater or brothel; therefore, the only thing he'll want to know about you is how you might look wearing nothing but a smile, and if you keep me satisfied in bed."

"You don't mince words, do you?" I'd commented irritably, wondering if he was picturing me in nothing but a smile.

"I was just giving you a truthful answer. It certainly wasn't meant to offend. You are a beautiful woman, and any man will have lustful thoughts about you within moments of meeting you. I'm sure you already know that." He didn't add that I was too old to play coy, but I'd blushed all the same, suddenly feeling naked under his gaze. Did he have lustful thoughts? Is that what he was telling me? I couldn't think about that. I was at his mercy, and I needed to believe that there were boundaries between us.

I sat still as Polly brushed, braided and twisted my hair, finally wrestling it into an elaborate coif.

"Will this do?" she asked shyly, twisting her hands in front of her.

"Yes, thank you, it's very nice," I replied. "Where did you learn to do that?"

"I used to be Lady Nolan's maid before she passed. She was

a beautiful lady who liked to look her best and wear all the latest fashions even when in the country."

"How old was Lady Nolan?" I asked, wondering about Polly's mistress.

"She had thirty-two years, madam, so not so very young." What Polly meant was that Lady Nolan was quite old. A woman was at her prime at twenty, middle-aged by twenty-five, and practically geriatric by thirty. Did Hugo think me old? I suddenly wondered.

"What did she die of?"

Polly seemed taken aback by my unnatural curiosity, but she answered nonetheless as she set about dressing me. "She had a weak heart. It just gave out one day." Polly shrugged as if that was the most natural thing in the world and went on with her work.

I couldn't help wondering what that meant in modern medical terms. Did she have a heart attack or maybe high blood pressure? I had no way of knowing, but I felt sad for the no-so-young, fashionable woman who had died before her time.

"Hold out your arms, madam," Polly instructed as she fixed the sleeves to her satisfaction, and then tied the laces of the bodice and tucked them beneath the bustle of my skirt.

I gaped at myself in the mirror. I was sure that somewhere in there was still the same Neve Ashley I'd always been, but the woman who gazed back at me was a stranger.

Polly insisted on applying some makeup to make me look "just the thing" as she put it. I rejected the thick, white paste for fear that it was lead-based but allowed Polly to coat my face with some rice powder and rub a little cerise powder into my cheeks. She would have gladly plucked out most of my eyebrows and probably a good deal of my hair as well to give me a larger forehead, but I stayed her hand and allowed her to just shape my eyebrows a little, leaving her clucking with disapproval.

I handed Polly the jewel case, sitting regally in front of the mirror as she draped the necklace over my powdered bosom and closed the clasp. "You do look lovely, madam. Do you have any patches?"

I was about to reply in the negative when there was a knock at the door and Hugo was admitted into the room. I rose from the settee shyly, standing in front of him like a child waiting for a parent's sign of approval. He was rather splendid himself in a suit of midnight blue, the coat liberally embroidered with a pattern in silver thread and a snowy cravat that frothed at his throat and offset the dark curls of his wig.

Hugo didn't have to say anything because his face said it all. His expression was one of surprise, admiration, approval, and pride all at once. "You look very beautiful, Mistress Ashley. That color suits your complexion. Shall we?"

I gave him a slight bow and took his proffered arm.

The dining room was ablaze with candlelight, the flickering light reflected in the numerous silver platters and goblets and setting the table aglow. I couldn't even begin to guess what some of the dishes were, but they looked exotic in the extreme, the presentation an art form in itself.

Our host, a man in his late forties by the look of him, came to greet us, his eyes devouring me in a way that left me feeling naked despite all the layers of clothing I was safely swathed in. He must have been handsome in his day, but age, poor nutrition, and overindulgence showed in the sagging of his jowls, the puffiness beneath the eyes, and the sallow complexion offset by his ginger wig, which was elaborate. He wore a patch on the right cheekbone, which suggested that he fancied himself quite the dandy.

A younger man, no older than twenty-five, was also present; his dress and manner more somber and practical. He didn't appear to be Sir Benedict's son, and I could tell by Hugo's expression that he hadn't expected him to be there.

"Lord Everly, it's been too long," Sir Benedict exclaimed. "Have you recently been at Court?"

"I was in London at Christmastide but was given permission by His Majesty to return to my estates at the New Year," Hugo replied.

"Allow me to introduce my secretary, Edmund Somerville. A most industrious young man. I don't make a single decision without him."

The young man blushed furiously and bowed to Hugo and me, clearly feeling a little awkward at being included. I gave him a sympathetic smile, feeling just as awkward myself. I was terribly nervous, but it seemed all I had to do was look pretty. No one expected me to converse or even think, which in this case was a relief. Since Sir Benedict was recently widowed, I didn't have to worry about being interrogated or snubbed by his wife. I was the only woman at dinner—an ornament.

"It's a pleasure to make your acquaintance, Mistress Ashley. It's been far too long since a beautiful young lady graced my table. Please, sit next to me. This seat used to be occupied by my dear wife, but she's no longer with us and I would see it filled, if only for one night."

"I hear you're to marry again," Hugo said as a servant placed a slice of venison on his plate. Hugo didn't decline, but I knew he wouldn't touch it since it was Lent.

"Yes, you heard correctly," Sir Benedict replied as he took a mouthful of venison and raised his eyes to the heavens in his apparent delight. "Delicious, as always. Do try it, Hugo."

"It's beyond compare," Hugo replied smoothly as he pushed the meat around on his plate. "Who is the lucky woman?"

"I'm afraid I must keep it a secret for now," Sir Benedict answered playfully, "but I will say that she's very young and very comely. Edmund here is still negotiating the marriage contract, and the lady's father is being somewhat unreasonable. I do hope to be wed soon. It's high time I had an heir. My dear wife was unable to give me one," Sir Benedict explained, giving me a petulant look worthy of a child. "I did so hope for a son. Three daughters were what the Good Lord granted us, but it's not a complete loss. Girls are useful for making valuable alliances," he said brightly, raising his cup in a toast. "To beautiful young ladies. May they delight us always."

I was loath to admit that Hugo had been right. Sir Benedict's eyes frequently strayed to my breasts, and I felt his leg brush against mine under the table. He'd dare go no further since he deigned me to be Hugo's property, but he wasn't averse to copping a feel if possible. I tried to discreetly move away, but it didn't work. Sir Benedict's fleshy hand brushed against my thigh, making me shift uncomfortably in my chair.

My eyes met those of Edmund Somerville across the table, and I felt a strange kinship with the man. He knew what Sir Benedict was doing and felt sympathy for me. He had such a pained look on his face that I couldn't help wondering if secretarial skills were all that were required of him. Perhaps Sir Benedict used him to procure other services discreetly, so as not to put off a future father-in-law.

Course after course was brought out, with Sir Benedict eating heartily and Hugo only tasting the fish and vegetable dishes. Despite the gorgeous presentation, the food tasted either bland or over spiced, made with a slew of ingredients that didn't, in my opinion, even go together, which was ironic since Sir Benedict boasted at length about his clerk of the spicery whom he'd acquired in London; a man knowledgeable in the various spices and their effects, as well as their uses in medicinals and tonics. I thought I just might need a tonic after the last concoction I tried, so decided not to eat any more and just move my food around the way Hugo did.

The men kept the conversation neutral for my benefit, exchanging bits of Court gossip, discussing the plays and musicals they had seen when in London, and commenting on the latest fashions. Sir Benedict wouldn't appreciate being quizzed on his loyalties in front of a courtesan; that conversation would come later. In the meantime, it was all light banter, with me chiming in from time to time when I felt it safe.

"Mistress Ashley, do you sing? Oh, I would love to hear you. Give us a song," Sir Benedict implored as he squeezed my knee. He probably did think I was an actress. "There's a pianoforte in the salon. Do you play? Say that you do."

I did play a little, and the promise of escaping our host's groping hand was quite an inducement.

What's a good seventeenth-century song? I thought frantically as I followed Sir Benedict into the salon with Hugo at my side. I could think of only one and hoped it would be all right.

I sat down at the instrument and tested out the keys while the men arranged themselves around the room. It was out of tune, but it didn't matter. Combined with my awful singing, it would probably make the men want to run for cover.

I began to sing "Lavender Blue," to the obvious delight of Sir Benedict.

"I love that one," I heard him saying to Hugo, who was watching me with interest.

I was glad I remembered the words. My mother used to sing that song to me when I was little since it always seemed to put me to sleep, and it was one of the nicer memories I had of her. She was still happy then, still in control. Thinking of my mum and the home I'd left behind nearly made me cry, but this wasn't the time to come apart. I blinked away the tears as I tried to concentrate on the words, putting home out of my mind for the moment. I had a part to play.

> Lavender blue, dilly, dilly
> Lavender green
> If I were king, dilly, dilly
> I'd need a queen

Who told you so? Dilly, dilly
Who told you so?
I told myself, dilly, dilly
I told me so

If your dilly, dilly heart
Feels a dilly, dilly way
And if you'll answer, "Yes"
In a pretty little church
On a dilly, dilly day
You'll be wed in a dilly, dilly dress of

Lavender blue, dilly, dilly
Lavender green
If you were king, dilly, dilly
You'd need a queen

Who told you so? Dilly, dilly
Who told you so?
You told yourself, dilly, dilly
you told you so

If your dilly, dilly heart
Feels a dilly, dilly way
And if you'll answer, "Yes"
In a pretty little church
On a dilly, dilly day
I'll be wed in a dilly, dilly dress of

Lavender blue, dilly, dilly
Lavender green
Then you'll be king, dilly, dilly
And I'll be your queen

I was surprised to see the expression on Hugo's face when I finally finished the song and took a little bow. He looked gutted; his face pale in the candlelight, a haunted look in his dark eyes as he drank me in, clearly surprised by my performance. He quickly regained his composure and clapped his hands along with our host and Edmund Somerville, who looked blank.

"You have a multitude of talents, my dear," Hugo said, smiling at me in approval. It was an innocent enough comment, but I saw the hungry look in Sir Benedict's eyes. He assumed that Hugo was referring to my talents in bed, and I shuddered with revulsion as he came closer and leaned over me, practically drooling onto my breasts.

"Oh, yes. That was lovely, just lovely," Sir Benedict breathed. "Give us another."

"I'm afraid Mistress Ashley is very tired after a long day in the saddle. Perhaps we can let her go get some rest, and you and I can have some of that wonderful brandy," Hugo suggested smoothly. It was time for the men to talk and for me to leave. Hugo was diplomatically suggesting that Sir Benedict excuse his secretary as well, and the point wasn't lost on our host, who waved a hand at the young man, signaling that he might depart.

"Edmund, escort Mistress Ashley to her chamber, if you will," he commanded as he reached for the decanter of brandy. "Lord Everly and I have much to discuss."

"Goodnight, gentlemen," I said, deeply relieved at being dismissed. I was exhausted and longed only for my bed.

Edmund didn't say much as he led me through the house. He seemed tired himself, grateful to get away from his demanding master.

"Goodnight, Mistress Ashley," he said as he stopped in front of my door. "You have a lovely voice."

"Goodnight, Mr. Somerville; you are too kind."

Edmund shook his head, his expression one of disgust. "If I were kind, I'd tell you to lock your door and leave this house as soon as you can. Sir Benedict drives a hard bargain, and I wouldn't be surprised if you were a part of it."

"What can you mean?" I gasped, suddenly afraid.

"Only that I hope that Lord Everly holds you in very high esteem," was all he said as he gave me a stiff bow and walked away.

Hugo and I had been put in adjoining rooms, as I feared, but there was no help for it, and after Edmund's warning, I wasn't as put out as before. I got undressed with Polly's help, washed my face free of makeup, pulled out the multitude of pins holding my coiffure together, slipped on a nightdress, and crawled into bed. I was exhausted, but sleep didn't come easily. I firmly put thoughts of what might be happening at home out of my mind, focusing on my escape. I could probably manage to slip out of the house, but even if I got to the stables, highjacked a horse, and got away undetected, I had no idea how to get back to where I needed to be, especially in the dark.

I tried to remember the way, but we'd been traveling all day and took more than one fork in the road. I'd be hopelessly lost within an hour, alone in the middle of the night with no protection and no money. I knew enough about the seventeenth century to realize that a woman alone was fair game and that although I didn't have much to steal, I could be raped or even killed, so I finally conceded that I had to stay. Sooner or later, Hugo would return home and I would seize my opportunity then. I only hoped that it would be sooner rather than later.

* * *

It must have been well past midnight by the time Hugo finally returned to his room. I was still awake, and I saw the glow of his candle beneath the door to his room. I hoped he would just go to bed, but he had other ideas.

Hugo tiptoed into the room and set the candle on the nightstand by the bed. He was wearing nothing but a shirt and I clearly saw the outline of his body as he turned to blow out the candle. I felt the mattress sag as his full weight settled on the bed. I must have tensed because Hugo moved a little to the side to put some space between us.

"I am a man of my word," he said, eyeing me in the dark. "I won't touch you."

"So why couldn't you just sleep in your room?" I whispered, inching away from him.

"Because our host would find that suspicious, and I don't wish to give him any cause to doubt me or to view it as an invitation to visit your room himself. You are quite safe, I assure you. By the by, you were a runaway success tonight, my sweet," he said, smiling in the dark. "Sir Benedict was very taken with you. He even suggested that I leave you here as a token of my good will in return for his support when the time comes."

"What?"

He chuckled but didn't reply right away. Instead, he made himself more comfortable, folded his hands across his stomach and pretended to go to sleep.

"What did you tell him?" I hissed, terrified that Hugo had agreed.

"I told him that you have captured my heart, and I would not part with you for any reason. He was somewhat put out, but I think he will get over it by morning."

Hugo closed his eyes and was asleep within minutes, but I wasn't as lucky. I hadn't slept with anyone but Evan in years, so lying in bed next to a strange man was awkward, to say the least. Hugo smelled of brandy, woodsmoke from the fireplace, and his own slightly musky smell that made me scoot to the other side of the bed until I was practically hanging off. I knew he was naked under the shirt, as I was naked under my nightdress, and I found the thought to be utterly disturbing.

"Go to sleep," Hugo suddenly said. I could hear the amusement in his voice, but he never opened his eyes or moved any closer.

"I can't."

"Need help?" he asked with a chuckle.

"No, thank you." I turned on my side, facing away from him, and pretended to go to sleep. I was certain he knew I was faking it, but it didn't matter. Fake it till you make it, Evan always said, and eventually it worked.

TWENTY-TWO
APRIL 1685

I woke up just as the first rays of sun tried to sneak between the closed shutters, providing just enough pearlescent light to bring the objects in the room into dim focus. The fire had gone out sometime during the night, and my breath came out in white puffs as I snuggled deeper under the quilt. I was surprisingly warm and snug, probably thanks to Evan's body heat. My back and legs were pressed against him, his arm casually thrown over my side and gently cupping my lower abdomen, his pelvis right up against my lower back. I could feel his arousal and moved against him suggestively just to be a tease.

"Good morning to you, too."

I nearly jumped out of my skin as I suddenly remembered exactly where I was and with whom. This wasn't a dream of the eighteenth-century inn Evan and I stayed at when we took a little holiday last year. This was frighteningly real, and the man next to me wasn't Evan, but my captor.

I elbowed Hugo in the stomach, and he moved away from me with a groan that sounded more like a laugh.

"I didn't want you to get cold during the night. The room

became glacial once the fire went out," he said with an expression of perfect innocence on his face.

"How kind of you," I spat out. "Do you think you might be persuaded to go back to your own room while I wash and dress?"

Hugo gave me a look that made me blush with embarrassment. He guessed I was dying to pee and didn't want him to watch me using the pot. Oh, what I wouldn't give for a private bathroom and a hot shower right about now. He was right though; the room was freezing, the chill seeping through the walls and ill-fitting shutters, the air acrid with the smell of ashes from the fireplace.

Hugo got out of bed and walked to the door without turning. "I'll leave you to it," he called out as he closed the door behind him.

I jumped out of bed and seized the chamber pot as if it were the pot of gold at the end of the rainbow. Funny how nothing seemed important when there were certain physical needs to be taken care of.

I dove back into bed, my feet icy after only a few moments against the cold floor. If it was this cold in late March, how cold was it in the dead of winter? I'd never realized how much we took for granted in our modern lives: running water, heat, and, especially, light. No matter how many candles were lit during the evening, the rooms were dim and full of shadows; the faces swallowed by the darkness the moment they receded from the feeble circle of light. No wonder Jem liked to sleep in the kitchen and get hot buns in the morning. It was the warmest place in the house, where the food was always hot, not merely warm as it was by the time it made it to the table.

I braced myself for the arctic temperature and jumped out of bed once more, determined to at least wash my face and hands, rinse my mouth, and possibly wash a few other parts as well. My resolve was quickly forgotten as I saw the thin layer of ice on the water in the pitcher, deciding that perhaps hygiene wasn't as important as not freezing to death.

"Good morning, madam," Polly cheerfully called out as she carefully entered the room, carrying a steaming pitcher of water and a small tray laden with breakfast, which she set down on the round table currently housing the pitcher and ewer. It was some kind of porridge, but at least it was warm.

"What time is it, Polly?" I asked as I gratefully sank my hands into the warm water.

"Oh, it's likely gone eight, madam. Yon men were up hours ago and breakfasted already. They're readying the horses, and yon little page is rearing to go. Sweet lad, he is."

"And smart, too," I remarked, smiling at the unbidden image of Jem sitting by the roaring hearth, stuffing his face with fresh bread and hot porridge.

TWENTY-THREE

The mud in the yard was coated with a layer of ice, which cracked loudly as the horses' hooves stepped on it and broke it into minuscule shards as sharp as glass. The horses snorted, unnerved by the slippery ground, their ears pressed back and their eyes rolling in their heads as they trod carefully over the frozen earth. A deceptively bright sun hung cheerfully above our heads, making the ice sparkle, the crystals dancing with light and mirroring the bright glare of the windows.

"There's always one last frost before the winter gives way to spring," Peter said wisely as he led my horse to the mounting block.

The thought of spending another day in the saddle was paramount to torture, but I mounted the horse and hung on for dear life as it picked its way toward the gates and the road beyond.

Sir Benedict had invited us to stay for another day, but Hugo had politely refused, telling him we had some business to complete before returning home for Easter. At least now I knew when he planned to go back to Cranley, information that gave me that tiny bit of control over an untenable situation. Easter was in three weeks; so, it was three weeks until I would have a chance at escape, and three weeks of cohabitating with Hugo Everly.

A sneaky wind managed to get beneath my skirts and into the folds of my cloak, filling the fabric with air and making me look like a ship in full sail, a fact that the men remarked on with glee, eliciting a hearty laugh from Jem. I tried to pull the cloak tighter around me, but there was nothing to fasten it with other than the clasp at the throat. The wind kept blowing the hood off my head, leaving my ears red and numb with cold. My back and legs were sore from riding, my head ached, and my eyes wept salty tears from the bitter gusts. How I wished I could be at home, on the sofa in front of the TV with a hot cup of tea and a few of my favorite chocolate biscuits.

"Neve?"

I looked up at the sound of my name, suddenly realizing that I'd been wallowing in my trance of misery for some time and probably hadn't heard him calling me before.

"Are you all right?" Hugo asked, a look of concern on his face. "You don't look at all well."

"I'm very cold... and achy, and hungry," I admitted. I wasn't normally a complainer, but I was feeling sorry for myself, and it was all Hugo's fault anyway, so I felt no need to spare his feelings.

"There should be an inn at the next village. We'll stop there," he promised and gave me a weak smile. "Come, ride next to me. Conversation helps pass the time, and you look lonely."

I was. I'd never felt so alone in my life. I enjoyed occasional solitude, but I always knew that friends were just a phone call or a tube ride away. Now I was in a place where I knew no one and no one knew me. There was no one to call; no one to turn to for help. If I died here, no one would know or care. I would simply vanish off the face of the earth as if I never existed, leaving nothing behind in my modern life but some books, clothes, and a handful of people who would mourn me for a time—or not. I had no husband, no children, and no extended family. There was no one I felt tethered to or who would feel the loss of me in any kind of deep emotional way. People would briefly wonder what had happened to me and then get on with their own lives, pushing the memory of me away, as human beings tended to do with unpleasant and unresolved things.

I wished I could tell Hugo all that, but I had to keep silent for my own safety. Instead, I pulled my horse closer to his and rode in silence for a few moments while I composed myself. I smiled in surprise as Hugo held out an oat cake to me.

"It's all I've got, but it might tide you over until the village. I always bring a few cakes for Ronan when we go on long rides. He likes to feel appreciated."

Hugo's horse gave me a resentful stare as I bit into the cake, but I ignored it and chewed gratefully. It wasn't very tasty, but better than the horrible porridge of this morning.

"Were you able to enlist Sir Benedict's support?" I asked as I finished the cake and licked the crumbs off my fingers.

Hugo smiled at me indulgently, as if I were an adorable child, and shook his head. "Sir Benedict is a shrewd man who will not commit to anything unless he's sure of its success. He professed support for Monmouth, but once a rebellion is under way, he will see which way the wind is blowing before declaring his support publicly. If Monmouth is sure to win, Benedict will say the duke had his support all along. If he looks to be losing, Benedict will very loudly exalt the king and condemn the bastard upstart. He did, however, make a contribution to Monmouth's coffers, which is the most I can hope for at this time."

"Is that the feeling of most people, that Monmouth is a bastard upstart?" I asked.

"No. There are those who are openly in support of Monmouth and will take up arms and risk all to see him succeed. Most people, however, will wait to declare their allegiance. They have too much to lose."

"And you? Don't you have anything to lose?" I was curious about this man and what drove him. I could understand a desire for religious freedom, but I sensed there was more to his resolve —something more personal.

"I have nothing to lose," Hugo replied flatly.

"How come you never married?" I suppose it was a rude and prying question, but I wanted to know. He had to be in his mid-thirties, and a man of that age in the seventeenth century would most certainly have a family, unless they'd died and he was the only survivor, and even then, he'd be likely to remarry very quickly.

"I have," Hugo replied. I could see the tensing of his jaw and the grim set of his mouth, but I was too curious to desist.

"And is your wife...?" I let the sentence trail off, unsure of how to phrase what I wanted to ask. It seemed callous to just ask if she were dead; besides, had he been married, it would have shown up in the family records, but Max had said that Hugo hadn't been wed.

"Alive and well," he replied as he skewered me with his gaze, "and married to someone else."

"But you are Catholic; you don't believe in divorce, do you?"

"No, I don't, which is why I still consider myself married," Hugo said with a shrug.

I could see the bitterness in his face, but now that I knew, he felt the need to explain.

"Catherine and I met at Court while my father was still alive. She was hardly more than a child then, but I'd got it into my head that I was going to marry her. She was so lovely and so pure. The fact that her family was one of the oldest Catholic families in England also contributed to my decision. I wanted my wife to share my faith and raise our children in the Church.

My father kept our religion a secret, convinced that one day the tolerant attitude of the king would be tested and criticized. He was right, of course. His wish was that I marry a Protestant, but then again, his faith was never very strong. My father worshiped power and freedom and was willing to bow to whatever God happened to be in fashion at the time. He thought it would be politically beneficial to play both sides."

"Your father sounds a hard man," I said, trying to picture a young, lovesick Hugo and the man who wanted to use his marriage to further his own ambitions.

"He could be harsh, but he knew what he was about, and there were many times after his death that I realized that he had been right all along. We argued incessantly, him and I, and he went to his grave thinking that I didn't love or respect him—a fact I have to live with."

"So, you married your Catherine anyway?"

"Catherine and I married in secret after my father died. Had I married before, he would have disinherited me, and I'd have had nothing to offer her. Like my own father, her father was against the marriage. He had someone else in mind for her and the marriage negotiations were already under way, so I had to act fast. I finally convinced her to marry me. I was sure that once we were wed, her father would accept me and everything would turn out well, especially since her family would want to avoid a taint on Catherine's reputation."

"What happened?" I asked. It seemed like Hugo had thought things through, but the marriage had obviously fallen apart.

"Two weeks after we were married, Catherine's father had the marriage annulled and had her married off to the man of his choice." I could hear the anger in Hugo's voice. He was still hurt after all these years.

"On what grounds?"

"Non-consummation," he spat out.

"Did you not...?" I let the sentence hang, suddenly uncomfortable about prying into his personal life.

"Oh, I did," he retorted. "Many times, but Catherine's father, Lord Wessex, bribed a physician to proclaim my wife *virgo intacta* after subjecting her to the humiliation of an examination. Not only was she not a virgin, she was already with child, but, of course, it was too soon to tell."

"I'm sorry, Hugo. Did she not resist her father?"

"She thought that her father would accept me once we married, but she wasn't ready for a rift with her family. Her father wouldn't even hear of accepting the marriage. Catherine's betrothed was a duke, a man with vast estates bordering her father's to the north. Her father wanted to procure a better title for his only daughter and consolidate the estates after his death, making Catherine and her husband one of the richest and most influential couples in Christendom. Had he had a son to inherit, we might have stood a chance."

"What of the child?" I asked, feeling a surge of pity for him.

"The baby died in infancy. A girl. I never even saw her. Catherine has since borne her husband four healthy sons," Hugo replied bitterly.

"Do you still love her?" I asked softly, watching the emotions shift in his face.

"No. Yes. No... I don't know."

"So, which is it?"

"I don't love the woman she is today. I love the girl she was when she married me. She was so beautiful and sweet. I'd have done anything to make her happy, but she never gave me a chance. She went off with her father like an obedient puppy, without a backward glance. She could have defied him; she could have trusted me to love her. He'd have come around in time; I'm sure of it."

Hugo turned to me, and it broke my heart to see the sadness in his eyes. Not only had this girl broken his heart, but she had destroyed his chances of marrying again. The annulment wasn't valid since the marriage had been consummated, so in Hugo's mind he was married until one of them died.

"And what about you?" he asked. "What of your family?"

I knew this question would come sooner or later. A woman of my age would almost certainly be married or widowed and would have borne children. Hugo was too tactful to ask me outright, but he wanted to know more about the woman who had the power to destroy him. I wondered what he would say if he knew that I'd lived with a man without the benefit of marriage, and then miscarried a baby whom he hadn't wanted. Would he think less of me? Why did I care anyway? I asked myself angrily.

"No, there's no one," I replied instead.

"Have you never married?" Hugo asked.

"No, no one has ever asked." Which was the truth.

I expected Hugo to make some caustic remark, but he just gazed at me with a look of such sympathy that I nearly burst into tears. I was glad to see the chimneys of the village come into view. I was no longer hungry, but I felt frozen, mostly inside.

TWENTY-FOUR

Hugo poked up the fire and threw on another log, watching the shifting shadows of the leaping flames cast a golden glow on Neve's face. She was curled up in bed, the coverlet all the way up to her chin, her fair hair fanned on the lumpy pillow. The inn had only one private room left, the only other accommodation available in public rooms where travelers shared a bed with strangers, packed together like mackerel in a barrel. The men had no problem sleeping six to a bed, since it was still warmer and softer than bedding down in the stables. Even Jem chose to sleep in the communal bed rather than make up a pallet in the private room, eager for the warmth and camaraderie of his companions.

The bed was hardly big enough for two people, so Hugo tried to make himself comfortable on the hard wooden chair, which squeaked pitifully every time he so much as shifted his weight. It had to be past midnight, since the inn had grown quiet about two hours ago. The last patrons had departed, and the owners quickly tidied up and went to seek their own bed, knowing that they had a limited amount of time to rest before they got up at dawn and their daily routine began anew. The inn was shabby but clean, and the food had been palatable, which was more than he could say for many places he'd stayed at. The innkeeper and his wife did their best, and it showed. He'd have to give them an extra coin come morning, just to show his appreciation.

Hugo was physically tired, but couldn't sleep, partly due to discomfort and partly to the ghosts that seemed to surround him; those of the dead and the living. He felt his father's presence, the old man staring at him with contempt, disgusted that he had allowed an insipid girl to prevent him from fulfilling his duty and producing an heir for Everly.

Have I taught you nothing, boy? his father's voice demanded in his head. *Your marriage was annulled, so, according to the Church, you were never married. The record of your nuptials has been expunged, just as you have been expunged from your wife's heart. You've wasted twelve years on self-pity and righteous recriminations. Do your duty!* his father roared.

What of my conscience, Father? Hugo demanded of the angry ghost.

To hell with your conscience! You are not the first or the last to have to bargain with yourself and the Almighty. He has more important things to concern himself with than one failed marriage. Your wife is dead to you, so find another. And what is this plot you've got yourself involved in? You'll end up with your head on a spike for your pains. What difference does it make who sits on the throne as long as we prosper? Put your idealism aside, learn to play the game, and produce a boy, for God's sake.

Hugo sat up straighter in his chair, his eyes fixed on the dancing flames, his back rigid as the chair let out another moan of protest. He hated to admit it, but his father was right to a degree. Catherine was dead to him, although not physically dead. All these years he'd lived with the memory of a precious young girl, but had she really been what he believed her to be or a product of his own over-romanticized imagination?

Catherine loved the idea of courtly love. She'd devoured his romantic declarations and kept the poems he'd written her under her pillow. She loved legends, casting herself as Guinevere and him her devoted knight, but what had she known of real love? She had been frightened of his ardor, shocked by the physical love she'd known nothing about. He'd been too young and foolish to realize that Catherine had been completely unprepared for the force of his desire, and he'd terrified her with his emotional and physical demands. He'd allowed himself to believe that the look he saw on her face as Lord Guilford had led her away was one of regret, when, in truth, it was likely relief. A life with him was too frightening, too intimate.

Hugo knew Catherine's husband well. The duke spent most of his time at Court, leaving his wife and children at home in the country. He only brought them to town on special occasions, such as a Christmas pageant or the coronation of the new king. He'd enjoyed several affairs with other men's wives and rarely went home to his own, but perhaps that was a life Catherine had wanted since her husband demanded very little of her, especially now that she had produced several heirs and was past her prime.

And what had possessed him to talk to Neve Ashley of his father and Catherine, the two people who still haunted him daily? Why did he feel the need to confide in her when he'd kept his regrets to himself for so long? And why was he suddenly unsure of his path, a path he'd chosen a long time ago and had followed without deviation, steadfast in his moral conviction and bound by duty?

"I can feel you brooding from across the room," Neve suddenly said, raising her head from the pillow. "Come to bed."

"I didn't wish to inconvenience you," Hugo replied, desperately wanting to just lie down next to her and escape his unpleasant thoughts.

"You inconvenienced me by forcing me to accompany you.

Now, lie down and go to sleep. You are driving me crazy with your fidgeting."

"You really are a most perplexing woman, you know that?" Hugo asked as he began to pull off his boots. Neve had been irate to find him holding her only that morning, but now she was inviting him into her bed, a bed that was a third of the one they'd previously shared. Surely, she knew that some physical contact would ensue.

"So, I've been told," Neve replied and gave him an impish smile before snuggling under the covers again.

Hugo hastily undressed and got into bed, stretching out next to Neve and sighing with relief. He hadn't realized how much his back ached until now. He was no longer used to spending days in the saddle the way he had in his youth.

"Goodnight, Mistress Ashley," he whispered.

"Hmm." Neve was already asleep, her breathing even and her mouth partially open. She moaned softly in her sleep and rolled onto her back, her face illuminated by the feeble light of the fire. Hugo tried not to stare but couldn't help himself. When awake, she looked guarded, and at times frightened, but now she looked like a little girl, trusting and sweet, and heartbreakingly defenseless. He'd refrained from asking her too many questions, seeing her stiffen every time he so much as brought up her past, so he'd left her alone in an effort to build trust. Sooner or later, people revealed everything he needed to know on their own, once they felt less threatened, but he couldn't figure this woman out.

She said she came from London, which might be true, but her appearance and demeanor did not fit into any category he could think of. She was clearly educated and cultured, but she didn't have the manners or bearing of a gentlewoman. She moved and spoke freely, meeting his gaze head on with no wiles or attempt at being coy. Perhaps that's why she had never married; she'd intimidate any prospective husband with her brazen manner and speech. However, Neve Ashley clearly didn't come from the lower orders either. Her hands were soft and smooth, her complexion unblemished, and her teeth straight and white when she smiled that charming smile of hers. This was not a woman who'd known hunger or disease, nor had she ever been subjected to hard physical work.

Perhaps she was the daughter of some wealthy merchant or scholar, one who'd had the financial freedom and unconventional thinking to educate a girl and use her talents in his shop, for lack of a son. That could explain the absence of a husband as well. She might have had to care for her father and help him in his business, making her unable to marry at the proper age. What was her age? Hugo wondered, looking at Neve more closely. She had to be past twenty, but he couldn't tell by how much. Her gaze was all too knowing for a young maid, but her physical appearance spoke of one much younger than thirty. Most women of his acquaintance, even those who enjoyed wealth and privilege, began to lose their bloom shortly after marriage. Numerous pregnancies, births, and the physical demands of life took their toll, making them appear older than they really were. Even Jane, who'd only had one child, looked like a woman in her middle years when she was still relatively young.

Hugo ran his hand through his hair, more puzzled than ever. He'd spent the past few days trying to work out this conundrum, but he was no closer to an answer than before. Who was this woman and where had she come from? Was he endangering himself by his association with her, and what should he do with her in the future?

These questions remained unanswered as his mind finally quietened down and his lids began to grow heavy as sleep claimed him at last. He dreamed that he was walking through a dark forest, the sky obscured by heavy tree limbs that intertwined over his head and blocked all light from the narrow track. He thought he was getting closer to the edge of the forest, but, in fact, he was pushing deeper and deeper into the dense growth, the track now all but invisible and the light completely gone. He heard the sounds of forest creatures and the screeching of owls as night settled, leaving him lost and frustrated. Every crack of a branch or cry of a fox sounded ominous as he sank against a tree trunk and looked up at the invisible heavens, searching for answers which never came.

Hugo woke up with a start, glad to find himself in the cold, dark room of the inn. Neve still slept peacefully, and he was glad of that as he rose to his feet and stretched out, easing the kinks in his back. The remnants of the dream swirled in his head, making him uneasy about the coming months. Was he walking into something dark and inescapable? Was Neve right in her prediction of his impending doom?

Hugo splashed some cold water on his face and took a sip of ale left over in the cup from the night before. It tasted bitter on his tongue, and he spat it out into the cold hearth. He was in a foul mood, suddenly unsure of just about everything.

TWENTY-FIVE

I reluctantly mounted my horse, knowing full well that I would be spending another day in the saddle. My limbs still ached, but a good night's sleep had helped. I felt somewhat restored in body and mind. The weather had changed during the night, the bitter cold of the day before replaced by a mild morning, much more appropriate to March and April. I could almost smell spring in the air as I turned my face to the sky, basking in the weak sunshine.

The village was already awake, people going about their business, calling out greetings and exchanging bits of news and gossip, and thin, dirty children playing tag or glancing balefully at the others as they were forced to help their parents with chores. The dooryard of the inn was busy, travelers preparing to leave, and the landlord trying to extract the last bit of coin before parting with his guests by offering to sell them some food for the journey, or a hot breakfast porridge being ladled out by his wife in the dining room. Hugo had ordered breakfast to be brought up, so I'd enjoyed some fresh bread and butter drizzled with honey and a cup of milk, grateful not to have to drink more bitter ale. Jem had come up to see if I was ready while I was eating, so I'd shared some of my bounty with him, even though he'd already had his breakfast downstairs.

"I like honey," Jem had stated as he licked his fingers and peered at the plate to see if any honey had oozed from the bread and could still be licked off. "I like it in porridge too, but there was none to be had, or even a dollop of butter," he'd complained. "Peter says that Mr. Finch is rich, richer than some dukes and lords even, so mayhap his kitchen will be a welcoming place," Jem had mused with a smile as he gave up on the honey and finished the last of my milk. "Could be they'll have some sweetmeats or even syllabub." He'd given me a dreamy look as I'd fastened my cloak and pulled the linen cap over my curls. It wasn't much, but it kept me warmer and prevented my hair from constantly being blown into my face. "Do you like syllabub?" Jem had asked as we made our way down the narrow stairs. I'd never had it, but from what I'd heard of it thought it sounded less than appetizing.

"No, I don't care for syllabub, but I do like fresh scones with clotted cream and hot-cross buns."

"Oh, I like those too," Jem had replied dreamily. "I'm still hungry," he'd added as an afterthought and ran toward his own mule, which was already waiting for him, its expression one of doleful compliance, much like Hugo's men.

Judging from the glazed eyes and downturned mouths, they'd had a night to remember and were now nursing legendary hangovers, exacerbated by the noise in the yard and the screeching voice of the innkeeper's wife as she called out to her husband. I nearly laughed out loud as Archie rolled his eyes in exasperation and sighed, his head clearly beating like a drum.

"Oh, would ye stop that bellowing, woman?" he growled. "He can hear ye, being only a foot away. He's just ignoring ye in the hope that ye'll finally shut yer trap."

The innkeeper's wife opened her mouth to reply, and I had to admit that I was curious to see what she would say, since the expression on her face was a most amusing one, but Hugo strolled out of the inn at just that moment and she curtsied instead, lost her balance and landed in a heap of manure, which sent the men into uproarious laughter.

"Serves ye right, ye wee besom," Arnold called out, "for not putting any butter or even milk into the porridge. It was dry as dust and twice as foul."

"Enough of that, lads," Hugo said quietly as he mounted his horse. He looked sullen this morning, no doubt exhausted after his broken night.

After the unexpected intimacy of the night at Sir Benedict's house, I hadn't been prepared to share the narrow bed with him, knowing that we'd spend the night in each other's arms, not out of passion, but out of necessity, but I'd felt sorry for him, seeing how uncomfortable he was. Thankfully, he'd kept to his side of the bed and was gone before I even woke up, allowing me some privacy to take care of my more personal needs.

I had seen the occasional glimmer of interest and desire in his eyes and didn't want to do anything to encourage him. I'd play his mistress when necessary, but that was all. I had to admit that pretending hadn't been that hard at Lord Benedict's house. Hugo easily took on the role of the lover, gazing at me with undisguised affection and smiling indulgently whenever I spoke or flirted with our host. He'd brushed my hand a few times and put his hand on my lower back when escorting me from the room, leaving our host in no doubt as to what our relationship was.

I, myself, found it easy to respond. All that was expected of me were a few coy looks and the occasional blush, which Hugo seemed to bring to my cheeks without even trying. He was a handsome man and reminded me greatly of Max, but the resemblance stopped at the physical. They were as different as two men could be. Max was easygoing and full of that self-deprecating humor which made him so likable. Hugo did not lack for humor, but his was of a different kind, directed more at the world around him and the people in it rather than at himself. I suspected that Max would always choose self-preservation over any kind of possible danger, but Hugo wasn't afraid for himself. He was a man of principle; one who would fight for what he believed in, possibly to the death. I'd told him what would happen, but even the possibility of execution did not deter him. How would I feel, knowing that I might have to walk up to the scaffold and lay my head on the block, knowing that within moments it would be severed from my body? And that's if I was lucky.

I'd read an account of Monmouth's execution, and it made me sick to my stomach. The executioner had been Jack Ketch, a man known for his inability to carry out the task at hand, whether due to incompetence or drink. Although he'd been handsomely paid to make a clean job of it, Ketch had hacked at Monmouth six times, leaving him screaming in agony, but still very much alive. As the crowd had roared in disapproval, Ketch threw down his axe and challenged anyone who thought they could do better to come up and finish the job. There were no volunteers, so he was ordered to continue. It took Ketch two more blows to finally kill Monmouth, but he failed to sever the head and had to detach it from the corpse with a butcher's knife, spraying the crowd with a shower of blood and leaving his audience outraged.

My stomach heaved at the thought of something equally horrific befalling Hugo. No man, no matter the crime, deserved such a gruesome death. I'd always thought that beheading was relatively humane compared to hanging, but after reading the account, I had my doubts.

I snuck a peek at Hugo as he rode silently next to me, lost in his own thoughts. What would happen to him in the next few months? I wondered. Would he truly disappear without a trace, or would it only be the record of what happened that vanished?

I'd known Hugo for only about a week, but that was enough to realize that he would not abandon his ideals. He believed this was worth fighting for, so the only chance of salvation rested in him not being labeled a traitor, which was unlikely since he openly solicited support for the Duke of Monmouth.

I sighed and turned to Hugo, needing to hear his voice instead of my own.

"So, where are we going today, my lord?" I asked, putting emphasis on "my lord" in a subconscious attempt to annoy him.

"We will be visiting the home of one Josiah Finch," Hugo replied. I didn't miss the tensing of the jaw or the grim set of his mouth as he said this, wondering what it was about Josiah Finch that literally set his teeth on edge.

"Is he a supporter of Monmouth?" I asked, hoping Hugo would be a little more forthcoming.

"Mr. Finch is not a supporter of anyone, per se. He's loyal to his king and country, but he would be equally loyal to Monmouth if he took the throne. Finch's main interest is his own gain."

"So, why are you soliciting him in particular?"

"Mr. Finch is as rich as Croesus but covets a title to go with his wealth. Monmouth can grant him one should he become king," Hugo explained, his eyes fixed on some point in the distance.

"Is it money that Monmouth is after?" I still didn't quite understand how this worked. It wasn't just about financial contribution, I knew that. There was much more at stake.

"An army needs funds. The men must be armed, housed, fed, and paid. Most men can't afford to fight for free; not when they have families to feed. Josiah Finch doesn't have much political clout, being hardly more than a glorified tradesman, but he is able to finance Monmouth's venture, should he choose to. He has several gunsmiths on his estate who could produce a goodly amount of flintlock muskets within the next few months, should Finch decide to support the cause."

I stared at Hugo, uncomprehending. He wanted Monmouth's rebellion to fail, yet he was courting a man who would supply Monmouth with arms and the funds to support an army. Would that not give Monmouth a greater chance of victory? I asked Hugo as much, and he turned his dark eyes on me, smiling at my naiveté.

"Your question makes perfect sense, of course, but you must realize that the Duke of Monmouth is no fool. He wishes to be a king, not a martyr. He will not attempt a rebellion unless he has the necessary manpower and arms to have a fair chance of success. Therefore, he must believe that he will have what he needs once he lands in England. No amount of muskets Finch can provide can stand up to the might of the Royal Army," Hugo explained patiently.

"I see," I mumbled, feeling sorry for poor Monmouth. I knew that the man wanted to usurp the throne and overthrow the rightful king, but I couldn't help but pity him. I knew his fate, and it was awful. Why couldn't he be content with the life he had? What was it about the throne that held such allure that men were willing to risk everything to attain it? Was it worth his life? I supposed so. He certainly wouldn't be the first person to risk everything to gain the throne of England. He believed he had a fair chance of success and had to make his play, since this might be his last opportunity to capitalize on the public's support.

"Would this be Monmouth's first open rebellion?" I asked. I vaguely recalled reading something about a previous attempt but couldn't remember the details.

Hugo glanced at me, a gleam of suspicion in his eyes. I shouldn't have asked that. Had there been a previous attempt, I would have known about it, as would most of the country. I was showing my ignorance, but Hugo's face relaxed as his eyes slid away from mine. I was a mere woman, so politics would be way above my head in his estimation. I might have heard something, but not understood or remembered. I gave Hugo a weak smile, hoping that he would be thinking just that.

"There was an attempt in 1683 dubbed the Rye House Plot," he replied. "I don't believe that Monmouth was personally involved in the plotting of the details, but the objective was to put him on the throne. The plot was devised by a group of fervent supporters who hoped to assassinate both Charles II and his brother on their way to London from the horse races at Newmarket." Hugo gave me a questioning look; no doubt wondering if that rang any bells.

"Oh yes, of course, I recall hearing about that, but I don't remember the details," I chimed in, hoping to put him off the scent.

"The plot failed," Hugo said flatly. "There was a fire in Newmarket about a week before and the races were canceled, so the king and his brother came back to London early. It did come to light, however, and the plotters were executed."

I nodded gravely, as if remembering the executions, and changed the subject. I was tired of talking about Monmouth. "Lord Everly, what do you do when you are not inciting rebellion?" I asked lightly, hoping to put him in a better mood.

Hugo glanced at me and chuckled, his eyes suddenly twinkling with humor. "Inciting rebellion is a full-time occupation," he said with an impish grin, "and I think you might call me Hugo considering that you've spent two nights in my bed."

"I believe the bed in question was actually mine, but all right, Hugo it is. I'm not one to stand on ceremony, and you didn't answer my question."

"I enjoy other pursuits," Hugo answered defensively.

"Such as?"

"Well, there's my estate, of course. That requires a fair amount of time. I have an estate agent, but I'm deeply involved in the day-to-day running of things, plus I have a responsibility to my tenants. Unfortunately, since I don't have a wife, I have to involve myself in things that are not altogether my domain."

"Like what?" I asked, curious as to what he thought a woman's domain was.

"The lady of the manor usually visits the tenants, particularly ones who are old and infirm, ill, or with newborn or numerous children. She sees to the well-being of the tenants, and when needed, offers whatever help she's able to. My father believed that a landlord holds the position of a parent to the tenants and they, in turn, reward him with loyalty and hard work. My mother was very involved with the women on our estate, and they esteemed her. Jane has been visiting the womenfolk since she's been back, and that has been a great help. I never know what to say to the women, especially when it comes to the children. It's customary to visit a tenant when they have a new baby. Truthfully, they all look the same to me," Hugo confided with a shrug.

"And what do you do for pleasure?" I hadn't meant to sound flirtatious, but that's the way it came out, and my tone wasn't lost on Hugo.

"Are you asking me if I have a mistress?" he countered.

"No, I'm not. I was simply asking what you enjoy doing." I knew I sounded a little prickly, but I didn't want to give him the idea that I was applying for the position for real.

"I enjoy hunting," he replied, "or were you inquiring about more civilized pursuits? I like to read, and I always visit the theater when I'm in London."

"Comedy or tragedy?"

"Tragedy. I prefer plays that make me think and feel rather than just laugh, although sometimes that's just what's needed. I like music as well. Jane used to play the harpsichord, but she's in mourning now. I enjoyed hearing you sing," he added wistfully. "Will you sing for me?" he suddenly asked.

"What? Now?"

"Why not? We have some hours yet. It will make the journey more pleasant."

"I don't know many songs," I replied.

"Just sing the one you sang before. I like it."

I was about to refuse him, but the expression on his face made me change my mind. He seemed so forlorn that I took a deep breath and began to sing softly. I'm not sure why, but I felt a need to make him feel better, if only for a few minutes.

TWENTY-SIX

By the time we reached our destination, the sun was sinking below the horizon, the sky a deep lavender slashed with blood-red streaks, a truly spectacular sight, particularly when seen from the open road with nothing but open space all around. The Finch house appeared almost black against the darkening sky, only a few lights reminding us that it was occupied. In truth, it was more of a fortress than a house. It must have been a castle at one point, but it had been built upon, and the new parts of the building were on either side of what must have been the keep. The tower stood stark and sullen against the evening sky; its crenellated top like jagged teeth taking a bite out of the heavens. The newer parts had somewhat larger windows and pleasing proportions, but the whole place gave the impression of being watchful and ready for a siege.

I dismounted and allowed the men to take my horse, while I followed Hugo to the massive front door, which was studded with iron nails and held in place by hinges that were probably as wide as my arm. The whole atmosphere gave me an uneasy feeling. I looked up at the arrow slits in the keep, almost expecting a few archers to be positioned there; ready to fire on us should we prove to be unwelcome guests.

The door was opened by a middle-aged woman, who bid us to wait in the chilly side room probably once used as an antechamber by the lord of the castle. It was made entirely of stone; cold and silent as a tomb, and almost bare, except for a wooden bench pushed up against the wall.

At last, our host appeared, and my feeling of dread dissipated. I'm not sure what I was expecting, but the man who came toward us was smiling in welcome, his eyes twinkling with mirth. He was bald as an egg but had bushy whiskers which hugged his generous jowls like the flaps of a hat.

"Lord Everly!" he exclaimed. "We've been expecting you. I trust all is well? And who is this enchanting young lady?" Mr. Finch took my hand and kissed it lightly as he smiled into my eyes. "You are most welcome, my dear. I'm glad to see Hugo has finally found some female company. He's in danger of becoming a monk." He gave Hugo a sly look, and I couldn't help wondering if he were in some way referring to Hugo's Catholicism, but Hugo didn't seem put out in any way, and I decided that his secret was probably safe. "Your room is ready, as is supper. We'll wait if you prefer to freshen up, but I must admit that I don't like my meat cold."

"I take your meaning," Hugo said, taking my arm and leading me down a narrow, dim hallway to what must be the dining room.

I would have liked to change and wash my hands at least, but I followed obediently, eager to sit down on something that wasn't moving.

The room was lit by a brace of candles, which did little to dispel the overall gloom. Much as the foyer, it was all stone, hung with several paintings and tapestries of hunting scenes. *We must be in the old part of the house*, I thought as I took in the small windows tightly covered with shutters against the spring evening.

"May I present my son, Lionel Finch, and his charming wife, Frances," Mr. Finch the elder announced for my benefit.

Hugo obviously knew Lionel Finch already. The two men gave each other a stiff bow, something unspoken hanging between them as they both sat down.

I smiled in greeting and made a small curtsy as I sat down on the hard chair. The candlelight was at eye level, so I was better able to make out the faces of Lionel and his wife. Lionel Finch looked nothing like his father. He wore an elaborate wig of blond hair and was dressed as if he were dining at Court. His face was narrow and lean, dominated by large eyes that appeared almost colorless against his pale skin and blond wig. He gave me a smile of welcome, but the smile never reached his eyes, which seemed to be studying me as if I were a particularly interesting specimen. I felt uncomfortable under that basilisk stare and turned my attention to his wife.

Frances Finch appeared to be no more than fourteen. She was slight and pale, but beautiful, in the way that a doll was beautiful; her features perfect, but somehow lifeless. Blond ringlets framed her heart-shaped face, and her wide blue eyes were huge in her face, the dancing reflection of candlelight reflected in her dilated pupils. Her lips slightly quivered as she shyly met my gaze across a platter of fowl. I wasn't sure if it was the work of the shifting shadows, but I thought I noticed a bruise on her cheek, unsuccessfully covered up with a layer of powder. Frances hastily averted her eyes and stared down at her hands, like a child who was expecting a talking-to. I tried to engage her in conversation, but her answers were hesitant and limited to monosyllables and practiced smiles.

I attempted to follow the conversation of the men, but I was too tired to really care about what was being said. Hugo was on the far side of the table, his gravelly voice washing over me as he answered Mr. Finch's numerous questions about Court and commented on some of the more prevalent political issues of the day. The younger Finch didn't say much, but I sensed an anger in him that seemed to be directed at his father. He appeared resentful of the old man, and his few comments were meant to undermine and disrespect. Mr. Finch seemed not to notice, but Frances stiffened every time her husband spoke, shrinking deeper into the huge chair. She reminded me of Alice in Wonderland after she drank the shrinking potion; everything appeared too large as she sat at the table, trying to become invisible.

After the last course was finished, Mr. Finch gave Frances a meaningful look and she hastily rose to her feet. "Mistress Ashley, if you would be so kind as to join me in the parlor," she said. I thought her voice shook, but I wasn't sure.

I followed her out, happy to leave the men to their talk and just sit quietly for a while. I didn't expect any meaningful conversation from the lady of the house, which was just as well since I was too tired to keep up the façade. I longed for a hot bath to drain the tension from between my shoulder blades and my lower back and a soft bed, but I'd have to wait.

Frances led me to a small parlor which was furnished with several chairs, a round table which might be used for dicing or card games, and a harp. The back wall was decorated with a large tapestry depicting some hero on a battlefield, surrounded by fallen soldiers who were either already dead or dying. The knight had his helmet off, a look of naked desperation on his face as his surveyed the carnage and evidently resigned himself to die fighting. Blotches of red thread depicted his wounds, which were bleeding profusely, the blood running down his shiny armor as he raised his sword, possibly for the last time. The scene was awfully depressing, especially for a room intended for relaxation and the pursuit of pleasure.

Despite the fire, the parlor was chilly, so I settled in a

chair in front of the fireplace, enjoying the warmth of the flames and the smell of burning wood. Frances took a seat in the chair opposite and tried to smile. Now that she was lit up by the firelight, I could see a dark shadow on her breast, which was also dusted with powder. She flinched as she saw where my gaze fell and opened her mouth to say something, but closed it again, suddenly shy. Her pupils were still dilated, but slightly less, and she appeared to be a little more animated.

"Have you been married long?" I asked, to draw her out.

"Just over a year," she whispered, her eyes not meeting mine.

"It must be daunting being the mistress of such a large house." I had no idea what to say to the girl, but we couldn't just sit there in silence, and she didn't seem inclined to pick a topic.

"Not really," she replied. "My husband doesn't want me involved in the running of the house. There are servants who see to everything, which is just as well since I wouldn't know where to begin. Lionel wants everything done as it would be at Whitehall Palace and gets very angry if something doesn't meet with his approval. He's not titled, you know, but he likes to pretend that he is, especially at home, where he can lord it over everyone." That was the longest speech I'd heard from Frances so far.

Encouraged by her desire to talk, I tried to continue the conversation. "Do you visit the tenants?" I asked, mindful of the conversation I'd had with Hugo earlier.

"No. I'm not permitted to leave the grounds." Frances finally raised her eyes to mine, and I thought I saw the shimmer of tears. "You are the first woman I've encountered in months, besides the servants."

"What of your family?"

"My mother died just after I was born, and my father was only too happy to see me married. I was a burden to him, you see. He has my brother to keep him company. I haven't seen either of them since my marriage."

"It must be lonely for you," I remarked, hoping I wasn't upsetting her.

Frances nodded; her eyes fixed on her folded hands.

I knew I shouldn't have asked, but I couldn't help myself. "How old are you, Frances?"

"Fourteen," she whispered. So, they had married this poor girl off at thirteen, or possibly even twelve, to a man who had to be in his mid-thirties. What was her life like in this tomb? She seemed so fragile.

"Frances, are you unwell?" I asked, still conscious of the strange appearance of her eyes.

"The drops make me feel somewhat muddled," she replied apologetically.

"What drops?"

"Lionel brought me drops from London. He said all the fashionable ladies use them at Court. I'm to put them in my eyes before I come down to dine. He says it makes my eyes more beautiful, but I start to feel confused and light-headed, and I can't see clearly. They are starting to wear off now, so I see you better. Does Lord Everly ask you to use them as well?"

It took me a moment to comprehend what Frances was referring to. I'd read something about ladies using belladonna drops in their eyes to make their pupils appear dilated and, in their estimation, more seductive, but I could have sworn that practice originated in Renaissance Italy and wasn't actively practiced in seventeen-century England. However, belladonna was a known poison, also referred to as deadly nightshade. If used improperly, it could kill, or, at the very least, cause disorientation, hallucinations, and nightmares.

"Frances, are they drops of belladonna?" I asked carefully.

"Oh, yes. Lionel says that belladonna means beautiful lady in Italian."

"Have you told him that these drops make you feel unwell? Surely he wouldn't want you to become ill." I wanted to scream at her that she should stop using them, but Frances was clearly under the spell of her husband and wouldn't listen to me anyway. At least her face wasn't coated with thick lead-based face paint which over time could kill her, but then, she was still very young. That was probably still to come.

"Lionel likes me this way. He says that the drops make me behave more appropriately in polite company. He says that children should be seen and not heard."

I nearly gagged at this statement, but I had to proceed carefully. I was a mere visitor in this male-dominated society and riling up poor Frances to rebel against her husband would only cause her harm. Most women of the age used their wiles and backhanded tactics to achieve their goals while playing the docile and obedient female in public. Perhaps Frances knew how to manipulate her husband to get her way, but it didn't seem like it.

"I wish I was dead," Frances suddenly said, raising her blue eyes to mine. "I'd take my own life if it weren't a mortal sin. I'd even considered drinking all the drops at once, but the thought of going to Hell scares me far more than the thought of living. So, I wish that I would die naturally. It would be a very welcome relief." She no longer sounded shy or afraid. Her voice was strong, and I got the distinct impression that she'd given this a lot of thought. To hear such sentiments from a fourteen-year-old child was disturbing, to say the least. What would make her wish for death? Her life didn't seem very fulfilling or fun, but by the standards of the day, she was a very lucky girl, one who had every comfort and security.

"Why, Frances?" I'd only met this girl a few hours ago, but I wanted to help her. She seemed so lost, so tragic. Perhaps it was just need for attention that made her say those things, but I couldn't just ignore what I'd heard.

"I begged my father not to agree to the marriage, but my husband paid handsomely for me. My father didn't have a dowry to give me, but I have a title, which was more desirable. My husband hoped to improve his prospects and thought that I would help him do that. He's been disappointed on that score."

"Is he unkind to you?" I asked, thinking of the bruises I'd glimpsed.

"I make him angry," she whispered. "He says that it's my fault that I haven't gotten with child. How can I when he can't do his part? He tries, but then says that I'm not woman enough to arouse him. He flies into a rage and hits me until I beg him to stop. He likes it when I beg. Sometimes that makes him..." Frances suddenly stopped, realizing that she'd said too much. She reached out and took my hand, her own cold as marble on mine.

"Makes him what?" I asked, terrified of what her answer might be.

Frances shook her head, unable to answer my question. She'd clearly spoken to no one about this, and ladies didn't discuss intimate subjects in polite company, especially with someone they'd just met. I could see that she'd been desperate to confide in someone, but now she was afraid that she had crossed a line. "I wish I was dead," she repeated softly, gazing into my eyes. "There's nothing for me in this world. One day he won't be appeased by my crying and he'll kill me in a rage. And no one will care or even notice. They'll just bury me and forget I was ever even here."

"What about the elder Mr. Finch? Does he know? He seems like a nice man. Surely he would come to your defense."

"Yes, he knows. I overheard him telling Lionel that he should beat me more carefully, so as not to leave bruises on my face or damage my womb. When we were first married, he stayed in the room and watched as Lionel..." A tear slid down her cheek as she looked at me, her eyes begging me for help.

Had this been the modern world I would advise her to leave, to get a divorce, to seek help, but what could I tell this poor, defenseless girl? At this moment, I was almost as helpless as her. I was at the mercy of Hugo Everly, and should he choose to beat me, I'd have nowhere to go and no one to turn to. The thought suddenly made me realize how dire my situation really was, but I pushed it away and tried to concentrate on Frances instead.

"Was he able to consummate the marriage?"

Frances nodded miserably. "He was. At first, he performed his husbandly duties almost every night. I thought I would die, but this is far worse."

"Was he kinder to you then?" I asked, curious about what caused Finch's impotence.

"Not by much, but at least he didn't beat me. He just took his pleasure and left my bed. He was brutal, but at least it didn't last long," she confided.

I was surprised that she would tell me all this, but this girl had obviously been isolated for a very long time, and she assumed that being Hugo's mistress, I was well-versed in the business of love, or in this case, hate.

"What happened to cause him to stop, eh...?" I wasn't sure how to phrase the question appropriately, but she got my meaning.

"It began to happen after I started my menses, and my body began to change. It seemed to repulse him," she said simply.

Now I understood. This guy was a pedophile. He wanted to have sex with a child, not a woman, and once Frances began to look like one, he lost his desire for her and blamed it on her. I felt sick to my stomach, imagining what it must have been like for her to be married before she even reached puberty. Poor girl. Her husband would either beat her to death one day or find himself some poor child to slake his lust on, if he hadn't already. There had to be plenty of children on the estate, some of them orphaned. Finch could have any of them as the lord of the manor, and no one would be able to do anything to stop him.

"Frances, is there anywhere you can go? Anyone you can turn to? Would your father listen?" I asked gently, trying desperately to think of a way I could help this child.

"No, he wouldn't. My father feels his duty to me has been satisfied. There's no one, mistress, no one at all."

She was about to say something more when the men came in, looking jovial and a bit worse for drink.

Lionel Finch gave me a hard stare before turning to his wife. "Time to retire, I think, my sweet." The tone of his voice when he said, "my sweet" sounded as if he were saying, "my dog," but Frances obediently rose to her feet and curtsied before leaving the room. I watched her go, my stomach in knots.

Hugo held out his hand and I took it, suddenly angry with him as well. I wanted to cry and rage, but I meekly allowed Hugo to escort me from the parlor and followed a servant up the spiral staircase to our room. I felt utterly helpless and scared. For the first time since I'd come to the seventeenth century, I allowed myself to wonder what would happen if I couldn't get back to my own time. Up until this point, I'd refused to entertain the idea that something might go wrong and I might get stuck here, but after my conversation with Frances, I was suddenly very much aware of my own vulnerability, and it left me terrified.

I sank down on the bed, tears coursing down my cheeks as a baffled Hugo threw his coat over a chair, removed his wig, and sank to his knees in front of me.

"What is it?" he asked. "Are you ill? Does something hurt?"

I shook my head, avoiding his eyes. I didn't want to look at him, didn't want to talk. I just wanted to go home and be away from all this. Forever. I lay down on my side and pulled my knees up to my chest, curling into a fetal position, but it gave me no comfort.

"Neve," he said gently, as he took my face in his hands and forced me to look at him. "What happened?"

"I just can't. I can't be here," I choked out. I couldn't say any more without betraying myself, so I closed my eyes and let the tears come again.

Hugo got off his knees and sat down next to me on the bed, pulling me into his arms and letting me cry as he handed me his handkerchief. "Is it Frances?" he asked softly.

I looked up at him, surprised by the question. What did he know? "Why do you ask?"

"I saw the bruises, and I know Lionel Finch. This wasn't the first time our paths crossed."

"What do you know?" I asked suspiciously, wanting to blame someone, but finding that I couldn't quite blame Hugo.

"I know that Lionel is a cruel man," was all that Hugo said, but from his tone, I guessed that he knew much more. Maybe that's why Lionel seemed to resent him. His preferences were not something he'd want as fodder for gossip. There were plenty of men who enjoyed the company of whores, but that was perfectly acceptable in this day and age, even for married men. Preferring children to grown women was something that most people would find abhorrent, even in this time, but it was a thriving trade in any age.

I'd read something about the prostituting of children in Victorian England. Men paid handsomely, and often even outbid each other, for the privilege of deflowering a child. Of course, once the children became a little older and less desirable, they wound up in regular brothels, working their way down in status and the fee they could command until they were turned out and solicited customers in doorways and parks; doing it behind a bush or against a wall for lack of a place to go. Life expectancy wasn't high, which was probably a blessing in their case.

"He beats her," I whispered. "She's just a child." The

memory of Frances's haunted blue eyes and fresh bruises tormented me, making me feel responsible for her plight somehow.

"Not enough of a child," Hugo said, confirming my suspicions. "He has something of a reputation for seeking out young girls, ones who haven't been touched. He pays handsomely, especially for girls under the age of ten. There are plenty of orphans, girls and boys, who are plucked off the streets and taken into brothels. They are clothed and fed and led to believe that they will be looked after. Then, they are sold to the highest bidder. The younger the child—the higher the price. I suspect Finch only married her out of a need to produce an heir. His interest in her couldn't last." Hugo said this so matter-of-factly that I wanted to hit him, or rage at him at the very least. How could a decent man be so accepting of such cruelty? But, deep down, I knew that he could do next to nothing to change the conditions of society. He was on a crusade of his own, and his had nothing to do with protecting children.

"We have to help her. We must."

Hugo shook his head, giving me a rueful smile. "We can't. We must leave them to it, and we will, come morning."

"We can't just leave. He'll kill her. I know it," I moaned, hoping that Hugo would take me seriously.

"Neve, Frances belongs to Lionel Finch. She's his by law, and he can do with her as he pleases. She's his property as much as his horses and his hounds. A man is permitted to beat his wife if he chooses, sometimes unto death. There's nothing we can do to stop him."

I jumped off the bed, my fists hitting his chest in helpless fury. "What do you mean he can beat her unto death? Are you mad? What kind of world is this where a man can beat a helpless girl, and no one cares?"

Hugo grabbed my wrists and pulled me to him, wrapping his arms around me to prevent a further assault. I was thrashing against him, my self-control finally gone, partly due to Frances's situation, and partly due to my own, for at this point, Hugo owned me just as much as Finch owned Frances. We weren't married, but I was entirely at Hugo's disposal. My very life dependent on his.

"It's the kind of world where a man can do as he pleases," he replied firmly. "A woman has to rely upon the kindness and decency of her husband or benefactor. That's the sum total of it," he said. His face was awfully close to mine, and I looked into his bottomless eyes, suddenly unsure of the type of man he was. What did I really know of him and his own tastes? I'd only known him properly for a short time and although he gave the impression of being a good man, I had no idea of his attitude toward women.

Hugo must have seen my thoughts in my face because he hastily let go, putting a respectable distance between us.

"I know that you don't know me very well, but I'd like to think that I'm a decent human being and an honorable man. I would never hurt you, Neve, so please don't be afraid of me. I will protect you with my life, if necessary. However, Frances Finch is none of my affair. I have no right to interfere, so please don't ask me to. Now, go to sleep. Tomorrow is another day, and you will see things in a more positive light."

TWENTY-SEVEN

Perhaps things would have seemed brighter in the morning, had I not been woken up in the middle of the night by desperate screams. At first, I wasn't sure what I was hearing since the sounds were muffled and swallowed up by the thick walls, but as I lay quietly for a few minutes, I heard Frances's pitiful crying. I couldn't make out what she was saying, but it sounded as if she were pleading with her husband. It went quiet for a moment, and I thought that maybe he'd finally had his fill, but then something went crashing to the floor and the sound that filled the narrow corridor was one of someone being torn apart limb from limb.

I flew out of bed and ran for the door in my nightdress, but Hugo's strong arms grabbed me from behind and lifted me clear off the floor, pinning my arms to my sides like a vise.

"You're not going anywhere, especially dressed like that," he said quietly as he set me down, turned me around to face him, and took me by the shoulders. "What were you planning to do?"

"She's hurt," I screamed at him. "She's fourteen, for God's sake. I have to do something."

"Neve, have you considered that you might actually make

things worse? Finch can't take his anger out on you, so he will take it out on Frances and punish her for your interference— and will continue punishing her long after we are gone. Think, woman!"

"I *am* thinking, and I can't just stand by and watch a helpless girl get abused by a man who's more than twice her age just because he can. He beats her to punish her for his own sexual impotence, and eventually he will either do irreparable damage or kill her. Or, she will kill herself, regardless of the consequences. I don't really believe in Heaven and Hell, but she does, and she will die knowing that her soul will forever be damned, and her body will be buried at a crossroads; her grave condemned to eternal desecration and shame. What kind of God allows that to happen to a mere child who has no say in her own fate?" I raged, staring Hugo down and daring him to give me one good reason for ignoring what was happening just down the corridor.

Hugo suddenly went very still, his eyes opening wider as he took in what I'd said. "You see this?" he asked. "You see her taking her own life?"

"Yes, I see it. I see it as clearly as I see you in front of me," I spat out, suddenly aware of the powerful weapon at my disposal. Hugo would not interfere in a domestic dispute between husband and wife, but if he believed that Frances was going to commit suicide, a mortal sin in the eyes of a Catholic, then he might be induced to act, driven by his faith to save her soul from eternal damnation and torment.

"Stay here." Hugo hastily pulled on his breeches and tucked in his shirt as he left the room, closing the door firmly behind him.

I wanted to follow him, but deep inside, I knew I didn't want to be a witness to whatever was about to happen in Finch's bedroom. Hugo probably resented me for forcing him to interfere, but I simply couldn't help it. I was a modern woman,

accustomed to justice and at least some sort of social responsibility. I wasn't naïve enough to believe that people in my own
time didn't commit atrocities or hurt one another intentionally,
but I simply couldn't stand by and let it happen, especially to
Frances, who had no one to turn to for help and no place to run
when things became unbearable.

This wasn't just a one-off; this was a regular occurrence, one
that would become more frequent and probably more vicious as
Frances grew older and resembled a child less and less. Perhaps
in time she would produce an heir and die in childbirth, if she
were lucky—but what would happen to the offspring of Lionel
Finch? Who's to say that he wouldn't abuse the child, especially
if it happened to be a girl, a useless commodity in a man's world;
one who might even arouse his desire and have no ability to
fight back should he attempt to force himself on her? The
thought made me shake with horror and rage, particularly when
I remembered how often I'd heard stories just like that in my
own time.

I put my hands over my ears as I heard another crash from
down the hall. The growl of raised male voices was muffled by
the sounds of struggle, shattering glass, and splintering wood. I
was suddenly afraid of what I had done. This wasn't just a
heated argument between two men; this was a brawl where
only one of them could come out victorious, and what if it were
Lionel Finch? Hugo had gone in there unarmed, but what if
Finch had a weapon at his disposal and used it on Hugo? He
seemed to be the kind of man who lost all sense of reason when
his passions were aroused and had no qualms about going as far
as murder. In the eyes of the law, he would be justified in
anything he had done, just as he would be justified in punishing
Frances and doing God only knew what to me if Hugo wasn't
there to protect me.

"Oh, dear God," I mumbled, "what have I done?"

I nearly jumped out of my skin when the door crashed

open, kicked in by Hugo, who was carrying the prone figure of Frances. He laid her gently on the bed and stepped aside, allowing me to sit next to her. His shirt was torn, and his face bore the marks of a vicious fight, but he seemed unaware of his injuries. Hugo carelessly wiped his bloodied mouth with his sleeve, smearing crimson across his chin and exposing his bleeding knuckles. He had a gash beneath his left eye, which was oozing blood and already turning a nasty shade of violet. A few millimeters higher and he might have lost an eye.

Hugo's gaze burned with an unholy fire, and the man himself seemed to be vibrating with a manic energy which could only be described as an adrenaline rush, fueled by anger and bloodlust. He could barely stand still as he looked around, grabbed his coat and strapped on his sword before turning toward the door.

"Help her," was all he said as he strode out, leaving me with Frances.

The fire had died out, but a feeble morning light was beginning to seep in, the rosy glow of the rising sun filling the room with a peachy haze which did nothing to liven Frances's ashen pallor.

She moaned and opened her eyes. They were filled with terror as she wildly looked around, expecting to see her husband advancing on her.

"Frances, you're in my room. Please don't be afraid," I said as gently as I could, brushing the hair off her forehead to calm her. Her lip was split, but otherwise her face appeared undamaged, angelic as ever in the pale light of the dawn.

Frances moaned again, her hand flying to her stomach as she winced and gasped with pain.

"Let me see," I said.

"No," she wailed, her eyes growing even more agitated. "Don't look." Frances clamped her hand over mine, but I shook my head and pushed her hand away as I lifted the ruined nightdress.

I gasped at the sight of her abdomen. A huge, blood-tinged bruise bloomed all over her belly, covering the area between her breasts and her pelvis. The taut skin was nearly black, angry red blotches bursting like muted fireworks through a thundercloud.

"He kicked me with his boots," she whispered. "He said I was useless anyway, so I didn't need a womb."

Never before had I understood the desire to kill as I did at that moment. I didn't consider myself to be a violent person, but the hatred that surged through me took me utterly by surprise; a tidal wave of rage that knocked me off my feet and left me breathless with a desire for vengeance. I couldn't speak, so I just patted Frances's hand, sprang to my feet and marched from the room. I had no idea what I was going to do, but I was on autopilot, my mind no longer in control.

I burst into the bedroom, but Finch wasn't there. There were noticeable signs of struggle: a silver candlestick with a gutted candle overturned on the nightstand, Frances's torn dress in a heap next to the bed, as ruined as the poor girl who had worn it, a chair in splinters by the hearth. An ewer and pitcher had been smashed to bits, shards of glass littering the floor like a colorful mosaic that could cut your feet to ribbons if you weren't careful.

I ran downstairs, looking in every room until I found Lionel Finch in the parlor, sitting in a hard-backed chair beneath the tapestry of the knight who was about to martyr himself on the battlefield. Finch was nursing a cup of something, a murderous expression on his battered face as he looked up, momentarily astonished by my disheveled appearance. His shirt was torn as well, liberally stained with blood—hopefully all his—his hand wrapped in a cloth which was quickly turning a shade of rust brown. He looked older without the elaborate wig, his thin brown hair cropped close to the skull and matted with blood just above the temple. His left ear seemed to be missing a piece, but I didn't look too closely for fear of being sick. My lust for murder seemed to have abated at the sight of him, but I was still enraged, desperate to hurt him in the only way I could. This man didn't deserve to take another breath, much less enjoy an existence in which he was master of his domain and everyone in it.

"You miserable swine," I yelled. "How dare you? What gives you the right to treat a human being with such cruelty? If I were a man, I'd drive my sword straight through your gut, putting an end to your pathetic existence, but first I would take a wooden club and sodomize you with it until you begged for mercy, so you'd know what it feels like to be violated and hurt in that manner." I was panting with fury, my hands clenched into fists, and my body shaking with outrage. I wasn't sure where that last bit came from, but it was the worst thing I could think of doing to him, short of murder, and it seemed to have an immediate effect.

Lionel Finch was on his feet in seconds; advancing on me with an expression of such menace that I knew I'd made a terrible mistake. He had no claim to me, but that wouldn't stop him.

I looked around frantically, but the house was silent, all the servants either still asleep or hiding in their rooms for fear of getting involved in whatever was happening. If he beat his wife so savagely, I feared to think of how he treated the people he believed to be inferiors. I was sure that more than one person had the marks of his whip on their back or lost a tooth or two to his fists.

I stepped back hastily to get away from Finch, but there was nowhere to go. A massive carved cabinet that took up almost the entire wall was right behind me, and the path to the door was blocked by an advancing Finch. I pressed myself against the cabinet, shaking with terror, when Jem came running into the room, his eyes round with fear. He was fully dressed, his wooden sword at his side, banging against his thigh as he made for Finch.

"You leave her alone," Jem screamed as he grabbed Finch's arm and tried to pull him away from me. "Leave Mistress Ashley alone."

Lionel Finch didn't so much as look at him as he seized him with both hands and threw him against the wall. I heard a terrible cracking sound as Jem's head collided with the stone wall, his eyes large and full of surprise as he slid down the wall and crumpled into a heap on the floor, leaving a trail of blood on the stone. His eyes fluttered closed and his skin turned gray, only a shade lighter than his blue-tinged lips.

"Jem!" I screamed. "Oh, Jem." I tried to get around Finch to get to the boy, but he drove his fist into my stomach, leaving me breathless with shock and pain as he grabbed me by the hair and drove his knee into the very spot he'd just hit.

I collapsed to the floor, gasping. I couldn't breathe, couldn't see, blood was roaring in my veins and obliterating all other sound but the pounding of my heart. I'd been in pain before, but that was a mere tickle compared to what I was feeling now. It was as if all my insides had been rearranged haphazardly, wrapped around each other and squashed up against my diaphragm. I felt as if I were suffocating, the air I was gulping not quite reaching my lungs.

I finally opened my eyes just in time to see Finch's boot coming toward my face, ready to smash it to a pulp. I threw my hands in front of me to protect myself from the imminent blow. I couldn't breathe, couldn't think, couldn't feel anything but heart-pounding terror. All I felt was the instinct to protect myself from this brutal man.

I cried out as the toe of his boot met my hands, but the blow wasn't hard, merely a glancing contact as Lionel roared in rage. I curled into a fetal position on the floor and peeked through my fingers to see what had caused him to spare me. Hugo had Lionel Finch in a chokehold as he dragged him away from me and pushed him against the wall. He was breathing hard, his eyes glazed and unseeing as he wrapped his hands around Finch's throat and lifted him off the ground, choking the life out of him. Finch kicked wildly, striving for purchase, but Hugo lifted him higher and pinned his legs with his own. Their eyes locked as Hugo held him in a death grip, his face only inches away from Finch's and twisted with fury. Lionel struggled for breath, his eyes rolling in terror as his face went from red to a mottled mauve, the whites of his eyes turning blood red from the pressure in his head. His kicks were becoming feebler as horrible suffocating sounds came from his open mouth, a trickle of blood running down his chin and onto Hugo's hand.

"Hugo," I screamed. "Stop, you'll kill him."

My voice seemed to bring Hugo to his senses. He released Lionel Finch and stood aside as Finch collapsed on the floor, gasping for breath and clutching at his bruised throat. Despite the air he was sucking in, he still seemed to be suffocating, possibly due to the swelling of his neck muscles.

Hugo paid him no mind as he rushed over to Jem and took him in his arms. "Jemmy, can you hear me?" he whispered. I could see that Hugo was crying, his voice a bare croak as he touched his forehead to Jem's, his tears falling onto Jem's cheeks. "Jem, wake up," Hugo pleaded. "Please, wake up."

Jem remained motionless in Hugo's arms; his dark lashes fanned out against his pale cheeks, which were so round and childish that they broke my heart.

I sank to my knees next to Hugo, silent sobs wracking my body as Hugo wrapped one arm around me, pulling me closer.

"It's not your fault," he whispered, as if reluctant to disturb Jem. "It's not your fault."

That made me cry even harder because I felt as if it were.

I'd done what I believed to be right, but what had I accomplished besides this terrible carnage?

I reached out and took Jem's hand. It was limp, but still warm, and as I moved my fingers toward his wrist, I felt a weak pulse.

"He's alive," I whispered urgently. "He's still alive." I sprang to my feet and grabbed the cup Finch had been drinking from. It contained what smelled like brandy. I held the cup to Jem's lips, urging him to take a sip.

He didn't, but the smell of alcohol seemed to revive him, and he finally swallowed a little and began to cough.

"Jemmy?" Hugo called out softly to him. "Jemmy, can you hear me?"

I nearly sobbed with relief when I saw Jem's eyelids flutter. He was still very pale, but color was coming back into his face as he tried to reply. He couldn't form the words, but he raised one small hand to Hugo's face and touched his cheek before closing his eyes again. His breathing seemed to be more even now, but he'd slipped into sleep.

"Don't let him go to sleep," I said as I struggled to my feet. "He's concussed. He needs to stay alert."

Hugo nodded and tried to rouse Jem, but he was dead to the world, his small body slumped in Hugo's arms. "Neve, grab your things and get Frances. We are leaving," he said without looking at me. "Now!"

I threw one last look at Lionel Finch as I fled from the room. He was still gasping, but his color was almost back to normal. His eyes were closed as he lay curled on the floor, but I knew that he was very much aware of everything that was happening. He was simply buying time in case Hugo changed his mind and decided to finish the job. I didn't have any time or compassion to spare for Finch, so I ran from the room, dimly aware of the pain in my middle and the pounding of my heart against my bruised ribs. I knew with an instinctive certainty that Hugo would have killed Finch had I not intervened. What I'd seen on his face was cold purpose. Another minute and he would have choked Finch to death, driven by fury, fear for Jem, and probably some regard for me.

It had been my interference in the first place that put Hugo in this situation, I thought as I choked back tears. A man might not be persecuted for beating his wife to death, but he would certainly be persecuted for murder, especially of someone as wealthy as Lionel Finch. Hugo could have been hanged because of me, which would have been very ironic since my initial intention had been to save his life—not endanger it. I didn't know what the penalty for attempted murder was, but I was sure that Lionel Finch would find out as soon as he was able, as he would no doubt accuse Hugo of abducting his wife.

I put my frantic thoughts on hold as I ran back to the bedroom, got dressed and helped Frances out of bed. She was shaking from shock, her face white from the pain in her belly, but I helped her dress and led her downstairs. I'd noticed several curious servants skulking in the corridor, but they were galvanized into action as soon as they saw us, going about their business as if nothing was amiss, their anxious gazes a testament to their fear of the master.

Hugo's men were already in the courtyard, the horses saddled, and bags packed. Hugo must have gone out to the stables to wake them when I confronted Lionel Finch in the parlor. What if he hadn't come back in time? I couldn't bear to think of what Lionel Finch would have done to me. He wouldn't have stopped with one kick; of that I was sure. He was furious, and slaking his rage on women was what he did best. He would have smashed my face in, possibly even killed me, a thought that left me shaking with post-traumatic nerves.

"Are you all right?" Hugo asked me as he helped me mount my horse. "Are you hurt? I should have inquired sooner, but the sight of Jem lying there just obliterated all thought from my mind," he explained.

"I'm all right," I lied. "Thank you. There's no need to apologize."

I wasn't all right, but all I wanted was to get away from this place and put as much distance as possible between myself and Lionel Finch.

Hugo gave me a curt nod, before turning to Frances, who looked as if she were about to swoon. Archie was standing right behind her in case she fainted, ready to catch her if necessary, but not presumptuous enough to lay his hands on her before the need arose.

Hugo lifted Frances onto his horse, then vaulted into the saddle behind her, putting a protective arm around her middle as he took the reins. Frances flinched but didn't utter a sound, just closed her eyes and leaned against Hugo. She was white as a sheet; her golden lashes fanned against her cheek as tears silently slid down her face. I couldn't begin to imagine what she must be thinking or feeling. There was no way this would turn out well, no matter what happened, and I was sure Frances was aware of that, as was everyone else, judging by the solemn look on their faces.

I was glad to see that Jem was awake. He looked like a rag doll as he sat slumped against Peter's wide chest, but he gave me a weak smile before closing his eyes against the morning sun. His head was haphazardly bandaged, but at least it didn't seem to be bleeding anymore as Peter's doublet was clean, at least of blood. Jem's mule was tied to Archie's horse and walked obediently, possibly relieved not to have to carry Jem's slight body. The hooves squelched in the thawed mud as we made our way out of the yard. The last thing I saw as I turned my horse toward the gate was Lionel Finch's face in the window. Hugo had made an enemy for life; of that I was certain.

TWENTY-EIGHT

We rode in absolute silence for over an hour. Frances had dozed off, her face pale against her blue cloak despite the rosy glow of the sun's rays. She looked even younger when asleep, her blond ringlets framing her face and rounded cheeks in a way reminiscent of a cherub in a painting.

I tried not to look at Hugo for fear that he would reprimand me for what I'd done, but he just stared ahead, his hands tense on the reins. I wanted to know what he was thinking but was too afraid to ask. Images of the events of the morning kept flashing before my eyes, my nerves stretched to breaking point and my back so rigid that it felt as if it would shatter like glass. My eyes burned from lack of sleep, and my head ached terribly, the nucleus of the pain somewhere right behind the eyes, the pain radiating into my temples.

The men rode behind us. Normally, they talked between themselves, their repartee filled with jibes and jokes, but this morning, they were silent and watchful, alert for possible pursuit and retribution. There didn't appear to be any, but it would have been foolish to relax—not that any of us could.

"Where are we going?" I asked at last, unable to keep silent any longer.

I cringed as Hugo turned to face me. His face was battered from the fight; his left cheekbone badly bruised and still oozing blood; his lip swollen where it'd been busted, and his expression wary and a trifle blank. It took him a moment to process the question since he couldn't seem to gather his wits enough to answer.

"I don't know," he said at last. "I need time to think. We must see Frances safe. There will be hell to pay for what I've done, and I must make sure she's out of Finch's grasp. If he gets her back, he'll kill her. And we must see to Jem. He requires a medick."

"I'm sorry, Hugo," I whispered, unsure of what I was apologizing for. I knew the brawl had been my fault, but what could I have done differently. Looking at the frail girl in the saddle, I couldn't be sorry for interfering, though I was remorseful for the position I'd put Hugo in. Of course, now there was no question of Finch's support for Monmouth's cause, and Lionel, being the vicious cur that he was, would want retribution for the injury he'd suffered, the humiliation, and the loss of his wife. I had no idea what he would do, but I was sure we wouldn't have long to wait to find out.

Hugo suddenly stopped at a crossroads and looked to his right, his face thoughtful. I looked at the weathered cross leaning drunkenly to the side with a single name scratched into the crossbar—"Agnes." Suicides were buried at a crossroads, denied a proper Christian burial in hallowed ground; their souls cast adrift for all eternity, their final destination Hell. Frances would no doubt have ended up like this in time, if her husband didn't kill her first, and Hugo was likely reminded of that as he noticed the cross.

Frances seemed to shrink into herself as she saw what Hugo was looking at, her face full of fear. She hadn't uttered a word since we'd left, but I was sure she was wondering what Hugo was planning to do now that he'd taken her from her husband. He could hardly take her to Everly Manor since that would be the first place anyone would look for her, and if they found her, she'd be returned to Finch to face the consequences of her escape.

Hugo seemed to make up his mind and turned his horse to the right, silently followed by the men. I trotted behind him, eager for the sound of his voice. I wanted him to talk to me, to reassure me that I'd done the right thing, and he wasn't angry with me; I needed his support, but he remained quiet, lost in his own thoughts. He didn't seem angry, just tired, in pain, and preoccupied.

I slowed down my horse and waited for Peter to come alongside me. Jem rested against his chest; his eyes partially open as he stared straight ahead. Peter had wrapped a blanket around Jem to keep him warm, and his little body was lost in the folds, his face a stark contrast to the dark colors of the wool.

"Jem?" I called out softly. "How are you?"

"My head hurts something awful," he replied. His voice sounded shaky, and another wave of guilt and fear swept over me. Jem needed all the equipment and skill of a hospital emergency unit. Instead, he would be lucky to get some medicine woman or a charlatan claiming to have medical knowledge. What could they possibly do for him other than give him some nasty concoction and proclaim him cured? He must be suffering from a terrible headache, disorientation, and probably some nausea. Being on a horse in bright sunlight was surely torture, but Jem took it like a man, shutting his eyes against the light and taking deep breaths of air to combat the queasiness.

"Jem, thank you for standing up for me. You were very brave," I said, but he seemed to have fallen asleep.

* * *

We rode on for several more hours. I was thirsty, hungry and bone-weary from a restless night and all the emotional upheaval, but it was too soon to stop. Pursuit was still possible, so we had to keep moving.

Frances had woken up with a start a little while ago, her face a mask of panic until she saw me and began to relax. She didn't ask anything, just accepted a drink from Hugo's leather flask and slumped back against his chest. She appeared too tired to even speak, almost indifferent to where we were taking her as long as it was far away from home. Hugo murmured something to her, and I saw her lips stretch into a tiny smile as she nodded and closed her eyes once again. I wished he would say something to me.

Sometime after noon, we passed a small village, where Hugo sent Archie into the inn to buy some bread, sausage, and ale. We ate in the saddle, not taking the time to stop in case of pursuit. I overheard Archie explaining something to Hugo, but I was too tired and upset to listen. I couldn't stand his silence. I would rather have him berate me and rage at me than shut me out this way. I wanted to know where we were heading and what we would do once we got there, but Hugo kept his counsel, taking his eyes off the road only to check on Jem, then turning away again, his face shadowed with concern.

By the time the sun began to dip toward the horizon, I had exhausted myself with worry. Hugo still hadn't said a word, his silent profile a constant reprimand as he stared straight ahead. He took a narrow track that led into the woods, motioning us with his hand to follow.

The woods were dense, the darkness gathering in the hollows and thickets, creeping across the ground and enveloping the thick growth in a cloak of night. The night was full of sounds: a screech of an owl, a cry of a fox, the snapping of a twig as something ran in the underbrush and rustled the leaves in its wake. I pulled my cloak closer, suddenly scared.

Where was Hugo going? Was he planning to make camp in the woods where we were less visible? It was too cold to sleep outside, but stopping at an inn made us vulnerable. I was sure that Lionel Finch could gather dozens of men from his estate if he wanted to. We had only four men.

I could glimpse the moon between the bare branches of the trees, its comforting light the only thing standing between us and pitch darkness. A terrible wave of nostalgia washed over me, making me wish for home with such overwhelming intensity that I felt a squeezing in my heart that took my breath away. I was so lonely and afraid; so isolated from these men who'd been silent all day.

Frances didn't seem to mind. She'd been in and out of consciousness all afternoon. I couldn't begin to imagine the pain she endured as we rode, her stomach a constant reminder of last night. What if Finch had damaged her internal organs and she was hemorrhaging? That thought put paid to my self-pity, and I glanced at her immobile profile. Perhaps that's why she was so languid. In either case, there was nothing I could do to help. She was in God's hands now, as was Jem.

I nearly choked on the thought. I would never have expressed such a sentiment in the twenty-first century, but here, it seemed right and true. There was no hospital to take them to, no X-ray machine to assess the damage, no surgeon to operate, and no painkillers to give. Hugo gave Frances succor for her battered soul, alcohol for the pain, and hope of escape from her marriage. There was nothing to give Jem other than time. The rest was unknown.

I almost cried with relief when I saw the high wall of some kind of settlement appear in a clearing. The moon shone brighter here, illuminating a small door with a metal grille set at eye level and blocked by a wooden panel. Hugo motioned to Archie, who slid off his horse and banged on the door until a frightened face appeared behind the grille. I couldn't hear what was being said, but it took several minutes for Archie to convince the person on the other side to open the gate and let us pass.

The woman who let us in was dressed like a nun, her weathered face framed by her white veil, the only bright spot in her otherwise black attire that blended into the night.

I looked around in surprise. There were several wooden buildings clustered around a large yard. Sounds of animals came from the barn, the pungent smell of manure and hay drifting through the slits between the planks. Directly ahead was what appeared to be a chapel, and to the left of the chapel was a long, low building with several tiny windows—a dormitory perhaps.

The men dismounted and allowed the horses a drink from the trough by the well, while Hugo lifted Frances out of the saddle and carried her into the hut indicated by the nun. Peter followed with Jem, who appeared to be asleep still, his feet dangling from under the blanket.

I sat down on a bench, saddle-sore and heartsick. Hugo hadn't so much as glanced at me as he walked away and disappeared inside the building.

"All right, Mistress Ashley?" Archie asked, seeing my despondent state.

I nodded, unwilling to discuss my feelings with him. "What is this place, Archie?"

"It's a closed religious order for women, Mistress," Archie replied as he led away the horses, presumably to the stable to be fed.

I remained sitting on the bench, alone and forgotten, until a young woman dressed as a nun came to fetch me.

"Good evening. I'm Sister Julia. Please come with me, Mistress Ashley," she said. Her voice was melodious and soothing as she spoke to me. "Your young wards are with our healer now. Sister Angela is very knowledgeable. If anyone can

restore them to health, it's Sister Angela. We've already had our
supper, but there's plenty left. Lord Everly asked that you have
supper and a bed for the night," the nun informed me.

"What about him and the men?" I asked, surprised.

"Oh, they can't stay here; men are not allowed. They will
make camp outside the wall, but we will make sure they are fed
and comfortable." The young nun smiled at me as she beckoned
me to follow.

I was led to a room with a long table flanked by benches,
which was the communal dining room. It was lit by several
thick candles, their light welcoming after the darkness of the
forest.

"Here you are," the nun said. She handed me a bowl of rich
stew, a large chunk of brown bread and a cup of cold milk. "You
must be hungry after your journey. I will show you to a cell
after you've eaten where you'll be able to wash and rest for the
night."

I didn't think I could eat, but the smell of the stew awak-
ened my senses and reminded me that I'd only a small piece of
bread and sausage hours ago. I finished the stew and the bread
and gulped down the milk, thirsty after a day in the saddle. I
was glad the men would at least get a hot meal, even if they had
to sleep outdoors. They were probably starving and exhausted. I
was so tired, I swayed as the nun led me to my room in the low
building I'd seen earlier.

The cell was tiny, with a narrow cot covered with a straw
mattress and coarse bedding. There was a low stool to put the
candlestick on and a pitcher and ewer for washing. The water
was freezing cold, but I washed my hands and face, and used a
wet cloth to wipe down other parts of my body. I would have
killed for a hot bath, but this was better than nothing. At least I
felt a little cleaner. I didn't even bother undressing as I fell onto
the cot, murmured a heartfelt prayer for Jem and Frances, and
tumbled into a dreamless sleep.

TWENTY-NINE

The men took their spots by the fire and went to sleep just after finishing their meal, looking like cocoons in their tightly wrapped blankets. The night wasn't particularly cold for the beginning of April, but sleeping on the ground always left one stiff and chilled to the bone by morning; the blanket and clothes damp and clammy against the skin. The nuns wouldn't let them sleep inside, not even in the barn, but at least they were kind enough to bring out some bread, stew, cider, and cheese. They were probably eating the community's provisions for tomorrow, Hugo thought guiltily, but couldn't refuse the bounty. They were hungry and thirsty, having had nothing but a little bread and sausage all day long.

On any other night, the men would have sat around the fire talking late into the night, but tonight was different. The whole day had been filled with a pregnant silence that left Hugo feeling as if some great beast was sitting on his chest, squeezing the life out of him. He knew well enough that the "beast" was guilt, which sometimes was the heaviest burden of all. He'd felt Frances's inert body against him all day, her warm weight a constant reminder of what had transpired and his own part in it.

At one point, he'd thought Frances had stopped breathing and discreetly placed his hand right below her breast. He'd felt her heartbeat echo through his fingers and let out a breath of relief. If Frances died, Neve would never forgive him, nor would he forgive himself—just as he wouldn't be able to live with himself if Jem suffered any permanent damage. He was a tough little boy, but beneath the cocky exterior was a lonely, frightened child who'd lost his mother and needed to feel that he belonged somewhere and was cared for. Hugo hardly knew him when he first took him into the household, but over the past year, he'd come to truly care for the boy, love him even, if he were honest with himself, and he was now responsible for the boy's well-being.

He'd been foolish in the extreme to go out to the stables to wake the men without first taking precautions to ensure that Neve, Frances, and Jem were safe. He hadn't expected Finch to attack Neve or hurt Jem, but that had been his mistake. He should have expected it, knowing Finch's vicious nature. He hadn't told Neve the half of it, but it wasn't something a lady should ever have to hear, especially not from him. Finch and his father would be useful allies to Monmouth because of their immense wealth, but no respectable member of the peerage would ever have any dealings with them, particularly Finch the younger. His proclivities were an open secret, as was his terrible cruelty. Hugo had heard rumors in London of several incidents which had left Finch banned from whorehouses for life. He'd broken noses, knocked out teeth, and in one instance had blinded a young girl after kicking her repeatedly about the head. Was it part of God's plan to create such monsters?

Hugo tried to avoid any dealings with the Finches, but Henry Howard, the Duke of Norfolk, who was also a disillusioned Catholic and one of Hugo's associates, had expressly asked him to visit the Finch estate, knowing full well that the desire for a title might induce the Finches to invest heavily in the Rebellion. They'd met at St. Nicolas some weeks ago, and Norfolk had been very clear on the subject, refusing to brook any argument from Hugo.

"Put aside your personal distaste, Hugo, and use your considerable powers of persuasion to enlist Finch's support. I know he's a deplorable scoundrel and a reprobate, but his contribution just might turn the tide in our favor, so keep your loathing in check. I expect to hear from you before Easter." With that, Norfolk had departed, leaving Hugo feeling angry and defiant, but in no position to refuse.

Hugo's initial plan had been to visit the Finch estate, make his case for the Rebellion, hopefully secure a healthy contribution, and be on his way by the following morning, but that was before fate had dumped Neve Ashley at his feet and made a dog's breakfast of all his plans. He could feel her eyes boring into him as they'd ridden in silence but couldn't bear to meet her gaze. He didn't blame her, as she so wrongly assumed; he blamed himself. He'd promised her his protection and, instead, stupidly left her alone in the house with Lionel Finch. Of course, he had no way of knowing that she would leave Frances and come flying down to berate him to his face, but he should have expected it. Neve was outspoken and direct, two qualities which nearly left her maimed and Jem dead.

Hugo stared into the flames; his mind unable to rest. Had he returned even a few minutes later, Neve would have been badly damaged, and he'd have only himself to blame. His blood boiled as he recalled the sight of her curled in on herself on the floor, covering her face with her hands and whimpering in fear as Finch towered over her, his eyes burning with hatred and his face contorted with rage. Hugo had seen firsthand what Finch had been capable of, the sight of Frances's battered body still in front of his eyes, and now he wanted to hurt Neve, disfigure her for life, possibly even kill her. Hugo had barely even registered Jem on the floor as he'd grabbed Finch, desperate to avert the blow that was aimed for Neve's face. He could hardly remember what he did next, all he could recall was going berserk, and trying to strangle Finch as Neve screamed for him to stop—and then he saw Jem.

Hugo threw another log on the fire and watched as a shower of sparks lit up the night sky, twirling and glowing for a moment before their light grew dim and was swallowed up by the night. That's what life was like; a tiny spark that glowed so bright against the darkness before it was snuffed out, Hugo thought bitterly. He'd had a lot of similar thoughts recently, no doubt brought about by Neve's prophecy of his impending doom. He'd always known that he was taking a great risk, found the odds to be acceptable, and forged ahead nevertheless, but suddenly he wasn't as steady in his resolve. Neve had said that there would never be another Catholic king on the throne of England. Was she right? Was it really possible that people who adhered to the true faith would never be allowed anywhere near the seat of power in the country he loved? Would sacrificing his life change that? Not very likely.

Hugo pushed his fists into his eyes until he saw stars of red and green dancing in front of him and his eyeballs ached, but he couldn't extinguish the bleak picture of the future that sprang to mind. What he was doing was futile; Jane had said as much. Despite their age difference, Hugo always listened to his sister. She knew him like no other and was the only person who had his best interests at heart. She'd begged and pleaded with him not to get involved with this scheme, telling him that he had to accept their situation for what it was.

"Hugo, listen to me," she had demanded as she'd paced in front of the roaring hearth on a frigid night in January. She'd just come to him after Ernest had died, needing a few months to regenerate her spirit after the years of her husband's illness. "You must forget this foolishness. England wants a Protestant king, and a Protestant king it'll have, one way or another. If

James has a son and secures the succession, there will be open rebellion. What we must do is ride out the storm. Charles was a Protestant king, and we were all right under his rule. Our family prospered."

"We prospered because we kept our religion a secret. We could never worship out in the open, get married by a priest, or have children baptized in the eyes of God without looking over our shoulder. Father forbade us to tell anyone that we are Catholic for fear of being discriminated against and ostracized. Have you forgotten about all the members of government who were ousted because of their faith to please Parliament? Janey, this is not you talking; these are Ernest's words. He always backed the winning side."

"Don't you disrespect the memory of my husband," Jane had hissed. "Ernest married me and was a good husband to me. I came to him pregnant with another man's child, and he loved me, cared for me, and treated my son as his own. Oh, he knew, Hugo," Jane had informed him, hands on hips, sneering at Hugo's look of surprise. "He knew Clarence wasn't his. You never told him the truth when you contracted the marriage, but he knew. Just as he knew that he'd never have a son of his own, at least not with me. My womb had been damaged by Clarence's birth, so there could be no more children. Ernest could have divorced me, but he remained loyal to me and left his entire estate to Clarence instead of his daughter. He didn't back the winning side in my case. He backed a lame horse."

"Jane, I didn't mean to imply anything about Ernest," Hugo had relented. Jane was rarely in a passion, but he'd provoked her this time. If only she knew the truth about Ernest, but she'd never learn it from him. Ernest was gone now, so there was no point in hurting Jane any further; no point in opening her eyes to something that had remained hidden all this time; something that Hugo would take to his own grave to protect his sister.

"Hugo, there's no right or wrong, only survival, and Ernest

knew that. Shouting his religious views from the rooftops would not have benefited him, so he kept quiet and went about his business, just like father. Have you ever considered that maybe you should do the same?"

"No, I haven't," Hugo had replied as he'd tried to keep his anger in check.

"Hugo, you're thirty-four. You need to get married, have children, and stop trying to change the world. It will change soon enough without you." With that, Jane had taken a seat across from him, a look of challenge in her eyes.

"You know I can't marry," Hugo had retorted.

"Yes, you can. Your marriage was annulled within the law. Legally, you can marry. If you feel some misplaced loyalty to a woman who's borne several children to her new husband, then you're just being a martyr and a fool," Jane had concluded, giving him a triumphant glare.

Hugo couldn't help but laugh, taking Jane completely by surprise. She'd opened her mouth to protest, red spots blooming in her cheeks as she'd stared him down, unsure of what she'd said to prompt his mirth.

"And what are you laughing at?" she'd demanded.

"I'm laughing at the way you just obliterated everything I hold dear. I should turn my back on my faith, forget my marriage vows, and just do whatever it takes to prosper. Correct?"

"In a nutshell, yes. You are too old for all this childish idealism."

Hugo had snorted with laughter, suddenly feeling lighter than he had in years. Jane had a way of making everything appear perfectly simple, and it was, as long as you didn't allow conscience to get in the way. Hugo loved his little sister, but he also knew her flaws. Jane had lain with a man promised to another, gotten with child, and then married another man without nary a qualm about deceiving him. She made out all right for herself though, so maybe she had a point about survival.

Hugo smiled ruefully at the glowing remnants of the fire as he remembered the argument. He'd forgiven Jane, of course; he always did, but perhaps his practical little sister had a point. Maybe he was just an idealistic fool, too old to keep with such outdated principles. Neve Ashley had told him as much. His father always said that women saw things more clearly, and perhaps they did, unhindered by men's notions of honor and duty. Their allegiance was to their family: a duty to love, protect, and nurture.

Hugo finally wrapped himself in a blanket and lay on his back, staring at the multitude of stars in a cold, black sky. He was far from happy, but his spirit felt more at peace. Frances and Jem would recover, Neve thankfully wasn't hurt, and he had some serious thinking to do about the future.

THIRTY

Sister Julia came to wake me before dawn. The sisters had finished their morning prayers and were now gathered in the dining hall for breakfast, to which I was invited. I would have preferred to have a little something in my cell, but it was rude to refuse, so I splashed some water on my face and hands, threw on my cloak, and tucked my errant curls into my cap before following Sister Julia into the foggy April morning. My face immediately grew moist as a gentle mizzle fell from the sky, coating my skin and cloak with a sheen of dampness. The flame from Sister Julia's candle moved in front of me, the tiny sphere of light distorted by the fog and seemingly floating of its own accord.

I felt terribly awkward as I entered the dining hall and everyone's eyes turned toward me, but the sisters smiled and behaved as if my presence there was the most natural thing. I was given hot porridge with honey and milk and more of the brown bread I'd had last night. The bread was too hard to bite, since without modern-day preservatives, it only lasted a few hours, and the fresh loaves hadn't been baked yet. The sisters tore off chunks and mixed it into their porridge, so as not to be wasteful. I did the same. The warmth of the porridge was most welcome. The cell had no heat, so I was chilled to the bone, especially after washing with the icy water. The nuns seemed unaffected by the cold, eating their breakfast in near silence and getting ready to go about their daily chores.

"Where's Lord Everly?" I asked the nun next to me.

"He's outside the wall in the meadow," she answered, giving me a searching look. I obviously wasn't Lady Everly, so the nuns drew their own conclusions. They were good at keeping their opinions to themselves, but I could see a few judgmental glances directed my way. Little did they know that our relationship was as platonic as could be, and not the sordid liaison of their collective imagination.

"And Frances and Jem?"

"Resting peacefully," the sister at the head of the table answered, giving me an encouraging smile. Perhaps she was the Mother Superior of this convent, if that's what it was.

"May I see them?"

"Certainly. Sister Julia will take you," the nun replied as she finished her meal and rose to leave. "God be with you, Mistress."

"And you," I replied automatically.

By the time breakfast was finished, it was fully light outside. The fog still swirled all around us, wrapping its fingers around trees and buildings and pooling in the hollows, but the mizzle had stopped, and a hazy sun tried to peek through the clouds.

I looked around me, wondering if anyone knew of the existence of this community. Were they completely self-sufficient? For someone like me, it was difficult to accept that someone could live without going to the shops or hearing the news of the outside world, and survive entirely on the fruits of one's labors in total isolation, but it seemed that the sisters were completely cut off, and that's how they liked it.

As I followed Sister Julia to the hut where Hugo took

Frances last night, I tried to get a good look at her face. She was older than I'd originally thought, perhaps somewhere in her mid-twenties, so around my age. There was something strikingly familiar about her large gray eyes. She wasn't very tall, but underneath her habit, her body seemed lithe and strong, typical of a woman who spent her life doing hard physical work.

"I'll leave you here, Mistress Ashley," Sister Julia said as she stopped in front of the hut. "I have to start on my chores now if I hope to finish by midday." She smiled and disappeared into the barn which was directly across. I could hear the bleating of sheep and lowing of cows that needed to be milked and allowed out to graze. A soothing voice was having an intense discussion with one of the cows, questioning its bad temper and asking it to stand still. I turned and walked into the hut, nervous, but eager to see the patients.

It was a two-room building, the low rafters of the front room hung with various drying herbs that gave the place a pleasant medicinal smell. There was a long wooden table beneath the high window, spread with assorted roots and leaves and littered with bowls and bottles. A sharp cutting knife lay forgotten, and a mortar contained some kind of greenish powder that smelled minty. A neatly made cot stood against the back wall, flanked by a low stool on which there was a candlestick, pitcher, and a prayer book. Sister Angela's cloak hung on a peg in the wall, looking like a giant bat taking a well-deserved rest.

The back room was Sister Angela's infirmary. It had two cots placed close to the hearth for warmth. Sister Angela was poking up the fire as I entered her domain, but came out to greet me, smiling in welcome.

"Good morning," she said as she met me halfway. "You must be anxious about your companions." She was an older woman, probably in her mid-sixties, but I could see traces of beauty in her face. I wondered if she had been a nun all her life, or if she had joined the order in later years after something, or someone, had left her weary of the outside world. She had a wonderful serenity about her, which radiated like a force field and made me feel slightly more optimistic.

"I am. How are they?" I asked, hoping that Sister Angela's cheery demeanor was part of the answer.

"Oh, they are much improved. I gave them each a drop of the juice of the poppy last night to help them sleep. Sometimes rest is the only thing I can truly offer, especially when the injuries are internal, but they both enjoyed a peaceful night." She beamed at me, and I felt a wave of relief wash over me.

"Will they be all right then?"

Sister Angela glanced quickly into the other room, took me by the elbow and led me closer to the outer door, to prevent her patients from hearing her answer. "Mistress Ashley, all I can do is offer some pain relief and sympathy, but the rest is really in the hands of the Lord. The young woman has suffered severe blows to her stomach, but there's no way to ascertain how extensive her internal injuries are. She's not bleeding, which is a good sign in my opinion. I pray that the bruising is mostly external and will heal in its own time. Whether she will be able to bear children in the future is something only time will tell."

"And Jemmy?" I inquired, tense with worry.

"Jem will be somewhat muddled and perhaps drop off to sleep at odd times for a week at least, I think, but I checked him before giving him the sleeping draft, and he seemed relatively alert and his vision unaffected. Had he been seeing double, then there would be cause for concern. He has a lump on his head the size of an egg, but I put a poultice on it, and it will go away in a few days. I don't think he will suffer any long-term effects, just a terrible headache and fatigue. He needs rest and peace and quiet." The three things we couldn't provide for him.

"May I see them?"

"Of course," Sister Angela replied and led me back toward the other room.

Jem was curled up on his cot, his mop of dark hair and one cheek the only things visible above the blankets, but his breathing was even, and his color appeared to be healthy.

Frances reclined on her cot close to the hearth, her face rosy from the heat, her eyes wide open and clear. She smiled as she saw me.

"Mistress Ashley," she called out. "Come and sit by me."

I looked to Sister Angela for permission, and she gave me an encouraging nod as she pushed a stool toward me. I pulled up the stool and sat down next to the cot. Sister Angela retreated to the table in the other room, where she continued to slice something as she kept an eye on her wards.

"Frances, how do you feel?" I asked as I took the girl's warm hand, partially as a gesture of comfort and partially to feel her pulse, which was steady and strong beneath my finger on her wrist.

"I'm much improved. My stomach still pains me, but I slept well for the first time in a year, I think," she replied, casting a grateful look at the nun who was happily grinding something in her mortar. "Every night, I went to bed and lay there terrified, not knowing whether Lionel would come to me or not. I don't know which was worse: having him come, hurt me, then leave, or not having him come and wonder if he would come later or in the morning," Frances said, looking to me for understanding. "This fear in me was like a snake, coiled in my belly, ready to strike at any time. Sometimes I would be sick from the anxiety, and Lionel thought I might be with child. He beat me when I began to bleed."

"Oh, Frances, I'm so sorry," I said, knowing how inadequate that sounded.

"Don't be sorry," Frances said as she smiled at me and squeezed my hand. "You saved me. You and Lord Everly saved me, and I will never go back again. Ever."

"Are you all right with staying here?" I couldn't offer her

any other alternative, but I wanted to know that she gave her consent to being left with the nuns. I would hate to think that she felt she had no say in her life. Again.

"Oh, yes," Frances replied happily. "I will gladly stay here forever."

Her answer surprised me, but I didn't question it. She might change her mind in the future, and I was sure the nuns wouldn't force her to stay against her will.

Frances obviously noticed my reservations about leaving her and laid her hand over mine. "Don't worry about me, Mistress Ashley. I'm happy to remain. This is a place of peace and love—two things I have never really known. My mother died when I was born," she explained sadly. "My father hired a nurse and forgot all about me until I was of marrying age. I think he blamed me for my mother's death; at least, that's what my brother liked to tell me. He could be very unkind at times." Frances grew quiet, no doubt remembering her childhood.

"And then you married," I prompted.

"Yes. I hoped that I would be happy. Lionel was courteous at first. He brought me little gifts and showed me off to his friends, but then, after about a year, everything changed. I thought his father might intervene, but he turned a blind eye. He's still the master, but it's Lionel who controls everything." Frances sighed as she gave me a sad smile. "So, you see, I've never been loved or known peace. I like the company of women, and I would much rather dedicate my life to God than to my husband. Besides," she added brightly, "staying here serves a dual purpose."

"How so?"

"As long as I'm alive, I'm Lionel's wife, which means that he can't marry or produce the heir he so desperately wants. If he doesn't know where I am, he has no way of knowing if he's free," she added simply. She would have her revenge on her husband in a way that enabled her to stay safe.

"You're a clever girl," I said with a smile, suddenly realizing that Frances wasn't as naïve as I first thought.

"Not clever, just disillusioned and bitter," she corrected me. "I crave revenge and retribution, but I hope that, in time, I'm able to forget all about that part of my life and find a higher purpose."

"I'm sure you will," I replied, rising to my feet. "I'll never forget you, Frances," I said, meaning it.

"Or I you, Mistress Ashley. You saved my life, and I will pray for you for the rest of my days."

"Goodbye then," I said and turned to leave.

"He's a good man," Frances called after me. "Don't leave him."

I wasn't sure what made her say that, but I just nodded and took my leave.

Don't leave him, indeed.

THIRTY-ONE

I said goodbye to Sister Angela and headed for the gate. I hadn't brought anything with me, so there was nothing to take. All I had were the clothes on my back. The men were already up, dismantling their makeshift camp and getting ready to leave. Archie was pissing against the tree and winked at me as I passed; Arnold and Peter were saddling the horses that were in no mood to be rushed and were enjoying a breakfast of fresh grass. Hugo was sitting by the fire, staring into the flames. I couldn't take his silence anymore, so I sat down next to him.

"Good morning," I said. "Did you sleep?" I knew the answer to that question before he even replied. Dark shadows beneath his eyes looked like smudges of ash on his pale skin, and a day's growth of beard, coupled with the bruises and grubby clothes, gave him a disreputable look.

"I tried," was the terse reply. Clearly, he'd failed.

"Hugo, I know you're angry with me, but I couldn't have acted any differently than I did," I began, needing to explain to him why I'd behaved the way I had.

"I'm not angry with you; I'm angry with myself," Hugo said gruffly, finally turning to face me.

"Why?" I asked, surprised that he would be so hard on himself. Things had certainly gone wrong, not that there was a graceful way of barging into someone's bedroom, kicking the living daylights out of him, abducting his wife, and leaving him gasping for breath after nearly choking him to death, but at least everyone was alive and almost well. I was about to point that out to Hugo when he finally spoke.

"Had I not returned in time, Finch would have hurt you very badly; partially because he would have enjoyed it, and partially to get back at me. When I saw you cowering on the floor with him towering above you, ready to strike, and Jem just lying there, white and broken, possibly dead, I felt a rage I'd never known before. Something snapped inside me, and I wanted to kill him," Hugo said simply. "You should have let me."

"No, I shouldn't have. You don't want a murder on your conscience, even if it's of someone as contemptible as Lionel Finch," I replied. "Leave the judging and punishing to God. You helped Frances, and that's what counts. Will she be safe here, do you think?"

"I'd like to believe she will. There's nothing more I can do for her; nowhere I can take her. Finch will be searching for her, and he won't give up. I only hope he won't come here."

"Is this a Catholic convent?" I asked. I didn't know much about religious orders in seventeenth-century England. Of course, I'd learned about Henry VIII's dissolution of the monasteries at school, but my education on the subject ended there. I'd assumed that there were no Catholic convents or priories left, but this place was hidden in the woods, so perhaps they managed to keep its existence secret. Or had they? Hugo had known about it, so perhaps Lionel Finch would too.

"The order is Anglican. I believe they call themselves the Convent of the Sacred Heart. I don't know if they are officially sanctioned by the Church, but they must have someone they answer to, like a bishop. These women joined together and decided to live in seclusion, devoting their lives to prayer and contemplation. I don't think they consider themselves married to Christ, and they don't take the same vows as Catholic nuns, but they do promise chastity, poverty, and obedience. They are more of a religious community than a convent."

"How did you know about it?" It seemed strange that a Catholic nobleman would know of a secret Anglican order of nuns living in the woods.

"I didn't," Hugo replied. "It was Archie who suggested bringing Frances here. Sister Julia is his sister," he replied. "A terrible tragedy befell her some years ago. She found peace here, and I hope Frances will too."

"It's kind of them to take her in."

"I made a sizeable donation to their coffers," Hugo replied, smiling at my naiveté. "They will take good care of her and keep a portion of what I've given for Frances, should she decide to leave in the future."

"That's very generous of you."

"Generosity has nothing to do with it. I took Frances from her home. I know what you're going to say," Hugo interjected before I had a chance to interrupt, "but Frances is now adrift in the world. She doesn't have the protection of her father or her husband, ironic as that may sound. She is penniless and powerless, with no one to turn to. My sister always knew that I would come to her defense, no matter what, but Frances can't expect that from her kin. Knowing that she has some funds, should she choose to leave, will give her some say in her future, which is something everyone should have, especially a girl of fourteen."

"She was right about you," I said with a smile. "You are a good man."

"Interesting that a fourteen-year-old girl had to point that out to you," Hugo teased, suddenly more like his old self. The cloud of despondency seemed to have lifted and I was glad to see him smiling at me.

"Hugo, what's going to happen?" I asked, afraid of the answer. We were going to be exposed and vulnerable as soon as we got back on the road.

Hugo shrugged, his eyes on the dying flames in front of him. "Lionel Finch has the power to destroy me, and now I've given him a good reason to do just that. He won't rest until he sees me dead, of that I'm sure. I just have to wait and see what form his vengeance will take."

"What do you mean?" I asked, horrified. I hadn't really thought past getting away from the house and taking Frances to a place of safety. I feared that Lionel Finch would gather his men and pursue us, forcing a confrontation in which we would be sadly outnumbered.

"He can publicly accuse me of treason and let others do his dirty work, or he can come after me himself and try to kill me for the insult I've given. I've interfered in his marriage, taken his wife from him, and caused him bodily harm. I'd say the man has reasons to want me dead, don't you?"

"Perhaps we should return to Everly Manor," I suggested.

"Perhaps," Hugo conceded. "Although that's the first place anyone would look for me." He got to his feet and tossed the remnants of his drink into the fire. "Let's get Jem and leave this place. Our business here is done, and the longer we stay, the more we endanger this community."

THIRTY-TWO
APRIL 2013

Max watched out the window as Detective Inspector Knowles skipped down the steps and walked to his car. Detective Sergeant Johnson was waiting for him, the light of his cigarette glowing in the gathering darkness of the April evening. Their questions had been perfunctory; their manner ingratiating. Max had offered them tea and they'd gratefully accepted, happy to turn the interview into a social occasion. Max knew the inspector well. D.I. Knowles was a drinking companion, captain of the rugby team, and a good man to go hunting with when the desire to shoot something arose, so Max had nothing to worry about; luck was on his side.

A stranger might have been more suspicious, might have even acquired a warrant to search the premises, but Knowles just wanted to get the interview over with, call it a day, and get back to his wife and baby girl, who'd just learned to say "Dada," which Knowles couldn't help boasting about. Seeing the joy on the inspector's face, Max had wondered if he might ever have the opportunity to boast about the insignificant accomplishments of his own offspring, but he'd directed his mind back to the inane questions, eager to get the officers out as quickly as possible.

It was all very routine, and all Max had to do was stick to his story. No, he had no idea where Neve Ashley had gone. No, she didn't seem out of sorts, anxious, or depressed. Yes, she'd said goodbye and promised to stay in touch. That was all he could tell them.

The police seemed to be under the impression that Neve had just gone off somewhere without telling anyone. Max couldn't help wondering if they'd even checked her credit card or bank activity. No one seemed particularly keen to find her, but clearly someone had reported her missing, most likely Lawrence Spellman, so it was good that he'd anticipated this and took it upon himself to perform some damage control. Having access to Neve's wallet and mobile phone made it ridiculously easy and diverted any suspicion from him, clearing the way for the scheduled film shoot.

The movie company trucks had begun arriving the day before. Already the car park of the museum was full to bursting, people darting to and fro and various pieces of sound and lighting equipment carried through the front door. The actors would be arriving soon, taking over the village and bringing much-needed business and exposure to shops and pubs greatly in need of new custom.

Max turned from the window and went to pour himself a drink. Everything was going according to plan—and yet he couldn't rest, couldn't sleep, couldn't find peace of mind, even when walking with Tilly or having a drink at the pub. Neve had vanished and Max's secure world had vanished with her. At first, he'd been worried about Neve, wondering what had become of her, and if she were safe, wherever or whenever she happened to be, but the worry had quickly turned into a quest for self-preservation. Max couldn't shake the idea that Neve could somehow, perhaps even without meaning to, upset the balance of his life and do irreparable damage to the timeline and the succession. Max had absolutely no proof that Neve had gone back in time, or that she'd even gone to a time period which might have a bearing on his own life, but there was nothing worse for fanning your worst fears than uncertainty.

Max took a seat on the sofa without bothering to turn on the lights. He liked sitting in the dark. It helped him feel safer somehow and made his actions seem somewhat less deplorable without the merciless glare of the lights on his conscience. He'd been over the argument a thousand times at least, but still he was at war with himself, torn between doing the right thing, and doing the thing that would benefit him the most. If Neve had been a victim of a crime, surely, she would have turned up somewhere by now, even if she were dead. She'd been missing for over two weeks now, no trace of her either in Surrey or in London. Had she turned up, she'd have come looking for her car and her handbag, would have called him or Spellman, or the police.

She was somewhere in the past, possibly wreaking havoc or getting herself accused of witchcraft or theft, which she would have to resort to if she wanted to survive. Since she hadn't come back, she was either unable to do so or unwilling. Was someone helping her? Was someone preventing her from going back? These and other questions burned in Max's mind day and night, driving him insane with their lack of answers. He had no way of knowing. None. He'd scoured the internet, searching for any mention of a Neve Ashley in the last few centuries. It stood to reason that if she'd been burned as a witch or married to a nobleman, there'd be some mention somewhere, but he found nothing.

And now that the film production was about to begin, he had a new dilemma. Neve had mentioned that a key scene would be filmed in the crypt. What if someone discovered the passage by accident? Max couldn't begin to imagine the pandemonium that would cause. He had to make sure that didn't happen, and the only way to do that would be to seal the door. But where was it? He'd gone down to the crypt the week before, staring at every inch of the wall until his eyes hurt, but he hadn't noticed anything out of the ordinary. He had run his hands over the stone walls, looking for some kind of mechanism, but didn't find anything at all. He had even tried moving some of the lids of the tombs in the hope that a passageway was hidden inside one of the coffins, but the stone lids weighed a ton, too much for one man to budge. There was no way Neve could have done that on her own, much less slid it back into place after she got in.

Max had turned the manor library upside down, looking for any blueprints of the church building. He had found the documents from the reconstruction of the church after the fire, but there were no original plans for the building. How was it even possible that a church built centuries before and rebuilt in the eighteenth century could share a passageway that led to the past? It was absurd, ludicrous, and completely outside the realm of possibility. And yet...

The only bright side to Max's failure to find the passage was that if he couldn't find it, chances were, neither would the actors or crew. But how had Neve found it? Had she known something about it? But from whom? Henry's story had been greeted with derision and ridicule. No one outside the family knew of his supposed escapade, and the story was kept secret, for fear of tainting the family name with the stain of insanity. The fact that his notebook survived was a miracle in itself, since any reminder of that period had been expunged from family history.

Max looked with dismay at his empty glass and got up for a refill. He was drinking too much, but alcohol was the only thing that calmed his nerves and helped him think straight. Max suddenly stopped and stared at his reflection in the mirror hanging over the drinks cart, an idea dawning. There were people at the asylum who had come into contact with Henry. He'd been there for nearly three years. Perhaps he'd told someone: a doctor, a nurse, an orderly. Could any of those people have been related to Neve, and was there a way to find out?

Max sighed in exasperation. An ancestor of Neve's could have had a different surname. A list of employees for the asylum would not be online, and the place had closed down at least one hundred years before. No, it was a dead end, just like every other idea he'd come up with.

"Neve, where the hell are you?" Max hissed under his breath.

He slumped back on the sofa and stared at the dark rectangle of sky visible through the window, a new realization dawning on him. At this point, if Neve returned, he'd have a lot of explaining to do. He'd lied to the authorities and Neve's boss, hidden her car, and accessed her bank account and mobile phone without her permission, with the clear intent of subverting an investigation into her disappearance. If Neve made any of this public, his political career would be dead in the water; his image tainted by dishonesty and sinister motives. If Neve was truly in the past, the only way to avoid discovery was to keep her there and hope that she perished without a trace—a lost soul who belonged to no one and didn't have a friend to turn to—and the only way of doing that was to seal up the passage. Since Max couldn't find the door, all four walls of the crypt needed to be walled up. Perhaps he could tell the vicar that the foundation wasn't sound and needed to be reinforced. That was a thought.

Max finished his drink in one gulp and headed upstairs to research masonry workshops in the area.

THIRTY-THREE
APRIL 1685

I was vastly relieved when we finally reached the outskirts of Guilford by nightfall. Traveling down the narrow, muddy roads between the villages left me feeling vulnerable and exposed, our silhouettes in stark relief against the open ground and bright sky. We saw the occasional farmer with a loaded wagon or a lone traveler, but, for the most part, we were alone.

Hugo seemed calm and in control, but I couldn't help worrying that we would be overtaken by Lionel Finch and his men, especially since our progress was slow due to Jem. Hugo had overridden Jem's feeble protests that he could ride on his own and insisted that Jem ride with him, which had left Jem torn between a desire to prove that he was all right, and the need for protection and comfort which he so desperately needed. He sat in front of Hugo, his bright face alternately alert and flushed with pride, and drowsy, his chin resting on his chest as he nodded off. Hugo gently pulled him against his own chest to make him more comfortable, and Jem smiled in his sleep as he felt Hugo's arm come around him and hold him tight.

I kept looking back, unable to believe that Lionel Finch would just calmly continue going about his business after what had occurred yesterday morning. He had to be raising an army to pursue us, all reason obliterated by his lust for vengeance. The men didn't bother to search the horizon for signs of pursuit, but they were alert, their backs stiff and their weapons at the ready should anything occur.

I fell in line with Archie at one point, eager for someone to talk to since Jem was asleep and I didn't want to disturb him by talking to Hugo over his head.

"How long has it been since you've seen your sister?" I asked, hoping Archie would be in a talkative mood and tell me what I wanted to know.

It took him some time to answer, his face a closed book as he stared ahead, deciding how much to divulge.

"It's been some time, Mistress Ashley," he finally replied. "I hardly recognized her."

"Has she been there long?"

"About five years now, I reckon. She seems happy, for what it's worth." I could tell by Archie's demeanor that he didn't approve of his sister's choice, but he respected it and was glad to see that she didn't harbor any regrets.

"Has she always wanted to devote her life to God?" I asked, trying to phrase my question in a way that wasn't as prying as asking him straight out what made his sister give up the outside world and shut herself away in a tiny community of nuns in the forest, possibly forever.

Archie mutely shook his head. "In my experience, there are two types of religious women: those who believe they have a vocation, and those who turn to God to escape from something. My sister is the second kind," Archie finally replied, spurring on his horse to indicate that the conversation was over. He didn't want to discuss his sister or the circumstances that had led to her decision to withdraw from the world, and I didn't blame him. He'd told me enough.

I looked around with interest as we rode through the

outskirts toward the center of town. Guilford wasn't like the sleepy villages we'd encountered on our journey, consisting of a cluster of houses, a village green, and a church. This was a bustling metropolis, its history stretching as far back as the Romans and Saxons who settled here after the end of Roman authority in the area. Guilford had grown exponentially over the centuries, becoming a center of commerce and progress, and even figuring in some works of fiction, such as Sir Thomas Malory's *Le Morte d'Arthur* and the *Doomsday Book* of 1086 as the holding of William the Conqueror.

The shadowy bulk of Guilford Castle could be seen rising in the distance, its unyielding Norman keep silhouetted against the darkening sky; just as it must have done when King John, Eleanor of Aquitaine, and Henry III visited it several centuries before. I wondered if it were occupied at the present, since not even a flicker of light could be seen in the narrow windows, giving the impression that the castle was just a solid block of stone. It had been initially built to intimidate the citizens of Guilford, and it still managed to do so, even in times of peace.

Hugo slowed his pace as he rode through the town, which was a warren of streets and alleys, some of them leading to the town center, where the market was held on Saturdays. It was growing dark, but the streets were still alive with passersby and traffic. Wagons rattled down the wider streets, while mounted riders and pedestrians navigated the narrower lanes. There was a smell of rotten vegetables, human and animal waste, and a whiff of rotten fish coming off the River Wey, but as we drew closer to the center of town, there was also the appetizing smell of roasting meat, fresh bread, and boiled vegetables wafting from nearby taverns.

Light spilled from windows and doorways, the sound of people talking, singing, and at times arguing erupting for a moment as the door to some establishment opened and then closed again. I was worn out and eager to reach our destination, but this was my first exposure to an actual seventeenth-century town, and I was curious despite my fatigue. Several torches burned in front of the entrance to the guildhall, but it appeared to be closed, the windows dark and shuttered against the coming night. I wondered where the Royal English Mint might be, although I wasn't sure if the Mint were still in existence in 1685. I'd have to look it up once I got back to my own time.

Hugo turned into High Street and I gazed around with interest, having read that in 1995, a chamber had been discovered in this very street which might have been the first synagogue in Western Europe. I peered into the gathering shadows to see if I might spot anyone who appeared Jewish. Would there be any Jews in Guilford in the seventeenth century or had they left and resettled someplace else? The article hadn't mentioned how long the chamber had functioned as a place of worship, only that it had been established as early as the twelfth century.

We passed several respectable-looking inns, but Hugo kept going.

"Hugo, where are we going?" I asked, wondering why he hadn't stopped at any of the inns on High Street.

"I prefer not to stay anywhere close to the hospital," he replied, silently indicating the solid, three-storied building across from Trinity Church at the top of High Street. "Too great a risk of infection with people visiting the sick or working at the hospital, and then coming to an inn for a drink or a meal or spending the night."

Jem perked up at the sound of the hospital being mentioned, his pale face round as a moon in the glow of the torches by the gates. Hugo hadn't said so directly, but now I began to guess why he chose to stop in Guilford. He would take Jem to the hospital if he weren't better by tomorrow.

I felt an overwhelming sympathy for Jem as he tried his best to look alert. The poor boy was terrified of being left behind and would do anything to convince Hugo that he was recovered. He did look a little better, but the bandage was crusted with dried blood at the back of his head, and his gaze looked a trifle unfocused in the gloom of the street.

Hugo sensed Jem's agitation and laid a hand on his shoulder in a gesture of reassurance, as he whispered something softly in his ear, which made Jem smile and visibly relax. Hugo pulled Jem against him and I was glad to see the boy didn't resist but laid his head on Hugo's chest and looked up at the sky which was barely visible through the thick smoke belching from every chimney in the city.

We finally stopped at a small, but comfortable-looking inn overlooking a canal. Several small boats lay moored, their elongated outlines just visible in the darkness, their owners at home for the night before their workday began at dawn. Guilford business owners were able to access the Thames through Weybridge, which gave them a boost of prosperity not yet enjoyed by many other landlocked towns.

I expected the canal to give off a dank, pungent odor of debris and human waste dumped in its waters, but it smelled pleasantly of fresh water, mud, and wood from the boats. We were no longer in the center of town, and the air was somewhat fresher here, a light breeze blowing off the canal and dispelling the stink of wood fires, refuse, and medicinal odors emanating from the hospital.

I had to admit that I was glad we'd be staying at an inn. Sleeping alone in the nun's cell last night had made me realize just how much I'd grown to rely on Hugo. He made me feel safe and protected; a shield against the cruel and senseless world beyond the walls. He'd been true to his word and never touched me inappropriately, but I was deeply aware of him as he rested next to me, his lean body warm and strong beside me.

I wasn't sure exactly when the realization had hit me, but I suddenly knew that I trusted him body and soul—something that I couldn't say of anyone I'd ever known before, not even my parents. Especially not my parents. Hugo had risked everything to save me and had been willing to commit murder against a man who had laid a hand on me.

A buried memory had come floating to the surface as we rode through the verdant countryside in the early afternoon. I'd suppressed it because I couldn't bear to think about it, but it suddenly popped out of nowhere, underlining the difference between Hugo and the man I thought I'd loved.

Evan and I had gone to see a show in the West End. It was a mediocre show with a thin plot and forgettable score, but it had been a lovely summer evening, and we were happy and in love. We'd only been dating a few months and, at that point, Evan was everything I'd always thought I wanted in a man: smart, ambitious, and very attractive. We decided to walk back to his flat and maybe stop for a drink somewhere along the way. The streets were still crowded at that time of night, and London had never appeared as magical to me as it did on that evening. We stopped at a pub, planning to get only a beer, but realized we were both starving and stayed for a late supper. It was well after midnight by the time we finally left and continued our walk.

The crowds had vanished, leaving in their wake a few passersby, who either walked unhurriedly arm in arm, or trotted at a brisk pace to get to where they were going. A nearly empty bus rumbled past us and several taxis slowed down in the hope of a fare. Evan put his arm around me and drew me to him as he kissed my temple. It was such a romantic gesture that I wrapped my arms around him and kissed him right there in the middle of the street, completely oblivious to the people around us.

We were only a few streets away from Evan's building when a young punk came toward us out of a shadowed doorway. By now, we were alone on the street, the lights not quite reaching that particular stretch of pavement. The boy couldn't have been more than sixteen, but he held a knife in his hand,

and his eyes were glazed in a way that suggested that he was high as a kite.

"Give me your wallet, guv, and no one gets hurt," he growled, inching closer. The boy's hand shook slightly, whether from drugs or from fear, but he advanced on us, ready to strike.

I didn't expect Evan to take him on or play the hero. No amount of money was worth a possible injury or death. The credit cards could be easily replaced, as could the cash, but not as easily replaced as my faith in Evan. As he fumbled in his pocket for his wallet, he took a discreet step back, putting me between him and our assailant. The boy had hardly looked at me before, but now I was directly in his line of vision, and he ordered me to empty out my purse.

He grabbed Evan's wallet and extracted whatever cash he could find before flinging it back in his face. My purse would be more difficult, since he'd have to lower the knife to open the clasp and look for my wallet.

"Take the money out," he barked.

I had only twenty pounds on me, but he yanked it greedily out of my hand before giving us a mock bow and making a run for it. He disappeared into the darkness within moments, but Evan stood rooted to the spot, afraid to move. He didn't ask me if I was all right or offer any comfort.

"He could have killed me," was all that Evan said as we finally walked away.

I guess I should have known then that Evan would always put himself first, but I was too naïve and too infatuated to clearly see the man that he was.

I smiled to myself now as I imagined what Hugo's reaction might have been. He would have made minced meat of that kid. The punk would be paying Hugo to let him go and not the other way around.

I snuck a peek at Hugo as he jumped off the horse and gently pulled Jem into his arms. I had no doubt that whatever

Hugo had whispered in Jem's ear had to do with food. The boy would sell his soul for a sweetie and Hugo had probably promised him a feast, complete with a jam tart or syllabub for dessert. I could see the hungry look in Jem's eyes as he looked toward the inn. He'd have a soft bed all to himself as well.

I wasn't sure if Jem even noticed, but Hugo kissed the top of his head as he held Jem close, his face softened by the light from the window and the love he obviously felt for the boy. I suddenly envied the child in his arms, wishing that just a little of that love could be directed at me. The realization made me feel vulnerable and suddenly very lonely. I was a woman alone in a world where no one loved me.

THIRTY-FOUR

The inn was practically a five-star hotel by seventeenth-century standards. It was probably full on market day, but being midweek, the innkeeper was able to offer us his best rooms and a supper that would have put any fine cook to shame. We had roasted partridge and a flaky pastry filled with wild mushrooms in cream sauce. There were also roasted potatoes, and a cucumber salad made with dill and a dressing of vinegar and oil. I would have eaten boiled mutton with a hunk of bread, having had nothing since morning, but this was a feast for the senses.

I smiled as Jem tucked into his jam tart, licking his lips and fingers when he'd finished, so as not to miss a single crumb. He looked much better after having eaten, but his eyes were heavy with fatigue, and despite trying to stay upright, he was leaning heavily against Archie, who was still grumbling about Jem not sharing his tart.

"I'll take him up," Hugo said as Jem's eyes finally fluttered closed and stayed that way.

"I'll do it," Archie volunteered. "You just finish your meal, Your Lordship." He scooped up Jem as gently as if he were a newborn babe and carried him upstairs to bed.

I was ready to go upstairs myself. The innkeeper's wife promised me some hot water, so I excused myself and left the men below to drink and dice. They needed to unwind after the tension of the past two days, and I was glad to see that Hugo opted to stay with them.

A young girl, possibly the daughter of the house, brought me two pitchers of steaming water, and I took advantage of my bounty to wash my hair and then scrub down every inch of my grubby skin. I would have killed for a shower, but in seventeenth-century terms, this was the next best thing aside from an actual bath. At least I was warm and clean.

I put on my nightdress, poked up the fire, and sat in a chair by the hearth to dry my hair. It was nice to have a bit of solitude after a day spent with the men, but I found myself feeling anxious and depressed. Any time I was alone, the magnitude of my situation began to overwhelm me, but now the direction of my thoughts had shifted, focusing more on Hugo and what would happen to him after I left—if I actually left.

Max had never told me exactly when Hugo vanished, but I knew it would be sometime soon. What was going to happen to him? I thought frantically. I couldn't bear the thought of him dying. He was so young, so strong, and so passionate about his cause. It was unfair that his life should be snuffed out so soon. I only hoped that whatever happened was quick, and he didn't suffer. I knew he'd take whatever came as stoically as he did everything, but there was only so much pain a man could stand before he broke, physically and mentally.

My thoughts were interrupted by a soft knock on the door. Hugo came in, a trifle worse for wear, and locked the door behind him. He wasn't drunk, but his normally controlled demeanor was somewhat more relaxed, his posture less rigid as he leaned against the door, taking me in as I rose to greet him. He was staring at me in a way he hadn't done before, and I belatedly realized that the leaping flames behind me made my nightie nearly see-through, illuminating my body in a rosy glow and giving Hugo a tantalizing preview of what lay beneath.

He didn't budge from his spot by the door, but his eyes drank me in, leaving me in no doubt that he found me desirable. The thought made me giddy, suddenly glad of the fire's unexpected bonus. I wanted him to say something, but he just stood there, rooted to the spot, a look of anguish suddenly creasing his face.

"Hugo, is something wrong?"

"You might say that," he replied, finally coming to life and removing his coat. He sat down to pull off his boots, but his eyes never left my face as he peeled off his stockings and tossed them to the floor.

"Well, what is it?" A few hundred horrible scenarios raced through my brain as I waited for him to answer, but he didn't rush to reply, instead looking away for a moment as if deciding how much to tell me. "Hugo?" I didn't mean to sound harsh, but my voice was laced with strain. What had happened in the short time I was upstairs?

Hugo finally turned toward me, his face alerting me to the fact that he was about to come clean. He'd decided to tell me whatever was on his mind, and I braced myself for the impact.

"After Catherine left me, I didn't care that I couldn't marry again; I didn't want to. She was the love of my life, the only woman I had ever wanted by my side. I suppose her betrayal should have cooled my love, but I wanted her all the more, choosing to believe that she still loved me and had been forced to leave me against her will. I believed it still when I heard that our child had died, and when she gave birth to a healthy son by another man. But, in time, my heart knew the truth. She never loved me the way I loved her. She married me because she was intrigued by me, but her feelings weren't strong enough for her to defy her father. She simply married someone else and made a life with him."

I nodded in understanding, feeling that no comment was necessary. Drink obviously brought out Hugo's maudlin side, and he just needed to talk to someone of his loss. Knowing what I knew of him, he'd probably kept it all bottled up for a decade, choosing to bury his pain rather than confront it.

When I didn't reply, Hugo continued.

"I've been alone for ten years. There were several mistresses, but I never loved them, and eventually they moved on to men who could give them what they craved. And now, when my life is nearing its conclusion, you appear to me as if out of thin air, and suddenly I want to live. I want to live more than I've wanted to live in ten years, because now I have something to lose. Only, it's too late, isn't it?"

I finally understood what he was telling me, and my heart nearly burst. He was declaring his love, and asking me to tell him that maybe there might be another outcome to the future I foretold, but what could I say? I wanted him to live more than words could say, but despite my professed "Sight," I had no idea what was about to befall him. But we had this moment, and it was unbearably beautiful, more so because we both knew it couldn't last.

I walked over to him and gazed directly into his dark eyes. He didn't say a word, but the emotions that played over his face told me everything I needed to know. He was smoldering, but beneath the heat of desire, there was vulnerability, apprehension about the uncertain future that lay before him, and fear of rejection. He'd bared his soul to me, and I could either accept his precious gift or reject it and leave him to face whatever was coming alone.

I reached up and cupped his cheek, and the relief on his face made me catch my breath. How could I have thought his man arrogant and vain? The thought flickered in my mind as I pulled him to me, brushing my lips against his.

Hugo's kiss was soft and tender, filled with a longing that

left me breathless. He wasn't just kissing me, he was asking for my consent, and I gave it wholeheartedly, melting against him as he pulled me closer, the kiss deepening and turning from tenderness to passion. All my reservations and insecurities fled as I felt the force of Hugo's desire and his overwhelming need for me. There was no going back now, and I had no wish to. Whatever happened, I wanted this as much as he did. There'd be a price to pay, there always was, but whatever it was going to be, I was determined to have this moment, and this man.

Hugo stood back and pulled my nightdress over my head, leaving me exposed to his hungry gaze. With Evan, I often felt self-conscious, but this time there was no embarrassment. Hugo looked at me not like a man who was searching for flaws, but like a man who wanted to worship every part of me, no matter how imperfect. He saw me as a whole, not a sum total of my parts.

I unlaced the ties of his shirt and pulled it over his head. His chest was smooth and warm under my hands, his stomach flat and taut as I moved my hand downward to unlace his breeches. This was unspeakably brazen behavior for the time, but I didn't care. I wanted him as much as he wanted me, and it was only fair to let him know that. I was no simpering seventeenth-century virgin. I was a grown woman who knew her own mind, and I was going to do this on my own terms.

"Not yet," Hugo murmured as he lifted me off my feet and laid me on the bed as if it were an altar and I was an offering to the gods. He gently pushed my hands away as I reached for him, instead pinning my wrists above my head and kissing me hard, his pelvis grinding against mine.

I wrapped my legs around his waist in order to spur him on, but he wasn't about to just take me and be done with it. He bent his head to my breasts and suckled each nipple in turn, while his hand slid between my legs, stroking and probing until I was panting with desire. I could feel his hard length against my thigh, but Hugo pulled back once again as I tried to take hold of him.

"I've dreamed of doing this since I first saw you," he whispered to me as he slid lower and pushed my legs apart. All coherent thought fled from my brain as I felt his tongue inside me, his thumb caressing the sensitive bit of flesh just above slowly and deliberately as I arched my back in ecstasy. Hugo's tongue followed the path of his thumb as his fingers slid inside me, making my legs bounce on the bed with mounting tension.

"Hugo, please," I begged. "I can't take it anymore."

He didn't reply, just slid back up and plunged into me in a way that made me cry out with exquisite pain. He began to move, my hips rising beneath his, urging him to go faster and harder until my body finally let go of all control and shuddered with unbearable pleasure. Hugo followed a few seconds later, allowing himself release now that he'd satisfied me. He rested his forehead on my shoulder, breathing hard as his heart rate began to slow down, and he grew softer inside my body.

I wrapped my arms around Hugo and held him close as he kissed me lightly, his eyes mere inches from mine. "You are mine, now and forever, and I swear that I will love you till my dying breath."

"I love you too," I murmured as silent tears slid down my cheeks.

THIRTY-FIVE

Gossamer fingers of sunshine reached through the unshuttered windows and caressed everything in their path, a golden haze settling on the bed. I stretched, smiled at the memory of last night, and promptly blushed, recalling some of the more intimate moments. I felt unusually languid, reluctant to get out of bed and start the day, but as wakefulness returned, the enormity of what I had done came crashing over me like a ton of bricks. Perhaps Hugo had experienced the same rush of panic, since his side of the bed was empty and cold, as cold as my heart suddenly grew.

Last night had been magical, but in the harsh light of day, I realized that I'd opened a Pandora's Box by acknowledging my feelings for Hugo and being weak enough to actually act on them. What was I supposed to do now? The plan had always been to make my escape as soon as we got back to Everly Manor, but how could I just walk out on Hugo without any explanation? I'd seen the vulnerability in his eyes, and knew the pain he'd been through and was yet to experience, so how could I just break his heart that way? Despite my growing love for Hugo, I'd always known I'd go back. There was never any doubt, but now the seeds had been sown, and I had to confront some very difficult questions, especially in view of what I knew would happen.

It was mid-April, and the Bloody Duke of Monmouth, damn his eyes, would be landing in England to stage his rebellion in less than two months' time. Between now and then, something terrible would befall Hugo, and I would either be far away in my own time when it happened or right there beside him, watching helplessly as the man I loved was torn away from me. And then what? Could I do anything to help him? Could I in any way prevent whatever it was that was about to occur? And if I couldn't, could I just return to my old life as if nothing had happened? How could I? Everything had changed, and, truth be told, there was no one waiting for me back home; a thought that I'd tried to push away ever since I'd got here. Apart from my job, which I'd no doubt lost by now, there were no pieces of my life to pick up. I had no family and few friends. Evan had been the center of my existence, but the thought of him made me angry and bitter, mostly with myself for wasting time on a man who didn't deserve my love or my grief.

I hadn't known Hugo for long, but I knew deep in my soul that he was as solid as they came; a man who would die before he would betray his principles or his family. Hugo was worthy of my love, but was I worthy of his? Had he bolted this morning before I woke up, sick with the realization that he'd made a terrible mistake? What did he know of me or my origins? What could he think of a woman who just threw herself at him without so much as a thought for the future? Of course, I knew that a future was impossible, but a man of his time would know the price of loving. A man either had a mistress or a wife, or possibly both, but took responsibility for his women. And the women did not give themselves lightly; they negotiated their surrender, making sure that they weren't left used up and destitute when their lover grew tired of them.

I had asked for nothing and promised nothing in return, and now I had no idea where I stood. All I knew was that if Hugo regretted last night, I'd be devastated, my heart torn to shreds after feeling the unbearable heat of his love.

Sitting up, I wrapped my arms around my legs, resting my head on my knees. I felt wretched and confused; the afterglow of last night long gone and the reality bitter as ashes on my tongue. I wanted to cry, but the tears wouldn't come. I was physically and mentally holding myself together, knowing that if I finally gave vent to my emotions, I might not be able to regain control. I knew that I should wash, dress, and make my way downstairs, but I simply couldn't face whatever was waiting for me when I got there. I wanted to hide, and this was as good a place as any.

I was so enveloped in my misery that I hardly heard the door open, and only looked up with a start as a bunch of daffodils appeared in my peripheral vision. Hugo was standing by the bed; the flowers frozen in his hand as he took in my expression. I must have looked haunted because he set the bouquet aside and sat down on the bed, searching my face for clues.

"I'm sorry, Neve," he finally said quietly, confirming my suspicions. He was sorry about last night, and he'd bought me a bunch of flowers to soften the blow. I felt as if a dull knife had been driven into my gut, twisting and turning and leaving total carnage in its path. I couldn't breathe, couldn't think. All I wanted was to get away from his soft gaze and his warm hands, which took my frozen ones and were rubbing some heat into them.

"There's no need to be sorry," I finally managed. "I will leave as soon as we return to Cranley. You need not worry. I expect nothing from you."

I risked a glance at Hugo's face. He was white to the roots of his hair, his eyes huge with shock.

"I don't take your meaning," he finally stammered.

"Isn't that what you want? You just said as much. You are sorry for last night," I mumbled, suddenly unsure.

Hugo just drew me to him and rested his chin on my head. "You foolish girl," he said, stroking my back. "That's not what I meant at all. I only meant that I was sorry I wasn't here when you woke up. I couldn't sleep and went for a walk along the canal. I needed to think."

"I thought you might," I replied, waiting for the axe to fall. He had to have been thinking along the same lines as me.

I pulled away from him so that I could see his face. I needed to. Whatever he was about to say wasn't going to be easy for him, but I needed to let him say it. He deserved that much, and I wouldn't interrupt.

"Neve, after you fell asleep last night, I just lay here, watching you. I'd forgotten what it's like to be happy, and the feeling took me utterly by surprise. I was so wound up, I couldn't sleep. All I wanted to do was wake you up and have you tell me again that you love me."

"Is that all you were thinking?" I asked suspiciously.

"No, not quite. I was thinking that I have no right to ask for your love when I can't offer you either security or the protection of my name. I was so sure that my cause was just, but if what you say is true, then everything I'm doing is in vain. If Monmouth wins, we'll have a Protestant king. If Monmouth loses, as you predict he will, William of Orange will eventually take the throne, and we'll have a Protestant king. I believe in what I'm doing, but I'm not fool enough to just throw away my life for nothing."

"Hugo, what are you getting at?"

"After you went up last night, I sent Archie on an errand, and he returned this morning with a message from the Duke of Norfolk. The rebellion is imminent; I have done what I set out to do. Remember what you said to me when you came to warn me? You said I should sail for France. I wasn't prepared to listen to you then, but I will listen to you now. I still have time to get away, but I will only go if you come with me. We can be married in France and start our life together." He looked so hopeful, it nearly broke my heart.

"Hugo, you know I'm not Catholic," I gently reminded him.

"Yes, I know." He didn't say anything more, but that was enough. He was prepared to marry a Protestant. That was a huge sacrifice for him and showed me the depth of his love for me.

"Do you really want me that much, Hugo?"

"I want you that much. And I would gladly prove it to you this minute if I didn't have Jem waiting for me downstairs. I'm taking him to the hospital."

"Is he worse?" I asked, alarmed. Jem had seemed so much better last night that I'd allowed myself to think that all would be well. If Jem suffered any lasting effects, it would all be down to me and my confrontation with Lionel Finch. I couldn't bear the thought of that little boy being hurt because of my own stupidity.

"No, no," Hugo reassured me as he saw my panicked face. "Jem is in fighting spirit this morning and still reminiscing about the jam tart in the hope that I'll get him another. I just want to be sure that he's recovering well before we leave Guilford. There's no qualified medical man anywhere near Cranley, so if Jem requires any treatment, this is the place to receive it. We shan't be long."

Hugo gave me a lingering kiss, which made me wish he wasn't in such a hurry. He reluctantly drew away and gave me a stern look.

"And please, don't rush to any conclusions while I'm gone. Neve, I don't give my love and take it away a few hours later. That's not the kind of man I am, and I know you know that. I realize you have fears, but where there's life, there's hope, and I prefer to believe that we have some say in our destiny. I'm not a marionette who dances to the bidding of its master. I will decide what happens to me, and I've decided to live."

"I'm glad to hear it. Hurry back," I called after him as he closed the door softly behind him.

Perhaps Hugo was right. About an hour ago, I felt as if my world had come crashing down on me, but now, despite my reservations, a flicker of hope was shining like a beacon through the darkness, our future still unknown, but perhaps a little less grim. I only hoped that Jem was all right, and that was one less thing we had to worry about.

I had no watch, but judging by the bright light pouring through the window it was already midmorning. I finally got out of bed and opened the window to let in some fresh air. Sounds of activity instantly filled the room; men calling to each other from their boats on the canal, water lapping gently at the sides as they rowed steadily, the boats filled with anything that needed transporting. The innkeeper was loudly arguing with someone in the yard, a loaded wagon stacked with barrels just beneath my window and smelling strongly of hops awaiting unloading once the argument was settled. His wife, ignoring the ruckus in the yard, was hanging out some washing on a line behind the stables and taking advantage of the fine weather to dry her laundry quickly.

I washed my face and hands, brushed my teeth with a willow twig, did up my hair, dressed, and made my way downstairs. The dining area was deserted, most people having eaten already and either gone about their business or departed the inn for good. The publican's wife beamed as she saw me and invited me to sit down at a table by the window, overlooking the busy canal.

"Good morning to you, Mistress Ashley," she called out as she wiped her hands on a rag, "I was just hanging out some washing," she explained, obviously eager for a chat. "Can I offer you some porridge and a cup of ale?"

She saw my look of dismay at the mention of porridge. I'd always hated it, doubly so since I'd been forced to eat it nearly every morning for the past two weeks. It was either soupy and bland or thick and gluey from being reheated so many times.

"Might there be anything else, Mistress... eh?" I asked timidly, belatedly realizing I didn't know the woman's name.

"Fanny is my name," she replied, dimpling at me. "I'm not a one for the porridge either," the woman confided, giving me a sympathetic nod. "Does a trick on my bowels, it does, every time. Why, I can barely make it to the privy in time."

That was way more information than I needed, but I nodded in understanding, knowing exactly what she was referring to.

"How about I make you a nice egg? Would you like that?"

"Oh, thank you, Fanny. I'd like that very much," I gushed, eager for something that wasn't oats. Now, if I could only get a cup of tea, I would be in absolute heaven. I could see why tea had been such a success once it'd been introduced to the masses. Drinking warm, bitter ale first thing in the morning didn't compare to a soothing, fragrant cup of strong tea with some sugar and a splash of milk. And toast. What I wouldn't give for a piece of toast.

Fanny was as good as her word. She brought me a plate of eggs scrambled in bacon grease, a piece of cold pork and a thick slice of bread, liberally buttered and still warm. I could have kissed her.

"You enjoy it, love," she said. "I'm just in the kitchen if you need me. Making a tart for the young master," she said with an indulgent smile. "He's a sweet little lad. Lord Everly was ever so particular about having it ready for him. 'He must have a treat,' he said. It's nice to see him take such an interest," she sighed, conveying that most people didn't, especially in those less fortunate and of questionable birth. "Is there something wrong with him then?" she asked, eager for gossip. "I washed out that bandage for him as his lordship asked."

"He had a nasty fall and hit his head against the wall."

"Poor mite. Well, if anyone will sort him out it's the medicks at the hospital. I hear they practice all sorts of strange methods of healing. Goes against God, if you ask me. But they take care of the elderly—something most folk don't care to bother with. Once you're no longer useful, you might as well be dead, I always tell my husband. So, he'd better be useful to me for a good, long while." She gave me a meaningful smile and finally departed for the kitchen, leaving me to eat in peace.

I was just finishing my breakfast when Archie came strolling through the door. "Good morning, Mistress. Hungry this morning, are you?" he asked, giving me a grin that spoke volumes. "And his lordship running around looking for fresh flowers at the crack of dawn. My, I do wonder what you fine folk get up to when we are not looking."

I knew he was teasing me, but I blushed scarlet, confirming his suspicions.

"No longer a mistress in name only?" Archie inquired, enjoying my discomfort. So, he'd guessed.

I wondered if Peter and Arnold knew as well, but somehow, I doubted it. They didn't seem like the type to question what they'd been told, nor would they care. They were like a team of oxen: strong, immovable, and indifferent to their surroundings.

"Not much gets past you, does it, Archie?"

"No, ma'am. I keep my eyes open, unlike some people," he replied, clearly referring to the other two. "I'm glad to see his lordship happy. Can I have a cup of ale, my beauty?" he called out to Fanny as she came bustling out of the kitchen.

She blushed to the roots of her hair, flattered by the compliment. A beauty she wasn't, but she had a pleasant face and a warm smile which bordered on suggestive as she took in the young man before her. The change in her was instantaneous. Fanny arched her back, which instantly lifted her breasts and made her look thinner and more graceful, put her hand on her hip, and gazed at Archie from under her abundant lashes.

I glanced back at Archie, who was sizing up Fanny with as much desire as I had just displayed for my eggs and bacon. Archie noticed my stare and winked at me; his meaning clear. If he hadn't bedded Fanny already, he was likely to do so before the day was out.

"Oh, go on with you. It's on the house," Fanny said as she reached for a cup.

Archie put away his coin, drained his ale, and turned back to Fanny, holding out the empty cup. "I just can't seem to get enough. Perhaps you can bring me another cup to the stables. I've been out all night on an errand for his lordship and fancy a kip."

"If needs must," Fanny replied, her answer shining from her eyes as she watched Archie saunter from the room.

I smiled into my cup, amazed by the ease with which the transaction took place. It was interesting to see that people hooked up in pubs since time immemorial.

I was distracted from the mating rituals of seventeenth-century England by the appearance of Jem, closely followed by Hugo.

"No running," Hugo called out as Jem catapulted into the kitchen, eager for the promised treat.

"Wash your hands," I called out after him, "and you, too," I said to Hugo, who looked surprised, but promptly went back out into the yard to wash his hands.

"How's Jem?" I asked.

"On the mend. He must avoid exertion and sudden movements. They gave me a tonic to be given at bedtime." Hugo held up a vial containing a murky liquid that looked highly questionable.

"What's in it?"

"Some herbs mixed with laudanum, I expect. The medick said it would tranquilize the mind and restore the natural balance of Jem's humors." In other words, the tonic would induce sleep, which would allow Jem's brain time to heal if there were any lasting effects of the concussion. I supposed that wasn't bad medical advice for the time. I just hoped Hugo wouldn't give the child too much.

"Does this mean we are ready to return to Everly Manor?"

"Yes, but our progress will be slow since Jem must avoid any jarring movements, such as trotting or galloping, but we must be back in time for Easter."

Hugo planted a sweet kiss on the top of my head and turned to leave.

"Where are you going?"

"To the stables to speak to Archie. I have a question or two that need answering," he replied.

"You might want to wait a half-hour," I advised him with an innocent smile. "I think Archie might be occupied at the present."

Hugo's lips spread into a knowing smile. "You'd think a sleepless night would deter him, but I suppose you can't keep a good man down," he said, chuckling as he went out.

THIRTY-SIX

The journey back to Everly Manor took several days—days during which I was surprisingly happy. The possibility of pursuit seemed less likely, and the tender new romance between Hugo and I left me feeling hopeful and giddy. Perhaps we did have some say in our future, and now that I was here with Hugo, he might not vanish at all, but remain at Everly Manor and grow old with me. I felt a twinge of pity for Max, since this turn of events might interfere with his future, but there was nothing I could do. I didn't suppose I could change any major historical events, but maybe I could change the history of one man and his family.

I smiled as I caught Hugo looking at me. It gave my heart a lift to see him happy. I hadn't realized how gruff and controlled he'd been until I saw this new, unexpected side of him; a side that made me want to jump off my horse right there and then and drag him into the woods for a half-hour of much-needed privacy. I felt as if my whole body was aflame, every nerve ending zapping with electricity and turning me into a conduit of the current that passed between us.

Hugo hadn't said anything to the men, but, of course, he

didn't need to. They saw the change right away and didn't miss an opportunity to make seemingly innocent comments loaded with double entendre. I thought Hugo might get angry, but he seemed amused, enjoying the camaraderie of our little party. Jem was back on his mule, his little face relaxed, and at times perplexed, as he sensed that something beyond his understanding had shifted among the adults.

The next hurdle would be Jane. Her son was Hugo's heir, so she might not look kindly upon a woman who might change that, but, then again, I saw genuine love between Hugo and Jane, so she might be pleased to see that her brother was happy.

The shadow of the coming rebellion hovered just over my shoulder, but I tried not to dwell on it, even though the wheels had already been set in motion. Only yesterday, April 17, a meeting had taken place in Amsterdam in which the Earl of Argyll had been appointed captain-general of the invading army that was due to sail for Scotland within two weeks. Their enterprise would be doomed, plagued by one setback after another, until the Earl of Argyll would find himself cornered, arrested, and subsequently executed, but, as of today, none of the perpetrators knew of the horrible fate that awaited them within the next two months.

Monmouth himself would land in Dorsetshire in mid-June and be executed by mid-July, the whole rebellion, which would start out with great momentum and buoyant hope petering out in less than a month and ending with bitter disappointment for everyone who threw their lot in with the Protestant hopeful. Hugo was already implicated, by virtue of trying to garner support for the rebellion, but if he failed to join Monmouth's forces in the West Country in June, he still had a hope of escape, which I was betting on. I told Hugo as much as I could without arousing his suspicion by giving exact dates and names, but some of my predictions had already been verified by none other than Norfolk himself, who'd written to Hugo, informing him of the latest developments.

For now, the plan was to get back to Everly Manor in time for Easter, which fell on April 22. Hugo, Jane, Clarence and all the servants and tenants would attend the Protestant service at St. Nicolas on Sunday morning. The service would be followed by an Easter dinner for the Protestants and a second service for the Catholics, where a Catholic priest would perform a clandestine Easter Mass at a private chapel on the Nash estate for the immediate family and their guests. I wasn't at all sure what the correct code of conduct would be for someone like me, who was an honorary member of the family, but not of the same religion. I thought it might be more tactful for me to stay back, but the expression on Hugo's face told me otherwise. He expected me to attend, particularly since he planned to introduce me to his closest friend and announce our plans for departure.

I was strangely apprehensive when I saw the towers of Everly Manor come into view. As long as we were on the road, the situation seemed manageable, but now that we were returning, anything could happen. I stole a peek at Hugo as he spotted his home. He seemed calm, but I could see the tension in his jaw as he stopped for a moment and just gazed at the solid old house sitting proudly on the ridge. The late-afternoon sun lit up the mullioned windows in a brilliant shade of crimson; the light shifting and writhing like a living thing and giving the impression of leaping flames devouring the house from the inside. It was an eerie image, one that would stay with me for years to come. I wasn't someone who believed in omens, but the fiery appearance of the place gave me a bad turn.

Hugo gave me a reassuring smile as we galloped toward the house, eager to be home at last, and just before Good Friday.

THIRTY-SEVEN

Being at Everly Manor this time around felt completely different. I was no longer a prisoner kept against my will by a suspicious man, but a welcome guest, one who was held in high regard by the entire household. Jane was overjoyed to see us back and noticeably tried to seek out my company; whether she wanted to forge a closer bond with me or test my feelings for her brother, I had yet to determine. She was at times warm and forthcoming, and at times reserved and distant, watching me from under her hooded eyes as if deciding if I were worthy of her trust. I wasn't sure how she would feel about Hugo's intentions toward me, since Hugo kept our forthcoming marriage a secret for the time being, allowing Jane to believe that I was his mistress, but I could tell that she genuinely loved her brother and wished to see him happy.

Hugo, on the other hand, was a mass of contradictions. He'd spent several hours locked in his study after we'd returned, plowing through his correspondence, writing numerous letters to his compatriots, and generally wearing out the floorboards in the room. I suppose he still hoped that my prophecies were wrong, but I knew that deep down he believed everything I said, especially about the future of Catholicism in England. The rebellion was only a few weeks away, and as much as I tried not to dwell on it, it was constantly in my thoughts. I was a half-mile away from the church and the bridge to my old life, but my desire to escape had cooled despite the terrible doubts that plagued me day and night. For the first time in my life, I was truly torn, my brain and heart constantly at odds over the destiny I was about to choose.

As I strolled through the garden on a glorious April morning, surrounded by budding rose bushes and the lush new greenery of spring, I couldn't help reflecting on the strange nature of reality. I'd lived in the future my entire life, and I desperately missed the creature comforts of the twenty-first century, as well as the more liberal attitudes and availability of information, but after spending nearly two months in this world, I felt as if my former life was but a dream. The things that had been so important to me, like my job, my friends, and, previously, my relationship with Evan, seemed like a long-forgotten dream that dissipated with the bright light of day.

I didn't miss the fast pace of city life, or the constant merry-go-round that was my life in the twenty-first century. There were no blaring televisions everywhere I went, no music pumped through speakers in every store, restaurant and pub, no constant checking of my phone for emails, messages, and the latest news. There was no rush to be anywhere or make a deadline. I'd come to realize over the past few weeks that most of my modern relationships were transient, built on common experiences or work commitments. It'd been a long time since anyone had shown a real interest in me and took the time to get to know the person underneath.

Having the benefit of hindsight, I realized that even my relationship with Evan had been devoid of depth. We'd started out much like any other couple, giving in to attraction and getting to know each other, but within a few months, real life had set in, and we'd had to make time to see each other and connect. Evan was a busy man who could rarely turn the world off for any length of time. He was ambitious and hardworking, which left little time for me. I, in turn, had my own job, and filled my free hours with pursuits which Evan had no interest in. I went to art galleries, foreign films, and often took day trips into the country, all the while telling myself that Evan simply didn't have the time to do these things with me.

I hadn't realized how lonely I really was at a time when I was in a new relationship and should have been walking on air. Perhaps that's why I had wanted the baby so badly. I wanted someone to love; someone who would love and need me for more than a few hours a day. Evan might have loved me in his own way, but he certainly didn't need me any more than he needed his daughter. He needed success and the recognition of his peers, not the demands of emotional females.

When I'd first met Hugo, I'd thought him an arrogant, chauvinistic specimen of seventeenth-century manhood, but over the past few weeks, I'd discovered the man underneath. Hugo didn't love many, but he loved passionately. His devotion to a girl who had left him after two weeks of marriage, his need to protect his sister from ruin, his desire to leave his estate to his nephew rather than the closest male relative were all signs of a man who took his obligations very seriously. I'd come to realize that Hugo had utterly lowered his defenses after our night together, letting me go where no one but Catherine had gone before. He would die for me, and kill for me, if necessary, but, most of all, he would live for me, which is what I wanted above all else.

But did my dissatisfaction with my former life and my deep feelings for Hugo justify remaining in the seventeenth century and renouncing the only life I had known? I would be giving up much more than running water, electricity, or a night in front of the TV. I would be giving up centuries of enlightenment and

progress toward personal and political freedom, modern medicine, women's rights, and the ability to be independent,
remaining instead in a world where women were at the mercy
of men throughout every stage of their lives.

Was I prepared to marry and have children in a time when
scores of women died in childbirth, and where a simple infection could carry off a child within hours without the benefit of
antibiotics? Was I ready to sacrifice everything and everyone I
had known in my modern life?

The answer was no, but when weighed against sacrificing
Hugo, I was right back where I started. As I lay in bed next to
Hugo, hearing his even breathing as he peacefully slept, I imagined being back in my flat, going to work, and making plans
with friends who had to do backflips in order to carve out time
from their families and jobs to so much as meet me for a drink.

Was I prepared never to see Hugo again? Once more, the
answer was no.

I was aware of Hugo in a way that I could only call primal.
My body seemed to feel him before my mind even registered
that he was in the room, and I felt a hunger that seemed to grow
stronger with every passing day. I counted the minutes until we
could decently retire, knowing that Hugo would come to my
room and make love to me until I lost all ability to think and
could only feel and respond on the most primitive level. Did all
women feel this way when they met a man they were truly
compatible with, or was this something special, something given
only to a chosen few, perhaps ones who'd been denied love for
so long that they threw themselves into it in a way that left them
incomplete unless they were together?

I smiled to myself as I recalled a conversation we'd had on
the first night of our return. Hugo was still on top of me, sated
and spent, a smile of contentment on his lips as he'd kissed me
thoroughly. I took his face in my hands, subconsciously memo-
rizing his features. How much control did we have over what

was about to happen? Was there anything Hugo could do to prevent the inevitable?

"I'm still here," he'd said, smoothing my furrowed brow. He had an uncanny ability to read my mind, particularly at times when I wanted to keep my thoughts to myself.

"I'm scared for you, Hugo." I tried not to bring it up, but I couldn't help it. I knew what the future held, and the day of Hugo's disappearance was drawing closer.

"I know you are, which is why we will depart by the end of next week. I need to get my affairs in order and then we will just go. Have you ever been to France?"

I had, in 2010, on a week-long holiday. My French was rudimentary, but I thought I could probably get by until I learned to speak properly. I didn't care where we went, as long as we were safe.

"Will I be traveling as your mistress?" I had asked, striving for a coy tone, but sounding rather needy even to my own ears.

Hugo had just smiled at me and kissed me lightly on the tip of my nose. "Only until we reach Paris. Then, we will find a place to settle, and I will get down on one knee and beg you to be my wife. What do you think of that idea?"

I knew he was teasing me, but suddenly, being his wife was the only thing I wanted in this world.

"Do you mean it?"

"I never say things I don't mean, at least not to you. I know you can see right through me. I have requested a copy of the document that declares my marriage to Catherine annulled. Once I have it, I will be free to marry you, and I can hardly wait." A dreamy expression had come over Hugo as he'd considered our future. I could guess what he was thinking about.

"You want a child, don't you?" I'd asked, seeing the answer in his eyes.

"I have never allowed myself to imagine what it would be like to have a child of my own," Hugo had said softly. "The idea of holding my son in my arms fills me with such longing, especially when I look at you and know that you will be his mother."

"And if we have a daughter?" I'd challenged him.

"Then I would love her with all my heart and protect her from anything and anyone who means her harm. No daughter of mine would ever be left to the mercy of some man." Hugo was still gazing deep into my eyes, a question forming on his lips. "Neve, I know you said you have no family, but isn't there anyone at all who should be informed that you are leaving with me? Will no one look for you?"

"No, there's no one," I'd answered flatly, and meant it.

THIRTY-EIGHT

It was a visit to the church that finally helped me come to terms with my decision. I'd walked there early on Saturday morning, hoping that it wouldn't be crowded on a day between Good Friday and Easter Sunday. I was right, and the building was deserted at such an early hour. I'd meant to walk straight up to the door to the crypt to test myself, but once I was halfway up the nave, my legs simply wouldn't carry me, turning to lead as I approached the moment of truth.

I sank into a pew and closed my eyes, trying to silence my thoughts and listen to the inner voice which came not from a place of logic, but from a much deeper, more primitive part of my brain, the part that never lied to me or had an agenda of its own. Did I just walk through that door and never look back, or did I walk out of that church, march back to Everly Manor and accept my new life without reservation?

I'd finally reached that state of inner silence when a voice at my elbow nearly scared me out of my wits. "Are you all right, child?" Reverend Snow asked, looking at me with concern. "You look troubled."

I opened my mouth to tell the reverend that I was perfectly

well and never more at peace with myself or the world, which was, of course, a blatant lie, when something entirely different came out of my mouth. I'd seen Reverend Snow only twice before, but he had a gentleness of manner and a sympathetic gaze that made him appear extremely approachable, particularly since he was no older than thirty.

"Reverend, do you ever feel lost?" I blurted out.

The look on Reverend Snow's face was one of such surprise that I was instantly sorry I'd said anything. This wasn't a modern-day clergyman who could admit to doubts and his own interpretation of "the word." This was a seventeenth-century cleric, who was most likely a zealot despite his kind demeanor. How could he possibly understand how bewildered I felt at that moment, torn between the logical solution put forth by my brain and the totally illogical one advocated by the heart?

"May I?" Reverend Snow asked as he gestured toward the pew.

I slid over and allowed him to take a seat next to me. I half expected a sermon, but the reverend rubbed the bridge of his nose and stared ahead for a moment, his eyes unseeing, before finally replying to my question.

"I feel lost more often than not," he said softly. "That is not an answer that my superiors would expect of me, but it's the truth. You'd think that being a man of the cloth would give me greater understanding or a deeper faith, but, if anything, at times it leaves me more baffled than most common men. You see, the average parishioner takes what I say on faith and believes that God has a greater plan, like a parent, punishing and rewarding as circumstances dictate. I, however, don't see it that way at all."

"How do you see it?" I asked, stunned by the heartfelt admission of a man who was supposed to lead his flock, not admit that he was wandering in the wilderness.

"When I was a young man attending the seminary, I

believed that when bad things happened, it was because the Lord saw fit to punish certain people for their transgressions or sacrifice others for the greater good. I was comfortable in my faith, and safe in my delusions. But then I was posted to a parish and came face to face not with doctrine, but with real people, and I realized that I could no longer accept that view. So, to answer your question, I feel lost every time I bury a young woman who has died in childbirth or visit the deathbed of a child who'd been in fine health only a few days ago but is now ready for the next world. I try to hold on to my faith, but I see no justice or wisdom in these pointless, random deaths, deaths that seemingly benefit no one and cause endless suffering to those left behind."

"So, how do you cope?" I asked, grateful for the man's honesty. I strongly suspected that a speech like the one he had just made would get him defrocked, if the term could be applied to a Protestant clergyman.

"I've come to understand that, in my arrogance, I try to interpret and judge the will of God, when my true purpose is to comfort, guide, and at times offer forgiveness. It's not for me to ask why, but it is for me to do everything I can to help those who rely on me. I try to live every single day in a way that makes my life meaningful, so, ultimately, I'm doing God's work." He smiled that disarming smile of his as he saw me nod in understanding. He hadn't been so much questioning God as questioning himself, and he came up with an answer that made his presence in this parish meaningful to him.

"Your parishioners are lucky to have you, Reverend Snow," I said, and meant it.

"You are my parishioner, are you not? So, tell me what's troubling you so?"

Of course, I couldn't tell him the truth, but talking to him had been comforting and oddly illuminating, so I decided that there was no harm in seeking his advice. "You see, Reverend, I find myself at a crossroads. If I go the way I originally intended, I will have safety, comfort, and most likely a much longer life span. However, if I go the other way, I will have uncertainty, possible danger, and might have to sacrifice many things that I've always taken for granted but which are important to me."

Reverend Snow gazed at me for a long minute while sizing up the situation. He opened his mouth to speak, closed it, glanced toward the Heavens as if looking for guidance, then finally turned back to me. "If I understand you correctly, the second alternative is as appealing to you as the first, or you wouldn't be torn, would you? So, what is it about a life of danger and uncertainty that is as appealing as one of safety and comfort? Surely, you are not telling me the whole truth."

Reverend Snow saw the panic on my face and held up his hand, in a gesture meant to stop me from speaking. "You don't wish to tell me, and that's quite all right. You are entitled to your privacy, my child. I will tell you this, however. Imagine your life already lived, a winding road that's mostly behind you as you walk the last steps toward your final destination. When you look back on the path you've traveled, which do you regret more, choosing an unpredictable, but eventful life, which clearly appeals to you or you wouldn't be here, or choosing a life of safety and predictability?"

I opened my mouth to reply, but the reverend patted my hand and rose to leave.

"Don't give me your answer. I don't need to know it, but considering the haste with which you were ready to reply, I can only assume that you knew the answer all along. God bless you, my dear, and I hope you never regret anything."

"Thank you, Reverend. I don't think I will."

I rose to my feet and walked out of the church into the April sunshine, as certain as anyone in my position could be of their decision.

* * *

Hugo was out when I got back, but Jane was perched on a settle in the sitting room, her crewel work on her lap, her gaze far away. She started as I walked into the room, picking up her work with the guilty air of one who'd been daydreaming.

"I can't seem to concentrate," she explained as she stabbed her needle into a flower.

"Jane, it's a lovely day outside. Why don't you join me for a walk in the garden? You hardly leave the house," I suggested gently. Jane seemed to have an aversion to the outdoors and spent most of her time either quietly sewing or quizzing poor Clarence on his academic progress. The boy was almost as pale as his mother, but certainly not for lack of trying to escape. He had a mischievous streak which I found endearing, especially since it made me wonder what Hugo had been like as a boy.

Jane looked as if she were about to refuse, but after glaring at her half-finished pattern seemed to change her mind. "Oh, all right. Just for a little while." She stowed away her embroidery, shut her work basket, and followed me outside into the garden with the air of one going to the gallows.

I usually preferred to walk toward the woods or into the village, but Jane seemed to like enclosed spaces, so the walled garden it was.

We walked in silence for a few moments, each lost in our own thoughts. There were many things I wanted to ask Jane but didn't want to overstep my bounds. My position within the household was an awkward one since I was neither wife nor just a guest.

"Will you stay on at the manor after we are gone?" I finally asked Jane. "Or will you return home?"

"I'd like to stay on," Jane replied. "This is my childhood home, you see, and it's full of good memories—unlike the house I spent most of my married life in."

"I thought you and Ernest were happy."

Jane didn't reply, just picked a flower and tore off the petals in a way that suggested some suppressed anger. "I ruined my life," she suddenly blurted out.

I was about to respond, but Jane turned away, embarrassed by her admission.

"Jane, you can talk to me, you know. I won't judge you."

"Won't you? Everyone else would if they knew the truth," she replied sadly. "And the truth is that I have no one to blame but myself. I haven't spoken of this to anyone, but I think I can tell you. You are my brother's mistress, a woman of flexible morals, so you might understand. You are not like the women I've been exposed to most of my life—rigid and only too eager to judge and condemn. May I confide in you?"

I wasn't sure that Jane hadn't just insulted me, but she seemed eager to talk, so I let the slight pass and invited her to sit on a bench in the shade of an ancient tree. It was pleasant and cool, but Jane seemed unable to relax. She sat on the edge of the bench as if sitting more comfortably might somehow make it impossible for her to speak.

"I was sixteen when I met George," she began. "He was the handsomest man I'd even seen—not that I'd seen very many. Father often brought Hugo to London with him, but I was always left behind, since he felt I was too young to be exposed to the intrigues of the Court. I didn't mind, really; I'd always liked my own company, and the time passed quickly. Hugo always told me stories of the Court when he came back and I enjoyed seeing it all in my mind's eye from a safe distance."

Jane grew quiet for a moment, no doubt remembering that safe and happy time. I just waited patiently until she spoke again.

"I knew George had been promised to someone else, but I was young and fancied myself in love, so I took a gamble and lost. I allowed him to seduce me, hoping that if I got with child, he would be forced to marry me. It would have been the honorable thing to do, but, alas, George refused. Turned out he wasn't a very honorable man."

Jane laughed bitterly before carrying on. Now that she was talking, she couldn't stop. She had to get her story out, and I strongly suspected that she'd never spoken to another female about any of this.

"Hugo blamed himself, you see, since he was the one who took me to London. He thought I would enjoy the entertainments at Court and the company of other women. He also hoped that I might catch someone's eye and make it easier for him to arrange a suitable match for me. Instead, he married me off to Ernest, so that I could keep my baby. Despite my foolishness, I did love George and couldn't bear to have my child taken away from me, which is what would have happened. I would have been confined to the country until the baby was born, and then the midwife would take it away and I would never see him again."

"He's a lovely boy," I said and was rewarded with a smile.

"Yes, he is. He looks much like his father."

"I thought your marriage to Ernest was a satisfactory one," I prompted, thinking back to all the things Jane had said about her husband. She seemed to have had genuine regard for him.

"I liked Ernest, and I was grateful to him for marrying me and accepting Clarence as his own, but he had his own reasons, you see. When we were first married, he never visited my chamber. I assumed that it was because I was with child and he found it distasteful, but he never came even after Clarence was born. He never consummated the marriage."

That was odd, especially since he'd been married before and had a child by his first wife. Could he have really been that disgusted by his wife who bore another man's child?

"In the beginning, I hinted that his attentions would be welcome, but he just smiled at me and retired to his own room.

He was always kind and respectful to me, but there was no intimacy between us, and he took no interest in Clarence or his daughter."

Jane grew quiet again, but her hand pleated the fabric of her skirt subconsciously, betraying her nervousness at revealing herself to me.

"Did he keep a mistress, Jane?" I asked carefully, not wishing to hurt her.

"Looking back, that would have been preferable, but there was no other woman. Ernest never really went out, at least not then."

Jane let go of her skirt and turned to face me, her eyes burning in her face with an emotion I couldn't quite name. I thought it might be defiance, but I wasn't sure.

"After two years of marriage, I decided to take action. I wanted another child, you see, but I also wanted a husband who cared for me. Ernest was just indifferent, and I thought I could make him love me if he saw me in that way. It'd been wonderful with George, and I thought that although it would never be like that, it would be better than nothing. So, I brushed out my hair, dabbed on a little scent, put on my prettiest nightdress and crept to Ernest's bedroom. He didn't even hear me open the door because he wasn't alone. I just stood there, frozen, watching my husband bugger his secretary, Mr. Spencer. After he'd finished, he kissed him most tenderly, and I realized that this must have been going on for some time. Ernest had what he needed and had married me to keep his secret and attain an heir. He wasn't the one who'd been duped; I was."

"Oh, Jane, I'm so sorry. It must have been awful for you," I said, taking her cold hand in mine. I wanted to offer her comfort, but I had no idea what to say.

"Oh, that wasn't the worst part," Jane said, smirking bitterly. "John Spencer died of syphilis a few years later. Have you ever known anyone who died of syphilis? It's a terrible way to go—

years of mental and physical deterioration until there's nothing left of the person, just a hollow shell, and a deranged mind. Ernest made sure his lover was cared for and comfortable until the end. He was devastated after Spencer died, not only because he had lost someone he loved, but possibly because he knew that he'd been infected as well. The physician never told me the truth of my husband's condition, but I knew. I couldn't even tell Hugo because I was too ashamed. Ernest begged for my forgiveness before he died, although his mind was mostly gone by then."

"And what of his daughter?"

"Oh, Magdalen wasn't his. His wife conceived after nearly a decade of marriage, and it certainly wasn't by Ernest. Magdalen was most likely the daughter of a groom or someone from the village. Can't say I blame the poor woman. She wanted a child, and she finally had one."

"Jane, Ernest is gone now, and you are still a young woman. You can marry again; it's not too late."

Jane just shook her head. "I'm thirty years old, Neve. I'm well past my childbearing years, and I don't ever want to be at the mercy of some man again. Ernest left me very comfortably off, so I plan to remain a widow and look after my son. Clarence needs me. I thought Hugo needed me too, but it seems he's got you now, although I still don't understand when all this came about."

I sensed her bitterness, but there wasn't much I could say. Someday Clarence would grow into a man and want a life of his own and Jane would find herself very lonely once again.

Jane sprang to her feet. "I must get back. Clarence will be finished with his Latin by now."

"I'll just stay out here a while longer."

Jane looked deeply embarrassed, but she smiled at me, and I could see that she felt some measure of relief at having told me her secret. "Thank you, Neve," she said. "It felt good to talk."

"You're welcome."

I watched Jane walk away, her back stiff and her gait steady. I wish I could have helped her, but I suppose getting things off her chest was as much help as she would accept. She was only a few years older than me, but she saw her life as being virtually over, which just seemed like a terrible waste. I sighed and left the garden, feeling suddenly suffocated by the stone walls.

THIRTY-NINE

Hugo accepted a cup of wine from Bradford and took a long swallow, thirsty after the gallop along the dusty road. Brad always had good wine, not like the swill they usually served at the taverns. It was good to see Brad again, and good to talk. Brad settled himself across from Hugo and listened carefully as Hugo recounted the events of the past few weeks, leaving nothing out. Brad shook his head in disbelief as Hugo finished and took another sip of wine, savoring the bouquet while waiting for him to comment.

"Well, my friend, you seem to have outdone yourself," Brad said with a sad smile. "The fact that Finch chose not to pursue you openly only suggests that he has other avenues of retribution in mind."

"Which is why I'm leaving England for a time. Brad, I have a favor to ask of you. Will you look after Jane? She's expressed a desire to remain at Everly Manor, so she might need a hand with the estate, as well as some company. You know what a recluse Jane can be. I'd feel better knowing that at least she had you and Beth."

"Of course, we'll look after her, but what of her own estate?"

"She has a competent man in place who can run things to her satisfaction until she decides to go back or send Clarence to run things. I don't think she ever means to go back."

"Shall we introduce her to some eligible bachelors once her mourning is at an end?" Bradford asked, giving Hugo a conspiratorial smile. "Jane can be a very eligible prospect for some man. She's still a handsome woman and has a large estate which produces a healthy income."

"Not unless she asks Beth to. Jane hasn't had a happy time of it, Brad, so I think she might enjoy being her own mistress for a time. I'd gone to visit Ernest before he died and had a word with his attending physician. Ernest died of syphilis, although Jane doesn't know."

"Syphilis?" Bradford repeated, gaping at Hugo. "Are you sure? I'd never thought Ernest was one for the whores. He hardly even went up to London, spent most of his time looking after his estate and conferring with that secretary of his—what was the fellow's name?"

"Spencer. John Spencer. Seems he died of syphilis as well. Perhaps they visited brothels together, who can say? I only hope that Jane's health hasn't been compromised. The illness takes years to show its symptoms and is usually not diagnosed until the later stages."

"I saw Jane only last week and she seemed to be in fine health. Don't worry, Hugo, syphilis is a man's disease," Brad stated, eager to reassure his friend.

"How can you say that when the brothels in London are rampant with it? The men get it from the whores, do they not? It likely kills as many people per year as the plague," Hugo replied, surprised by his friend's naiveté. Bradford rarely left Surrey, so perhaps he wasn't aware of the disease and squalor of London, comfortable and safe as he was on his estate.

"Perhaps you are right. I didn't think of it that way." Bradford set down his cup and ran his hand through his thick, fair hair—a sure sign that he wanted to discuss something with Hugo but didn't know how to broach the subject.

"What is it, Brad?" Hugo asked, bracing himself for whatever unpleasantness was to follow. Brad was a great friend, but he was also someone who never minced words, and, in Hugo's opinion, that was his greatest quality. Brad always told him the truth and forced him to take a good, long look at his choices. Hugo had a fairly good idea of what was coming.

"Have you told Jane that you mean to marry?" Bradford finally asked.

"No, not yet. I'll write to her after the deed is done."

"Why are you keeping it a secret from your sister? Could it be because you know she'll disapprove of you marrying some trollop who just happened to stagger into your life?" Bradford demanded, all pretense at diplomacy gone.

"Brad, you will not speak of my future wife in those terms. Ever!" Hugo's voice was low, but he was angry, and Brad knew it.

"Hugo, we've known each other far too long not to be truthful with each other. Only a few weeks ago, you were deeply suspicious of this woman and her motives, and now you are ready to make her your wife. Why? Just bed her and discard her when you grow tired of her. Why offer her marriage? What do you know of her? Who are her people? Where does she come from?"

Hugo was just about to answer, when a flustered servant burst into the room. The girl was no more than fifteen, and her eyes were round with excitement in her flushed face. "Master Nash, sir, it's time. The pains have started. The midwife bid me to inform you, sir," she added, nearly getting the message wrong.

The change in Brad was instantaneous. He was on his feet, desperate to go to his wife, but knowing that he wouldn't be admitted until it was all over. Already, there was the sound of running feet as the household prepared for the birth.

"Dear God, Hugo, I'm terrified for her. There's a part of me that just wants it to be over, but what if she doesn't come through? What if by this time tomorrow I have lost my Beth? And I haven't even seen her for weeks. I've only spoken to her through the door. Oh, I miss her, Hugo. What would I do without her?" Bradford's hands were shaking violently, his eyes haunted by fear for his wife.

"Shall we go for a ride?" Hugo asked, putting his arm around Bradford's shoulders. "It might do you good to be away from the house for a time."

"No, I can't leave. What if I'm needed? I'll just stay here until it's over. Will you wait with me?"

"Of course," Hugo replied as he poured a liberal amount of wine for his friend. "Here, have some wine. How about a game of chess then? You need something to focus your mind."

"Right. Chess," Bradford mumbled as the sharp voice of the midwife carried through the house, calling for fresh linens and hot water.

FORTY

I got up on Easter Sunday feeling tired and out of sorts. It was time to prepare for the Easter service, which I had no desire to attend, but had no choice about as church services were mandatory. Jane was already up, taking breakfast with Clarence and dressed in her customary mourning attire. Clarence looked miserable. A boy his age would be hanging out with his friends, playing computer games, and texting inappropriate things to girls in the twenty-first century, but in this time poor Clarence did little more than study with his tutor, sit with his mother, and occasionally escape the house for a ride through the countryside. The prospect of hours spent in church followed by a second service was probably as appealing as being drawn and quartered. I couldn't help feeling pity for him.

"Did you not sleep well?" Jane asked as she put down her spoon and eyed me suspiciously.

"I was listening for Hugo, but it seems he never returned home last night." This was the first time that Hugo hadn't come home, and I was worried. What if something had happened?

"He spent the night at Nash House. There was a message last night. Seems that Elizabeth Nash finally went into labor, and her husband needed some male company," Jane replied smugly. She might have let me know, but, for some reason, she chose to keep the information to herself, probably to remind me of my position within the household. She was mistress here, and she owed me nothing. "Hugo will join us in church this morning," she added as she rose from the table, ready to leave. "No time for breakfast, I'm afraid. We must go. Come along, Clarence."

I trailed after Jane, feeling strangely miserable. Why was she so snide this morning? Was it because she was sorry to have confided in me yesterday? I'd honestly wished she'd kept her secrets to herself if she were going to punish me for knowing them. It seemed that women were equally catty in every century.

I donned my hat and cloak and followed Jane out to the carriage. I would have gladly walked to church, but Jane felt it unseemly, so Jane, Clarence and I rode inside, while Jem rode on the back of the carriage, and the rest of the household simply walked.

The church was already full by the time we made our way to the front and settled in a pew, leaving room for Hugo. A ripple of anticipation went through the congregation as Reverend Snow stepped up to the pulpit, ready to deliver his Easter sermon. He had just opened his mouth to speak when Hugo slid in next to me, wearing yesterday's clothes and smelling strongly of drink.

"Where have you been?" I hissed, annoyed at him for not sending word to me.

"It's a boy—Robert," he whispered joyfully. "Mother and child are both fine, and the father is senseless with drink and joy. I kept plying him with wine to keep him from panicking. The baby was a long time coming."

Hugo seemed very cheerful, so I just squeezed his hand and settled in for the service, but not before I saw the look of annoyance from Jane, who'd been watching me. I ignored her and braced myself for the lengthy sermon. This was going to be a long day, and if Jane chose to be upset about something, she'd have to deal with it on her own. I still had a Catholic service to sit through.

FORTY-ONE

MAY 1685

As our departure date approached, I grew more hopeful. In a few days, we would be on our way to Portsmouth to find a ship bound for France. According to Archie, who was coming with us, the journey to Portsmouth would take somewhere between ten and fifteen hours, depending on the weather, road conditions, and traffic, which moved at the breakneck speed of about eight miles per hour. The road to Portsmouth was a congested one since it was a direct route between London and the busiest port in England. We'd be joining the road midway, but there were sure to be many coaches, as well as mounted travelers, headed in that direction. In later years, the road would become known as Sailor's Highway, the most famous traveler being Admiral Lord Nelson who made the journey from his home in London to board HMS *Victory*, which would take him to the fateful Battle of Trafalgar, but it was a long while until Nelson would even be born.

This time, we would be traveling by coach since there would be too much luggage to travel on horseback. We would have to stop somewhere for the night and change horses before reaching our destination. Hugo didn't want to frighten me, but I knew that traveling by coach at night wasn't safe. There were countless highwaymen on the road to Portsmouth; the threat of the noose not much of a deterrent since they were well aware that most people who traveled in that direction were bringing goods and valuables. No one bothered to rob the sailors who were Portsmouth-bound, but the passengers and officers of the navy were ripe for the picking.

Jane took charge of my trunk, making sure that I had whatever she thought I might need for the journey and beyond. She called in a seamstress from the village and terrorized the poor woman and her teenage daughter into sewing well into the night to produce undergarments, two day gowns, and a fur-lined cloak made of midnight blue velvet trimmed with ermine at the cuffs and hood. The inside was made of fox pelt and would keep me warm once the cold weather set in again. I would take the gown that Jane had previously lent me, plus two more that she was gifting me, certain that I would need them when Hugo and I visited the Court at Versailles. I had half a dozen pairs of silk stockings, shoes, gloves, and nightclothes. I felt like a queen.

"Now, this should last you for some little while," Jane instructed me as she once again took inventory of my possessions, "but once you're settled, you should find a fashionable dressmaker and order several new gowns. I have no doubt that the fashions in Paris are simply divine, miles ahead of what the ladies of the English Court are wearing. Oh, I do wish I could come with you," Jane added wistfully. "I so long to visit Paris again. I went once with Ernest, you know. It was during the month of May and Paris was in bloom, the sweet smell of roses wafting through the window as I sat at my dressing table and gazed over the flowing river. The water was sparkling in the sunshine, and little boats drifted on the current, right past Notre Dame de Paris. It is a most impressive cathedral, Neve, the likes of which I've never seen, not even in Canterbury. You should see the windows. And the gargoyles. They are like something straight out of a vision of hell—monstrous and evil. Gave me quite a turn. Ernest said I was being foolish. He said they were used to keep the rainwater away from the walls when it rained. Fancy that, carving those monstrous things for such a mundane purpose."

Jane's petulance seemed to have dissipated after Easter, but I'd decided to keep my own counsel. I was friendly and polite, but there would be no more confidences if I could help it, and I tried to deflect Jane's numerous questions about my relationship with Hugo the best I could. I reminded myself that she wasn't a friend, but a woman whose son would lose out on his inheritance if Hugo and I had a child, a blow Jane wouldn't take lightly. Perhaps I was being paranoid, but I'd seen a side of Jane that put me on my guard, something that didn't happen to me often.

Jane held up one of the new dresses and gave it a critical once-over, making a small hmmph noise in her nose. "I suppose Mrs. Higgins is adequate for a village seamstress, but this would never do in London, much less Paris."

"Don't worry, Jane," I tried to calm her. "These gowns will be just fine for every day, and Hugo promised me a whole new wardrobe once we're settled." I wasn't the type of woman to waste good money on frivolous gowns, but I wanted to humor Jane. She seemed so concerned with minutiae. I had other things to worry about. "Jane, do you not mind that Clarence will no longer be Hugo's heir if Hugo has a child?" I asked carefully.

"Of course not, you silly goose. It's only right and proper that Hugo should have a son and heir. Clarence will inherit his father's estate, and that will be enough for him. His future is assured either way, so don't you give it another thought. Are you with child?" she asked carefully, averting her eyes so I couldn't see the panic there.

"No, I'm not," I replied, sounding rather terse. I should

never have brought the subject up, but I wanted to see Jane's reaction.

"So, nothing to worry about then, is there?" she said happily, turning her attention back to the quickly filling trunk.

No, there was nothing to worry about on that score. I couldn't help noticing the disappointment in Hugo's eyes as I gently pushed his hand away and told him that he'd have to wait a few days until my menses were over. I knew it wasn't the waiting that upset him, but the fact that I wasn't pregnant. He would have dragged me to the church and married me that very day. I couldn't help chuckling at the thought of Reverend Snow's face if he were presented with such a request, particularly after our recent conversation. He'd probably insist on calling the banns for three consecutive weeks and make us wait a month to marry.

Truth be told, I wanted to get married first anyway. After feeling so alone and betrayed by Evan when I found out I was pregnant, I wanted to know that Hugo wanted to marry me for me, and not just for the child I might carry. I wanted it to be right this time, even if the religious factor might be a problem. Hugo was all right with my Protestantism as long as the child could be raised a Catholic, a prospect I didn't relish, but couldn't really deny him. I'd never been much of a churchgoer anyway, and religion was not something that had any immediate effect on my life. But this was the seventeenth century, so religion affected just about everything and everyone, making being the mother of a Catholic rather a daunting task, particularly in England.

My thoughts were interrupted by the arrival of Mrs. Higgins, who was bringing a dress for me to try on. Each fitting took a minimum of two hours, with Jane and Mrs. Higgins clucking in approval and eyeing me like two hawks who'd spotted a juicy squirrel that they'd like to devour.

"I need some air," I blurted out as I bolted from the room,

nearly knocking poor Molly Higgins off her feet and making her drop the bolt of fabric she'd been carrying. Let them think what they would, but I simply needed to get away from them for a little while. I'd hardly had a moment alone this past week, what with the preparations and all, and it seemed as if Jane was constantly at my side. There were times when she seemed sad that Hugo and I were leaving, but at other times, it appeared as if she couldn't wait for us to go. The more I got to know Jane, the more perverse she appeared to me, and I almost began to wonder if the story she'd told me about her husband was true, or just a bid for attention and sympathy.

The most logical explanation for Jane's behavior, of course, was that she was jealous of Hugo's love for me. Hugo had been the only man in her life who genuinely loved her and was loyal to her, and now she had to share him with me—a woman who had no family, connections, or money. In Jane's estimation, I was beneath her brother, which is probably why he chose not to tell her of our plans to marry. I suspect that Jane was sincere when she said that she wanted Hugo to marry, but it seemed that she wanted him to marry more out of a sense of duty than love, then his heart would still belong to her, or so she thought.

I was thrilled to see Hugo coming out of the stables. He was plainly dressed in dun-colored breeches, shirt and coat, his head uncovered and wigless. This was the way I liked him best, and I told him so.

"Are you secretly attracted to stable boys?" Hugo asked with a grin, his eyes sliding back to the stable in invitation. "Hay can be very prickly and uncomfortable, but if you insist, I will suffer it for you."

"And what do you know of lying in the hay?" I teased him.

"Enough to know I'd rather not do it again," he replied, taking me by the arm. "Were you looking for me?"

"No, but I'm glad I found you all the same. Take me for a walk, and not in the gardens. I want to walk outside. The garden makes me feel claustrophobic," I blurted out, instantly realizing that Hugo would have no idea what that meant.

"Did you just make that word up?" he asked, turning to face me. "I had no idea you knew Latin or Greek."

"Ah, I don't," I stammered, wishing I'd kept my mouth shut.

"So, how did you just put those two words together? 'Claustro' means 'shut-in place' in Latin and 'phobia' comes from the Greek word for fear. You do surprise me sometimes," he mused as we walked through the gate. "I wish I knew more about you, Neve. You're so secretive about your past. I know you were afraid when you first came here, but you have nothing to fear now. I won't hold anything against you, you know." We'd had a similar conversation once or twice before, but I couldn't tell Hugo anything more than he already knew, for obvious reasons.

"A woman should always remain a mystery," I teased him as I filled my lungs with the fresh May air. Here, away from the house, there were no odors of horses or dogs or smells of cooking that emanated from the kitchens. The air was fragrant with wildflowers and grass, underlined by the comforting smell of rich soil and pine from the nearby forest. It felt incredibly liberating to just walk without being surrounded by walls.

Hugo drew me to him and gave me a sound kiss. "All right, you can hold on to your secrets—for now," he whispered as he caught my earlobe with his teeth and made me squeal.

I tried to push him away, but he froze as his head snapped to the right.

"What is it?" I cried.

Hugo's hand immediately went to his left side, but he wasn't armed. "Damn," he hissed under his breath as he realized that he wasn't wearing his sword.

I was about to ask again when I heard what Hugo had heard a few moments before me—several horses galloping down the country lane toward us. I could just make out four riders, and they didn't appear friendly.

There was no way we could get back to the manor before they reached us, so Hugo just stood his ground, watching warily as the horsemen drew nearer. One man came to a stop just before he reached us, but the other three took positions on either side and behind us, preventing escape. My heart pounded in my chest as I looked up at the man above me. He was wearing a steel breastplate and helmet, the kind I thought was called "lobster tails," and had been popular during the Civil War. The polished armor glinted in the spring sunshine, making it difficult to look directly at the rider.

From what I could see, he was middle-aged, bearded, and in top fighting form. He sat astride his horse as if he were an extension of the animal, his hard muscles clearly visible beneath the fabric of his breeches and the doublet beneath the breastplate. The other three men were younger, one of them a pudgy youth whose face was covered in spots and a sparse growth of beard. He was probably no older than sixteen, but judging by the tension with which he kept his hand on the hilt of his sword, he was eager to prove himself, which made him dangerous.

"Lord Everly?"

"Yes. Whom do I have the pleasure of addressing?" Hugo asked. I thought "pleasure" was a bit of an overstatement, but I kept quiet, hoping that this wasn't what my mind was clearly telling me it was.

"I'm Captain Humphries of His Majesty's Royal Guard." He didn't bother to introduce the other men as he drew out a rolled-up document from his pouch. "Hugo Edward Thomas Everly, you have been accused of attempted murder, kidnapping, and high treason. You will be taken to the Tower of London, where you will be incarcerated until your trial and subsequent execution," Captain Humphries announced, glaring down at Hugo from atop his horse.

"So, the outcome of the trial is a foregone conclusion?" Hugo asked calmly.

"It's not for me to say, but there's considerable evidence to suggest that the trial will not go your way."

"And may I ask who has made these accusations against me?" Hugo inquired.

Captain Humphries looked a trifle uncomfortable, realizing that he'd said too much already. "I'm not at liberty to divulge that information, sir. You will find out more in due course."

"Miller, fetch Lord Everly's horse from the stables, and Banes, search the house for any incriminating correspondence. Dowson, you are with me."

The two men left immediately, while the pudgy youth remained behind, hand still on sword.

"Lord Everly, I see no reason to have you fettered, but if you do anything to resist arrest, I will quickly change my mind. The men will be back shortly, so you have a few moments to say goodbye to your lady."

"Neve, I only have a few minutes, so please listen to me. I have made provisions for your future, should I be found guilty and executed. Bradford Nash will pay you a stipend for the duration of your life. You will want for nothing."

"Want for nothing?" I repeated stupidly. "But I want you. Don't you see, this is exactly what I predicted? This is it, Hugo."

"Neve, this is an arrest, not a conviction. I've destroyed anything that can link me to the other conspirators. If I can beat the charge of treason, the other two charges don't carry a death penalty. Finch is alive and well, and perhaps I can find a way to justify the abduction. Please, don't worry about me. England has the best justice system in the world."

I nearly burst into hysterical laughter. The modus operandi of the British justice system in the seventeenth century was to execute first and ask questions later. Hugo had almost killed Lionel Finch in his own home, abducted his wife, and openly solicited support for Monmouth's Rebellion. He was guilty as charged, and we both knew it.

I glanced down the hill toward the church. It was less than a quarter mile away. I stared at it, an idea beginning to form in my terrified brain. This was it. This was the start of whatever was going to happen to Hugo, and there was only one way to stop it. Once the soldiers got Hugo to London, there'd be no way to help him, even if the most competent defense lawyer could be found. Hugo was guilty, and I had no doubt that Finch would produce as many witnesses as he needed. He had coin, which was all the persuading some people required to pervert the course of justice, not that Finch's accusations weren't just under the law of the land.

I had to do something, and I had to do it this very minute before the other two came back. Memories of my miscarriage were still fresh in my mind, and I tried to recall the pain and the terror I'd felt, putting everything into my performance. I swayed, my hands flying to my belly as I doubled over, gasping and panting with pain. "Oh God," I wailed, "I think I'm bleeding. Help me. Please, get the midwife from the village." I didn't wait for the men to react as I began to fall, hoping that Hugo would catch me before I hit the ground. He did. I felt awful for what I was doing to him, but I had no choice. I screamed as if my body was being torn apart, a new life being expunged from my womb, the miscarriage caused by the shock of having my lover arrested.

"You're better off losing yer brat, ye silly trollop," the pimply youth sniggered. "Who needs another bastard who'll never meet its sire and have to live with the stain of his treachery?"

"Shut your mouth and go for the midwife," Captain Humphries barked as I continued to writhe in Hugo's arms, my eyes rolling into the back of my head with supposed agony.

Hugo looked terrified as he tried to talk to me, unsure if what I was experiencing was real and I hadn't told him or just a ruse. "Neve, can you hear me? What can I do?"

"Take me to the church," I mouthed. "Now. I need to get to the church."

Hugo lifted me up and turned toward the church, but Captain Humphries was instantly in front of us, blocking our path.

"You will remain here until the midwife comes," he ordered, clearly unnerved by what he was witnessing.

"I will take Mistress Ashley to the church, where she can be more comfortable and have access to Reverend Snow, should it become necessary. Now, get out of my way," Hugo barked, really angry now.

"I order you to halt," Humphries spat out, reaching for his sword.

"Or what? You will kill me for trying to help a pregnant woman?"

I could feel the tension coursing through Hugo as he stepped around the dancing horse and walked quickly toward the church. I was still clutching my stomach and gasping with pain, then slumped like a rag doll against Hugo's chest.

The captain seemed somewhat at a loss. As a gentleman, he felt a duty to help me, but as a soldier, he was bound to carry out his orders. His hesitation cost him dearly, since by the time he dismounted and reached the church, we were already inside the church porch.

"Stop," Humphries roared, but Hugo stepped into the porch and turned to face the irate captain.

"Sanctuary," he called out, his voice clear and calm.

"You bitch," Humphries growled as he realized that he'd been duped. "You go on and claim sanctuary. Much good it will do you. I will have this church surrounded day and night and no one, you hear me, no one will be able to bring you food or water. I will starve you out, and once I have you, I will take you both to London, and I promise you, Your Lordship, your lady will have a most uncomfortable journey. I will give her to my men to share and make you watch as punishment for what you've just done. You have my word of honor, sir."

"Do what you must," Hugo replied and kicked open the door to the church, carrying me into the dim interior. He set me down on one of the pews and kissed my brow. "Are you all right, sweetheart?"

I tried to sit up, but my heart was racing, and I truly felt faint. I closed my eyes and took several deep breaths in order to calm myself. I'd imagined all kinds of scenarios, but this hadn't been one of them. I'd gotten Hugo to the church, but now there was only one thing I could do.

Hugo sat down next to me and pulled me close to steady me. He seemed calm, but I knew that inside he must be aware of the implications of what we'd just done. Things looked very grim.

"Neve, there's no way out. Humphries meant what he said. He will starve us out, so going into sanctuary will buy us only a few days at most," he said gently. "I know you meant well, but we are trapped. I will surrender myself to Humphries on the condition that he let you go unmolested. Go to Brad. He knows what to do."

"Hugo, there's a reason I maneuvered you toward the church, and it wasn't because I wanted to go into sanctuary. I can get you out of here," I breathed, terrified of what I was about to do. I got to my feet and took Hugo's hand. "Hugo, just trust me on this one."

I pulled Hugo toward the door to the crypt, praying that the passage was open, and nothing had happened in the past month to prevent us from leaving.

"There's no way out from the crypt," Hugo insisted as he followed me through the door. "Neve, this might be the last private moment we have. Let me say goodbye properly," he said as he tried to turn me around.

"Hugo, please; just follow me," I hissed at him. I pulled him through the dark crypt toward where I knew the passage to be. I prayed fervently as I groped in the dark for the tiny knob that opened the doorway. I heard Hugo's gasp as the stone door slid open, revealing the dimly lit steps leading upward. I pushed Hugo though the door and pushed the knob, closing the passage behind us.

And now I knew exactly how Hugo Everly had disappeared.

FORTY-TWO

Hugo was just about to say something when we emerged into the church, which was thankfully empty. Brilliant light shone through the Jubilee window, sending rainbows of color onto the wooden pews and the stone floor of the church. I heard Hugo's sharp intake of breath, but I didn't have time to explain. We needed to get away and fast. I knew exactly the place, but it was imperative that we get out of the church unseen. My holdall hadn't been behind the knight's tomb where I left it, so I knew that my disappearance was known. The police might be looking for me, so for them to find me dressed in a seventeenth-century gown with a man who had no identification would not bode well for either of us.

I pushed open the side door that led into the graveyard and beckoned Hugo to follow. He stood rooted to the spot; his eyes glued to where he expected Everly Manor to be. It was still there, but completely overshadowed by the new house which sat proudly atop the hill. From our vantage point, I could see activity by the museum, people coming and going, various vehicles parked in the car park, and two cars just exiting the gates of the new manor house. Shooting was obviously already in progress; the place overrun with crew and actors.

Hugo watched silently as the cars sped away from the manor and disappeared around the bend. He sank down on a stone bench by one of the graves, a mournful-looking angel gazing down on him with undisguised pity. "Neve, I don't understand," he mumbled. "Is this some kind of witchery? What have you done?"

I sat down next to him and put my palms on his cold cheeks, forcing him to look me in the eye. He was clammy to the touch, and his pupils were dilated with panic. He'd been perfectly calm when faced with arrest and imminent execution, but this was so far beyond his realm of understanding that his defenses finally broke down and he looked ready to faint. It was hard enough going into the past even if you knew something of the history and customs; having seen the way people lived in films and read about in books. But, to go into the future and be confronted with things you'd never even imagined, much less seen, would be infinitely more difficult. I would have to tread carefully when explaining myself, but at this moment I needed to get Hugo to a safe place.

"Hugo, listen to me. I will explain everything just as soon as I'm able, but right now, we need to get away from here. I know a place where we can hide until nightfall. Get hold of yourself, man," I said more sternly as he continued to sit there.

"And what happens after nightfall?" he finally asked as he roused himself and followed me from the graveyard.

"I haven't figured that out yet," I replied in a light tone. "This wasn't exactly the plan, was it?"

"Was there a plan?"

"Yes, we were going to go to France, get married, and live happily ever after," I quipped, hoping to make him smile, but the jest was lost on him.

"Is this where you came from?" Hugo asked, his head

swiveling as he tried to take in his surroundings which were so familiar, yet so different.

"Yes, it is."

Hugo didn't say anything else; he simply walked beside me like an automaton, looking around him with awe. I maneuvered him into the woods as soon as I could, trying to remember the exact location of the hunting lodge. Max had shown it to me when I first came, but I wasn't interested in the structure since it was built long after the time period of our film. It was a Victorian addition to the estate, one that saw many hunts and informal meals, but had rarely been used on such a grand scale since the First World War. Max's father, Roland, had gone there often, according to Max, so the place had been kept up and stocked with food. I wasn't sure if anyone had been there since Roland's death. A key was stored, predictably, under the flowerpot by the door, which made it unnecessary for us to break in.

The lodge was just as I remembered it: a two-storied wooden structure with several stone chimneys and numerous gables that jutted out every which way. It reminded me of the cottage of the seven dwarfs from *Snow White*, hidden from view by the tall trees which had grown unchecked for the past several hundred years. There were several outbuildings, one having been the stables for the horses, an icehouse, and a shed. All were presumably empty now since no one had used the lodge in years.

Roland Everly had been an amateur taxidermist and kept a workshop at the lodge. His wife, understandably, had forbidden him from practicing his hobby at the manor, so he'd spent many hours at his hideaway in the gruesome pursuit of the perfect stuffed animal. His handiwork was everywhere; glassy eyes staring from every wall as we entered the house.

I meant to stay in control, but as I sank down onto the sofa by the cold hearth, I began to shake, tears streaming down my face as I wrapped my arms around Hugo. His response was somewhat wooden, but he held me and let me cry it out before dealing with his own confusion.

I finally pulled myself together and went in search of the bathroom. I saw Hugo's look of shock as I turned on the water and splashed it over my puffy face. He came in behind me and stuck his hand under the water, his face registering pure amazement.

"It's warm," he said. "Where is it coming from?"

I shocked him further by flipping the light switch. Electric light flooded the small bathroom, bringing into stark relief our faces in the mirror. Mine was blotchy; Hugo's was ashen. He bent his head and looked under the light fixture, where an innocent little bulb burned bright and steady.

"That's called electricity," I explained. My voice sounded shaky, but it was easier to focus on trivial things rather than go into an explanation of what had occurred only half an hour ago.

"What's that?" Hugo asked, pointing to the commode.

"It's a toilet. It flushes. Look." I flushed the toilet, and we both watched as the water gushed and swirled in the bowl.

"Hmm," was all that Hugo said.

I turned off the light and walked to the kitchen. As I expected, there was nothing in the fridge, but I did find several tins of biscuits which were miraculously not expired, and an unopened box of tea bags. There was even some sugar. It looked questionable, but it'd have to do. It would have been nice to have some milk, but beggars couldn't be choosers, I reminded myself.

I found the kettle and put it on to boil while I washed two mugs and found a plate for the biscuits. Hugo just watched in amazement as I turned on the stove but didn't comment. I think he knew I was stalling, so he went back into the front room and began leafing through a hunting magazine from a few years ago. I could see him through the doorway and couldn't help smiling at the expressions passing over his face. I couldn't even begin to imagine what he was feeling. I had gone back into the past knowing exactly what to expect, but Hugo had literally gone down the rabbit hole. He had no warning, no books and pictures to look at, no movies that depicted life in the future. He'd had no inkling of what was to come. I had to admire his reserve. I would have been running in circles and screaming by now, but he just sat there calmly, waiting for me to finally explain.

I poured tea into the mugs, added a generous helping of sugar and placed a dozen biscuits onto the plate, before bringing the tray into the front room and setting it on the coffee table in front of the sofa.

"Careful, it's hot," I warned Hugo as I handed him a mug.

"What is it?" He looked at the brown liquid with suspicion.

"It's called tea. It comes from China and India. It's the most popular drink in Britain. You can have it black, with or without sugar, with milk or with a slice of lemon." I suddenly felt foolish and closed my mouth. Here Hugo was, shocked, scared, confused, and I was prattling on about tea.

Hugo took an experimental sip and set the mug down.

"You don't like it?"

"It's strange," he said and reached for a biscuit, which he finished in two bites. "So, are you going to explain, or do we just pretend that nothing happened?" He picked up the mug carefully and took another sip, swirling the tea in his mouth to experience its full flavor. It seemed to make a better impression the second time around and he took another sip.

"I don't know where to begin," I said.

"Begin at the beginning, if there is one. If not, start with the day I found you."

"I suppose the beginning would be my birth in 1986, but that's neither here nor there," I said with a nervous giggle.

"1986?" I was glad Hugo had already swallowed the tea, or things would have gotten messy. "What year is this?"

"It's 2013. Twenty-first century."

"Go on." Hugo calmly reached for another biscuit, but I could see a slight tremor in his hand. He was doing his best to keep it together, and I felt overwhelming sympathy for him, but knew that feeling sorry for him was not what he needed right now. I had to give him an explanation that made sense, or at least sounded plausible.

"Hugo, I came to Everly Manor at the beginning of March as part of my job. Yes, I work," I added in response to his questioning stare. "I'm a location scout for a movie production company. A movie is kind of like a theater play, but it's filmed and shown on a screen rather than performed live. Many movies are shot on location, so scouts go to various possible locales and choose the one that's most appropriate and fits into the production budget."

Hugo didn't say anything, so I continued. "While I was down in the crypt, taking pictures—that's like a painting that you can capture on film—for a scene that was to be shot down there, I accidentally pressed against one of the flower carvings in the wall behind the knight's tomb. It opened a passage. I had no idea that the passage led anywhere other than another part of the church, but when I came up the steps, I saw you, and the church as it was in the seventeenth century."

"So, you followed me?" Hugo asked, sounding more curious than angry.

"No. I fled back down the steps to the crypt in a panic. I thought I'd experienced some kind of hallucination. You see, I knew who you were. Max—that's the current Lord Everly—showed me your portrait and told me of the mystery surrounding your disappearance. No one knew what had happened to you. You simply vanished one day in May 1685."

"Am I correct in assuming that I vanished to the twenty-first century?" Hugo asked. I was glad to see that he was smiling at the absurdity of it all.

"I suppose so, but I didn't know that at the time. I went back through the passage just to prove to myself that what I saw that first time was real. That was the day you nearly ran me down."

"And when you ran away, you went back home?" Hugo asked.

"Yes, but I kept thinking about you and Jane, and I felt awful for just disappearing like that, especially when I knew what was in store for you. I came back to warn you. That's all I wanted to do. And you prevented me from leaving."

"So, you don't have the 'Sight,' you have actual knowledge," he correctly deduced.

"That's right. I knew exactly what was going to happen. It's all been copiously documented."

Hugo set down his mug and stood up, going to the window. He stood with his back to me for a few minutes, digesting what I had just told him. I could see the rigid set of his shoulders and the proud way he held his head. He was feeling defiant and angry, and I couldn't blame him. I wanted to say something to reassure him that I hadn't tricked him or lied to him, but it wouldn't do any good. He had to see that for himself.

Hugo finally turned to face me, his anger under control. "Neve, I bear some of the responsibility for what happened to you, and you have, without question, saved my life. I would have been executed had I been taken into custody, but I simply can't comprehend any of this. Do people in the twenty-first century routinely travel through time? Has the world really come so far in its exploration of scientific matters, or is this some kind of black magic? And if such a thing is possible, can I go back if I wish, and would I return to exactly the same time that I left? Is there a way to navigate it, or do you simply show up sometime in the past? You were able to come back three times to the same time period, so you must have controlled it somehow."

I had to admit that for a man of the seventeenth century, his mind was processing this admirably well and coming up with all the right questions. I'd asked all those questions myself and was no closer to an answer.

"Hugo, the honest answer is that I simply don't know. There are some theories about ley lines—points where they intersect are supposed to hold some power—but none of that has been proven or put to the test. I'm not aware of navigating through time, but you were on my mind, so it's possible that I somehow influenced where I wound up, but I strongly doubt it. I wasn't thinking of you at all when I was taking pictures down in the crypt. If anything, I was wondering about the knight whose tomb I was photographing, so I suppose I should be thankful I didn't end up joining the Crusades. I couldn't deal with desert heat," I said, in a failed attempt at a joke. "I assume you can go back if you wish, but you will be arrested and taken to the Tower. I couldn't bear to lose you, Hugo, especially not in the horrific way they executed traitors. You know what would happen to you, don't you? Hanging or beheading would be a blessing compared to the torture that you would be put through."

Hugo nodded in acknowledgement. He knew exactly what would be done to him. He would be publicly drawn and quartered, his body parts displayed around London as a warning to others, while his entrails and private parts would be burned in front of him while he died of shock.

Hugo sat down next to me and drew me to him, kissing the top of my head. "You're not going to lose me, Neve. You deceived me, but you tried to help me in the only way you could, and for that, I'm very grateful. I know that your feelings are genuine, as are mine."

I breathed a sigh of relief to hear him say that. For a moment, I thought that he might charge right back to the church and return to 1685 to face his fate, partly out of anger, and partly out of some misplaced sense of responsibility. At least he was being sensible.

"What now?" he asked, reading my mind.

"We wait till it gets dark and all the film people have gone, and then we'll go see Max. He's a lovely man, Hugo. I think you'll really get on. There's such a strong physical resemblance between you, it's uncanny. I'm sure Max will be happy to help."

Hugo sat back and studied me for a moment, his mind clearly not accepting my proposal. "Assuming this Max is willing to help me, what type of help are you envisioning? Money? What am I to do here? I have nothing."

"You have me," I stated simply. "You will always have me."

"But why would you want a man who has nothing to offer you? In 1685, I could offer you wealth and position, assuming I lived long enough to marry you. Here, I'm no one."

"You are actually less than no one," I corrected him. "In this time, you can't simply show up somewhere and start a new life. Everything is documented and everyone has certain forms of identification which can be verified at any time. Every person has a National Insurance number which is unique. Someone with the right access can pull up all your personal information, starting with your birth and continuing to everything you have done since. There's an electronic trail that every British citizen has. Actually, it's not just in Britain; it's all over the world. Governments track every single person who enters and leaves the country in order to protect its citizens."

"I see," Hugo said, although I was sure he didn't. "So, how can Max Everly help?" he asked again. Perhaps he did see.

"I'm not sure, but he's your descendant, actually Clarence's descendant. Perhaps he can think of something. He has plans of standing for Parliament; he knows people."

"Standing for Parliament?" Hugo asked with interest. "So, Parliament still exists then?"

"Oh, yes. And the monarchy doesn't have the kind of power it once did. The Queen is more of a figurehead rather than a ruler. She's a public servant."

"Remarkable," Hugo said as he tried to take this in. "So, she doesn't have the power to dissolve Parliament?"

"No, she doesn't. No one does."

* * *

The next few hours passed in conversation. Now that Hugo had had a little time to get his bearings, he was curious about the world he found himself in and eager to learn as much as possible before we left our bolt-hole. I tried to explain television, radio, telephones, satellites, various forms of travel, and anything else that came to mind. And as long as we were talking about progress, Hugo wasn't asking me any personal questions. I wasn't ready to explain about Evan or the baby I'd lost. Of course, I didn't have to tell him, but I felt it would be dishonest to lie about my past. I'd deceived him enough already, so I owed him the truth.

"My head is spinning from all this information," Hugo announced. "It all feels very theoretical at this point, since I haven't actually seen any of the devices you spoke of."

Unfortunately, the lodge didn't have a TV or a telephone. There was a radio, however, so I turned it on and found a station playing pop music, curious to see how Hugo would react.

"What is that noise?" he asked.

"It's the type of music that's popular today. You don't like it?"

Hugo shrugged. "I suppose it takes getting used to, like anything else. Do you like it?"

"I like some of it. There are other kinds of music as well." I found a station playing a Mozart concerto and watched Hugo relax. This was something he could relate to. He closed his eyes and reclined back, pulling me along with him so that my head rested on his chest. I could hear the beating of his heart, which was a bit erratic. Perhaps he wasn't as calm as he wanted me to believe. "Hugo, are you all right?" I asked, worried.

"I honestly couldn't say," he answered as he held me closer. "I can go back and await my execution, or I can stay here and feel like a fish out of water for the rest of my days, assuming we find a way for me to stay. I'm not sure which option is more appealing. Now that you are back in your own time, there's nothing to keep you from leaving me. You are free to do as you please."

"Do you think that I pretended to love you? I was going to stay with you in a time that's not my own. I was going to give up everything. Is that what you really believe?" I demanded, outraged that he would think that.

"I don't know what to believe. You need to give me a little time, Neve. A lot has changed since breakfast," he added ruefully.

"I know," I conceded. "Why don't you take a hot bath? That might relax you. And I'll see if I can find us some clothes. Arriving at the manor dressed like actors in a play might not be the best thing."

"All right." Hugo got up and walked to the bathroom, where he just stared at the tub without turning on the light. "Am I meant to get water from the sink and pour it in here?"

"No. You turn on the taps, like so, and get the water to a temperature you like. Just let it fill the tub, then turn them off. Should I turn on the light?" I asked carefully.

"No. Just leave the door open. The light is too bright."

I handed Hugo some soap, a fluffy bath towel, and a bottle of shampoo, and left him to his own devices while I went to search the rest of the house. Roland stayed here for days on end, according to Max, so there had to be some clothes left behind, unless everything had been cleaned out after his death. The lodge was pristine, if a little dusty, but judging by the biscuits, tea, and toiletries, it was still in use by someone.

I found what I presumed to be Roland's bedroom. It was very masculine and devoid of any personal items. I opened the drawers of the dresser but found nothing at all. The closet proved to be just as empty. All of Roland's things had been disposed of.

The next bedroom was furnished in much the same style. This wasn't a place where women stayed, I gathered. This was a masculine domain, filled with stuffed animals and guns. The gun cabinet in the other room was locked, but I could see various firearms through the glass doors.

I opened the drawers and was gratified to find a few pairs of briefs, socks, and several T-shirts. Of course, this wouldn't do any good without trousers, I mused. I pulled open the closet door and grinned. Two pairs of jeans, a tracksuit in navy blue, and a cashmere blazer hung in the closet, as well as several dress shirts. Judging by the style, I thought they might belong to Max. This was a fortuitous find indeed.

I left my treasure trove and went to check out the third bedroom, hoping against hope that it belonged to Lady Everly and I might find some feminine attire, but the room was bare. Lady Everly probably hadn't spent a single night here.

Returning to Max's room, I undressed and pulled on a pair of briefs before trying on his jeans. They were too tight in the hips and way too long, but they did fit. I put on one of the T-shirts and looked in the mirror. It was odd to feel so confined from the waist down after weeks of wearing nothing beneath my skirts. I could see the outline of my nipples through the thin fabric and suddenly felt terribly self-conscious. It would have to do, though. My seventeenth-century gown was a bit over the top. Of course, there were no shoes, so I had to keep my own, which made my outfit even stranger.

I pulled the pins out of my hair and watched it tumble around my shoulders. I hadn't worn my hair loose except at bedtime, so it was liberating to just let it curl around my face. I stared at my reflection. It was difficult to reconcile the woman I had been only that morning to the one that was staring at me now. I suppose I should have felt more comfortable to be wearing modern clothes, but I felt odd, incomplete somehow, and less feminine.

I turned from the mirror as Hugo walked into the room. His hair was damp from the bath, and the towel was wrapped around his waist in a way that made me wish he'd just take it off. He stared at me for a moment, his head cocked to the side, as if appraising a painting.

"You look different," he said. "Is that what women wear these days?"

"No, these belong to Max. I couldn't find anything appropriate. I have some clothes for you. I hope they fit." I handed Hugo the briefs, socks, jeans and a shirt. He understood what to do with the jeans and shirt, but the underwear and socks left him perplexed.

"You put those on under the breeches," I explained. "And those go on your feet."

"Why do I need to put these on under my breeches?" he asked, clearly confused as to the purpose.

"Men wear underwear under their clothes. It's just more hygienic and keeps things in place."

Hugo gave me a strange look, but obediently dropped his towel and pulled on the underwear and socks, followed by the jeans. They fit him well, but I had to show him how to work the zipper.

"These breeches are awfully snug."

I could see he was uncomfortable, so I handed him the tracksuit instead. "Try this. It's not as confining."

Hugo put on the tracksuit with a T-shirt and a pair of trainers I'd found in the closet.

"Are the shoes too tight?"

"No, they are remarkably comfortable," Hugo said as he

took a stroll around the room and froze in front of the mirror. "How strange I look."

"Not nearly as strange as you would look in your seventeenth-century garb in the present day. You actually look great."

"Do I?" I could see by his expression that he couldn't say the same for me. He was outraged by my attire but kept quiet on the subject. Of course, he thought I looked odd; it was only natural, and I didn't want to aggravate him any further. My mind was on our meeting with Max. I hoped he was at home.

"We'd better get going. It will be dark soon, so it should be safe now."

Hugo just inclined his head in agreement and left the room. I wanted to reassure him that everything would work out for the best and Max would help him, but I held my tongue. I had no idea what Max's reaction would be, nor did I expect everything to fall into place anytime soon. It would take Hugo a very long time to acclimate to this world, and his pride would suffer a severe blow. To go from being the lord of the manor to being nobody would be hard for anyone. I couldn't even think of any job he could do, other than manual labor of some sort, but even that required skill.

We walked through the forest in silence, finally emerging not too far from the new house. Several windows were lit, and Max's car was in the drive, which was a good sign. I'd tried to come up with a plausible explanation, but all I could do was tell him the truth. Nothing could explain my disappearance and reappearance with his long-dead ancestor.

My hand shook as I rang the bell, while my other hand reached for Hugo's. He didn't pull away, but he didn't intertwine his fingers with mine the way he would have only this morning. He was still angry, and most likely scared to death. He was literally between a rock and a hard place, and he knew it.

Max himself opened the door; his tall frame illuminated from behind by the lights in the foyer. I couldn't see his face clearly, but what I glimpsed was enough to show me the shock, amazement, and apprehension that flitted over his features before he forced them into a smile.

"Neve. My goodness, where have you been? I was worried sick." Max pulled me into a warm embrace and kissed me on both cheeks, but his eyes were trained on Hugo, a barely perceptible glint of malice putting me on my guard. "Are those my clothes?" He held me at arm's length, admiring the way the T-shirt clung to my breasts. "They never looked this good on me. Do come in. Mother isn't here. She's visiting an old friend in Cornwall. It's lovely this time of year."

He was prattling on to hide his nervousness, but I could sense his animosity toward Hugo. It was as if he knew exactly who he was.

Max ushered us into the sitting room and invited us to sit down.

"I'll call for some refreshments, shall I?" He vanished down the corridor before I could say a word, leaving me feeling baffled.

"He's just surprised; that's all," I said to Hugo as he sat stiffly next to me and looked around the room.

"Was he your lover?" Hugo asked suddenly, spearing me with his gaze.

"No, he wasn't. He was interested in me, however, I won't deny that. He wanted to get to know me better." I wasn't going to justify my previous life to Hugo. That all happened before I'd met him, so I had nothing to feel guilty about. It was not as if Hugo hadn't had mistresses.

"I see," was all that Hugo had time to say before Max came back into the room.

"Stella will make some sandwiches and tea. I'm sure you two could use a bite. You do look the worse for wear, if I might say. Now, where have you been? Spellman has been looking for you, as well as Evan. He called here several times demanding to know where you had gone."

Oh, why did he have to bring up Evan? I thought as I took a sideways look at Hugo. He sat still as a statue, waiting for me to introduce him.

"Look, Max, something extraordinary happened to me back in March. While taking photographs down in the crypt, I came upon a passage that led me to the seventeenth century, where I met Hugo. Max, this is Lord Hugo Everly, your ancestor."

I expected Max to be shocked, but he simply nodded to Hugo.

"I know," Max said. "I recognize him from the portrait, only he looks less pompous in my tracksuit and without that ridiculous wig."

I glared at Max, angry that he would try to humiliate Hugo rather than make him welcome. Max heard me loud and clear and put on a welcoming façade.

"Of course, I'm thrilled to meet you, Hugo. I'm just understandably shocked. It's not every day that someone who died over three hundred years ago waltzes into your life. I do hope you understand, old chap. Oh, you really are an old chap, aren't you?" Max laughed, amused by his own wit.

"The pleasure is all mine," Hugo replied with undisguised sarcasm.

Oh, this wasn't starting off well at all.

"Max, you don't seem surprised by my time traveling," I said, suddenly realizing that he hadn't so much as batted an eyelash at my admission that I was in the seventeenth century, keeping company with his ancestor.

"No, I suspected you might have gone through the passage, although I wasn't sure. I found the bag with your clothes, phone, and keys behind the tomb, and then saw your car parked in the street not too far away from the church," he admitted.

"Did you take my things?" I asked, shocked that Max would

just assume something like that. What if I'd been kidnapped or hurt?

"I took your holdall and used the car keys to drive your car to the lodge. It's in the stable. I assumed that you went willingly and didn't want to alert anyone to what you'd done. It would certainly raise a lot of awkward questions, and every cheap rag would send a reporter down here to investigate."

"But how did you know about the passage? Have you ever gone through?" I demanded.

"I actually didn't know about it. I heard a tale long ago of an uncle who disappeared for months, then came back rambling about the Civil War and his encounters with Oliver Cromwell. Everyone thought him mad, and he spent some years in an institution for the mentally insane. He did manage to get out eventually, once he learned to stop speaking of his experiences. When I saw your clothes and your phone hidden behind the tomb, I went looking for his journal to see if any part of it could have been true. His musings were very convincing, and I couldn't find any other explanation for your disappearance. Some women saw you going to the crypt alone with a large bag. You never came out and there was no sign of a struggle. There's no other way out from the crypt, and no one saw anyone else about that day. So, what year did you wind up in?"

"1685, where I met Hugo. He can't go back, Max, and we have to help him."

"Ah, the plot thickens," Max said, his eyes on Hugo. "You disappeared without a trace in May of 1685. Am I to assume that this is where you disappeared to?" There was that sarcasm again, but I couldn't afford to antagonize Max. He was our only hope.

"It would appear so," Hugo replied.

At that moment, Mrs. Harding appeared with a tray bearing a plate of sandwiches, tea, and some little cakes that smelled heavenly. She threw me a weird look, but barely even looked at Hugo as she took her leave.

"Help yourselves, darlings," Max said as he reached for a cake and popped it in his mouth.

I poured Hugo a cup of tea and placed several sandwiches on a plate for him. I didn't think he'd help himself, since Max wasn't particularly hospitable, but Hugo was sure to be hungry. The gesture wasn't lost on Max, who gave me a knowing little smile.

"So, what now?" asked Max, pouring a cup for himself. "What's the plan?"

"I don't know," I stammered. "I was hoping you can help Hugo somehow. He's family, after all."

"Hmm, he is indeed, isn't he?" mused Max as he helped himself to another cake. "I suppose I can make a donation to the cause, but I can hardly get involved in any kind of shady enterprise that might damage my political prospects if anyone got wind of it. You might be better off going to London. It's much easier to get lost among the masses than here, in a place where everyone knows everyone's business. People would be remarking on the resemblance before the week was out. Of course, you can stay the night, and you can use the lodge for as long as you want, if you are not ready to go back. I can provide foodstuffs and whatever else you need; assuming you stay out of sight."

"That's very kind of you, Max," I said, trying to keep the venom from my voice, but Max just shrugged his shoulders, effectively washing his hands of the whole thing.

"Stella will show you to your rooms," he said, dismissing us.

"One room will be sufficient," Hugo informed him just as Mrs. Harding came in.

"Oh, like that, is it? Well, don't let me stand in your way, old man."

I wanted to slap the smirk off Max's face, but simply got up and walked out of the room. He clearly wasn't going to be much help, so Hugo and I were on our own.

Hugo silently followed me up the stairs and to the room Mrs. Harding opened for us. It was the room where I'd stayed before, and it felt sadly familiar. I wished I had my things, but I had nothing aside from Max's clothes on my back. Well, tomorrow I would reclaim my car, get my suitcase out of the boot and change. I'd have to charge my phone and call Lawrence Spellman. I was probably fired anyway. The thought made me cry with frustration. I suddenly felt so lost.

Hugo pulled me to him and held me, his chin atop my head. "Neve, it will be all right. I will do whatever it takes to make this work, I promise. I'm sorry if I was distant earlier; it won't happen again. Just say that you still love me," he asked softly.

"Of course, I still love you, you fool," I sobbed. "I love you even more, if that's possible."

"Then come to bed and let me make you feel better."

"That's the best idea I've heard all day," I replied and shed my clothes.

FORTY-THREE

Max waited until Neve and Hugo departed before pouring himself a large drink, which he gulped down in seconds. He'd behaved badly, but he couldn't control himself. The appearance of Neve was bad enough, but Hugo's was simply catastrophic. He hadn't been able to seal the passage as he'd planned. He'd consulted several so-called professionals, who'd informed him that the church was a historic building, and plastering over the walls of the crypt would not only serve very little purpose but would cover up the original texture of the stone, as well as the elaborate carvings that dated all the way back to the fourteenth century. Since there was nothing structurally wrong with the crypt, they'd never be able to obtain a permit.

As the weeks had passed, Max began to believe that everything would be all right. Neve hadn't come back in nearly two months, so it was safe to assume that she was staying in the past —whether willingly or not, he didn't much care. Max wasn't sure what year she'd ended up in, but Clarence had inherited Hugo's estate in 1685, and that was sure to happen anyway since Hugo did his vanishing act. Max had reasoned that since he was still Lord Everly in 2013, whatever Neve did in the past didn't affect him since the present would have been altered. Everything went on as before, thankfully, so the most likely scenario was that Neve had caught some nasty disease, or behaved strangely enough to arouse suspicion, and met her end in some unpleasant way, her life extinguished like a candle, with very little fuss. He had to admit that he'd felt sorry at the thought, but there was nothing he could have done. He'd looked for the passage, and had he found it, perhaps he might have even gone to look for Neve and do the chivalrous thing by bringing her back. Oh, who was he kidding? He liked her, he'd been physically attracted to her, but the first rule of survival was self-preservation, not chivalry.

The fact that no one appeared to be looking for Neve very hard certainly hadn't hurt. There was absolutely no evidence of foul play: no body, no car, and no bag. Phone and bank records would show that calls had been made since Neve's disappearance, and her bank account had been accessed from several different ATMs in the London area. Like most people, Neve had used her birthday as a code, making it ridiculously easy for Max to access her account. He'd made sure that he wore a cap pulled low over his face in case security cameras caught him accessing her account at the time of the transaction and kept the hat on long after he'd left the bank, acutely aware of the all-reaching access of CCTV. Consequently, the evidence suggested that Neve Ashley had simply taken off without telling anyone—irresponsible, certainly, but not a victim of a crime. Lawrence Spellman had questioned Max several times, clearly concerned for Neve, and her irritating boyfriend had come round, but they had both quickly given up, realizing that Max knew nothing. It'd all gone according to plan—until this evening.

Hugo Everly showing up on Max's doorstep was more than

Max's mind could accept. He needed a little time to understand the implications of having his ancestor in the present day. Technically, there wasn't much Hugo could do, but one never knew. He was Lord Everly and could conceivably make some claim to the estate, if he were able to prove his identity. And what if he went back to his own time and managed to avoid arrest? He was obviously in love with Neve—that slag who'd rejected him, but promptly fell into bed with a horse-smelling, sword-wielding traitor—so if she agreed to go with him, he might very well marry her and sire an heir, who would leave Max out of the line of succession. Despite his uncertain status, Hugo could do much to destroy Max's life.

Unless, of course, Hugo vanished again; as he was meant to, Max thought bitterly. As of now, Hugo had no identity and no legitimacy in the twenty-first century. If something happened to him, no one would look for him except Neve, since he didn't officially exist. But what would she tell the police; that she'd brought a seventeenth-century man through a passage in a church? Who'd believe her? They would think she'd lost the plot and would send her for a psychiatric evaluation, one that she would fail unless she retracted her story.

Even if Hugo's corpse turned up somewhere, no one would be able to identify him or find his killer, since no one would be able to tie him to the Everlys. It could be the perfect crime—a crime that would set Max free and clear his path to power. Now, all he had to do was keep Neve and Hugo from leaving. He could invite Hugo to go hunting and shoot him accidentally on purpose, or he could take him fishing and drown him in the stream, which was an even better idea since the body could float down the stream, washed clean of any evidence.

Max poured himself another drink but sipped it slowly this time. He needed time to work out the details, but that shouldn't be too difficult. He'd ruffled some feathers tonight, but he would smooth things over come morning and put his plan into action. The sooner, the better too, since his mother would arrive home within a week, and there was no need to involve her in his scheme.

FORTY-FOUR

I woke up just as the fuchsia rays of the rising sun began to color the conservatively decorated bedroom, making it look like a punk-rock dream of a teenage girl. Everything glowed a reddish-pink and the effect was dazzling, especially on Hugo, who looked like some god crowned with a blood-red halo.

Unfortunately, he didn't appreciate the artistic effect and rolled away from the light to avoid the sun on his face. I smiled and stretched contentedly, briefly remembering last night. A few moments later, I was abruptly brought back to reality when I remembered the encounter with Max. I hadn't expected Max to be thrilled, but I certainly did not anticipate the venom I could almost see dripping from his tongue. I'd trusted Max, and thought of him a friend, but the side of him I'd witnessed last night was like nothing I'd seen before.

Did Max believe that having Hugo in the twenty-first century somehow threatened his position and future plans? But how? Hugo had no claim to anything, being dead for over three hundred years; so why did Max feel so threatened? He'd taken my car and bag and hidden them, making certain that no one who looked for me would find any sign of my disappearance.

Was that a helpful gesture, or a way of disguising something sinister? What if I hadn't gone through the passage but had been assaulted by someone or kidnapped? The police would never know since Max hadn't lost any time in disposing of the evidence. And if he had known that I'd stepped back in time, was he happy to leave me there and forget I'd ever existed?

These revelations made my head spin. I had to get Hugo out of here as soon as possible. London was the best place for a person to get lost in, so to London we would go. I just had to collect my car from the lodge stables, change into my own clothes, and disappear before the cast and crew descended on the manor house for a day of shooting and spotted me wandering about. I would speak to Lawrence when I was ready and present him with a plausible explanation for why I'd gone walkabout.

I rolled onto my side and fitted myself to Hugo before kissing his bare shoulder and wrapping my arm around his waist. "Hugo, time to go," I whispered in his ear. My voice had an immediate effect. Hugo placed his hand over mine without turning around, but I knew that he was now fully awake, his mind going full speed.

"We must leave," he said, "now?"

"Yes, we must, but I'm afraid I must see Max before we go. I need to get my car and purse from the lodge."

The mention of the car made Hugo turn around and face me, his eyes full of anxiety.

"Exactly how fast does a motorized vehicle ride?" he asked.

"It doesn't ride—it drives, and it's much faster than a horse. Don't worry; it'll only feel strange for a few moments until you get your bearings. It will be fun."

"Fun?" he echoed. "I never really thought of things as being fun, but I suppose under the circumstances, I might just reconsider the meaning of that word." He was trying to be sarcastic, but I detected a note of panic in his voice. A galloping horse could go as fast as thirty miles per hour, so I didn't dare tell Hugo how fast a car could drive down a motorway. He'd find out in due course.

We dressed in near silence and went in search of Max. I forgot all about the portrait, but Hugo stopped and stared at the only thing left of his time on earth. His likeness glared at him with all the charm of a belligerent bulldog.

"I never did like that portrait," Hugo said conversationally. "I never wanted to sit for it, but Jane insisted, saying that it was only right and proper that every Lord Everly have his place in the gallery. She said I should look imposing and masterful. What do you think? Did I manage to accomplish that?" he asked with an impish grin.

"Oh, yes. You are the very picture of a feudal overlord about to whip his serfs." I couldn't help teasing him, especially when I knew that despite his cool demeanor, he was probably worried about what was to become of him now that we had no plan to fall back on.

"A job well done then, to be enjoyed by future generations of Everlys for years to come." Hugo took my arm and led me to the stairs, where we nearly collided with Max.

"Are you off so soon?" Max asked innocently, his face wreathed in smiles. "Please, stay for breakfast at least, and then I will drive you to the lodge and open the stables. I insist."

"Very well," Hugo said and followed Max to the dining room, where a hot breakfast was waiting on the ornate sideboard.

Max handed Hugo a plate and then went on to fill his own with eggs, sausages, and fried tomatoes. Racks of toast and hot tea were already on the table—a fact that I found telling. Max didn't want Stella to serve breakfast as she normally did. Perhaps he'd realized the possible implications of having someone witness Hugo's presence at the manor. Stella had been there last night, but she'd hardly noticed Hugo. This morning, with the May sunshine bathing the room in a golden haze, she was sure to notice that her employer's guest looked like his long-lost brother, which might raise a few questions, particularly if she happened to mention it to Lady Everly on her return. I had to admit that the resemblance was even more pronounced in the daylight. Perhaps that's what scared Max. Did he think that Hugo would try to impersonate him in some way?

Max took a few bites and pushed his plate away, making a show of being unable to eat. "Look, old chap, I'm afraid I was rather unwelcoming last night. The shock of seeing you and all that... I'd like to make it up to you. Why don't you stay for a few days? Get the lay of the land, so to speak. You can stay at the lodge if you prefer. I'm sure Neve has things to attend to after her extended absence, so you and I can get to know each other better; we are family after all. Do you enjoy fishing?" Max asked, smiling at Hugo in an ingratiating way.

"Not particularly," Hugo replied, the chill evident in his voice.

"What about hunting?" Max tried again.

"I thank you for your kind offer, Lord Everly, but Mistress Ashley and I will be on our way."

I smiled into my eggs because at that point, there was no doubt who the real Lord Everly was. Max looked like a chastised schoolboy next to Hugo, who was every inch the lord. I could see spots of color appear in Max's cheeks. Hugo hadn't said anything offensive, but Max felt slighted; that was obvious.

"Max, if you would be so kind as to give me the key to the stable, we'll be going. And thank you for breakfast." I took a last sip of tea and rose to leave, followed by Hugo.

"I'll drive you there," Max suggested, but Hugo wasn't about to have his first automotive experience in the presence of Max.

"I think we'll just walk to the lodge," he said. "It's a fine morning outside. Shall we meet you there?"

"Of course," Max conceded.

* * *

I was relieved to be outside. The drops of dew on the grass sparkled like shards of crystal, and a peachy haze enveloped the park and village, blurring the edges and making everything appear soft and beautiful. My feet were wet within minutes, but I didn't care as I walked with Hugo toward the woods. At this moment, all I wanted was to retrieve my things and be gone. A plan was forming in my head, but it would take some finessing, so I wasn't ready to share it with Hugo just yet.

Max was already at the lodge by the time we arrived; the padlock hanging listlessly off the thick chain and the doors to the stables open to reveal my car. Max tossed me the keys and turned to Hugo, a bright smile on his face. "May I show you around while Neve collects her things?"

I knew that Hugo wanted to refuse, but he was too much a gentleman to reject Max outright again, so he gave a slight incline of the head and followed Max into the forest. I wasn't sure what Max wanted to show Hugo, but I had a few things to do before we left. I rummaged in my holdall until I found my mobile and my wallet. My clothes were a bit wrinkled, but wearable, so I changed right there in the stable, and went to the lodge to return Max's togs. I was about to leave when I remembered our seventeenth-century clothes, so I hastily collected our things, washed out the tea mugs and plate, making sure to leave no trace of our stay behind.

I came out of the lodge and glanced around. Max and Hugo were not back yet, so I turned on my phone, fully expecting it to have a dead battery. The telephone buzzed to life with an announcement that I had seventeen missed calls, ten messages, a dozen texts, and countless emails. I glanced at recent calls, surprised to see that there were several calls placed within the past two months from my phone. A few were to Everly Manor, and several others were to my flat. If my mobile had been in the car all along, how was it possible that calls were made, and why was the battery still charged, if low?

I would answer these questions later, but first I decided to bite the bullet and listen to my messages. There were two calls from Evan, sounding haughty and demanding to know where I was; five messages from Lawrence, the last one telling me that I was fired; and several other messages from various friends as well as one from my bank. The clerk informed me that as of my last withdrawal on April 20, I was overdrawn by ten pounds.

My hands began to shake as the realization of what must have happened hit me. Max had my car keys; he'd found my personal belongings. He must have made the calls and used my account to give the impression that I was still in the present, rather than in the seventeenth century. I couldn't understand how this might benefit him or why he would feel the need to perpetuate this charade, but whatever his reasons were, he clearly had something to lose now that I was back.

I threw my things back into the car and ran in the direction that Max and Hugo had taken.

FORTY-FIVE

Max tried a few different topics before he finally stumbled on one that Hugo found interesting. The man wasn't a fisherman or a huntsman, and he seemed reluctant to talk about seventeenth-century politics, given that he was shoulder deep in treason and about to be executed in his own time, but he was curious about the modern-day running of the estate. Max prattled on about farm equipment while his brain whirred like a crazed bumblebee. This was his one chance to get rid of Hugo. Once Neve took him to London, he would be in a vast, populated place where committing a crime of this magnitude would be nearly impossible without detection. With all the nosey passersby and CCTV cameras on every bloody corner, someone was bound to see something, and, with Max's luck, even get images that would be played on every television station and get a gazillion hits on YouTube; solidifying his guilt and ruining his brilliant future. Max and Hugo were alone in the woods, walking toward the stream, so this had to be it. No one could say that it wasn't premeditated, but Max was utterly unprepared. He'd meant to get a gun from the lodge, but never got the chance, so he'd have to improvise.

"Did you have the grist mill in your time?" Max asked, feigning interest. "I'm not certain when it was built, but it's actually still there—disused, of course. It hasn't been utilized since the Industrial Revolution. Oh, I do beg your pardon, you wouldn't have heard about that. I'm sure that Neve told you that everything these days is run on electricity and monitored by computers." Max allowed himself a moment of enjoyment as Hugo tried to process what he was saying and not to appear to be an absolute dunce. Hugo just nodded in understanding, making Max even angrier than he already was.

"Yes, Neve did explain that to me. I must confess that I don't quite understand the workings of it, but it sounds most efficient."

Bastard! Bastard! Bastard! Max thought as he pointed toward the old mill in the distance. The building was all but rotted away; the old wheel covered in slime and weeds after centuries of neglect. The whole thing was a grotesque reminder that the past belonged in the past, like the specimen that was picking his way along the slippery path next to Max, his face alight with curiosity.

Hugo turned to ask a question, and Max was suddenly struck by the resemblance. It was like looking in the mirror and seeing a slightly more weathered version of oneself. Hugo was about the same age, possibly even a few years younger, but decades of living in a place devoid of proper nutrition, medical care, and creature comforts was bound to age a man. Of course, Hugo had never seen the inside of a tanning salon, Max thought savagely, and a golden tan could be so becoming and appealing to the ladies.

"It didn't work on Neve," his inner voice commented, but he ignored it and continued walking, a sinister thought forming in his mind. If Hugo resembled him so greatly, he could easily take his place. Hugo could kill him and claim to be Lord Everly, which he technically was, in his stead. It would take him a bit of time to acclimate to this century, and of course, he could never fool his mother, but it could be done with Neve's help.

Max trained his eyes on the path, searching for what he needed. It came along a few minutes later, within a few feet of the mill. The stone was the size of Max's fist, a jagged edge sharp and pointy sticking up at one end, perfect for bludgeoning someone's unsuspecting skull. If the body washed under the wheel of the mill, it would rot in peace without anyone ever suspecting the secret it held. Even better than floating downstream. No one came this way anymore, so the body would never be discovered.

Max dipped down and picked up the rock without missing a step and held his hand behind his back. *Dear God*, he said in his head, *please forgive what I'm about to do and guide my hand so that I get it right the first time. This man is an obvious threat to me, so this is self-defense*, he added, just in case God needed to hear his reasons.

Max took a deep breath and raised his hand behind an unsuspecting Hugo.

FORTY-SIX

I ran as fast as I could, my heart hammering against my ribs and my mind spinning out of control with fear for Hugo. I wasn't sure what Max intended, but at this point, I strongly suspected it wasn't a scenic tour of the grounds. How could I have been so wrong about him? So taken in by his phony charm?

I stopped for a moment to catch my breath, but after a few quick sucks of air continued to run. Max and Hugo had at least a twenty-minute lead, so I had no idea how far they'd gone. I'd heard Max saying something about the stream earlier, so I ran toward the barely audible rush of water, praying all the while that I was completely insane, and Max was just enjoying a nature walk.

As I burst through the gap in the trees, I saw the hulking black outline of what was left of the mill. The giant wheel was lazily turning, trapped in eternal motion caused by the water that flowed beneath it. The bank of the stream was muddy, and I slipped and landed hard on my butt, avoiding falling into the water by mere inches. My hand was scraped, and my jeans were muddy and wet, but I sprang back up and continued running toward the mill in the hope that Max had taken Hugo there. They could have gone a different way, but I had followed the trail, and thought it would have made sense for the men to walk the path rather than crash through the woods, pushing branches and brambles out of their way.

I finally spotted them ahead of me. The path was too narrow for two people, so Max solicitously walked behind Hugo, playing the gracious host. Hugo was looking around with interest, no doubt comparing the spot with his own memory of it. He must have gone hunting in these woods more times than he could remember, and despite telling Max that he didn't enjoy either hunting or fishing, he had fished this stream, most recently with Clarence, only about a week ago. Clarence had been thrilled to escape from the classroom and caught a few middling fishes, which he presented with flourish to the Cook. She must have tossed them to the cats as soon as Clarence turned his back, but she made all the appropriate noises of astonishment and appreciation, making Clarence blush pink with pleasure.

I couldn't hear what Max was saying, if he were saying anything at all, but I suddenly noticed the large stone he held in his right hand behind his back. My heart plummeted to the ground, and my throat seemed to close up just when I needed more than anything to scream and warn Hugo that he was in danger, but the sound that came out was nothing more than a whimper, a tiny scream that wouldn't carry more than a foot or two—a squeak rather than a battle cry of warning.

Tears of fear and frustration ran down my face as I tried to fill my lungs with air and let out a roar, but I felt as if I were choking, my throat constricted, and my vision blurred. I angrily wiped the tears away and tried screaming again, but nothing came out, save a hoarse croak. *Oh Hugo*, I thought, *please hear me*. But Hugo just walked on, oblivious to my anguish and Max's evil intentions. What in the world did Max have against Hugo? What could Hugo do to alter Max's life? If Hugo went back, he'd be executed, and everything would go on just as it had already happened. And if Hugo remained in this century, he'd be no threat to Max whatsoever. Max was the current Lord Everly, the man who had it all. What could he possibly fear from a displaced seventeenth-century man who, at this moment, didn't have a farthing to his name or anything other than the clothes on his back, which didn't even belong to him?

A desperate sob tore from my chest as I saw Max raise his hand to bring the rock atop Hugo's head. This couldn't be happening. I'd tried to save Hugo, and instead I'd led him to his death. Was it destiny that Hugo should die in May of what was in his time 1685? Was it not possible to cheat fate? Was this the day of his death in his actual life? It couldn't be, since he'd likely just arrive at the Tower of London, but perhaps he'd tried to fight his captors and died in the attempt.

All these thoughts raced through my head in the mere seconds it took for the rock to come down, but I shut down my brain and forced myself to look up. I needed to see Max committing this crime so that I could be a witness to what happened. He wasn't going to get away with it. The tableau seemed to play out before my eyes in slow motion. Max brought down his hand with all his strength, but the rock never made contact with Hugo's skull. Hugo executed a graceful dip, making Max lose his balance and come tumbling down onto the bank of the creek face first. Hugo kicked Max's wrist savagely, forcing him to release his hold on the rock, which fell into the water with an audible splash. I watched as Max flipped over, his face contorted with rage as he tried to grab Hugo's legs and bring him down, but Hugo danced out of the way and grabbed a fallen branch. Before I knew it, he was sitting on Max's chest, the branch pressed against Max's throat in a way that made him turn first pale with fear, then puce with the lack of oxygen. I knew I should do something to stop Hugo, but I didn't. I knew deep down that Hugo wasn't a murderer; he wanted to scare Max, and it was working admirably.

Max was croaking something, his hands trying to push at the branch and his legs flailing helplessly as his eyes pleaded with Hugo for mercy. All Hugo had to do was push down harder and Max would suffocate.

I tore my gaze away from Max and looked at Hugo. I couldn't see his face, but his shoulders were tense, and his thighs straddled Max in a way that prevented him from moving.

Hugo suddenly turned around as if sensing my presence.

"Come join us, Neve," he called. I was surprised by how calm he sounded, considering that he'd just escaped death by stoning.

I stumbled toward him, blinded by panic and fear. What was he planning to do?

"Hugo..." I breathed, but I had no idea what to say.

"Should I do it?" Hugo asked dispassionately. "According to you, I don't exist in this time, so no one would ever think to accuse me of Lord Everly's murder. I am invisible, am I not?" Hugo asked me. He kept the pressure on the branch, but it appeared as if reasoning this out was his only concern.

"Hugo, please, don't do it," I pleaded. "I saw what he did, and he deserves to be punished, but not by your hand."

I was surprised to see a brilliant smile light up Hugo's face. "But think about it," he called out to me, "I could simply take Lord Everly's place. The resemblance is uncanny, you said so yourself. Of course, people would be put off by my mannerisms and lack of certain personal knowledge, but they would try to rationalize it away, never even imagining that the real Lord Everly is tied beneath the old grist mill, sleeping peacefully for all eternity."

My mouth dropped open in shock, but Hugo winked at me before turning back to Max. He was just tormenting Max for what he'd done, no doubt having figured out that he'd just outlined the fate Max had in store for him. It was quite clever actually, because Max went from beet-red to pea-green, his eyes bulging with shock and fear. Hugo wasn't as thick as he'd taken him to be, his mind working as fast, if not faster than Max's. He was enjoying this cat-and-mouse game, making Max pay for his treachery.

"What do you think, Max?" Hugo asked. "Is that what you had planned? No one would look for a man who doesn't exist, would they? No one would care, except Neve, who would be written off as being mad. She'd disappeared for weeks, and no one knew where she'd gone. People would think she had some sort of mental collapse, wouldn't they?"

Max was croaking something, but I couldn't understand what he was saying.

"Did you say something?" Hugo asked politely and shifted the branch a little to allow Max to draw a deep breath and speak.

"Hugo, please," he pleaded. "I don't know what came over me. It was a moment of madness. Please, I beg you, don't kill me. You are not a murderer."

"How do you know? I didn't think you were a murderer either, but here we are." I could tell by the twinkle in his eye that Hugo was having fun at Max's expense, but I was horrified. What were we to do now?

I was surprised when Hugo sprang to his feet and kicked Max into the creek. Max would be wet and muddy, but very much alive. I hoped he wouldn't try to harm Hugo again, but Max showed no inclination to get out of the stream. His head bobbed above the water as he watched Hugo warily.

"What now?" Max asked, clearly still scared.

"Now we leave," Hugo replied over his shoulder.

FORTY-SEVEN

Hugo sat perfectly still as I put the key in the ignition and started the car. I knew that he was nervous but didn't want to make things worse for him by telling him that his fears were unfounded. I'm sure that if I were about to go up in a spaceship, I'd be nervous as well, and after traveling all his life at less than 30 mph, this was pretty much the equivalent.

I let the car roll out of the stable and down the dirt road at a very slow speed, allowing Hugo to get comfortable with the motion. He looked at the dashboard with interest, asking me about the various displays and buttons, probably in order to distract himself. I answered calmly, while gradually picking up speed.

By the time we got on the motorway, Hugo had a slightly greenish hue to his face, but he stared ahead resolutely, fixating on one spot in order not to be overwhelmed by the cars zooming past us. I was dawdling in the slow lane, but eventually I got tired and switched lanes, the car now traveling at just over the speed limit. It was a beautiful spring day, so I opened the windows and a fresh breeze caressed our faces as the sun played peek-a-boo with the trees on the side of the road. The air smelled of grass and pine with overtones of petrol and hot rubber.

I noticed that Hugo was no longer staring ahead but was looking at the passing cars; his head cocked to the side as he noted the different models and shapes. He was breathing deeply and evenly, which led me to believe that it was safe to talk to him.

"So, what do you think of your first car ride?" I asked with a smile, feeling as if I were talking to a toddler.

"I think it's *fun*," Hugo replied promptly, making me laugh. "Now, tell me about all the different vehicles that we're passing. What's that one, for instance?"

We spent the next few minutes discussing the various types of cars on the road before I tried to describe to him what London was going to be like. A sleepy English village, even one that was four centuries ahead, was nothing like the city he was about to encounter. London in the seventeenth century was dirty, overcrowded, and full of horses and carts jostling for space on the narrow, muck-strewn roads bracketed by wooden houses with overhanging upper floors, but it was something Hugo was used to. Arriving in a city of millions with heavy traffic, double-decker buses, skyscrapers, and shops and restaurants lining every commercial avenue, and boasting everything from televisions to kebabs, was bound to be a trifle overwhelming.

"Is Evan in London?" Hugo suddenly asked, taking me completely by surprise. I should have known he wouldn't just let it go, and now that we were relatively safe and almost at home, he needed to know what he was up against emotionally, not just physically.

"Yes, he is, but I won't be seeing him," I replied, knowing that this wasn't the end of it.

"What is his relationship to you? Max implied that he was rather important."

"He was, for a time, but things are long finished between us." I took Hugo's hand and gave it a squeeze. "Hugo, he's no threat to you."

Hugo nodded, but wasn't quite ready to move on from the topic. "What was your relationship with him?" He didn't pull away his hand, but he didn't return my squeeze of affection either. His hand just rested in mine as noncommittal as his facial expression.

"We lived together for nearly four years. Does it bother you that I had lived with another man?"

Hugo shrugged and gave me a rueful smile. "I married a blushing maiden, and she left me without so much as a backward glance. Innocence doesn't guarantee loyalty or everlasting love. I never assumed that your life was a blank page; besides, given my current situation, your previous cohabitation with another man is the least of my worries. But why did he never marry you?" Hugo asked, incredulous. "What kind of man would live with a woman for four years and not offer her his name or financial support? Did he lie to you? Make promises?"

"No, he didn't. Hugo, marriage is somewhat different in the twenty-first century. People still marry, of course, but for different reasons. Women are independent and self-sufficient, so they no longer need the protection or support of a man. They marry for love, or out of loneliness, but not out of fear or duty. An unmarried woman is not looked down upon or considered to be a withered old spinster. Single women have lovers and lead a full life. Sometimes they even have children out of wedlock, and no one thinks of them as bastards. They have the same rights as anyone else. There's no stigma or shame. As a matter of fact, some women choose to have a child on their own."

"Why?" Hugo asked, utterly shocked.

"There are many reasons. Some women don't want to marry the father; others are lesbians and want to raise the child with their partner, and some would like to marry, but are never asked, so they have a child in order to have something of a family rather than being alone."

"Did you have a child?" Hugo asked suddenly, as if reading my mind.

I was about to tell him about the miscarriage, but something stopped me. He'd had enough shocks for two days, and I had a right to keep something of my life private. The miscarriage did not affect him in any way, so there was no reason for him to know. Besides, speaking of it was painful, and I had no wish to rake that all up again.

"No, I never had a child," I replied, my voice strangely flat.

"But you might have..."

"Yes, I might have in time. Evan has a daughter from a previous marriage, so he wasn't all that interested in having more kids."

"He didn't want a son?" Hugo asked, still perplexed.

"Sons don't have the same value they once did. Most people leave their estate to all their children. They divide it between boys and girls. There's no longer the law of primogeniture, so being a younger son is no worse than being the eldest, unless there is a title, which few people have."

"Hmm, I see," Hugo said. "So, you didn't feel insulted by his lack of desire to marry you?"

"I would have accepted had he asked, but it wasn't uppermost in my mind. I'm only twenty-five, which in modern terms is very young. Most people tend to marry closer to thirty. I wasn't in any tremendous rush."

Hugo stared at me. Now I'd really shocked him. "People think twenty-five is too young to marry? So how old are these women when they have children?"

"People are having children well into their forties, fifties even. There are now ways to help women get pregnant artificially, and sometimes even without men." I couldn't help chuck-

ling at the look of astonishment on Hugo's face. He thought I
was having him on, but I assured him I was quite serious.

"So, what you are telling me is that the role of men has
diminished significantly over the past few centuries. We are no
longer needed for protection, marriage, or even conception.
What do men do with themselves?" He was joking, but I could
see that the information really affected him.

"They have careers; they pursue their interests, such as
sports, arts, and so on. And, of course, they have families, which
are just as important as ever, only different. Nowadays, men
help with the raising of the children. They do everything from
changing nappies to feeding the babies and giving them baths.
Once the children get older, they spend time with them.
Fathers are involved in every aspect of their children's lives,
even that of the girls. They take them to dance lessons, shop-
ping, and even play dress-up. It's a different world, Hugo. Come
to think of it, I'd really like to see you play dress-up."

"One thing at a time, sweet," Hugo grumbled as we pulled
into the outskirts of London.

He grew quiet as he gazed around, his face alight with
wonder and worry. I just let him be, knowing he needed time to
take it all in. There'd be plenty of time to explain things to him
and educate him on how different things were in the twenty-
first century. For now, he was on sensory overload, so I just
turned on the radio and let it play quietly in the background as
Hugo sank deeper into his seat, his knuckles white as he let the
full force of London hit him.

Surprisingly, Hugo took it all in his stride, but what really
shocked him was my flat. I carefully inserted the key in the lock,
all the while praying that the flat hadn't been burglarized in my
absence, but everything appeared to be just as I'd left it. Thank
God I had no pets, or I would be coming back to a slightly
different smell than that of dust and spoiled food in the fridge. I

collected everything into a bag and took it to the trash bins outside before returning to find Hugo walking around in consternation.

"Is this it? Is this where you live?" he asked, confused.

"Yes, why?" I was rather proud of my lovely flat in Notting Hill. It was a trendy neighborhood with lots of shops, restaurants, and young people; just the type of place I wanted to live in. I'd never have been able to afford a flat in Notting Hill on my salary, but my foster parents had helped me sell my mother's house after her death and invest the money wisely; something I didn't think was important at the time, but I'd been pleasantly surprised to find that I had a tidy sum by the time I finished uni —enough for a down payment on the flat and a nice holiday abroad. I'd subleased the flat for three years, but moved back in as soon as the lease was up since I could no longer stay with Evan.

I could hear the bustle from the street through the open windows, as the May breeze cleared out the stale odor of the past two months and filled the front room with the smell of flowers and spicy Indian food wafting from a nearby restaurant.

"There are only two rooms?" Hugo asked suspiciously; obviously still thinking that I was having him on.

"Yes, only two rooms and a bath. This is actually a very expensive neighborhood and flats come dear."

Hugo nodded in understanding, but I could just see the gears turning in his head. He'd lived alone at Everly Manor until Jane and Clarence came to stay, and here I was, a working woman, living in an apartment the size of his bedroom. I plonked down on the sofa, suddenly seeing the flat through Hugo's eyes. It was tiny, and far from luxurious. He must have expected so much more. He probably thought I had a maid. Well, finding out that I had to clean, wash, lug groceries, and cook would come as a surprise.

Hugo sat down next to me and pulled me to him, kissing the top of my head. "I'm sorry, sweetheart; I didn't mean to upset you. It's a lovely—what did you call it?—flat. I'm sure we'll be very happy here. By the by, what is that smell? It's rather appetizing, in a revolting kind of way." That made me laugh.

I had to stop feeling sorry for myself. At least I was in my element, whereas Hugo was like a blindfolded man thrashing through the jungle. He had no idea what things were or what to expect from them.

"Would you like to try it? It's coming from the Indian restaurant. I get takeaway from them all the time."

"What's takeaway?"

"It's when you order food, and they prepare it for you and give it to you to take home. Or you can just eat there. Which would you prefer? Or would you like to eat something typically English?" I asked, wondering if something so radically different might make him ill.

"I would very much like to try the takeaway," Hugo replied, "but I was under the impression that you were overdrawn at the bank."

I gazed at him in surprise. "Ah yes, but I do have a savings account, so I will transfer funds to my checking. As a matter of fact, I'll do that right now." I pulled out my laptop and turned it on, ready to access my online banking.

Hugo watched in amazement as I clicked a few keys.

"Voila, done," I announced.

"You don't need to visit the bank?"

"No, everything can be done electronically now."

"Right, I should have guessed." Hugo looked a bit crestfallen, but I just pulled him to me and gave him a tender kiss.

"Are you finding all this manageable or are you ready to run screaming back to the crypt?" I knew that he could hardly just go back, but I had to ask.

"I am more than all right," Hugo replied with a smile. "This is the adventure of a lifetime."

"Really?"

"Really. Now feed me."

FORTY-EIGHT

My heartbeat quickened as I stepped out of the lift, greeted the receptionist, and made my way toward Lawrence Spellman's office. I was surprised that he was in London during the shooting of the series, but he'd come up for the weekend and stayed through Monday, taking care of some paperwork before returning to Cranleigh tomorrow morning. I would have gone back to Surrey to speak to him, but this was preferable. I wasn't ready to face the rest of the crew, or Max, whose reaction to seeing me could be volatile.

I still burned with anger every time I thought of Max. It was one thing to be a self-serving ponce, but to attempt murder against an innocent person was monstrous. The depth of his hatred frightened me, and I found myself frequently looking over my shoulder, expecting him to be lurking in a doorway or turning the corner, his desire for revenge against Hugo clouding his judgment—if he had any—and driving him to commit a terrible crime.

"Enter," Lawrence called out, and I timidly stepped into his office.

Lawrence Spellman always reminded me of an undertaker

or a clerk in some Dickensian law firm. He was slight and balding, his round spectacles perched on his nose, and his "uniform" a black suit with a white shirt and conservative, dark-colored tie. For a creative person, he looked like anything but. Lawrence had never been married, had no children, and as far as anyone at the office knew was probably still a virgin, despite being in his early fifties. He made wonderful films though, full of romance, passion, and longing.

"She lives!" Spellman announced as I walked into his office and took a seat.

"Lawrence, I'm so sorry," I began.

"Neve, you know that I'm not a stickler for company rules, but you could have at least called—or texted. You don't just disappear for nearly two months without a word to anyone." Spellman tried to look stern, but his gaze was one of concern. "Are you all right?" he asked kindly.

"I think so," I mumbled, putting on my best "girl trying not to fall apart" act. "I just had some sort of breakdown. You know; Evan, and all that..." I let the sentence hang since Lawrence knew of my miscarriage.

"Neve, I know you haven't had an easy time of it, but you can't just vanish. We were all worried about you. I called the police, but they informed me that you were just hiding somewhere. Where were you?"

I made a vague gesture with my hand, indicating that I was here and there, but nowhere precisely. "Lawrence, I know you are angry, but please, can I have my job back? I promise it won't happen again. I've been a model employee for years. This was my first transgression," I pleaded. Being out of work right now was not an option.

"All right," Lawrence replied gruffly. "You can have your job back, but if you so much as disappear for a few hours without notifying me, you're out."

"So, what projects are coming up?" I asked, hoping to distract him from my inexplicable behavior.

"There's a World War Two drama in the works, but I've sent the script back to be tweaked, and a series about a posh hotel right here in London. Naturally, it will be filled with the shenanigans of the staff and the guests," Lawrence said happily.

"Naturally," I replied, smiling. Lawrence was the only person I knew who'd use the word "shenanigans," but if I knew the man, "shenanigans" would be an understatement. This was just the kind of thing Lawrence loved: developing characters who would grow and change throughout the series and take viewers by surprise when they least expected it.

"Of course, the series will be filmed mostly on set since we can hardly take over an actual five-star hotel for the duration. I will, however, need you to find me some suitable locations for filming right here in London—clubs, spas, restaurants, places where wealthy guests would go while in London. You can start next week. Why don't you take the rest of the week off and get your head on straight? You look a bit peaky."

"Thanks, Lawrence. I appreciate it," I replied, grateful for the extra time off, which I assumed would be paid. I needed to figure out what to do with Hugo. "Is Glenn here?"

"Yes, he's in his lair, I believe," Lawrence grumbled, already caught up in reading some letter.

I made my way through the office as unobtrusively as I could. Everyone knew of my disappearance, and the last thing I wanted was to answer a bunch of questions from nosy co-workers. Thankfully, most people were in Surrey on location, so the only people around were those who saw to the administrative duties of the company and were too comatose on a Monday morning to pay much attention to a woman who'd pulled a disappearing act but had the audacity to come back and ruin a perfectly good mystery and source of water-cooler gossip.

Glenn Coolidge was in his studio, surrounded by equipment and tooling with something as I came in. His black spiky hair was wilder than ever, and his intelligent gray eyes danced with mirth as he saw me enter. Glenn was the resident computer genius, the person who supervised the Special Effects department and could create, hack, or manipulate any data he could get his hands on.

"Neve, you're not dead," he announced. "Did you bring me a cuppa?"

I set a cup of black coffee in front of him and gave him a kiss on the cheek.

"No, I'm not dead, thank you for noticing. Only you would skip comments about the weather and just blurt that out."

"I'm American; I don't do comments about the weather. Where've you been?" Glenn invited me to sit down and took a sip of coffee. No one ever came to see Glenn without bringing a cup of black coffee with two sugars.

"I've had some personal problems. You know how that can be." If anyone knew about personal difficulties, it would be Glenn. He was currently part of a triad with a married couple, sharing their flat and bed, and battling his ex-wife in court for visitation rights with his daughter. His living situation did not make a custody hearing any easier, nor did it help him make a favorable impression on the judge. I'm not sure how I would feel if the father of my child was openly living in a ménage à trois, but it was none of my affair, and I liked Glenn enormously, no matter what he did. He was one of the funniest, craziest guys I knew—and a real friend.

"What is it, my girl?" Glenn asked as he studied me over the rim of the cup. "You look like you want to ask me something, but don't really know how to phrase it." No one could ever accuse Glenn of being obtuse. He practically read people's minds as if he could access a microchip in their brain and download all the data, à la *Star Trek*.

"Glenn, how difficult would it be to obtain a... eh... fake passport?" I stammered.

"For whom?" Glenn asked suspiciously.

"For a friend," was all I was willing to volunteer.

Glenn set down his cup and leaned back in his chair, folding his arms behind his head and studying me as if he'd just discovered that I wasn't at all what I'd been pretending to be. He was about to say something, then changed his mind, shaking his head as if arguing with himself silently.

"Glenn?" I prompted.

"Look, Neve, I might know of some people who could furnish you with a fake British passport for a large sum of money, but you're my friend, and I would not advise it. If there is any other way—take it."

"Why wouldn't you advise it, and how much would it cost?" I asked.

Glenn rubbed his chin as he looked at me, trying to gauge how serious I was about getting involved in criminal activity. "Look, years ago, a passport was enough to establish an identity, but things have changed. We live in a digital world where your electronic trail begins before you're even born. I'm sure MI5 could pull up pictures of your mother's ultrasounds and determine whether you have your father's nose or your mother's ears before you were even born. A person needs more than just a form of credible identification. When the fake passport is scanned by a customs officer or a prospective employer, all kinds of flags will be raised. Where was this person born, where did they go to school, when did they get their driver's license, and where is the record of their previous employment? You need a whole file to go along with your passport; you need a life."

"I see. They make it look so easy in American movies," I quipped, feeling hollow inside. What was I to do now? This was my only idea to date. "Is there any way to make it work?"

"I'm not really sure, but I think that if you use your fake passport to drive across the border in some remote spot, you might have a better chance than leaving from, say, Heathrow. The officials on the other side of the border will not be as interested in your past exploits as long as the passport looks legit, but re-entering the country might be tricky. Neve, what are you up to?"

"Nothing. It was just a rhetorical question. I'm trying to write a crime novel," I improvised. Glenn liked to gossip, so although I knew he wouldn't blab about something as sensitive as this, I didn't want to give him any ammunition against me, just in case.

"Really? I tried writing once. I like horror, like Stephen King, but nothing I wrote was even remotely scary. I read a passage to my wife—ex-wife—and she just laughed in my face," Glenn recounted with a grimace.

"Is that why you divorced?"

"No, we divorced because she caught me in bed with a man, which was apparently much scarier than anything I could write," he said bitterly. "It had nothing to do with her. I still loved her as much as ever."

I wasn't sure what to say to this, so I just thanked him and left, gutted that my clever plan had just gone up in smoke. I couldn't risk Hugo getting arrested the minute he used his identification, and without it, how could he do anything? If Hugo were to stay with me in the twenty-first century, he needed to work. I'd thought that perhaps I could send him to some computer course, which would teach him the basics and enable him to get some sort of employment, but now I knew that wouldn't work. Without legal ID, all Hugo could do was some sort of manual labor which paid cash, such as loading trucks or washing dishes for someone who was willing to cheat the government. And that would never do.

I felt despondent as I walked down the street, reluctant to

go home and tell Hugo that my grand plan had failed. I honestly had no idea what to try next, and I knew that Hugo was too much of a man to just live off me and accept a life of idleness and utter insignificance. The world had changed much over the centuries, but some things remained the same. A person couldn't just drop into a place and build a life for themselves without help. From the beginning of time, people have belonged to families, tribes, guilds, unions, and churches. Without the connections forged over a lifetime, a person would be relegated to living on the fringes of society, and that was never easy. Hugo had grown up a nobleman, a man who was secure in his position and comfortable financially and physically. He'd never done a day's work. How could I tell him that he'd have to unload trucks or stock shelves in some grocery, not temporarily, but possibly for the rest of his life? He wouldn't complain, but I knew it would be a terrible blow to his self-esteem and would ultimately change him into someone neither of us barely recognized.

FORTY-NINE

By the end of May, our life had settled into a kind of strange routine. I went to work, while Hugo, armed with *London A-Z*, my library card, and a bagged lunch, went off to explore. He refused to accept any money from me, so walked all around London on foot. At first, he picked particular destinations, but later on, I think he just walked wherever his feet happened to take him just to have something to do. He must have covered miles as he crossed the capital from side to side, but he couldn't bear to stay cooped up in the flat, and he needed something to tire him out enough to allow him to sleep at night and not dwell on his situation. Hugo was in Limbo, and in turn, so was I.

Hugo had discovered St. Francis of Assisi Catholic Church in Notting Hill Gate and went regularly. I hoped that he'd speak to the priest and maybe find some solace without revealing too much, but we both knew the situation was untenable. Hugo never complained, but he'd grown more silent and less affectionate, his lovemaking more aggressive than tender. I could understand how he felt, and my mind rarely strayed very far from the situation at hand. I'd saved his life, but what kind of life could I offer him in return? The excitement and wonder of this new world quickly waned, leaving Hugo feeling out of place and out of time. He wasn't the type of man to be content with simply being alive; his basic human needs taken care of by someone else. Hugo needed to feel useful and productive; he needed to take pride in his achievements and be the man of the house, the protector and provider, not a kept man, living in a two-room flat with his girlfriend.

It was quite by chance that I came upon a solution, albeit a temporary one. I had to take a ride out to Hawthorne Stables in Bayswater, a place I visited often since most of our costume dramas required the use of horses. The owner, Dmitri Kouros, was a second-generation Greek immigrant, who never forgot the hospitality of his native land. He always invited me into the office and plied me with ouzo and his mother's homemade baklava, despite my protests. I really couldn't abide ouzo, but the baklava was a weakness of mine, and Maria Kouros made it like no other. I was on my third piece when Dmitri went into his usual tirade about the lack of help at the stables.

"Young people don't want these types of jobs," he grumbled. "They want to dress in a fine suit and go sit behind a computer terminal all day in some tiny cubicle. Show me a young man who wants to muck out stables, in London of all places? I get some animal-loving teenagers during the summer, but they all leave by fall, and I'm short-staffed again." Dmitri took a sip of ouzo and snorted with disgust. "I have to do half the work myself. At least I still have a few riding instructors left, but for how long?"

"Dmitri," I began, accepting a glass of the hated ouzo and making great pretense of admiring the aroma. "I have a friend who's very good with horses and needs a job, but he's not quite legal... yet. Is there any chance...?"

I was gratified to see Dmitri perk up a bit. "Good with horses, you say? He has experience, this friend?"

"Oh, yes. Used to own a stable full of horses in his homeland, but times are tough." I took a sip of ouzo and nearly choked. It was like drinking spiked cough syrup.

"Where's your friend from?" Dmitri asked.

"Here and there," I replied and winked at Dmitri. "What do you say? Give him a try?"

"All right, bring him in, and I promise I won't ask any questions. It's eight to six, six days a week, fifty pounds a day. That's my offer. If he gives me any trouble, he's out on his ear."

"Deal. I'll bring him tomorrow." I shoved the last piece of baklava in my mouth and gave Dmitri a sticky kiss on the cheek. "See you tomorrow then."

* * *

I wasn't sure how Hugo would take to doing such a menial job, but I thought he might be pleased to have something to do. I was right; Hugo was thrilled. The prospect of earning three hundred pounds a week was most welcome, since he still tended to think of money as having the same value it had in his own day. Three hundred pounds was a lot of money in 1685, so Hugo didn't quite realize that he wasn't going to be making a fortune. In either case, I was glad that he was happy and eager to contribute something to the running of the household. Hugo would have been wonderful at teaching adults and children how to ride, but he'd have to come into contact with customers, who might unwittingly cause trouble for us. He needed to stay behind the scenes, and he understood that.

Hugo started the following day, and I kept checking my phone all day to see if there might be a message from Dimitri, but all seemed to be well, and Hugo arrived at home by 7 p.m. He was hot, smelled strongly of horses, and was starving, but he had a smile on his face, something that had been in short supply of late.

"How was it?" I asked as I presented him with chicken

parmigiana and spaghetti with marinara sauce. I enjoyed introducing him to new foods, which he tried without complaint. I knew he didn't like many things, but this was one of his favorites and he tucked in. Hugo's hair was still damp from the shower, and the T-shirt stretched across his wide shoulders, reminding me of just how attractive he was, especially when happy. He'd grudgingly permitted me to buy him some clothes, and his wardrobe now consisted of T-shirts, jeans, and trainers.

"It was good. Felt nice to be around horses again."

"And Dmitri?"

"He's a nice man," Hugo replied cautiously. "Likes to talk."

"Did he pump you for information?"

"He tried, but I just gave him vague answers. Don't worry, Neve, I understand what's at stake."

"I know you do," I replied in a conciliatory manner. "I just wanted to make sure you had a nice day."

Hugo gave me a loaded look over his wineglass. Mucking out horseshit was not what most people would think of as a nice day, but beggars couldn't be choosers, could they?

And so, a new normal had begun for us, but it didn't last long.

FIFTY

Hugo sat down on a bale of hay, rested his head against the sun-warmed wood, and closed his eyes. The smell of horses was in his nose, but he didn't mind. It reminded him of home and the life he'd left behind. He tried not to burden Neve with his feelings, but sometimes when he was alone, like now, he couldn't help feeling a wave of bitterness wash over him. Truth be told, Hugo really liked the twenty-first century. Everything had seemed strangely accelerated and bewildering at first, but he'd gotten used to the constant movement of vehicles all around him and the sounds of modern life. The seventeenth century was so quiet by comparison. Here, there were sounds everywhere: traffic, blaring horns, music playing in shops, restaurants, and open car windows, multitudes of people walking, talking on their mobiles, singing along to their iPods, the rumbling of the tube, and the revving of double-decker buses as they passed him on the street. He had found it all overwhelming to begin with, but now it was just background noise, the soundtrack of a busy life.

Having a little money in his pocket made Hugo feel marginally better, but what he was making wasn't enough to live on or support a family; not that he could have a family. As a non-entity, he couldn't legally marry Neve, not even in a church; he'd asked Father Martin. The priest likely thought he was a bit strange, but never allowed his feelings to get in the way. He offered whatever comfort he could, and when Hugo had asked for the sacrament of confession, he did so with all the pomp due his office. Hugo couldn't tell him the whole truth, of course, but he did confess that he was in the country illegally and couldn't secure a good job or take any kind of course that might make him more proficient in modern technology.

Father Martin had told him that it wasn't a sin to want a better life, and that many before him had tried to immigrate illegally in the hopes of a more promising future. *If only he knew*, Hugo had thought ruefully.

Well, at least he was still alive, which was something, especially today of all days. It was July 15—the day James Crofts, Duke of Monmouth, was beheaded on Tower Hill in 1685, following the failure of his short-lived rebellion. Hugo would have been executed right alongside him had Neve not spirited him away. He was grateful, of course, but the thought of living his life on the fringes of society, never earning enough to support a family, and never being able to practice any of the freedoms this wonderful new world afforded was a terrible irony.

Hugo took a drink of cold water and went to change his clothes. The day was over, and the stables were closing in a few minutes. He wished Dmitri and the other lads a pleasant evening and set off across Hyde Park. Hugo enjoyed his evening walk; it gave him time to rein in his thoughts and feelings before coming home to Neve, who gazed at him in that searching way to gauge his mood. She wasn't the same woman he'd met only a few months ago. In the seventeenth century, she'd been frightened and defiant, but she wasn't defeated. Now she looked as if the world was resting squarely on her shoulders, and he couldn't take that. How long would she be willing to live with a man who couldn't give her a proper life?

A conversation they'd had last night as they lay in bed returned to haunt Hugo as he walked past the glittering ribbon of the Serpentine, winding through the park like a mythical pathway to a better world. But this was the better world, Hugo thought bitterly; only he couldn't truly be a part of it. Neve had asked him what he'd want to do, had he been born in the twentieth century, and the question had stumped Hugo. There were so many choices for a young person in this day and age. When he'd been young, his only choice had been to follow in his father's footsteps and pander to the king, or just play the lord of the manor and spend his days in pursuit of pleasure while others toiled on his estate and filled the coffers.

"I think I'd like to have been a doctor," Hugo had replied, surprising Neve.

"Really? I thought you might have wanted to be an engineer or even a policeman. You have such a desire to see justice done." She had snuggled closer to him, enjoying her little fantasy.

"You are right, both of those occupations are high on the list, but my first choice would be medicine," Hugo had answered, trying to picture himself as a healer.

"Why?" Neve had asked.

"I've never told you how my mother died, have I?" Hugo had asked, not really wishing to relive those horrible days, but wanting Neve to understand why he felt so strongly about his choice.

"You said she died in childbirth," Neve had replied quietly.

"So she did. But before she died, she suffered as no human being should ever have to. I remember hearing her screams echo through the house day after day as she tried to bring the child into the world. I was too young to understand any of it, but I knew something was horribly wrong. Jane was almost two at the time, and she cried and cried, sensing, as children do, that something dreadful was happening. The child was coming out the wrong way, you see, and every time it so much as moved downward, it was pulled up again. My father took me out on the estate—something he never did because he thought me a nuisance, but he felt it his duty to remove me from the house. He told me many years later that the cord had been wrapped around the baby's neck, preventing it from being born. Of course, the child died, as did my mother after four agonizing days of labor. She literally bled to death as the child tore her apart."

"Oh, Hugo, that's horrible," Neve had breathed, no doubt imagining the scene.

"Had there been a qualified doctor, the kind you have in this century, my mother would have lived and so would my baby brother. I wouldn't have lost her, and been left with a sister who was too young to share my grief, and a father who was too cold and controlled to show me any sympathy or affection. I howled for days after my mother passed, until my father threatened to whip me if I didn't stop."

"Did you?"

"Yes, but I never stopped mourning on the inside. I begged God every night that he would give my mother back to me, and in a strange way, he did. I started having dreams of her. She came to me as I slept, telling me that she loved me and would watch over me for the rest of my life. She looked happy and beautiful in the dreams, her voice soft and melodious, just the way it had sounded when she used to talk to me before I fell asleep. My mother wasn't one of those women who birthed a child, passed it on to the nurse, and forgot about it until it could walk and talk. She genuinely loved Jane and me."

"Is that why you took in Jem? Because you understood how he felt?"

"I came to the house after Jem's mother died to find him huddled in a corner, crying as the women laid her out for burial.

No one paid much attention to him, and I knew that once his mother was put in the ground, this child would be lost. He'd die of disease or neglect, but he'd never see adulthood. So, I took him away with me. Jem doesn't seem to remember that time. He slept in my bed for two weeks after the funeral and often thought I was his mother when he woke in the middle of the night. I was a very poor substitute, but I was happy to have been able to offer him some comfort. Jane relegated him to the kitchens once she came. She didn't think it appropriate to have Jem living in my room, but I didn't mind. I miss him," Hugo had sighed. "I can't imagine how sad he is thinking me dead."

"Do you miss Jane as well?" Neve had asked, probably to distract his mind from Jem.

"I do, but not in the same way. Jane's lived with her husband for the past thirteen years, so I saw her infrequently, and I saw Clarence even less. He was always in the nursery or at his lessons. He will make a good master once he reaches maturity. He's a smart and hard-working boy."

Thinking of Clarence had brought Hugo's mind to Max. Max Everly was the direct descendant of Clarence, the product of Hugo's treason and subsequent disappearance. Strange how life worked, especially when you were granted a chance to see for yourself how it all turned out.

Neve could have had Max, murderous villain though he was, thought Hugo bitterly. He'd seen the look of lust in Max's eyes as he'd stared at Neve in her modern clothes. He'd wanted her, and wanted her badly, and could never forgive her for choosing Hugo instead. Had she chosen Max, Neve could have been Lady Everly, and now she was just plain Neve Ashley, unwed, unprotected, and financially unsupported by her man. Perhaps the best thing to do would be to set her free. Hugo could always just disappear one day or go back to his old life and let himself be arrested and taken to the Tower. Perhaps now that Monmouth was dead, they'd be more lenient if enough money changed hands, although he'd be branded a traitor, and his family would be shamed by association. He couldn't do that to poor Clarence.

Hugo sighed and exited the park, walking along Kensington Road. He'd be home soon, and he had to stop feeling sorry for himself and try his best to put on a brave face for Neve. She'd have cooked something for their supper, and he was starving. He had to admit that he did enjoy the food. It was so much more diverse than the cuisine of the seventeenth century. Neve was constantly surprising him with new culinary delights. He'd hated sushi and couldn't stomach Indian spices, which seemed to permeate his entire body and ooze out of every pore, making him smell like the Indian restaurant down the block, but everything else had been generally to his liking, especially ice cream. He still couldn't believe the amount of flavors it came in and had aspirations of trying each and every one. So far, strawberry was by far the favorite. Maybe he'd get some ice cream tonight. Neve had a real "sweet tooth," as she called it, and he liked indulging her, although she seemed to fret about her weight.

Hugo was about to stop into a grocery owned by a nice Pakistani fellow when an advertisement for a film caught his eye. The movie was called *Master of Disguise* and depicted the same actor appearing as several different characters. Hugo was about to walk right past when he stopped in front of the poster and stared at the pictures more closely, ice cream forgotten. He stood for a few minutes, stroking his chin as he studied the different faces of the actor.

Hugo finally walked away, his step suddenly jauntier.

FIFTY-ONE

I closed the lid and sat down on the toilet, my head in my hands. I'd known I was feeling off for a few weeks, but stubbornly told myself that I was just tired from the summer heat and stressed by the situation with Hugo. Now I could deny the truth no longer. I was pregnant, probably at least a month along, and once again I was about to be confronted by a less-than-thrilled father-to-be. I knew how badly Hugo wanted a child, but not under these circumstances. This was the absolute wrong time to bring a baby into the world, and the thought of Hugo's despair at not being able to marry me and give the child his name made me swallow back a sob. Why did life have to play such cruel tricks? I wanted this baby more than anything, yet felt anything but happiness at the prospect.

I blew my nose on a tissue as I heard the door slam and Hugo's footsteps in the corridor. I wished I could hold off on telling him, but he'd be hurt if I didn't share the news with him —and what was the point of waiting? Things weren't about to change, were they?

Taking a deep breath, I let myself out of the loo, walking into the front room like a woman going to her execution. Hugo was sitting in his favorite chair by the open window overlooking Portobello Road. He'd found it grating at first, but now the bustle of the street seemed to amuse him, presenting him with a never-ending parade of sights and sounds. Hugo had poured us some wine and was holding his glass, the drink forgotten as he focused on something just outside.

I slid onto Hugo's lap, wrapped my arms around his neck, and lay my head on his shoulder, feeling like a small child in need of comforting after some small disappointment. Hugo wrapped his arms about me and rested his chin on top of my head. He'd changed his clothes, but I could still smell a combination of horseflesh, sweat, deodorant that I'd bought him, and the fruity bouquet of Cabernet Sauvignon on his breath.

"How was your day, sweetheart?" he asked softly. "You look tired."

"I am." I was tempted to leave it at that and just sit quietly with Hugo for a while, but he took my wineglass from the windowsill and handed it to me, giving me the perfect opening. "I can't drink that," I whispered, raising my eyes to his.

"I thought you liked this one." He glanced at the label on the bottle to see if he'd gotten it wrong.

"I do, but I won't be drinking for a while," I said, realizing that the statement would mean nothing to Hugo. In his time, women drank all through pregnancy and while they nursed, the effects of alcohol on fetuses and infants not known to them. "Hugo, I'm pregnant," I mumbled as I watched his face for a reaction. I wasn't sure what I expected, but Hugo's face broke into the most radiant smile, one of such joy that I suddenly felt my heart lift as well.

"How long?"

"About a month."

"How can you tell so quickly?" he asked, puzzled.

I showed him the plastic stick that clearly said "pregnant" in the little window.

Hugo took the pregnancy test and looked at it more closely, marveling at the message. "And how does this plastic tube know that you are with child?" he asked. He was curious about the workings of everything.

"It measures certain hormones in the urine," I replied, giggling as Hugo quickly handed the stick back to me, unsure of how my urine got inside, but not willing to find out. "Hugo, are you upset?" I asked, although clearly, he wasn't.

"I'm overcome with joy," he replied and kissed me soundly. "I can't wait to be a father, but first, we must be married."

"You know that's impossible," I replied. In his excitement, Hugo seemed to forget that, according to the British government, he didn't exist, therefore couldn't enter into a legal union with someone without first proving his identity.

"No, it isn't." Hugo seemed unusually happy as he looked at me, his eyes dancing with merriment.

"Hugo, what is it? Have you thought of something?"

"As it happens, I have."

I sat up in Hugo's lap and faced him, eager to hear what he had to say. What could have changed between this morning and now?

Hugo took a sip of wine, prolonging the suspense and watching me with undisguised glee.

"Well?" I asked, punching him lightly on the shoulder. I hated when he did that. He had a real penchant for drama, something he'd probably picked up over the years at Court.

"Well, I was walking past a cinema today and saw an interesting advertisement for a film called *The Master of Disguise*. And, it got me thinking. Actors change their appearance all the time for different roles, yet we never thought of what that really means," Hugo announced triumphantly.

"Hugo, I'm not following."

"Darling, in the seventeenth century, there are no cameras. People don't take a picture and forward it to others or post it on social media for three hundred of their closest friends to see. By the by, I still don't understand how that works. At any rate, how many people in the seventeenth century, aside from those who've met in person, really know how I look? The soldiers who have the warrant for my arrest know to take into custody Lord Hugo Everly, who's dark-eyed, dark-haired, somewhat above-average height, and of average build. How many of them have ever seen my likeness?"

"Not many, I suppose, other than the ones who had actually met you, like the captain who came to arrest you at Cranley," I replied, the light suddenly beginning to dawn.

"If I change my appearance, I can be anyone I choose to be. I can be Mr. Smith or Mr. Jones, or even Monsieur Dauriac, if I so desire. No one would be the wiser. There's no hair color or eye-color-altering lenses in the past. If people saw a blond man with blue eyes, they would never associate him with me, don't you see?" Hugo was practically bouncing in the seat, his excitement contagious.

"But, Hugo, say you do color your hair and change your eyes, then what? You still can't go home and claim your rightful place," I said, feeling bad for raining on his parade.

"Oh, but I can. I've been using your library card to great effect. In November of 1688, William and Mary will land in England, depose King James II, and take the throne. The people of England will refer to this as the Glorious Revolution. Once a Protestant monarch is on the throne, the charge against me will become void since I will no longer be considered a traitor, but a hero who wanted to put a Protestant on the throne of England. I will be able to go home," Hugo announced.

"And until then?"

"Until then, we can go to France as we planned and live there for three years in relative comfort, since I will be able to stop by Everly Manor and collect what I need, as well as inform Jane that I'm still alive and that you're with child. She'll be so happy. This is what she wanted for me all along." Hugo's face suddenly grew serious as he took my face in his hands. "Neve, I will stay here if that is what you want. I will never leave you or try to force you to go back against your will. This is your time and your life, and you will be forsaking so much more than I have a right to ask, and I wouldn't dare ask if I didn't know that you'd planned to give it all up for me before. The decision is yours, and I will abide by it."

Yes, the decision was mine, but now things had changed. A few months ago, I'd made a heart-wrenching decision to stay with Hugo in the seventeenth century, but although I knew that I might get pregnant at some point, I wasn't pregnant at the time, so it was all hypothetical. Now, there was a child growing inside me, tiny though it might still be, and that brought to the forefront all the fears of my last miscarriage and the lack of medical care in the seventeenth century. I was no fool; I knew the statistics. What was the likelihood of me surviving a birth? Maybe fifty-fifty, if there were no complications. I was scared, and Hugo knew it.

"Neve, I know you're frightened, and I would be too, knowing what type of medical miracles you would be leaving behind, but I promise you, I will find you the best accoucheur money can buy. I will abduct the queen's own physician if I must, to keep you and our child safe."

I leaned forward and rested my forehead against Hugo's, my eyes closed as my mind raced through all the objections which my neurons were firing at lightning speed. Any sensible person would stay here and try to find a way forward. After all, Hugo wasn't the first illegal to land on the shores of England, but I couldn't keep him from his life or his birthright. He had to go back, and I could either stay here, alone, heartbroken, and pregnant, or I could take my chances and go with him; all the while praying and hoping that I wasn't making a terrible mistake, a mistake that would cost me my life.

"Yes, Hugo, I will go back with you, but this time, I will do it right—if there is such a thing. I must make provisions for my flat, my car, and my job. I can't just disappear without a trace," I said, already thinking of what would need to be done. Focusing on the mundane was one way of keeping at bay the magnitude of what I was agreeing to.

"Because you hope to come back?"

"Because I don't think it's right to disappear again. I owe Lawrence Spellman that much. I also need to schedule an appointment at the clinic to see a doctor before I leave. I want to make sure that everything is all right and get a script for prenatal vitamins. I'd like to see a dentist as well, as should you. You don't have a National Health Service card, but there's a private dentist I know who will gladly see you. It's not like you'll have another chance," I said with a sad giggle. "When do you want to go?"

"As soon as you are ready. How long would it take to alter my appearance?"

"Not long. I can get some lenses from the makeup artists, and we can buy hair color at any pharmacy. It might be helpful if you grow a mustache and a beard, which we will color as well. Do you think I need to alter my appearance too?" I asked, suddenly conscious of the fact that Lionel Finch and the captain of the guard had seen me with Hugo.

"I think that as long as you are dressed simply and are traveling with your 'husband', no one will make the connection between you and Lord Everly's sumptuously dressed mistress."

I was suddenly overcome with excitement. If we could pull this off, we could travel to France as we'd planned, marry, have our child, and live in the style Hugo was accustomed to until it was safe to return to England. It was a simple plan, but one that should work.

FIFTY-TWO

I smiled at Hugo as we slipped into Cranleigh church at dusk on September 1. I was still trying to get used to his new appearance. Underneath, it was the same old Hugo, but the man who smiled back at me looked completely different. Hugo's hair was now a dark blond, as was his moustache and short beard. I'd picked the lightest shade of blond I could find, but when applied to his own naturally black hair, the effect wasn't as drastic as I'd expected. The light blue lenses did their job, and Hugo's gaze was now more of a cornflower blue, the vibrant color accentuated by his dark eyebrows and lashes. He still wore his jeans and a T-shirt but would change back into the clothes he'd fled in once we were down in the crypt. Thankfully, the clothes had been plain, not the ostentatious outfits that a nobleman might wear at Court, so the disguise should work. My own shift, stockings, dress, and all its parts, and shoes were also in the bag. I also had an embroidered little satchel that I'd picked up at a stall in Portobello Road which held my prenatal vitamins in a leather pouch and a dozen pills of an antibiotic I had left from my previous bout of sinus infection.

I'd also brought a key to the safety deposit box where I'd stored all my valuables in a bank in London. If ever I needed to come back, I would be able to access them. I'd asked Deborah to keep an eye on my flat and help the tenant, should any problems arise, telling her that I was leaving the country for a while to travel the world. She was skeptical of my sketchy explanation but promised to look after things in my absence. Deborah was convinced that I'd met some man during my recent absence and was running off with him to live a life of hedonistic pleasure, possibly in America. I let her believe what she would, since I couldn't very well tell her the truth.

Lawrence Spellman had been less understanding, but I gave him two weeks' notice and promised that, should I ever want my job back, I wouldn't expect any more favors from him. It felt strangely heart-wrenching to walk down the corridor toward the lift for the last time, knowing that I had now severed my ties to everything and everyone in my modern life.

I'd even written a brief email to Evan, telling him that I was moving on and wishing him luck with his silk application, the result of which was due to come through any day now. I was sure he'd get it and call me to boast when he did, but I wouldn't be there to take the call or read the email. I would be in seventeenth-century France, a place where no communication could ever reach me.

The candles in the church were lit, casting shifting shadows onto the nave and the Jubilee window, its colors now darker and richer due to the gathering darkness outside. Hugo and I took a seat in the last pew and waited for Evensong to end. There weren't many people and, of course, Max and his mother were not among those attending.

The service finally ended, and Reverend Lambert walked out of the church without noticing us and took his place by the door to bid goodnight to his few parishioners. I heard his deep voice outside, asking after someone's mother and her failing health.

As soon as the last person, who was an elderly woman with a stout walking stick, shuffled toward the door, Hugo and I descended into the crypt. We changed in silence, stowed our modern clothes behind the farthest sarcophagus, where they were unlikely to be found, and pushed the center of the flower. The heavy door slid open, revealing the dark passage beyond. Hugo took my hand, and we ran up the steps, the door closing behind us with a finality that left a jagged mark on my heart. This time, I wasn't planning on coming back. This was it.

I could hear Hugo's sigh of relief as he gazed upon the church of his own time. It was also lit with candles, but the building seemed much darker, the atmosphere close, for lack of windows and proper ventilation. Evensong was finished, the Reverend Snow still outside, talking to someone in the church porch whose comments we couldn't quite make out.

We slipped quietly from the church into the graveyard, nearly invisible in the purple smudges of dusk, which settled between the gravestones and beneath the trees whose shaggy heads nodded in sympathy to those who'd died. Hugo's gaze was directed toward his home, which sat proudly atop a hill, feeble light just visible in some of the windows. I could feel his longing and his excitement at being back, but he held himself in check, waiting for Reverend Snow to retreat into the church before we could slip through the gate and be on our way. My heart was pounding with excitement and fear, but I forced myself to calm down by breathing the fresh country air of the seventeenth century, unpolluted with the gas fumes of the nearby motorway.

We walked briskly toward Everly Manor, our hearts beating in unison as we finally approached the gate. All seemed normal and quiet, the house settling into peaceful slumber as night approached and everyone prepared for bed. The dogs began to yelp, but quickly quieted, recognizing their master in the stranger who approached and held out his fist for them to sniff.

Hugo stepped into the stable as I went to the door, my heart in my mouth as I banged the heavy knocker. We'd decided that it was safer for the servants not to see Hugo at all, so I asked a startled Liza if I might have a word with Jane. Liza threw me a filthy look, no doubt blaming me for the disappearance of her master, but invited me to wait inside and went to summon Jane.

I couldn't help noticing that she looked radiant, her cheeks blooming with good health and her eyes sparkling in a way I hadn't noticed before. Perhaps Liza was being courted by someone whose attentions she welcomed, I speculated as I waited for Jane. I'd never liked the girl, but I was happy for her if that were the case. Everyone deserved a chance at happiness, especially a servant who wouldn't get many opportunities to escape the bounds of domestic servitude before the bloom wore off and she became one of those family retainers who worked in the house for decades, completely devoid of any personal ties of her own.

"Dear God, Neve," Jane exclaimed as she came rushing into the foyer. "I thought you were dead. What's happened to my brother?" she cried. "We've had no word since the soldiers came to arrest him in May. They came here, demanding to know where he'd gone, but I couldn't tell them. They said he simply vanished from the church, like a spirit. Captain Humphries asked Reverend Snow to pass a message to Hugo after you'd gone into the church, and the reverend came back saying that you were nowhere inside. The soldiers went in and searched every inch of the place, but there was no trace of either of you. They eventually left, but several men were posted in the village, in the event that Hugo returned; ready to take him into custody. They are still there. But where is Hugo?"

"Jane, Hugo is in the stables, and he looks somewhat different than usual. We were in hiding for a while, but Hugo deems it safe to make our way to France now. We'll just need a purse full of coin, two horses, his signet ring and sword, and change of clothing. Nothing ostentatious; just the simplest things you can find. Hugo will write to you once we've settled."

"But where have you been all this time?" Jane asked as she gaped at me. "Monmouth has been executed, God rest his soul," she intoned, crossing herself automatically.

"We were in London. Jane, please, time is of the essence. We'd like to be in Portsmouth by noon tomorrow. I will wait for you in the stables since I don't want anyone else to see me. They might betray us to the soldiers."

"Of course, give me a few moments. I will meet you there."

I found Hugo sitting on a bale of hay in the stables. The horses were restless, shifting in their stalls and sniffing at the air. I sat down next to Hugo and rested my head on his shoulder. I knew he was anxious to see his sister, whom he thought he'd lost forever, but I just wanted to get away as quickly as possible and put as much distance between us and Everly Manor as we could before we had to stop for the night. But I was glad that at least now Jane could be at peace, knowing that Hugo was alive and well. She'd assumed the worst, as anyone in her position would have, and with the death of Monmouth, her fears were justified.

Jane sidled into the stable carrying a worn leather satchel and Hugo's sheathed sword beneath her arm. I heard her sharp intake of breath as she saw Hugo, a look of naked disbelief on her face as she drew closer and gaped at the stranger before her.

"Janey, it's me," Hugo said gently, giving her time to get accustomed to his appearance. "It's really me."

"But how?" she mused, touching Hugo's blond hair and looking into his now much lighter eyes. "What kind of magic is this?" she asked, her eyes slanted and peering at me in the dim light of the lantern. "You *are* a witch, aren't you?"

"Jane, Neve is not a witch. She saved my life; you might do well to remember that. And now she's saving my life once again by disguising me. I will write as soon as we get to France," Hugo promised. "Take care of yourself and look after Clarence."

"Will you be married in France?" Jane asked carefully, unsure of how things stood.

"As soon as possible," Hugo assured her, "with plenty of time to spare before the child arrives."

"Oh Hugo, is it really true?" Jane spun around and took in my still-flat stomach. I couldn't tell if she was pleased or dismayed.

"It is. Now, we must be away. Jane, please don't tell anyone I was here, not even Clarence, and especially not Jem. How is he?" Hugo asked wistfully.

"A nuisance as usual," Jane replied coolly. I couldn't help wondering what life had been like for poor Jem since Hugo disappeared. Jane would have no use for a page, but she'd know that Hugo wanted the boy looked after.

"Jane, please see to Jem for me. I will come back, and I expect to find him waiting for me," Hugo instructed, seeing his sister's skeptical gaze. "You heard me."

"Yes, of course. As you say," Jane muttered. "What should I say about the missing horses?"

"Just make something up," Hugo advised as he slid the sword securely beneath the harness of the horse he'd already saddled. It wouldn't do for a simple merchant to be seen carrying such a fine sword.

Jane handed him a fat purse, his ring, and the satchel. "I will pray that you find a ship to carry you to France quickly and be away from danger. Godspeed."

Hugo embraced his sister and kissed her on both cheeks. "Thank you, Janey. Everything will be well."

"Yes," Jane replied. "Now that I know you are living, everything will be well. Take care of him, Neve."

"You know I will."

Hugo led the horses out of the stables and helped me mount, then vaulted into the saddle himself. We'd be riding until about midnight, then stop over somewhere for a few hours' rest and continue first thing in the morning once it was safe to be on the road again. Of course, the traffic toward Portsmouth would slow us down, but it would also be beneficial in helping us lose ourselves among other travelers and blend in with the crowd. We waved to Jane and set off through the gates.

* * *

Jane walked back into the house and bolted the door behind her. The smile of farewell turned into a scowl of discontent as she considered the implications of Hugo's miraculous survival and the news of his impending marriage and child. She'd grieved her brother, more than she'd ever grieved her husband, but she'd made peace with his passing and had come to accept that her son, who was now thirteen, was Lord Everly and the heir to both the Hiddleston and Everly estates. Since Hugo was never formally charged or tried, the title and estate were secure, something that Jane had been very grateful for.

Of course, she was overjoyed that Hugo was alive, she told herself as she climbed the stairs, but Neve's pregnancy changed everything. She'd encouraged Hugo to marry over the years, knowing full well that he never would. He'd been so besotted with that brainless trollop that no other woman could ever take her place in his affections. Seeing him with Neve changed all that, but Jane hadn't been particularly worried. Hugo had had his share of mistresses over the years, but none of them ever had captured his heart. He was a man after all, and he had some basic needs which he needed seen to. Nothing wrong with that, and having a mistress was so much more practical than lying with whores.

Neve was different, however. Hugo was in love, but Jane had assured herself that it would burn out in time. The woman had no money and no family, and she was well past her prime; so, a marriage was about as likely as a unicorn prancing into the yard, especially with the shadow of Catherine still hovering over proceedings. And, with Hugo's disappearance, Jane's worries had dissipated like morning dew on summer grass. Now, the situation had changed once again, and the only thing that could stop Clarence from losing his inheritance, was either Neve miscarrying or giving birth to a stillborn, which was not entirely unlikely. God was good, and he rewarded his faithful servants, as Jane had been. Jane genuflected and put the thought of the unwelcome child from her mind. Hugo had said that all would be well—perhaps it would, but not in the way he thought.

Jane sighed and rang the bell for Liza. She would have a cup of wine before she retired, since she was too overwrought to fall asleep. Jane removed the pins from her hair and shook it loose over her shoulders, surprised to see Harriet, instead of Liza, hovering in the doorway. The girl had become even more insolent than she'd always been, particularly since that captain began courting her. Liza thought Jane didn't know, as if such a thing were possible. Jane snorted with contempt. Liza's lover would be off to London sooner or later, and she'd be lucky if he didn't leave her full in the belly. She'd dismiss her on the spot, the little strumpet, Jane thought savagely as she turned to face Harriet.

"I'll help you undress, madam, if that's all right. I can't seem to find Liza anywhere. Perhaps she is unwell," Harriet suggested, implying that it was Liza's time of the month.

"Yes, fine, but first bring me a cup of wine, Harriet. I feel quite overcome tonight."

"Is there a reason for your high spirits, madam?" Harriet asked. She always was a curious girl, Jane thought as she shooed her out of the room.

"None at all, Harriet; none at all. Now be quick about it, girl."

FIFTY-THREE

SEPTEMBER 2013

Max Everly stared open-mouthed at the notebook before him. God, he'd been a fool; a fool of epic proportions. He hadn't been able to see the wood for the trees, but the answer had been staring him in the face this whole time. He'd meant to ask Neve about the secret passage, but never got the chance, and the last few months, Max had lived in constant fear of Hugo Everly coming back to exact his revenge. Max had looked over his shoulder all through May and June, finally beginning to regain some sense of calm by July. If Hugo hadn't come for him by then, or made an accusation of attempted murder, he wasn't likely to. It seemed Hugo had gone on to London and got lost in that sea of humanity that was the capital. Perhaps he'd stay there for the rest of his days, working as a delivery boy for some seedy restaurant or unloading packing crates. As long as he remained there, nothing he did mattered.

The filming had finished, and the trucks and equipment disappeared as quickly as they arrived, leaving Max with his profitable museum venture and a fat check already deposited to his bank for the film fee. The village seemed strangely quiet once the movie people had left, leaving Max feeling despondent and listless. He hadn't looked at Harry's notebook in months, but had pulled it out again two weeks ago, rereading his favorite passages and scouring for clues as to the location of the passage. Neve had found it and used it several times. It had to be fairly easy to operate if she could go back and forth without any difficulty and bring that—Max nearly choked on his fury as he thought of Hugo—buffoon, was the best he could come up with. Neither one of them seemed to have suffered any ill effects from traveling through time. The damn passageway had to be right there, in front of his nose.

Max had leafed through the notebook again and again, looking for patterns, anything that resembled a code, phrases that could be a double entendre. It had to be there. Harry couldn't have put all his experiences in writing and not mentioned how to open the damn passageway. He'd been such a clever boy, Max had thought as he turned back to the first page yet again. And that's when it had dawned on him.

It was so simple, it made him laugh. Nearly every page held a little sketch to illustrate Harry's narrative. And at the top of the first page, as well as on the very last page when Harry returned, there was a picture of a six-petaled flower with the center shaded in neatly. That had to mean something, since all the other drawings meant something as well.

Max shoved the notebook in the drawer and practically ran to the church, praying all the while that Reverend Lambert wouldn't be skulking around, gasping for a cup of tea as usual and looking for a willing victim to join him in a tin of biscuits and an ecclesiastical discussion.

Max catapulted into the church and raced down the stairs to the crypt, desperate to check his theory. His heart pounded as he stood next to the tomb of the knight and looked for the flower. There were several flowers carved into the frieze around the crypt, but only one—one—had six petals. Max reached out his hand. A tremor went through him as he lightly touched the center of the flower. This was it; his last chance to find the way to the past. If it worked, he might be able to change what had happened, might even be able to get rid of Hugo Everly before he came to the present, depending on what year he landed in.

Max took a deep breath and pushed the button, shaking with excitement as a scraping noise accompanied the opening of the panel. He found the corresponding flower on the inside to make sure he could open the panel again, and slowly walked up the stairs into the church, his heart hammering wildly against his ribs.

Max leaned against the wooden door, surveying the building he stepped into. Dear God, he'd done it. He'd *done it*! Max turned around and sprinted back down the steps to his own time. Now that he knew how to work the mechanism, he had to think things through, but first, he needed a little tour of reconnaissance. He'd grab some period clothes from the museum and come back later with a few coins in his pocket. A walk to the village and a drink at the public house would be a nice start. He'd learn what year he was in, pick up some local gossip, and find out something about the lord of the manor. Then, armed with pertinent information, he could go about formulating a plan.

Max grinned wolfishly as he patted Tilly's head when she ran out to greet him at the gate. "We're in business, old girl," he said. "And this time, I'll get it right."

FIFTY-FOUR

SEPTEMBER 1685

By the time we left Everly Manor, it had to be past nine, but it might as well have been the dead of night. The road was deserted, the only light cast by a sliver of the moon, hanging at a jaunty angle in the pitch-black sky. The night was hazy, so the heavens appeared like a pool of tar spilled over the universe, not a single pinprick of starlight visible through the muggy air. The road wasn't safe after dark, but Hugo had his sword and a dagger at his belt.

We had to put as much distance between us and Cranley as possible before we stopped for the night. Hugo knew of an inn where we could bed down, but it was at least two hours away. After about an hour's ride, my eyelids began to grow heavy, and my body felt as if it were welded to the saddle, my center of gravity somewhere right around my lower belly. I wasn't showing yet, but pregnancy was already making itself known. I felt unusually tired, had to go to the bathroom every hour, and experienced an ongoing nausea which was relieved only by the intake of food, which in turn made me feel even sicker. Seventeenth-century fare wasn't going to make things any easier, but we couldn't afford to wait. We hoped to reach France before I started my second trimester and settle somewhere where I could pass the rest of the pregnancy in calm surroundings.

Had Hugo been alone, he would have galloped at break-neck speed, but I was too afraid to suffer another miscarriage. Our pace was stately, which meant that we weren't covering more than two to three miles per hour. The gentle swaying of the horse began to lull me to sleep; my eyes closing of their own accord as the night around me grew more silent, the nocturnal noises muffled by the humid air. Hugo periodically reached out and shook my shoulder to make sure I was awake and didn't slide off the horse. He was worried about me, but we couldn't afford to luxuriate at Everly Manor with soldiers stationed in the village.

Hugo heard the hoofbeats long before I did, his body growing stiff in the saddle and his hand automatically going for his sword. No one would be on the road at this hour unless they were either escaping or pursuing their quarry.

Two men materialized out of the darkness, their occupation instantly recognizable by the reflection of feeble moonlight on their breastplates. They were soldiers, likely ones from the village, but neither of them had been with Captain Humphries when he came to arrest Hugo in May.

Hugo deliberately removed his hand from his sword and forced himself to relax, his demeanor one of surprise rather than apprehension. "Good evening to you, gentlemen," he called out as the soldiers drew abreast, their eyes narrowed in appraisal of the situation.

"Your name, sir," one of them demanded.

"Richard Tully, and this is my wife, Alice."

Had I not been shaking with nerves, I would have found it amusing that Hugo had chosen Alice as my pseudonym. I'd told him of my love of *Alice in Wonderland* as a child and how I'd felt as if I went down the rabbit hole when I wound up in the seventeenth century. Clearly, he hadn't forgotten.

"Who do we have the honor of addressing?" Hugo asked, his voice deferential.

"I'm Captain Norrington of His Majesty's army," the man replied, failing to introduce his companion.

Hugo gave a nod of acknowledgment, his head tipped to the side as if waiting for the man to state his business.

"We've been informed that a woman known to be Lord Hugo Everly's mistress was seen this evening in the vicinity of Everly Manor. State your name, madam," he ordered, addressing me.

"Mrs. Alice Tully, sir, as my husband just told you," I replied rather more saucily than I should have, but I was annoyed with the man. He was so pompous and sure of himself.

"And do you happen to know Lord Everly, madam?"

"No, sir. Whoever informed you that I might was mistaken. May I ask who summoned you?" I inquired, despite Hugo's look of warning.

"A maid from the manor came running into the village earlier, claiming to have seen a woman known in these parts as Mistress Neve Ashley," the captain replied, his gaze never leaving my face.

"Well, she was mistaken," Hugo cut in. "This woman is my wife and has been for the past seven years."

"And where are you bound, Mr. Tully, at this hour?" Captain Norrington asked.

"We are bound for the next village, Captain, where we will seek shelter for the night," Hugo replied smoothly. "My wife is tired, so if there's nothing else, we'll be on our way."

"Goodnight to you both," Captain Norrington replied and turned his horse around. "You shouldn't be on the road at this hour. It isn't safe, Mr. Tully. I suggest you find lodging as soon as possible. There's an inn about a mile down the road, I hope you will avail yourself of the accommodation."

"Thank you for your concern, Captain. We will most certainly do so."

Hugo watched as the two soldiers trotted away from us in the direction of Cranley, then gave me a wide smile and dug his heels into the flanks of his horse. "Just a little while longer, my sweet Alice," he said. "Like the man said, there's an inn just down the road."

I tried to reply, but my hands shook violently as I tried to spur on my horse. I knew the risks, but I hadn't expected to come face to face with soldiers so soon after coming back.

"It's all right, Neve," Hugo said gently. "Everything is all right and we can be on our way now."

"How in the world did they find out so quickly?" I asked, needing to rationalize what had just happened.

"Liza must have run to the village and informed them," Hugo replied casually. "Damn her eyes."

"Why would she do that?" I couldn't imagine why a loyal servant would run all the way to the village with night coming on to inform the soldiers of Hugo's possible presence. What was in it for her?

"I assume there's a monetary reward for any information leading to my capture," Hugo suggested, unperturbed. "Liza always was an ambitious girl."

"How well did you know her?" I asked, suddenly suspicious. Did Liza have any motive besides the monetary one? Of course, a monetary reward, no matter how insubstantial, would equal Liza's yearly pay, if not more, so to her it would seem like a fortune. That would motivate any a poor girl, especially if she had aspirations of leaving the service.

"I know her well enough to know she can't be trusted. Now, come on."

I was still pondering Liza's motives as my head sank onto the lumpy pillow, and my body tried to get comfortable on the straw mattress provided by the inn. It was better than wondering if anything crawly might be sharing the mattress with me. Hugo sat in the chair by the window, a faraway expression on his face.

"Hugo?"

"Hmm? Does Liza have any reason to despise you?" I asked.

Hugo might have answered, but I didn't hear what he said since I was already asleep.

FIFTY-FIVE

By the time I woke up, the sun was shining through the little window set high in the wall, the air in the room close and warm. Dust motes swirled in the golden shaft of light which culminated in the not-so-clean floor. I could hear sounds coming from the yard below: men talking loudly, horses neighing, water pouring as someone drew a bucket from the well and likely filled the trough. I wanted to get up, but every molecule of my being begged to stay in bed. It'd been a long time since I'd sat on a horse, and I was achy and tired. If Hugo hadn't woken me, then there was no rush, I thought and closed my eyes again.

Suddenly, a tremor of fear passed through me. *Hugo.* Where was he? What if he had been arrested while I slept?

I shot out of bed and grabbed my clothes, ready to get dressed and run downstairs, but I was forestalled by a knock on the door and Hugo's smiling face as he entered the room and set down a wooden tray on the scarred table.

"Where've you been?" I shrieked. "I thought something awful had happened to you."

Hugo just pulled me into his arms and gave me a reassuring

hug. "I didn't see any reason to wake you, since we've already had our encounter with the soldiers, so I went out to find you some breakfast. I didn't think you'd want ale and hard biscuit, so I went to the nearest farm and bought some fresh milk, bread and butter. Come and eat something. We have a long day ahead of us."

I allowed myself to be led to the table, where Hugo buttered a thick slice of bread for me and poured me a cup of milk. "Thank you," I said through a mouthful of bread. "That was very sweet."

"When you said you couldn't have anything alcoholic and needed to eat well for the babe, I was paying attention," Hugo said, pretending to be affronted.

"I'm glad. I was starving. When are we leaving?"

"As soon as you're ready. I hoped to get to Portsmouth before noon, but since we've been delayed, we have to get there before they close the gates at nightfall."

I nodded and took a sip of milk. Hugo sounded calm and confident, but my insides were jumping. We were literally heading into the lion's den. Portsmouth was the home of the Royal Navy, a town crawling with military presence, where someone could recognize Hugo despite his elaborate disguise. I had no idea how long it might take to find a ship to carry us to France, but I hoped it would take days rather than weeks.

I watched Hugo as he trimmed his beard in front of the tiny, cracked mirror on the wall. I had to admit that he looked very different. Hugo's eyes were a vibrant blue, the lenses hiding his own dark eyes, and his thick mane was a honey-blond any girl would envy. There were moments when he looked like a stranger even to my own eyes, but the disguise would last for only a few weeks before Hugo's natural dark hair began to show. It'd be easy enough to shave off the beard, but the roots in his hair would be harder to hide. The sooner we got to Portsmouth and found a ship, the safer we'd be.

I finished my breakfast, collected our belongings and pulled my linen cap over my curls. "Let's go," I said, suddenly feeling more confident. "Today is the day we get to Portsmouth."

"It certainly is," Hugo agreed and took the satchel from me.

FIFTY-SIX

The road to Portsmouth was more traveled than I might have imagined, with numerous wagons piled with various goods moving at glacial speed, carriages carrying naval personnel, families en route to somewhere, and mounted riders like us. I was eternally grateful that we weren't traveling by carriage. I couldn't begin to imagine being cooped up in a wooden box with no ventilation on a warm day like today.

By late afternoon, I was exhausted and achy, but I kept quiet, following Hugo's mount through the throng. We only had a few more hours to go and I was determined to get to the port city today. There was safety in numbers, and the amount of people traveling in the same direction gave us the best protection. No one paid attention to two travelers among the multitudes.

The slanted rays of the sun were no longer as bright as the evening approached, mellowing the landscape around us and painting everything in a golden haze. I could just make out the shape of the Round Tower rising behind the solid barrier of the city walls. Portsmouth was a fortified city, one that had been attacked repeatedly over the centuries and had withstood admirably every time. The tower and the walls had been rebuilt time after time by various monarchs, starting with wood and dirt and ending with solid stone, which greeted us now.

I sighed with relief as we finally rode through the city gates. I hoped we would be able to find accommodation, given so many people seemed to have the same idea, but Hugo beckoned me to follow him down the high street and away from the crowd pouring through the gates which would be closing in an hour or two. He stopped in front of a place called the "Greyhound" and went inside to check if there might be a room available. For the right price, there was, so we surrendered our horses to the groom and went in.

I hardly paid attention to my surroundings as I collapsed on the bed and closed my eyes, my back vibrating with tension after hours in the saddle, my inner thighs on fire from the friction against the horse. The bed was not exactly comfortable, and the room was so stuffy, I could barely breathe, but at least it was accommodation. Hugo forced open the window and a rush of briny sea air filled the room, dispelling the sour stink of previous occupants and the smell of mouse droppings, which were probably hiding under the bed.

"How in the world were you able to get a room so quickly?" I asked, stretching luxuriously now that my back had stopped convulsing.

"This is not the most popular inn in town," Hugo replied, as he reached under the bed for the chamber pot.

"Why? It's no worse than the rest—better even." The stone house looked solid and respectable, and the smells emanating from the kitchen made my mouth water.

"People have superstitions about certain places," Hugo said, shrugging his shoulders.

"What kind of superstitions?" I asked warily. "Is this place haunted?"

"Some say so. The Duke of Buckingham was murdered

here in 1628 by John Felton—stabbed to death. Not that he didn't deserve it, that villainous reprobate. Some say Buckingham's ghost still haunts the tavern, unable to rest after the violent manner of his death." Hugo gave me a smile and kissed my forehead. "But we don't hold with such nonsense, do we, my sweet? Hence, we get a room."

"I don't care if Buckingham comes during the night and climbs in between us. I'm not budging from this bed for at least twelve hours, but I wouldn't say no to some supper. Do you think I could convince you to go downstairs and see what you can procure?"

"Your servant, madam," Hugo replied with an exaggerated bow and made himself scarce. I hoped that whatever he got would be plentiful. I'd always had a healthy appetite, but once the nausea abated a bit, I was hungry around the clock, craving solid food rather than little snacks. I hadn't gained any weight yet, but I'd have to watch myself, especially in France, where food was so rich and delicious.

I suddenly giggled to myself. Here I was, in a naval town crawling with soldiers—with a man who had a price on his head —the only thing standing between him and an arrest being a bottle of dye and some colored lenses, and I was worrying about my weight. That was just too twenty-first century, I thought as I reclined back on the bed, hoping Hugo wouldn't be long.

FIFTY-SEVEN

I stood on the quay of Portsmouth, my eyes shielded against the sun by my hand as I took in the hulking shape of the *Mathilde*—a merchant vessel which would carry us to France. It would be sailing on the tide in two days' time, and we would be in France by this time next week. Hugo had been lucky to find a ship, since there seemed to be no other vessel scheduled to leave for France anytime soon. The *Mathilde* wasn't going to Le Havre, as Hugo might have liked, but it really didn't matter. Once we docked, we'd travel by coach overland to Paris, where Hugo had acquaintances who'd take us in until we found a home of our own. All that was left to do was to sell the horses and pay the inn bill.

Hugo took me by the arm, and we strolled along the quay in the direction of the nearest inn. "Let's have a drink to celebrate our imminent departure," Hugo said. "I'm parched."

I didn't really want anything except a nice cup of tea, which wasn't on offer, but I walked along with Hugo, happy to see his relaxed smile and eager for the two days to pass quickly so we could finally sail away from this place where Hugo was constantly in danger.

We found a table in the corner, away from the rowdy sailors who were enjoying tankards of ale and singing loudly, their voices anything but sober, but still strangely harmonious. Hugo ordered a tankard of ale and I asked for some apple cider—the least alcoholic drink I could have at a tavern. I took a sip, enjoying the taste of fermented apple on my lips. It was cold and refreshing, a nice change to the milk I'd been drinking since coming back to the past. The innkeeper thought it was strange that Mrs. Tully wanted nothing but milk, but kept his counsel, charging us more for the milk than he would have for fine French brandy.

Hugo leaned back in his chair and took a swig of his ale, his face suddenly growing alert as the conversation of two men at the next table reached us in the lull between sailors' songs.

"You just came from Cranley, you say?" one of the men asked.

"Oh, aye, quite a to-do there last night. It seems Lord Hugo Everly was finally apprehended, that traitorous knave. Just walked into the tavern, cocky as you please, and ordered himself an ale. You can just imagine the hullabaloo that caused, after him disappearing like that a few months ago. Must have thought he was free and clear now that Monmouth was hacked to pieces."

"So, what happened?" his companion asked, eager to hear the story, his eyes round with curiosity.

"What do you think? The soldiers just happened to be there, nursing ales of their own, them having nothing to do but skulk around the village in the hopes of that blackguard showing up. They arrested him on the spot with the intention of taking him to London the following day. And you know what the very best part of it all was?" the man asked, relishing the telling of his story. "The fool had the gall to tell the soldiers he wasn't Hugo Everly. Kept insisting his name was Maximilian. Him, sitting there in all his glory, claiming to be someone else.

Why, only the bluebloods are mad enough to think they can get away with such tomfoolery. They hauled him right off, they did, and a good thing too, if you ask me. There's no greater crime than treason, is there?"

I hardly noticed the spilled cider pooling on the table and making a rivulet of golden brown as it ran off the table. Hugo sat perfectly still, his face set in a mask of determination I knew only too well. He avoided my gaze, turning instead to the window, where the bustle of the quay was dying down as the day faded into evening, and the dusky hues of twilight settled on the town. I couldn't move, afraid that if I did, I'd alter this moment and everything would fall apart, like a broken vessel; fragments of glass flying everywhere as the glass hit the floor and shattered into a thousand pieces which could never be put back together.

"We must go back," Hugo said, his pained expression telling me that this wasn't an easy decision for him to make. "We can't let Max take the fall."

"He tried to kill you," I hissed at Hugo, desperate to make him change his mind. I didn't want Max to be held accountable for Hugo's actions, but I knew what going back would mean, and I couldn't bear to think about it.

"We have to go back," Hugo repeated.

"And do what? Turn yourself in?"

"I won't turn myself in, but I can't let him be executed in my place. It wouldn't be right, Neve, and you know it."

Yes, I knew it wouldn't be right, but every cell in my body screamed in protest, knowing that there was no possible way this could end well for any of us. I suddenly felt very cold, the full implications of what Hugo was planning to do finally sinking into my resistant brain.

Hugo took my quivering hands in his but didn't say anything. What was there to say?

EPILOGUE

Max desperately tried to hold on to the reins of the horse with his fettered hands, the chains making a jangling noise that reverberated right into his bones. The captain looked incredibly pleased with himself, riding ahead, his back straight and his helmet glinting in the morning sun and blinding Max with its glare; his sidekick riding behind and bringing up the rear. Max's ribs felt as if they would crack from the beating he had received last night; every breath was agony, every mile hell. The more he'd denied being Hugo, the harder they'd hit him.

Max's mind was numb, partially from the pain of his injuries and partially from shock. He'd lived a pampered and safe life, always knowing that there was nothing that couldn't be solved with money and connections. He had no connections in the seventeenth century, or money for that matter. There was no one to call, no one to ask for help. He was completely alone and helpless. He'd been arrested on a charge of treason, abduction, and attempted murder. There was only one outcome for this situation. Death.

A LETTER FROM THE AUTHOR

Huge thanks for reading *The Passage*, I hope you were hooked on Neve and Hugo's epic journey. It continues in book two, *Wonderland*. If you want to join other readers in hearing all about my new releases and bonus content, you can sign up for my newsletter!

www.stormpublishing.co/irina-shapiro

If you enjoyed this book and could spare a few moments to leave a review that would be hugely appreciated. Even a short review can make all the difference in encouraging a reader to discover my books for the first time. Thank you so much!

Although I write several different genres, time travel was my first love. As a student of history, I often wonder if I have what it takes to survive in the past in the dangerous, life-altering situations my characters have to deal with. Neve and Hugo are two of my favorite characters, not only because they're intelligent and brave but because they're fallible, sensitive, and ultimately human. I hope you enjoy their adventures, both in the past and the present, and come to see them as real people rather than characters on a page.

Thanks again for being part of this amazing journey with me and I hope you'll stay in touch – I have so many more stories and ideas to entertain you with!

Irina

Made in the USA
Middletown, DE
01 August 2024

58345770R00243